D0956167

About the author

Chris Manby grew up in Gloucester and published her first story in *Just Seventeen* at the age of fourteen. She lives in London and writes full-time.

Chris Manby

Seven Sunny Days

CORONET BOOKS
Hodder & Stoughton

First published in Great Britain in 2003 by Hodder and Stoughton
A division of Hodder Headline

A Coronet paperback

9 10 8

A CIP catalogue record for this title is
available from the British Library

ISBN 0340 819006

Typset in 10.5/12.75pt Sabon by
Phoenix Typesetting, Burley-in-Wharfedale, West Yorkshire

Printed and bound by
Mackays of Chatham Ltd, Chatham, Kent

Hodder and Stoughton
A division of Hodder Headline
338 Euston Road
London NW1 3BH

For David Garnett.
My guru.

Acknowledgements

Love and thanks as always to Mum, Dad, Kate and Lee. And big kisses to my nephew, Harrison, who distracted me during the dark deadline days by smearing a banana all over my soft furnishings. Thanks to the gang at Hodder, especially Carolyn Mays, for their continued support and professionalism. Thanks to Ant and James at Antony Harwood Limited, Sheryl Petersen at Don Buchwald Associates, Mary Rickard and Tony Gardner for agenting me so enthusiastically all over the world. Thanks to the members of the board for their advice on music to write to, review blues and how to get a party wall agreement. Thanks to Jane Brown for a great research trip to Club Med! Thanks to our fellow Club Medders, who will of course not recognise themselves herein! Thanks to Frank Strausser for helping my own American dream come true. Thanks to Guy Hazel and Jennifer Matherly for being two true friends. Thanks to Ryan Law for providing sanctuary from next door's builders. And thanks to next door's builders for fixing the hole in my roof . . .

August 2002

Why was it, Rachel Buckley wondered, that every time she passed a policeman she suddenly felt guilty? In her twenty-nine years on earth she had never so much as stolen a packet of chewing gum from a corner shop and yet, every time she saw that navy uniform, or heard the siren of a police car as it careered up to swoop past her Renault Clio in hot pursuit of a joyrider in a stolen BMW, Rachel froze, went as red as Santa's underpants and got a sudden urge to confess to every major robbery from the Great Train one to Brinks-Mat.

Customs officers were even worse. Now Rachel was actually sweating with anxiety as she waited in the queue to put her hand luggage through the X-ray machine at Gatwick's south terminal. She had read and reread the notice about passengers only being allowed to take one item of hand luggage on board the plane and felt a tickle of panic as she wondered whether the WH Smith carrier bag containing one magazine and a packet of Hula Hoops would count as a second item alongside her blue rucksack. In front of her, an altogether less considerate traveller had already jammed a huge trolley case through the X-ray machine and was attempting to fit a large cardboard box in after it. The customs officers didn't bat an eyelid.

'They'll find a goat when they X-ray that,' said Rachel's best friend and travelling companion, Yaslyn Stimpson. Yaslyn chewed gum nonchalantly and noisily as she tossed her own little black handbag on to the conveyor. When the metal detector arch beeped in alarm as Yaslyn sauntered through it, she merely grinned and said, 'That'll be the hand grenade,' before she stepped back out, unloaded her house keys and her gorgeous, real Cartier watch and passed through again to approving silence.

Rachel, on the other hand, removed her watch, her necklace *and* her earrings before she walked through. She was even momentarily convinced that her single mercury filling might cause some kind of reaction, though it never had before. But airport security was tighter than ever these days and she was ready to point out her occluded back molar.

'Hurry up,' said her other fellow traveller, Carrie Ann Murphy. 'We'll meet you over there in duty free.'

And with that, Yaslyn and Carrie Ann were gone in search of two hundred Marlboro Lights and some tax-free tubs of Estée Lauder. They didn't notice Rachel being pulled aside and asked whether the rucksack was her bag. Had she packed it herself? Had anybody asked her to carry anything for them since she arrived at the airport? And would she mind opening it up so the man behind the counter could take a proper look inside?

If Rachel had been blushing as she stepped up to the X-ray machine, she was emitting more radiation than the machine itself as she unzipped her rucksack now. Thank God it was the beginning of her holiday and not the end, she thought. Thank God the spare knickers

2

she'd packed in her hand luggage – since she'd heard that checked-in luggage went astray more frequently than usual on package tours – were clean and plain black cotton and nothing to be embarrassed about. All the same, the customs officer peered into the dark interior of the rucksack and gave a worried frown.

'I can't see what's going on in there,' he said. 'I'm afraid you'll have to empty the whole lot out on to this bench.'

And so, with three officers looking on – the first guy must have tacitly summoned assistance – Rachel emptied out her bag. Spare knickers, sponge bag, leather wallet, spare 'mugging wallet' (containing five-pound note and a supermarket reward card). One carton of apple juice (sugar free). Two packets of M & Ms (definitely not sugar free). And holiday reading including the new Marian Keyes and *Captain Corelli's Mandolin* (this year, she vowed, she would actually finish it).

'Is that everything?' asked the first guy.

Rachel nodded. 'Yes.' Even her tampax holder was open for all to see.

'You're sure that's everything, madam?'

'Of course I am.'

'Only we think we saw rather more when the bag came through the machine.'

'That's everything I packed,' Rachel assured him.

'Then you won't mind turning the bag inside out.'

Rachel did.

And there was a loud clatter as the very last item in Rachel's rucksack bounced off the carpeted bench and on to the floor, breaking in two and relinquishing its battery as it did so.

'Forget we packed this, did we?' the customs officer asked as he picked the little vibrator up with diligently rubber-gloved hands.

'I . . . I . . .' Rachel could only stutter.

''S all right, love. You don't have to explain yourself to me.'

'But I swear I've never seen it before in my life!'

'That's what they all say,' he told her. 'And believe me, darling, I have seen it all before.'

'I don't even know what it is!'

'Yeah, yeah.' He wasn't bothering to suppress his grin now. He placed the two halves back together carefully and twisted them until the hideous thing emitted an angry buzz. Then he dropped the vibrator, still buzzing, back into Rachel's cavernous rucksack where it was invisible once more – black, glittery plastic camouflaged against the rucksack's glittery waterproof interior.

'It isn't mine,' she said feebly as the officer zipped the rucksack up again and wished her a pleasant holiday.

'Hope she's coming on our flight,' said the man standing behind Rachel in the queue.

'Watch it, you,' said his wife as she swatted him with a handbag.

Rachel was still in shock when she found Yaslyn and Carrie Ann sitting in the terminal's Costa Coffee concession, mainlining double espressos and trying to get the cellophane off the new box of fags they were supposed to be exporting intact.

'What took you so long?' Yaslyn asked disingenuously.

'I got searched.'

'Oh, no,' said Carrie Ann. 'I wonder why they picked you?' But the smile was already playing about her eyes.

It was seconds before realisation set in. 'You bitches!' squealed Rachel. 'You know exactly what they found because you put it there! I can't believe you'd do that to me. You let me walk through customs with a vibrator in my bag!'

'Happy hen week,' the girls chorused.

'I had to come through carrying nipple clamps,' said Carrie Ann.

Rachel's annoyance didn't last long. Three glasses of champagne at the terminal bar later, she found the whole incident almost as funny as her friends did.

Well, she had to. Ritual humiliation is part and parcel of any hen party. Rachel had no reason to expect that her friends would let her get away without it. At least they had insisted on doing something different to the usual London hen affair of a cheesy nightclub, pina coladas and excessively greasy male strippergrams. It had been Yaslyn's idea to send Rachel off in real style by turning the hen night into a 'hen week'. Carrie Ann lobbied hard in favour of anywhere but Ibiza.

They settled on Turkey. Bodrum. And the flagship resort of French all-inclusive holiday chain *Club Aegee*. The pictures in the brochure looked fantastic. And word on the South London singles circuit was that, if you picked the right resort, a night at Club Aegee made the goings-on at the court of Emperor Caligula look positively sedate.

'You get a better class of people,' Carrie Ann assured her friends when they went to book the trip. One of Carrie Ann's neighbours, a very unassuming personnel officer with more hang-ups than the Holding Company, had gone to a Club Aegee resort in Sicily and came back engaged to a millionaire bonds trader from New York.

'Not the kind of man you meet at Club 18-30,' Yaslyn observed.

'Especially if you don't qualify for 18-30 any more,' the travel representative added as she tapped Carrie Ann's date of birth into the computer.

While the girls waited for their flight to begin boarding, they worked each other into a frenzy of excited expectation about the adventure that lay ahead. Yaslyn threatened Rachel with the prospect of mixed-sex Turkish bathing followed by a brisk rub-down from a eunuch. Carrie Ann, meanwhile, was scanning the luggage tags of every able man under fifty to see whether they were heading the same way and might be worth chatting up on the plane.

'What about him?' Rachel pointed out a good-looking chap in smart chinos.

'Nope,' said Carrie Ann. 'British Airways luggage tags.' The girls were travelling charter.

'What about those two?' suggested Yaslyn next. The two young men in question looked barely old enough to have their own passports. They were wearing black T-shirts sporting logos for bands the girls had never heard of. Their baggy jeans, slung low enough to reveal their underpants, gave the impression they were both still in nappies. You can tell you're getting old when fashion starts to look ugly, thought Carrie Ann.

'Not bad for starters,' said Rachel.

'They'd barely make an hors d'oeuvre.'

Yaslyn blew a kiss at the taller of the two, who promptly turned as red as his baseball cap. 'Lock up your sons!' she whooped at him. 'It's Rachel Buckley's hen week!'

The three girls chinked their champagne glasses and toasted Rachel's 'impending doom'.

'Thanks a lot,' said Rachel.

'OK,' amended Carrie Ann. 'To Rachel and Patrick for ever.' She drew a little heart in the air.

'And here's to you finding true love in Bodrum too,' Rachel responded to her freshly divorced friend.

'Or at least some casual sex,' said Yaslyn.

The holiday had begun.

'I didn't even want to come on this bloody holiday,' Sally Merchant whined. 'Let's just go home and forget about it now.'

'He'll be here any minute,' said Marcus, trying harder than ever not to shout back.

'The flight leaves in half an hour,' said his wife. 'We are never going to make it. Of all the things anyone could have forgotten to pack, only *you* could have forgotten to pack the passports.'

'I put them on the mantelpiece with the tickets. Right behind them. You picked the tickets up, didn't you?'

'Oh, right, so you're blaming me now,' Sally snapped.

'I am not blaming you,' said Marcus. Though in truth he really couldn't understand how Sally could possibly have picked up the tickets and *not* the passports, he was determined to keep out of conflict. This holiday, after all, was meant to be a break from the trouble, a break from all the arguing. This holiday was meant to prove that, away from all the stresses of everyday life, they still had a marriage worth fighting *for* rather than *about*.

'Come on, Charlie,' Marcus muttered. 'You can do it. Come on, pal.'

When the Merchants discovered at the check-in

desk that they didn't have their passports, Marcus had called their neighbour Charlie back in Surrey and begged him to drive the passports down to the airport. Fortunately Charlie was a freelance journalist who was never at work before lunch-time. And he loved a good crisis. Even better was a crisis in which he could play the role of hero and save the day. It was as close as he got to being the war correspondent he once dreamt of becoming.

'I know what this holiday means to you,' Charlie told Marcus on the phone. 'I'll be there in forty minutes.'

It really wasn't far. And Charlie really did know what the holiday meant to Marcus. The previous Thursday evening, over a couple of pints at their village pub, Marcus had told him all about it. Everything. The whole sorry lot.

At the time Charlie was researching an article on what women look for in a man.

'Money, looks, sex appeal? What do you think they look for?' he'd asked.

'I wish I bloody knew,' Marcus mumbled into his pint. Half an hour later, Charlie was considering whether he might not be the perfect volunteer for relationship counselling.

Marcus knew he should have felt embarrassed, telling his next-door neighbour everything that had (or rather hadn't) gone on between him and Sally over the past eighteen months. But he didn't. Somehow, telling Charlie about his marital problems felt like the most natural thing in the world. Why hadn't he had a conversation like this before? he wondered. A girly sort of conversation, involving feelings and painful emotions. How the tables had turned since Marcus first learned about the differences between girls and boys . . .

These days, whenever Sally had her girlfriends round for a video night and Marcus got home from his banishment to the pub early enough to catch the tail-end of their evening, it struck him that women now talked as he had imagined men were supposed to. Their conversations seemed to revolve around sex. Not loving, tender, life-affirming sex either. He'd felt sick to the stomach when he heard Sally's best friend, Victoria, give her husband of seven years marks out of ten for presentation, originality and performance.

'Nil. Nil and thrice nil,' she'd shrieked. 'Thank God for power tools!'

Power tools, he'd soon come to learn, were vibrators. Victoria had even taken to carrying one in her handbag.

A few days later, while browsing the Internet on their home computer, Marcus discovered that Sally had added a new site to her favourites: 'www.hushhhh.com'. *An erotic emporium for women.* A little further sneaky investigation revealed an order confirmation from the site amongst her e-mails. Marcus waited hopefully for Sally to surprise him one day wearing nothing but a feather boa and a pair of crotch-less knickers. But that day never came. And neither did Sally. Not any more. Not when Marcus was with her, anyway.

'Twenty-five minutes,' said Sally, looking at her watch. 'You might as well hail a cab to take us back home now.'

'He'll be here,' said Marcus, willing his new best friend Godspeed.

'Marcus, relying on Charlie to get us out of this mess is like relying on a chocolate fireguard,' Sally continued. 'He'll never make it. That stupid car of his can do twenty miles an hour at the best of times. And then he's got to find the right airport.'

'Why do you always have to be so negative?'

'Why do you always have to be so pathetic?'

Marcus opened his mouth to answer but he had just been rendered speechless. Pathetic? Sally looked at him as though challenging him to answer. 'Go on,' said her hard-eyed expression. 'Come back from that one, you sap.'

Thankfully, he didn't have to. Charlie's ancient blue MG spluttered to a halt at the kerb in front of them while Marcus was still formulating his defence.

'Your knight in shining armour *est arrivé*!' Charlie called out to his neighbours through the passenger window. 'Bet you're glad to see me, eh, Sal?'

'You'll never know . . .' she muttered back as she snatched the passports from his outstretched hand. 'Come on,' she said to her husband, before turning on her heel and heading for the departure lounge without wishing Charlie so much as goodbye.

'Thanks, mate,' said Marcus. 'I guess I owe you one.'

'My pleasure. Good luck,' Charlie told him. 'Looks like you'll need it!' He gave a mock salute. Marcus saluted him back, feeling every inch the soldier on his way into battle.

They made it to the gate with seconds to spare. The stewardesses wrestled their luggage from them to stow it at the front of the cabin (the overhead lockers were packed) while Sally and Marcus made the long trip to their seats at the back of the plane.

'This is so embarrassing,' Sally hissed. 'Everyone is looking at us.'

They were the last to board.

A large, middle-aged lady was already sitting in the aisle seat on their row. She got up to let them past with a grumble, as though they could have chosen to sit somewhere else. Sally took the window seat. Marcus stepped on their neighbour's pig's trotter of a foot as he tried to squeeze by too.

'Ow!' said the woman. 'Be careful.'

'For God's sake, Marcus,' Sally snarled. 'Watch where you're going.'

Marcus felt his cheeks grow red under glares from all directions.

Before the stewardesses had disconnected the boarding platform and sealed the doors for take-off, Sally had located her eye mask and blocked her travel companions out. Marcus watched the stewardesses' safety demonstration, though there was little chance of getting out past his corpulent neighbour in time to survive a real emergency.

Demonstration over, Marcus picked up his Lonely Planet guide to Turkey, flicked through the first two pages and put it down again. The words had gone all blurry in front of his soft brown eyes. Either he was going short-sighted in his old age or he really was about to cry.

3

Right then, on the other side of Europe, Axel Radanne felt like crying too. He hated Tuesdays. He hated saying goodbye to one lot of clients and heading to the airport to pick up another bunch. It wasn't that he grew particularly attached to the people he looked after. Oh no. Far from it. For the most part, the holidaymakers who stayed at Club Aegee made him want to grab the controls of the bus they travelled in on and steer it off the edge of a cliff. No, Axel hated the enforced jollity that was part of his job as a holiday rep. The 'goodbye' song they had to sing as each bus departed, for example. Who had instigated that stupid tradition? He especially hated that.

No wonder Axel's parents expressed surprise when their moody youngest son told them he was going to spend the summer as a Club Aegee holiday rep in Bodrum.

'You're not the kind to be a holiday rep,' they told him. And there was no doubt that he didn't fit the stereotype. He wasn't interested in sport, or singing and dancing, or hospitality. He had no ambition to become a tennis coach, or go to stage school at the end of the season. He just wanted to get as far away from France as possible. He wanted to be on the other side of an ocean. Preferably a large one. But he didn't have enough money to travel to India with the backpacking crowd from university (assuming they would have asked him). He didn't like the idea of teaching French to spoiled fat kids at a summer camp in the States (assuming they would have had him). So, Club Aegee Turkey it would have to be.

To be honest, if Axel's parents were surprised at their son's decision, they weren't half as surprised as he was when he learned he had the job. At the Club Aegee interview they had asked so many questions he could answer only in the negative. *Do you like to play team sports? Do you like to dance? Can you play a musical instrument?* This last was especially important. Club Aegee resorts were famous for their semi-professional evening entertainment. Some of the best-known media stars in France had started out on the Club Aegee cabaret stage. It was a well-trodden route to success.

'Well, what *do* you like to do?' the Club Aegee interviewer asked with a faint air of exasperation.

'I like to play chess,' said Axel flatly.

And that was what won him his place on the team.

It turned out that the Club Aegee marketing people were keen to add intellectual pursuits to their fabulous roster of activities. So at the beginning of May, Axel flew to Bodrum to begin work as Club Aegee's first ever *chess* rep, offering one-to-one tuition in the game and overseeing a weekly tournament for the more cerebral Club Aegee guests (assuming there would be more than two per week).

'It's going to be a wonderful experiment,' said the woman who gave him the job.

'It's going to be a total nightmare,' Axel assured his family before he caught the plane.

But when he arrived at the resort, Axel was quietly thrilled. Even to someone as prone to dwelling on the dark side as he, there was no denying that the place was incredibly beautiful. Someone looking very closely might even have discerned Axel's famously elusive smile as he stepped off the staff bus from the airport and surveyed the place that was to be his home until October (assuming he could stick it that long).

Dozens of white-rendered cottages nestled in landscaped gardens that were a riot of colour even at the beginning of the season. The huge swimming pool at the centre of the village was one of those infinite-edge pools, giving the impression that it offered a continuous aqua passage to the cerulean blue sea beyond. A path that had been carefully cleared of rocks and weeds led down through the beautiful gardens to a tranquil, private cove where the Aegean waited like a vast warm bath. Before the guests arrived, it truly was heaven on earth. And for a moment, Axel could forget all about France. And Natalie . . .

Unfortunately, Axel's contentment was to be short-lived. His status as chess rep meant that he wasn't expected to join the raucous team games round the swimming pool every morning, but it seemed that this was the only concession. Axel would be expected to take part in the nightly cabaret.

'But I can't sing!' he protested.

'You can mime,' said his boss, Cherie, *chef de village*.

And he would have to take his turn picking up guests at the airport too. On that front, he got the worst deal of all. As one of very few reps able to speak English fluently enough to deal with lost-luggage complaints and the accompanying swear words, Axel got the Tuesday run, picking up new arrivals from Gatwick. If he had to hear one more wiseass ask him where his beret was, or his onions . . . It didn't help that the Club Aegee uniform included a stripy matelot shirt . . .

Sybilla, the only Austrian rep at Club Aegee, said she would walk out if she ever had to do the airport run on a Tuesday. The Brits never waited long enough to hear more than her accent before they greeted her with a Nazi salute.

That morning, Axel waved off twelve Britons in the direction of the Home Counties. They hadn't been such a bad bunch, conforming to stereotype only in that they all got too much sun on the first day and spent the rest of the week looking as if they'd been dipped in scalding water. There was just one guest Axel went out of his way to avoid this time – a matronly woman called Sonia, holidaying alone, of course, who booked herself in for a two-hour chess tutorial every morning and always wanted to stay longer to engage Axel about his 'sad, sad eyes'.

On her last night, Sonia polished off a bottle of the terrifically rough red wine that accompanied the all-inclusive meals and made her daring and desperate lunge. Axel was horrified and angry when she hungrily attached her pink lips to his down the dark path that led from the swimming-pool bar to the toilets. Angry with himself. If this was the kind of woman he attracted, he thought as he peeled the drunken Brit from his shoulders, then no wonder Natalie didn't think he was worthy of her altogether superior love. As Sonia pressed her talcum-powdered face against his, he wanted to shout at her.

'Leave me alone. You're not Natalie. You look like a carthorse beside my dearest, darling deer.'

He didn't say that, of course. He just told Sonia that company policy prevented him from getting involved with the visitors, much as he would have liked to. Gilles, the tennis coach, his untidy room-mate (and the last person Axel would have chosen to share his abode with), laughed so hard he almost choked when Axel told him what had happened.

'Company policy! Ha! That's a good one. You should have slept with her, though,' Gilles added. 'A bit of the nasty with a woman like that will get you over Natalie double quick.'

But it just made the ache of her absence worse. Just brought home the gaping chasm in quality and style between Axel's deified beloved back in France and the mere mortal girls who would be more than happy to have him in Turkey.

'Get yourself laid before it seizes up,' Gilles concluded. 'You're only twenty-three.'

But Axel would never 'get himself laid'. He wanted to *make love* to Natalie or he would never make love again. Never. He couldn't bring himself to defile her perfect memory by sleeping with any other girl. And that was the thought that was clouding his expression as he waited for that morning's arrivals from Gatwick to tumble out towards the transfer buses like refugees from a war-torn land. Only pastier. And more badly dressed . . .

'Is this the Club Aegee bus?' asked Carrie Ann.
   '*Oui*,' said Axel.
   'Great,' said Rachel. 'Where are your onions?'

4

As Carrie Ann climbed on to the bus that would take
them from the airport to the resort, she felt as though
she had walked all the way from Gatwick to Turkey.
When your flight leaves at nine o'clock in the
morning, she concluded, it is not a good idea to neck
three glasses of champagne in the terminal bar before
boarding. The combination of altitude and dehy-
dration had given her a warp-speed hangover that
was hardly eased by the unrequested lumbar massage
she got from the passenger in the seat behind her.
The passenger in question was a five-year-old child.
The seat pitch in the cramped charter plane was just
the perfect distance for him to be able to kick Carrie
Ann in the kidneys every time he moved. Which was
often.

Somehow, Yaslyn and Rachel had managed to sleep
for the entire journey. Having checked in slightly late,
the three girls had been seated separately, but Carrie
Ann could just about see Yaslyn and Rachel from
where she was sitting between the passengers she
dubbed 'Jack Fat and his wife Crimplene'. As they
boarded, Yaslyn's neighbour for the flight had chival-
rously relieved her of her fashionably light hand
luggage and stowed it away in the overhead locker for
her. At the end of the flight, the dashing salt-and-
pepper-haired gentleman had fetched Yaslyn's bag

back down again too. In contrast, Carrie Ann's neighbour, Mrs Fat, had leapt out of her seat before the plane finished taxiing and, in her haste to retrieve her duty-free fags, let a very heavy vanity case drop on Carrie Ann's head.

It was Carrie Ann's own vanity case. She couldn't help but wonder if that was a sign.

'Good flight?' Rachel asked when the three girls were reunited on the tarmac. Yaslyn smiled, stretched like a kitten, and popped on her Gucci shades to protect her wrinkle-free eyes from the bright sunlight. Carrie Ann grumbled, felt her bones crack when she tried to straighten up and promptly dropped her own fake Ray-Bans lens down on the gravel.

'The bloke sitting next to me is on his way to meet his brother's yacht in Marmaris,' Yaslyn explained as she showed them his business card. 'He said we could join them if we want.'

'We?' Carrie Ann sniffed.

'I told him I'm travelling with my very best friends. There's plenty of room, he said.'

The yacht-owner's brother was still gazing hopefully in Yaslyn's direction.

'Only you could get an invite to stay on a yacht before we've even arrived in the country!' marvelled Rachel.

'Yeah,' Carrie Ann agreed. And not for the first time that morning, she wondered at the wisdom of going on holiday with a bride-to-be and a bikini model just a week after the arrival of her own decree absolute.

In the normal scheme of things, Carrie Ann and Yaslyn probably wouldn't have become friends. Carrie Ann was working as a senior manager at Office Angels with Rachel, then in her first personnel job as a graduate trainee. Rachel often talked about Yaslyn, a friend from her schooldays, and Carrie Ann grew to hate the very sound of her name. Yaslyn's was the face that launched a thousand women's magazines and became synonymous with 'Hard Hold Hairspray'. Even her name whispered beauty (and pretension). Carrie Ann did her best to avoid meeting the model, content to assume that her pretty face masked a hideous personality, until Rachel's twenty-third birthday. Rachel was celebrating at a karaoke bar. She wanted Carrie Ann *and* Yaslyn to be there.

Carrie Ann fretted over what she would wear to that party for a week. She imagined Yaslyn arriving in a limo, dressed in head-to-toe Gucci, ready to sneer at Carrie Ann's Oasis shift dress. In the event, Carrie Ann arrived just in time to see Yaslyn spill a glass of red wine down the front of her white Gap T-shirt. Two glasses later, Yaslyn confided that she had just been dumped by her stockbroker boyfriend, her agent had told her to shift seven pounds off her arse, and her exotic name was actually a combination of Yasmin, her father's choice, and Lynne, favourite of her grandmother, who thought that Yasmin sounded 'too foreign'.

The thaw in Carrie Ann's heart was completed when Yaslyn let out an enormous, stinky fart. 'Cabbage soup diet,' she admitted. 'I'm sorry.'

That was six years ago. These days, Carrie Ann rarely thought about the way Yaslyn looked any more. She didn't notice the soulful violet eyes that had garnered Yaslyn comparisons to a young Liz Taylor, or the mouth so perfect it had appeared ten feet wide on cinema screens throughout the world advertising toothpaste. Yaslyn was just Yaslyn. As insecure, neurotic and funny as the rest of them. Except at moments like this, when the one man Carrie Ann might have fancied out of a plane carrying three hundred people had eyes only for her beautiful friend.

'He is gorgeous,' confirmed Rachel, as she checked Yaslyn's new friend out from behind her sunglasses.

'Isn't married,' said Yaslyn. 'Right age. Loads of money. Perfect for you, Caz.'

'Yeah,' Carrie Ann muttered. If he could get the big Yaslyn-shaped splinter out of his eye first. It was hard when one of your favourite people rendered you invisible to the opposite sex. Especially now, when Carrie Ann needed all the superficial flirtatious encouragement she could get.

The divorce papers had arrived the previous weekend. Signed, sealed and thoroughly finished. Unbelievable. Two long years of communicating with her husband through solicitors were over. Two years of squabbling by post. Their marriage was over. Carrie Ann had her freedom. Even if he did have the marital home, the car, the furniture, the dog . . . The dog! Feckless hound. That was the worst bit.

Carrie Ann still couldn't understand why it was that he was entitled to all that. He was the bloody adulterer! That was the problem with being a high-flying woman, her friends reminded her. The under-achieving men in your life got intimidated and left. And they took half your worldly goods with them when they went . . .

Ah well, thought Carrie Ann. She would build up her empire again.

Though she had just jettisoned a thirteen-year marriage, Carrie Ann was still only thirty-four. She had her own temporary employment agency, with a staff of four (three of whom she could almost trust to wipe their own bottoms in her absence). She'd always had a good head for business – despite her ex-husband's harsh opinion to the contrary. And since Greg had dealt her such an almighty blow by ditching her for the woman she had previously considered her best friend, Carrie Ann had been working on the requisite 'body for sin' (*à la* Melanie Griffith's *Working Girl*) to go with it. Though she knew she would never look quite as good as Yaslyn, in the two years since she had found a pair of Mairi's knickers at the bottom of her marital bed, Carrie Ann had crunched her way to a stomach that wouldn't shame La Perla.

Shame, then, that she'd had to replace the La Perla miracle bikini she'd left behind on the dressing table in Battersea with an orange two piece from the airport concession of Warehouse.

'You'll look lovely in orange,' Yaslyn had promised her. Yaslyn would say that. Yaslyn would look lovely in a sack.

*

At last the Club Aegee rep was satisfied that all his happy campers were on board the bus. There were just five of them this morning. Carrie Ann, Rachel, Yaslyn and the couple who were last on the plane. As the woman passed, Carrie Ann attempted a friendly smile which wasn't reciprocated. The couple took their places on the back seat. Him in one corner, her in the other, looking in different directions and not saying a word.

Carrie Ann was instantly reminded of her last package holiday with Greg. Two weeks in Crete. A final attempt to save their marriage after the revelation of Mairi's underwear. Greg spent the fortnight listening to a CD Mairi had burned for him on his portable CD player. A CD of bloody love songs, of course.

Another reminder of Greg and the thump of her premature hangover made Carrie Ann feel very dark indeed. But it was hard to stay miserable once the coach pulled out of the airport and on to the road into Bodrum. It was hard to stay miserable when the sky was that blue and the clouds so far away and fluffy, as if their only purpose was to add a decorative touch to what might otherwise have been a boring scene. It was especially hard to stay miserable when Rachel peeped over the back of her seat and threatened to break into a rendition of 'The Wheels On The Bus' if Carrie Ann didn't smile at once.

From the front seat, Axel the rep was running through the amenities available to the guests on-site at Club Aegee Bodrum. 'Swimming pool, Turkish bath, tennis lessons, archery . . .'

'We could stick a picture of "he who shall not be

named" on a target and take turns,' Rachel suggested with reference to Carrie Ann's ex.

'Sounds like fun,' said Carrie Ann.

'And I am the rep for the chess,' Axel continued.

'Chess?' mouthed Yaslyn. 'Chess??? These Club Aegee types really know how to have a good time.'

5

'Come on, everybody! We are 'ere to 'ave a good time!'

'*You all ready for this . . . der der der . . .*'

Six Club Aegee holiday reps bounced into action like champion cheerleaders at the first bars of some 1995 club classic as the bus carrying the latest group of inmates turned into the camp.

'Oh my God.' Sally Merchant slunk lower into her seat as she clocked the frenzied dance routine in the car park. 'What are they doing, Marcus? What is this place?'

'I guess this must be the welcome meeting,' he said.

'Tell them to stop,' said Sally.

When the bus pulled to a halt, the reps finished their routine with a gigantic cheer and lined up by the bus door like a guard of honour to clap their new guests towards reception.

'I'm not getting off the coach until they've gone,' said Sally, remaining firmly in her seat while Marcus gathered together their belongings.

'Come on,' said Marcus. He almost added 'Don't be miserable' but thought better of it. At least she was talking to him now, even if it was only to moan. They had passed the entire flight in silence.

'This is absolutely retarded,' Sally concluded as she unwillingly followed her husband into the fray.

*

Cheesy dance routine aside, Carrie Ann had been right that these were a better class of holiday rep than the type that had made her life a living hell on her last girls' holiday in Ibiza seven years before. Rule of thumb if you're thinking of booking an 18-30s holiday – if you're old enough to go, then you're probably way too old to enjoy it. Carrie Ann would never live down the fact that she'd nearly had a punch-up with an over-enthusiastic 18-30 staff member who tried to drag her from her bed at six in the morning to join a water-park excursion. There would be no such excursion hard sell here.

Disembarkation over, reps and guests lined up on opposite sides of the courtyard like boys and girls at a junior school disco shyly regarding each other across the assembly hall. In the middle, Cherie, the *chef de village*, was like the headmistress, trying to encourage both sides to cross the invisible line.

'Welcome to Club Aegee!' she began with a whoop. The guests were soon to discover that the words 'Club Aegee' elicited an automatic cheer from the reps (and the more enthusiastic visitors), like the magic word on that children's TV classic *Crackerjack*.

The reps were introduced one by one, bouncing forward to take a bow when their names were called. First came Gilles, the tennis instructor, with his shimmering golden fringe. Then Pierre, the dancing instructor, who demonstrated his qualifications for the position by grabbing one of the female reps in an impromptu tango swoon. Xavier, in charge of wind-surfs and catamarans at the beach, bore more than a passing resemblance to Russell Crowe.

'If you look at him like this,' said Yaslyn, screwing up her eyes and turning her head sideways.

There were three female reps to match the boys. Carrie Ann didn't bother to take note of their names, dubbing them instead the 'Go-Go girls', which was pretty clever, she thought, considering that the village's term for reps was GO – short for 'Gentil Ordinateur', like the reps at Club Med.

These three girls might have been sisters. All had identical shoulder-length chestnut hair and smooth brown skin that really did look as though it had been brushed with honey. Carrie Ann suddenly felt very orange. The fake tan she had applied to her legs the previous evening was more tangerine than toasted caramel, as it had claimed on the bottle.

The 'trademark Club Aegee welcome cocktail' Axel had spoken of thoroughly unenthusiastically on the journey from the airport was an equally bright orange brew of indeterminate fruit flavour. 'And definitely no alcohol,' Rachel announced with a wince. She took a polite sip and then looked about for a plant pot to dispose of the rest in. A glass of water would have been nicer.

For some unfathomable reason, the sun-bunny reps had set up their table of refreshments and excursion leaflets in the least shady part of the courtyard, so that the chocolate biscuits set out to go with the drink were now a pile of crumbs in a shallow brown puddle. Carrie Ann, who had inherited her Irish mother's translucently pale skin, shrank back against a nearby wall like a creature that had grown up in the dark, while one of the Go-Go girls explained in broken English that they should leave their bags in the courtyard so that they might be delivered to their rooms later on. In the meantime, they would be escorted to their rooms.

'Not her. Please not her,' Yaslyn hissed when a second Go-Go girl jumped forward to introduce herself and escort the first group of happy campers to Block A.

'Not as if she could make you look fat,' said Carrie Ann.

The miserable couple from the bus were the first and only guests on the Go-Go girl's list.

'Mr and Mrs Merchant. *Allons*-y!' the Go-Go whooped and skipped off down the path. By the time the guests she was to escort had gathered themselves together, she was almost out of sight.

Yaslyn, Rachel and Carrie Ann got Gilles, the tennis rep.

He didn't so much skip as sidle over to them, Carrie Ann thought. And there were no prizes for guessing who got the first benefit of his centre-court smile.

''Allo, beautiful,' he said to Yaslyn, picking up her hand and bestowing it with a kiss. 'You look like you would like to play tennis? Am I right?'

'Oooh, yes,' said Yaslyn, with a wink back towards Carrie Ann. 'I don't mind the occasional knock-up.'

Gilles laughed and took Yaslyn's handbag for her, carrying it as though he were Lord Chancellor carrying a sceptre in front of the queen. He carried Rachel's rucksack in his other hand. Carrie Ann was left with her vanity case and a bad taste in her mouth which wasn't entirely due to the 'welcome' cocktail. It was amazing the effect Yaslyn seemed to have on men, like a latter-day Guinevere, turning every one of them into a gallant knight.

'Me! Me! I like tennis too!' Rachel jokily mouthed to Gilles' broad back as they set off in the direction of the guest huts. But he'd been blinded by the *Yaslyn Effect*.

'Your room.'

After what seemed like a Duke of Edinburgh Gold Award hike through the gardens, Gilles eventually pushed open the door to one of the little white huts.

'Now I know where you are,' he told Yaslyn, 'I will sing outside your window every evening until you promise to marry me.'

'She's already attached,' said Carrie Ann flatly.

Yaslyn and Rachel looked at Carrie Ann with surprise.

'Well, you are,' Carrie Ann reminded Yaslyn.

'Thank you,' said Yaslyn. 'I know.'

'See you on the tennis court,' said Gilles, as he departed with a bow.

'What a dreamboat,' sighed Yaslyn.

'What a slime ball,' said Carrie Ann.

'What do you think?' Yaslyn bounced into the room and headed straight for the doors that led to the balcony. 'Two pairs of trunks on the balcony below,' she announced moments later.

'What?' Rachel was investigating the bathroom of their surprisingly capacious little suite. The complimentary toiletries were pretty impressive too.

'Two pairs of trunks downstairs,' Yaslyn repeated. 'It means we're on top of two lads. So to speak.'

'Probably one lad with two pairs of shorts and a girlfriend.'

'Nope.' Yaslyn dismissed Carrie Ann's doomy prognosis. 'Don't you think that the kind of girl who goes out with the kind of boy who has two pairs of shorts would have at least three bikinis, two of which would be drying on that balcony right now?'

'Your logic is impeccable,' Carrie Ann conceded. 'Which bed are you having?'

'Whichever,' said Yaslyn, sauntering back into the room. 'That one.' She pointed at the bed on to which Carrie Ann had already put her case. The one beneath the window and farthest away from the air-conditioning unit which would doubtless make plenty of industrious-sounding noise but actually be quite hopeless when it came to conditioning air. Rachel had bagged the bed in the middle. Carrie Ann moved her case on to the bed directly beneath the air con with a sigh.

'Not bad, eh?' said Yaslyn, bouncing on her mattress. 'And we've got a sea view. If you lean as far over the balcony as you dare and risk tumbling into the lap of one of our neighbours.'

'Perhaps you should try it, Caz,' said Rachel. 'Good way to break the ice. Start throwing yourself at the men. Hey, wouldn't it be great if Carrie Ann found love with one of the guys downstairs?'

'Not if she's noisy in the sack, it wouldn't,' said Yaslyn.

Carrie Ann scowled.

'Oh, for God's sake,' said Yaslyn. 'I was trying to

make a joke. What's wrong with you? You haven't smiled once since we got here. You can't be miserable here, Carrie Ann. I simply won't allow it. Or, if you are going to be miserable, kindly do so from the opposite side of the pool.'

'No one's going to be miserable,' Rachel intervened, to keep the peace. 'We're all just a bit tired from the flight. I know I hardly slept at all last night because I was afraid I'd sleep through my alarm and be late getting to the airport. And I can never get any sleep on a plane,' she lied.

Carrie Ann forced a smile. Yaslyn gave a little shrug.

'This is going to be the best holiday ever,' Rachel assured Carrie Ann, suddenly leaping up to give her a hug. 'By the time this week is over we'll have had so much fun I'll probably be wondering why I'm bothering to get married at all.'

'*Because you've met a real Prince Charming.*' Carrie Ann and Yaslyn paused in their unpacking to sing out one of Rachel's favourite lines about the wonderful Patrick.

'Yes, well. I suppose I have. But I envy you your freedom too. The single life is the way forward, Carrie Ann,' she added unconvincingly.

'And food,' Carrie Ann interrupted. 'Lots of food. Let's get to the restaurant before they stop serving lunch.'

6

'We'll have to change rooms,' Sally announced, when the Go-Go girl who had escorted them there was safely out of earshot.

'What's wrong with it?' Marcus asked. It seemed perfectly fine to him. He was already unzipping his backpack.

'Marcus, it's a tip. That's what's bloody wrong with it.'

'It looks all right to me.'

'What?' Sally ran her finger along the window sill. 'Look,' she said, showing him her ever so slightly grimy fingertip. 'And look.' She dragged him into the bathroom and made him look at an invisible pubic hair on the bathroom floor. 'They haven't cleaned this place since the last guests were here. I'm sure they haven't. I can't possibly sleep here knowing that.'

'What do you want me to do? Get them to send a cleaner round again?'

'Just phone reception and get them to move us.'

'I think the camp's full. They might not be able to.'

Sally picked up the telephone receiver and slapped it into his hand.

'Try.'

*

'They've got no more rooms with double beds,' was the advice Marcus passed on when he got through to the concierge. 'Only singles.'

'That'll do,' said Sally.

'What? A room with two single beds instead of this one?'

'You'll be asleep when you're in it. What difference does it make?'

'I suppose we could push them together,' said Marcus.

'Yeah,' Sally replied vaguely. She was already dragging her case back outside. 'You can sort this out, can't you? I'm going to have a walk round the gardens. I need to get some air after that flight.'

'Don't you want to see where they're going to put us first? What if you don't like this other room either?'

'I'm sure it will be fine,' she said, and set off away from him down the shady path that led towards the beach.

Marcus remained on the threshold of the unsuitable room and watched his wife until she was out of sight. What had that been about? Dirt? Pubic hair? The room was spotless, as far as he could see. What had happened to the girl he had travelled round India with whose only stipulation had been that the cockroaches were swept out of her bed before she got into it?

They had met at a party during their first year at university. Marcus hadn't seen Sally around the campus at all until that night. He didn't really mix with the arty crowd throwing the fancy-dress bash for Hallowe'en. He was only going along as moral support for his friend Aimee. Aimee suspected that her ex-boyfriend might be at the party and wanted the rat in question to think she had already got herself a new man. Marcus was playing the new bloke, of course.

Aimee's ex-boyfriend *was* at the party. The ex-lovers ignored each other for all of three minutes, then spent the rest of the evening locked in the downstairs loo of the grotty student house 'working things out'. Marcus would have left at that point but he suspected that if he did he would only get a call from Aimee in the middle of the night asking him to come and fetch her. And he knew that he would have to go and fetch her. Marcus was more than a little bit in love with Aimee Lawson at that time. No one else could have persuaded him to don a sheet and dress as a Roman on the coldest night of the year.

'Hail Caesar!'

Those were the first words Sally Tyrrell said to him when she found him lurking in the corner of the sitting room.

'Want to fiddle with my asp?' she said then. She was dressed as Cleopatra.

Marcus held her plastic snake (not actually an asp but a cobra, he would point out later on) while Sally rolled herself a joint on top of a speaker cabinet. And that was it. Aimee Lawson began to fade from his consciousness immediately. Sally was as beautiful as the legendary Nefertiti in her black wig with a blunt fringe that drew his attention to her expertly outlined eyes. What colour were they? Marcus asked himself. And six years later, as they stood side by side in a register office, he was still wondering. Were they blue? Were they violet? They seemed to change colour when she smiled.

'Do you smoke?' she asked that evening, holding the neat little joint towards him.

'I never have,' he told her.

'Want to try?'

'I don't know,' he said. The fact was, he was nervous. When he said that he'd never smoked, he wasn't just referring to joints. He'd never even so much as sniffed at a Marlboro Light behind the bike sheds when everyone else was on ten a day by seventeen. 'Hurts my throat,' was his excuse.

'Then let me give you a blow-back,' she said.

'What?'

Was she propositioning him? Marcus didn't have a clue. But when she inhaled and moved her mouth towards his, he instinctively softened his own mouth in readiness for a kiss. When she didn't kiss him back but blew smoke in through his open lips instead, he immediately felt his throat seize up in surprise. His lungs went into shock. He fell over.

When he came round from his faint, Cleopatra was kneeling over him. As were Napoleon, Marilyn Monroe and a second-rate Captain Caveman.

'Caesar?' Sally was calling him. She still didn't know his name. 'Caesar? Are you OK? Caesar? Speak to us. Can you hear me?'

Marcus eased himself into a sitting position. He'd hit his head hard on the speaker cabinet as he fell. When he put his fingers up to the place that hurt, they came away bloody and he fainted again. Marcus never could stand the sight of blood.

'I'd better take you to the accident unit,' said Cleopatra when he came round a second time.

She drove him there in her bashed-up Mini and left him by the door. Marcus fully expected he would never see his Egyptian princess again.

But next day Sally collared him outside the library.

'I've been so worried,' she said.

'You can't have been that worried. You left me alone at the accident unit,' he pointed out.

'I'd been smoking grass,' she reminded him. 'I didn't want to bump into a policeman. Did they give you any stitches?'

Marcus showed her the neat row of butterfly strips across his temple.

'Ouch.'

'Ouch indeed,' said Marcus.

'Can I make it up to you?' she asked. 'Buy you a drink in the Union?'

He let Sally buy him three pints before he forgave her.

Four years after their inauspicious start, Sally and Marcus moved down to London together and were married in the Chelsea Register Office on the King's Road two years later. The butterfly strips applied so diligently at the accident unit hadn't been able to stop the gash on Marcus's head becoming a small white scar. But he didn't care too much about that. In fact, he was rather fond of it.

'I'll always be reminded of the day I *fell* for you,' he said, whenever Sally touched it and looked contrite.

Four years after the wedding and their 'Rome meets Egypt'-style reception, Sally and Marcus were living in a small house in the suburbs, both commuting to London to work. They left the house at 6.30 in the morning every morning to catch a train into Waterloo. They didn't talk on the train into London (Sally wasn't a morning person) and increasingly they found they weren't catching the same one home again. Sally's most recent promotion was keeping her at the office later and later.

The commute was taking up too much of their day, all but eradicating the time they once had to spend together during the working week. The weekends were taken up with DIY now. The charming cottage had turned out to be a bottomless money-eating pit in disguise riddled with dry rot and dodgy electrics. Tiredness was the reason they hardly had sex any more. Money worries were the reason Sally couldn't get excited about spending a week in the sun. There were concrete reasons, weren't there, for the way things had been between them lately? Problems that could be attended to if they took a bit of time away from it all. It wasn't just that they were falling out of love . . .

7

Walking into the restaurant that first lunch-time, Rachel, Yaslyn and Carrie Ann felt like the new girls at school, recognisable not by their spanking-new uniforms but by their glaring lack of tan. Heads swivelled as they stepped into the buffet area. Carrie Ann wanted to duck under a tablecloth. Yaslyn, who was slightly more used to being checked out by complete strangers, was unashamedly checking them back.

'Six o'clock,' she hissed through the corner of her mouth. 'The guy in the red T-shirt. He's yours, Carrie Ann. What a stud!'

Carrie Ann fell for it, turning oh so subtly to see her target. She found the red T-shirt, all right. Then she found the face of the guy who was wearing it. He was an Italian stallion. Forty years ago . . .

Rachel and Yaslyn cracked up at the thought.

'Brown paper packages,' said Rachel, referring to a line from a ridiculous self-help book that had been part of the 'divorce kit' she and Yaslyn had brought along on the trip for their friend. It was a thoughtful but not altogether appreciated present. Carrie Ann had smiled wanly when she opened the beautifully wrapped gift and found what was inside. She had hoped for some fantastic toiletries. Some funky jewellery. Instead, the kit contained a big box of

Kleenex, a pair of 'lucky' red knickers and a voodoo doll complete with pins to which Yaslyn had already helpfully attached a photo of Greg's smug face.

The self-help book – chosen by Rachel – was called *How to Get Over That Man and Find a New One*. It was written by one Margaret Mayday, whose author picture suggested she probably hadn't got herself a new man since 1978. It was not the kind of book Carrie Ann would have picked for herself, or ever intended to read. Luckily, Rachel had flicked through the tome and made a note of the more important advice for her. 'Brown paper packages' referred to the fact that the very best presents often come in unassuming wrapping paper. It was a variation on 'Never judge a book by its cover', 'Don't look a gift horse in the mouth'. Or, as Carrie Ann quipped mournfully when she heard it, 'Recently divorced beggars can't be choosers, right?'

Fortunately for Carrie Ann, the old Italian nag in the restaurant that lunch-time was joined by his mare before Yaslyn and Rachel could insist she introduce herself. The girls moved around the sumptuous buffet tables loading their plates. The fruit and cheese table looked like something out of a Caravaggio frieze. Carrie Ann went straight for the chips.

'Hangover,' was her excuse/explanation.

Yaslyn turned away from fried temptation as usual and headed straight for a big bowl of watercress.

'I hate salad,' she muttered as she loaded her plate.

'Then why are you having it?' asked Rachel. 'You're on holiday. Have some chips. Go mad.'

'Been putting a bit of weight on,' said Yaslyn vaguely.

Yeah, right, thought Carrie Ann when she heard that. Yaslyn still had a stone's grace before she looked half as big as Kate Moss.

Plates loaded, they chose a table in a shady corner of the restaurant's courtyard and continued their survey of the other guests. The air was filled with the sound of delightfully cosmopolitan chatter. French, Italian, Spanish. Not a British accent complaining about the weather/food/locals to be heard.

The Continental influence was clear in the way the clientele looked as well. These were holiday guests straight out of central casting. Well groomed with beautiful bodies no matter what their age (and the majority of them were a little older than the girls had expected) and elegant. No football shirts worn to lunch at Club Aegee. No prominent and badly drawn tattoos. No decent swimming trunks . . .

'Ugh,' said Carrie Ann and Rachel simultaneously as a fellow guest strolled past them wearing nothing but a pair of Speedos – the swimwear that Britain thankfully forgot.

'You'd think they'd have a rule about that,' said Rachel.

'You know,' said Yaslyn knowledgeably, 'in some parts of France it is illegal for a man to get into a swimming pool if he *isn't* wearing Speedos. You're not allowed to wear baggy shorts for reasons of hygiene.'

'No!' Rachel cried. 'That can't be true. I think I've just discovered a new diet,' she added as she pushed her plate away. 'The Speedo diet. For when you need to get into that bikini. Just try to eat a big lunch opposite a man wearing nothing but a pair of Speedos and a grin . . .'

'Sick!' said Carrie Ann.

'You will be.'

'But what if your Speedo model looked like him?' Yaslyn jerked her head in the direction of a young buck strutting across the restaurant courtyard as though he were crossing the red carpet at Cannes. 'French or Italian?'

'French,' said Carrie Ann. 'He's got that confidence.'

'Italian,' disagreed Rachel. 'He's ever so slightly camp.'

'French men are easily as camp as Italians,' Carrie Ann protested.

'No. Gérard Depardieu,' Yaslyn offered in evidence.

'Antoine des Caunes,' Carrie Ann volleyed back.

'How are we going to settle this?' asked Rachel. 'Go up to him and ask him something in French.'

'Nooooo!' Carrie Ann squealed. 'I can't.'

'This is a hen week,' Yaslyn reminded her. 'We've all got to do dares. Your first dare is to go up to Mr Gorgeous and ask him if he *parlay-voos Anglay*. Could be the start of something beautiful.'

'When I've had a drink,' Carrie Ann insisted.

'Do it now,' said Rachel. 'He's sitting on his own. You've got no competition.'

Then, as if Rachel had reactivated some ancient curse, the competition arrived. Mr Gorgeous looked up from his lunch tray like a man who had seen the face of God. Carrie Ann blinked to ensure she wasn't suffering from heat-induced double vision. Unfortunately not. Mr Gorgeous really had been joined by not one but two equally jaw-droppingly gorgeous girls.

Even Yaslyn stared. These girls must have mugged a baby giraffe for their legs. They both had straight blonde hair hanging down to their waists, which, despite the sun and the sea salt, was still quite unfeasibly soft and shiny.

'You know how magazines are always telling us that Barbie's proportions couldn't possibly exist in a real woman?' Rachel groaned. 'It appears they were wrong. To the power of two.'

Mr Gorgeous offered a chair on either side of him to each of the young girls. They shook their heads sorrowfully, laughed at a feeble joke and turned to leave. And now came the killer blow. One of the girls wrapped her arm around the other's waist. She was rewarded with a kiss on her cheek.

'They're not . . .' Carrie Ann breathed. 'They can't be. This is the end of my finding-Mr-Right-in-Bodrum fantasy. I can't believe we've picked the same bloody holiday site as the Swedish Lesbian Twins . . .'

Axel Radanne didn't notice the ostentatiously Sapphic embrace that held every other man in the restaurant transfixed. He was heading for the buffet in his usual fashion. Head down, eyes front, determined not to catch anybody's attention on his way between salad bar and table with his daily plate of watercress and grated beetroot. He didn't even look up to acknowledge the twin blonde girls' apology as they stumbled momentarily into his path. Mealtimes at Club Aegee were a form of torture for Axel. A Club Aegee rep was *always* on duty, Cherie had told them at the start of the season. And that went for mealtimes as well.

'Sit with some different guests every day,' she instructed. 'Show an interest. Get to know them. Building personal relationships like this is the best way to fend off complaints before they arise.' In fact, Cherie was proud to be able to tell all her new staff, Club Aegee Bodrum had *never* received a letter of complaint under her leadership.

Gilles took Cherie's instructions as *carte blanche* to spend two hours each lunch-time honing his chat-up lines to perfection. For Axel also, lunch-time was an opportunity to hone his skills. His skills of camouflage and evasion. On his way into the restaurant he would try to ascertain where Cherie, his boss, was sitting. He would make sure that she saw him arrive to give the impression that he was about to do his duty as a sociable rep. Then he would deliberately choose a table obscured from her vision by pillars. There was a group of three tables that guests very rarely chose to use. They were too close to the kitchen door. Too shady. Perfect for a wallflower like Axel.

Today he felt even less inclined to be sociable than usual. Because today there had been a letter in Axel's pigeon-hole in the staff room. He checked his pigeon-hole so often that now he was able to stand by the staff-room door and pinpoint his own personal mailbox without having to step inside. When he saw the unmistakable edge of an envelope there, his heart leapt sixty feet. He crossed the room in two bounding steps, snatched the letter up, tore it open and . . .

His own handwriting greeted him. He looked at the envelope in confusion. Unfamiliar handwriting declared 'not known at this address'. Natalie's name had been scribbled out in the same red pen.

The letter that Axel had taken such pains to craft was back in his pocket again. All the heartfelt protestations of love, the apologies, the promises to change, had winged their way across a continent and promptly been winged straight back at him.

Sitting at his table in the shade, Axel spread the sad pages out in front of his lunch tray.

'Dearest Natalie,' the letter began. 'This is the seventeenth letter I have written since I arrived in Turkey two months ago . . .'

It was the seventeenth letter to go unanswered. And unread . . .

8

Sally's short walk around the grounds had lasted all afternoon. Once he had safely moved their belongings to the new room, Marcus set out to look for her but could find her nowhere in the camp. He spent the afternoon trotting between the new room (which in his opinion was worse than the first) and reception to ask the receptionist whether his wife had been in to find out where they had been relocated to. She hadn't. He was just about to make another trip to reception when Sally finally turned up.

'Hello.'

'Nice walk?' Marcus asked, biting back the temptation to ask her why it had taken so bloody long.

'Yeah,' she said.

'Is this room OK?' he asked.

'Yeah,' she said, again, without even looking round. 'I'm going to have a shower.'

She showered for a whole half-hour. And when she came out of the bathroom, she had already changed into evening clothes. She must have taken them in with her. Marcus was faintly surprised. She'd always changed in front of him before.

'What was lunch like?' she asked as she towel-dried her hair.

'I didn't go to lunch,' Marcus told her. 'I was waiting here for you.'

'Sorry. You should have gone ahead and had something.'

'I thought you might want to have lunch with me.'

Sally shrugged. 'Ah well, it's dinner-time now. We can make up for it. Ready?'

Marcus followed her to the restaurant. At dusk, the resort seemed to change character. Flaming torches lit the winding path from the swimming pool to the buffet. Fairy lights twinkled above the pool bar.

The reps had changed out of their stripy sports gear into altogether smarter attire in black and white, to match the theme for the evening. Every evening had a theme, it transpired. The French guests were dressed as though for dinner at the captain's table on some majestic ocean-going yacht. Many of them wore black and white too.

'I feel underdressed,' Sally whispered.

'You look lovely,' said Marcus.

'I wish you'd told me it would be like this,' she replied, swiftly reintroducing an element of blame.

The lunch-time buffet of salad and fried food had also undergone something of a makeover for the evening. The chef who had doled out chips at midday now stood behind a huge poached salmon, sharpening one deadly knife against another.

'Feesh,' he said as Sally passed.

'This looks great, doesn't it?' Marcus stopped in front of the magnificent pale pink fish and attempted to engage Sally in conversation about the food.

'Hmmm. Wonder if they've washed that salad in sterilised water,' Sally replied. 'Last thing I need is a dose of Turkey tummy.'

'You weren't that bothered when we were in India,' Marcus pointed out. 'You ate pretty much everything there without worrying.'

'Yeah. And look what happened. That was the worst trip of my life.'

Sally had thrown that last comment over her shoulder as she simultaneously found herself a plate and started picking over the vegetables.

The worst trip of her life? Marcus wondered whether he'd heard right. Their holiday to India had been their best holiday ever, surely. They'd plastered their house with photos of the trip upon their return. Furnished their bedroom with knick-knacks they'd picked up in Kerala. Whenever anybody so much as breathed the word 'India' in her presence, Sally would practically swoon with delight and insist that everyone should go there at least once in a lifetime. She could sing the country's praises for an hour without stopping to draw breath. And now suddenly it was the worst trip of her life?

'Women revise history according to how they feel about you.' A comment Charlie had made over a pint in the Nightingale now echoed in Marcus's head. 'When I started seeing Caroline,' Charlie said by way of illustration, 'she said she liked the fact that I was dominant in bed. Six years later I was just another selfish bastard.'

Revising history in the light of her feelings. Was that what Sally was doing now?

That first evening in Bodrum, Rachel, Yaslyn and Carrie Ann had an early intimation of the circumstances that would come to test their friendship over the next few days. The room they had been given was big enough for three women and their various accoutrements. The bathroom, however, was not.

By the time the three girls had unpacked their wash-bags and vanity cases, the bathroom looked like the Boots 17 counter at the end of a Saturday afternoon. Though the mirror stretched all the way along one wall, there simply wasn't enough elbow room for two girls to do their make-up at once, let alone three. While she and Rachel were struggling to see their reflections, Yaslyn had already managed to knock Carrie Ann's expensive night cream off the shelf above the basin and into the lavatory.

'It'll be OK!' Yaslyn insisted, wiping the jar dry on some toilet paper. 'At least the jar was closed.'

'The germs in a toilet are microscopic!' Rachel breathed in horror. 'Something is bound to have got in.'

'Sssh,' Yaslyn hissed. 'She doesn't need to know.'

'Need to know what?' Carrie Ann called from the bedroom.

'Nothing,' the others chimed on cue.

'We're going to have to devise a rota,' suggested Yaslyn when they were finally ready to leave their room for the evening.

'Well, I need at least an hour to get anywhere near able to compete with you,' said Carrie Ann, gazing enviously at the model's simple black crêpe dress, flowing like water over her textbook curves. 'How do I look?' she asked, smoothing out the creases in her own linen shift.

'Fantastic,' Rachel assured her. 'Watch out, boys.

Do you think the competition will be allowed out this late at night?' she asked, referring to the Swedish Lesbian Twins.

'I hope not,' said Carrie Ann. 'I need to find my single stockbroker before the end of the week.'

'Ladies,' said Yaslyn then, 'I think we need to have a "going out" ritual while we're all here in Bodrum. Something that will make sure the night goes with a swing. Every night.'

'A mantra,' suggested Rachel. 'Like cheerleaders?'

'Cheerleaders have cheers, not mantras. Anyway, I was thinking more along the lines of a couple of shots of this.'

Yaslyn got out the bottle of Goldschlager she had picked up in duty free. Goldschlager is the kind of drink one only ever picks up in duty free en route to a hen party. The thick, gloopy aniseed-flavoured schnapps was speckled with flecks of *real* gold leaf. A bargain at less than ten pounds for a litre.

'That cannot be good for your digestion,' said Carrie Ann, eyeing the bottle suspiciously.

Nevertheless, Yaslyn poured out three measures into the tooth mugs she retrieved from the bathroom.

'Down in one,' she insisted.

'This isn't much of a ritual,' said Carrie Ann. 'We do this every time we go out back home.' Usually they started an evening with a couple of shots of flaming sambuca.

'OK.' Rachel snatched up the vibrator that had caused her such mortification at customs. 'What about . . . We have to down our schnapps while holding on to this. It's like our Olympic torch for the holiday. Our totem pole.'

'I'd have got a bigger one if I'd known,' said Yaslyn.

'We have to hold the lucky vibrator, down the schnapps and make a wish.' Rachel was really getting into the swing of things. 'I'll go first. I wish for a really happy hen week.' She attempted to chug her schnapps down in one and ended up coughing half of it back over Carrie Ann.

'Thanks a lot,' said Carrie Ann, picking gold leaf off her shift dress. When the totem was passed to her she said, 'I wish for a gorgeous bloke with a big brain, a big heart and an even bigger wallet.'

'Hmmm. I think I'll have one of those too,' said Yaslyn.

'Yaslyn,' Rachel reminded her, 'you're attached!'

9

It was widely agreed that Yaslyn had one of the best boyfriends in the world – the kind of man who convinced single women over the age of thirty-five, depressed by the statistic that they were more likely to die in a terrorist attack than marry, that suicide was not the only option. Kind, sensitive, handsome, generous. *Not the type to play games.* That was especially important, Carrie Ann pointed out. Yaslyn hadn't spent three months in telephone-vigil hell with Euan. Not that she had ever spent any time in telephone-vigil hell for any man ever. Yaslyn simply wasn't that kind of girl.

Yaslyn was the kind of girl who always got served first at a bar no matter how long everyone else had been waiting.

'What's a nice girl like you doing in a place like this?' were the first words Euan said to Yaslyn when she squeezed her way between two other punters at his bar.

'Aren't you supposed to ask me what I'm having and leave the chatting-up to the men who can afford to buy me a drink rather than sell me one?' Yaslyn replied. 'Vodka and tonic. Belvedere if you have it. And a bottle of Bacardi Breezer for my somewhat tasteless friend over there.'

Rachel turned to look at Yaslyn as though she knew

her name was being taken in vain. Then Rachel spotted Euan.

'Euan! What are you doing here?' Rachel hauled herself halfway over the bar to kiss him on both cheeks. 'Yaslyn, this is the bloke I was telling you about. Euan. He was at university with Patrick. He's just come back from travelling round the world. He worked in an orphanage in Tanzania,' Rachel added.

'Very worthy,' said Yaslyn, barely concealing a yawn.

'So, how are you finding it back in Blighty?' Rachel asked him.

'Not sunny enough. Until your friend here arrived with her dazzling smile.'

Yaslyn had actually been pouting all the while. She flashed her straight white teeth at Euan in a sarcastic approximation of a grin.

'How long have you been doing this?'

'Started yesterday,' Euan told Rachel. 'It's not exactly a great career move but it will keep me going until I can make some contacts on newspapers and stuff.'

'Euan is a photographer, really,' said Rachel for Yaslyn's benefit. 'Yaslyn is a model.'

'I think I recognise you,' Euan told her.

'Did we meet when you shot me for *Elle*?' Sarcasm was positively leaking from Yaslyn's pores that evening. She'd had a bad day, losing out on a big advertising campaign to the girl her agency had been selling as 'the New Yaslyn', for God's sake.

'No. I recognise you from that show.'

Yaslyn nodded and forced a smile. 'That show'

at the time was a game show called *Friends and Family*, a daytime TV rip off of *Who Wants to Be a Millionaire?* Yaslyn's job was simply to stalk backwards and forwards across the studio carrying the golden envelope that contained the million-dollar question. It wasn't what you could call a challenging role.

'It pays the bills,' she said dismissively.

'I like it . . . You're the best thing on it. Obviously.'

'You're too kind.'

'Of course, I won't have time to watch it now I've got a job.'

'You won't have a job for too much longer if you keep all your customers waiting as long as us,' Yaslyn pointed out.

'Sorry.' Euan scuttled to the fridge behind the bar and brought out Rachel's Bacardi Breezer. He popped the top off the bottle and garnished it with a paper umbrella that made Rachel laugh with delight. Then he poured out Yaslyn's vodka, holding the bottle high in the air and flicking his wrist at exactly the right time to ensure she got a perfect double shot.

'Would you like an umbrella too?' he asked her.

'What do you think?' said Yaslyn.

He added a yellow umbrella to her drink and hung a green plastic monkey from the side of the glass for good measure. He handed the drink over with a big cheeky wink.

'How much do I owe you?'

'This one's on me.'

'Thanks, Euan!' Rachel grinned at him. 'Will we see you at our house Sunday lunch-time?'

'I'll be there. Wouldn't miss your roast potatoes for the world.'

Rachel followed Yaslyn into the crowd.

'If I didn't have Patrick . . .' Rachel sighed. 'Isn't he lovely?'

'Who's lovely?' Yaslyn asked.

'Euan.'

'He's OK.'

'He definitely liked you. Perhaps I should fix you up with him.'

Yaslyn winced. The Hard Hold Hairspray campaign wasn't the only thing she had lost to 'the New Yaslyn' that week. It seemed that Yaslyn's on-off boyfriend, an actor called Simon, also thought it was time to upgrade to a newer model. Yaslyn had been getting tired of Simon's thespian philosophising in any case (his claim to fame was a six-week stint in a soap about firemen, for God's sake) but that hardly made it any easier to be pushed when she was still considering her jump.

'Yaslyn,' Rachel interrupted Yaslyn's daydream about strangling Simon with his own fire hose. 'Why don't you come over for lunch on Sunday too? I need another person to make even numbers.'

'I'm washing my hair,' said Yaslyn pointedly.

'Well, if you change your mind . . .' said Rachel.

Yaslyn didn't change her mind before Sunday. But Rachel was on a mission. She ignored Yaslyn's lack of enthusiasm that night in the Booze Bar and told Euan that Yaslyn wanted him to have her phone number. A week later he was standing on her doorstep with a box of chocolates and that goofy grin even bigger than she remembered. She took the chocolates as graciously as she could. No point telling him she hadn't eaten chocolate since 1994 as she figured he wouldn't have the opportunity to bring them again. This was going to be a one-off. A date because she felt sorry for him. And because Rachel would never stop going on about him if she didn't. With a bit of luck Yaslyn could be home before ten.

'I've booked a table at this gastropub I know,' Euan said proudly. 'It gets really busy. They do great steak and chips.'

Mix protein and carbs? thought Yaslyn in horror. Never. 'Great,' was what she said, hoping they'd have some sort of salad on the menu. They didn't. Steak and chips it was, then, and an appointment with some laxatives later.

It should have been a disaster, but there was something in the way Euan could tell a story about the industry Yaslyn knew only too well (he had worked as a fashion photographer before travelling) which had her sitting in that pub past her self-imposed ten o'clock deadline. She couldn't help but lap up his tales about other models he had known.

'Can you believe I went on a date with one girl who said she couldn't mix protein and carbs when I offered her a bacon sandwich for staying overnight?' Euan winked.

Yaslyn snorted into her plain black coffee.

'They're the reason why I left London,' he continued. 'Models. I've done too many catalogue shoots. Seen too many identical pouts and poses.' He pulled the chin-down-eyes-up posture that Yaslyn used on a daily basis. Those weren't the kind of photos Euan saw in his future now. 'I wanted to see something real,' he said of his time in Africa and India. He'd taken loads of pictures there. Eventually, he wanted to be known for his reportage and travel photography. He said the best smile he'd ever seen was on the face of a child living in the slums of Calcutta.

'But you've photographed some of the most highly paid models in the world,' said Yaslyn.

'Empty rictus grins.' Euan sighed. 'Ten thousand pounds a day couldn't make them smile like that girl did when I gave her a half-worn-out Biro.'

Yaslyn nodded politely.

'Do you want to see the photo?'

'You've got it with you?'

'I always carry it,' he said, as though it should have been obvious.

'Go on then.'

He opened his wallet and pushed the snap, a tiny picture snipped from a contact sheet, across the pub table towards her. Yaslyn gave it what she considered to be the right amount of attention and pushed it back.

'Gorgeous, eh? Couldn't you just take her home with you?'

Yaslyn nodded again. The child was sweet enough. But then Yaslyn had never really liked the idea of children. All that noise, the sleep deprivation, losing your waistline . . .

'Can I see you again?' Euan asked suddenly. 'Over the weekend, perhaps.'

'I don't know,' she said, his directness taking her by surprise. 'I'm quite busy at the moment.'

'I know what that means.' Euan laughed as he tucked the photo back into his wallet. 'You're a rules girl, right? Rachel told me all about it at Sunday lunch. You can't go out with a guy at the weekend if he doesn't ask you before Wednesday and tonight is Thursday so I guess I've missed my chance until next week.'

'That's so 1990s,' Yaslyn replied. 'I genuinely am busy.'

'Not on Sunday, surely? No one works on a Sunday. Especially not models.'

'I've got, er, stuff to do,' she told him. Her argument was weakening. 'Things around the house. Housework. And things . . .'

'Let me take you for a picnic,' he persisted.

'A picnic?'

'Yeah. How about it?'

'What . . . A picnic? Really?'

'Outdoors. Blankets. Sandwiches. You know the drill.'

Yaslyn did. But she hadn't been for one of those since she was twelve. Unless you counted the time

Antonio had the skipper of his yacht drop them off in a secluded bay with a wicker hamper full of lobster and ice-cold Krug.

Yaslyn's expression darkened as her brain flickered between two memories. The afternoon on white sand with Antonio the telecoms magnate, who had since turned his attentions (inevitably, it seemed) to her younger doppelgänger. And that picnic when she was twelve; during the summer when her mother and father tried to patch up their marriage by taking her on holiday to Cornwall. It had been lovely for two whole days. A really happy family. Then the rowing started again. And there was no way to block out the sound in that caravan, where only a curtain separated her bed from her parents, as they downed half a bottle of whisky apiece and apportioned noisy blame.

'Nah, you're right. It's a cheesy idea,' said Euan, misreading Yaslyn's distance for lack of interest. 'A girl like you doesn't want to get on the back of my bike and eat cheese-and-pickle sandwiches in the middle of the New Forest.'

How long would it be before she stopped being blind-sided by memories like that? Yaslyn wondered.

'I'd love to,' she said out of the blue. 'What do I need to wear?'

Euan was momentarily confused. 'You mean . . . ?'

'I said I'd love to come for a picnic. But I've never been on the back of a bike before so you'll have to tell me what to do.'

'Brilliant.' Euan couldn't hide his excitement. 'You don't need to do anything except hold on and try to remember to sway in the direction I do and not try to counterbalance me. That's when people fall off.'

'Do you want me to bring some food?' she asked.

'I think I can sort that out,' he said. 'This is going to be brilliant.'

And it was. There were no cheese sandwiches to be seen. The proper wicker basket that Euan retrieved from the plastic box on the back of his bike was as beautifully packed as any he could have picked up ready made at Fortnum and Mason. First he shook open a blanket and laid it on the flattest piece of ground he could find. Next he gestured that Yaslyn should sit upon it while he arranged a couple of place settings complete with linen napkins.

Finally, he brought out a bottle of champagne and two crystal glasses.

'I can't believe they survived the journey,' Yaslyn commented. Her spine felt as though they had been riding over cobblestones all the way from London to this particular clearing in the trees.

'Hold the glasses,' said Euan as he prepared to open the bottle. He ripped off the foil, untwisted the wire and was easing the cork out of the narrow neck before Yaslyn thought to say, 'Stop! It's probably been . . .'

The rest of her sentence was lost as the cork exploded from the bottle and Yaslyn was drenched in champagne. In his panic to contain the explosion, Euan only made it worse, jerking the bottle about like a Grand Prix winner on the podium. When the fountain finally subsided he stared at Yaslyn in horror. With her long hair hanging about her face like curtains, she looked like an Afghan hound that had come off worse in an argument with a garden hose.

'What I meant to say was it's probably been shaken

up on the journey,' she told him. 'And it might just go everywhere.'

'I, I . . .' Euan struggled to formulate an apology. Yaslyn could tell from his expression that he was convinced he must have blown it. He still held the bottle, the smoking gun, pointing towards her. Yaslyn cast her eyes down to the ground. Should she make him suffer? Her shoulders started to shake. He thought she was about to cry. But then the laughter erupted from her with even more force than the cork from the bottle. She stood up, took the bottle from his hands and tipped the last of it over his head. When a solitary drip reached the end of his nose, she stuck out her pink tongue and licked it away.

'Good job it's warm today,' she said. Then she peeled off her sodden cardigan, knowing only too well that her T-shirt was clinging like a second layer of skin to her breasts.

They stayed in the forest until it was dark that night. Side by side on the blanket, looking up at the stars.

'There's a shooting star!' Yaslyn said excitedly.

'Nope,' said Euan. 'That's a satellite.'

'You know so much about things,' Yaslyn told him. 'You're not at all what I expected.'

'Neither are you,' he said, propping himself up on his elbow so that he could look down on to her face, kissed silver by the moonlight.

'Do you mean that in a nice way?' she asked.

'I mean it most sincerely.'

Yaslyn knew it was a compliment. And then she kissed him.

*

That was how it started.

Rachel was almost more delighted than Euan that Yaslyn had finally seen his charms and immediately set about organising double dates for the pair of them with herself and Patrick. It was perfect symmetry in Rachel's opinion. Yaslyn was her favourite girl in the world and Euan was Patrick's best friend. When it came to organising the wedding, Euan was the obvious choice for best man. Yaslyn would be Rachel's chief bridesmaid.

Rachel nearly exploded with joy when Patrick confided that Euan had shown an unnatural interest in the ring-choosing process. She had a feeling that she and Patrick wouldn't be the only people making their love official on 27 July. In fact, she was sure of it. Yaslyn was going to be the second-luckiest girl in the world. Euan would propose to Yaslyn during his best man's speech. Rachel knew it. She couldn't wait.

Four bottles of all-inclusive beer into that first evening at Club Aegee, Carrie Ann was beginning to revise her opinion of her chances of pulling.

The girls had moved from the bar by the swimming pool to a smaller bar situated down on the club's private beach in the hope that the talent from which Carrie Ann had to choose her single victim might prove to be more promising.

'At least there are more men down here,' said Rachel.

'Maybe we're just seeing double,' Yaslyn quipped. 'Hey! There's your man, Caz!'

Carrie Ann whipped round on her bar stool like a World War II gunner locating an enemy plane. But Yaslyn was just pulling her leg again. A man with a lump of gold where some of his canines should have been was busy excavating the contents of his ear in blissful ignorance of Carrie Ann's attention.

'Will you stop raising my hopes like that,' Carrie Ann complained.

'One day we'll find you the right one,' said Rachel in an attempt to be comforting.

'Yeah, yeah. I've heard the myth a thousand times,' said Carrie Ann. 'Somewhere out there is the man for me. There's someone for everyone,' she added tritely, slamming her beer bottle down on to the bar so that foam spurted out of the top and all over her hand.

'There really is,' Rachel insisted. She'd met her own man on Millennium Eve – the worst night in the past thousand years to find yourself single at a party, as she constantly reminded Carrie Ann.

'But my man isn't here tonight. Look, buy me another bottle of beer and I'll dance with the most unattractive man here this evening.'

A few merry holidaymakers had started practising their lambada skills with Pierre, the dance instructor, near the water's edge.

'The beer's free,' Yaslyn reminded her. 'But perhaps it's time you did a dare anyway.'

'Why not?' agreed Carrie Ann gamely. 'He may have a very attractive friend. And that book you gave me . . .'

'*How to Get Over That Man and Find a New One?*' said Rachel gleefully.

'*How to Get Over That Man and Find a New One* by Margaret Mayday,' Carrie Ann confirmed in her very best Southern Belle accent, 'says that you should flirt even when you can't find a soul you want to flirt with. We overlook too many fabulous presents because they don't come in the right wrapping paper.'

'Good girl,' Rachel applauded. 'Let's find that brown paper bag of a man.'

Yaslyn and Rachel had their victim picked out within seconds. He was leaning against the other end of the bar, not looking much like a holidaymaker at all – in his crisp short-sleeved shirt and immaculately pressed grey trousers – more like an office worker who had simply taken his tie off at lunch-time. Despite the sand under foot, he was wearing lace-up leather shoes.

Perhaps he wasn't a guest at all, but some official Club Aegee auditor come to count the empty bottles.

As if by some sixth sense, the victim seemed to realise that three women were suddenly staring at him. He turned towards them and smiled the kind of 'warm and welcoming' smile that might have been prescribed at one of those body language seminars socially impaired businessmen seem to be so fond of. It had the effect of making him look a little bit more like a disgruntled actuary about to go mad and gun down everybody in the building.

'God, no,' said Carrie Ann, taking in the inappropriate outfit, the psychotically tidy hair, the glasses that weren't quite the right shape for his face. Or anyone's face for that matter. 'Anything but that. I think I've changed my mind.'

'Are you forgetting the teachings of Margaret Mayday already?' Yaslyn teased. 'I don't know if this is even worth a bottle of free beer. It's not as though you've got to make him try hard to want you. He's clearly up for anything.'

'He's winking at you,' Rachel confirmed.

'I'm not sure he can even see this far,' said Carrie Ann. 'It's probably just a tic.'

Yaslyn held her hand out, ready to shake on the bet. 'Think you can pull it off, Caz? You have to dance with him for a whole song to get the beer.'

'Three minutes for a free beer? I can do it.'

The DJ promptly put on an eleven-minute-long mix of Kylie's 'Can't Get You Out Of My Head'.

Luckily for Carrie Ann, she had no idea how long the mix was when she set out on her mission. She took a fortifying swig of her half-finished Budvar and headed for her target. At least he was modest enough to look behind him in a slightly bewildered fashion as Carrie Ann approached. It was as though he didn't think she could possibly be making a bee-line for him. Either that, said a little part of Carrie Ann's brain, or he was looking for an escape route.

The music was so loud it took a while for Carrie Ann and her new friend to work out that they didn't speak the same language. Carrie Ann started out in English, then tried French, then Spanish, before she used her single phrase of German and hit the mark.

'*Sprechen sie deutsch?*' she asked.

The man's grin widened. '*Ja, ja!*' he said. He spieled straight into a minute-long sentence that could have been a compliment or a brush-off. Carrie Ann didn't have a clue.

'British,' she told him, pointing at her chest. 'From Lon-don.'

'Oh. Norwegian,' he said. 'Oslo.'

'Not German, then. Do you speak English?' Carrie Ann asked.

The man nodded.

'Great.' Carrie Ann grinned back. 'Can we speak in English instead? My German isn't that hot, you see. Or my Norwegian. In fact, I don't know any Norwegian at all. Like to dance?'

She gave a little wiggle. He nodded more enthusiastically than before. Then at least they were speaking body language.

Carrie Ann took her victim's hand and they took to the floor – or rather the centre of the sand. She turned to face him and began to boogie in time with the music. He emulated her movements, but apparently to the beat of a different song. Carrie Ann slowed her actions to single time instead of double to give him a chance to catch her up. He slowed down too. Just a bit too slow. Or perhaps he was deliberately doing 'robotics', 1980s style.

Carrie Ann decided that she needed to take matters in hand before her partner started doing the Moonwalk. Around them, other dancers were looking on with obvious amusement. Out of the corner of her eye, Carrie Ann caught somebody mimicking her dancing partner's 'coconut shaker' hand movements. The only way to stop him was to grab him and hold him close.

He didn't object. And at that moment Carrie Ann had a strange sensation of déjà vu. It was the 'Last Lager Waltz'. That point in the evening at which everybody settles for the nearest warm body to lean against for a final stagger around the dance floor.

She didn't even know this man's name and yet he was nuzzling his nose against her bare shoulder. She didn't know what colour his eyes were and yet he seemed totally at ease with the idea of squeezing her buttocks as they circled awkwardly around the other dancers. Part of her wanted to push him away and cuff him around the head with her clutch-bag. Another part . . .

It had been so long since anybody had held her. Yaslyn and Rachel gave her hugs from time to time, for sure. And there had been plenty of cuddles during the decree absolute weekend. But this type of holding was different. There was intent in this position. This man found her attractive. He wanted her. Even if she wouldn't have crossed the street to spit on him if she'd seen him in Battersea . . . Maybe that was her problem. Maybe she had been setting the bar too high since splitting from her husband. Maybe she had been over-looking the brown paper packages. Maybe a man like this could make her happy.

Stop! It was the drink talking.

Kylie finished warbling. The DJ wasn't as good at mixing as he thought he was and there was a moment of definite silence between the song Carrie Ann had contracted to dance for and the next. The Norwegian bloke stepped away from her awkwardly, as though the music had been like a kind of darkness, making his behaviour acceptable only for the time it filled the air.

'Er, shall we get a drink?' Carrie Ann asked him.

He looked at her blankly. She searched his face for evidence that this might be the start of her big holiday romance. That he might be worth a nightcap. That he understood a word she had been saying . . .

'Morten,' he said.

'Carrie Ann,' she replied. Assuming Morten was his name and not the Norwegian word for 'no way'.

'I am not married,' he said then.

'What?'

'I am *not* married.' More emphatically this time.

The next tune began. Before they could entwine themselves again, Carrie Ann and her Nordic dance partner were separated by the Go-Go girls, congoing through the crowd. As they passed by, the last girl in the chain wiggled her bottom at Carrie Ann's man. He dutifully fastened himself to her behind.

*

'You lost him!' Yaslyn was indignant. 'You let him go!'

'What was he like?' Rachel asked eagerly. Carrie Ann's friends were even keener to overlook obvious incompatibilities than she was if it meant that she would have a special someone again.

'I don't know what he's like. Didn't speak a word of English,' said Carrie Ann. 'OK. Perhaps that's not entirely fair. He spoke four words of English,' she clarified.

'Which were?' Yaslyn asked impatiently. 'Which four words were they?'

'I am not married,' said Carrie Ann.

'Hmmm. He came prepared. More schnapps?' said Yaslyn.

'Good idea.'

Axel stood at the edge of the beach bar feeling as though he were looking at a living, breathing Bruegel painting. The half-naked bodies on the dance floor. The bacchanalian excess of it all. Somewhere in the middle, Gilles was dirty-dancing with a couple of girls from Lyons. They would be flying back to France in the morning. A safe bet for a fling in Gilles' little black book.

Axel wanted to get to bed too. But on his own. That evening, however, he was on the late shift. It was his duty to stay up and stay sober until every one of the guests had staggered back to their rooms. In particular, he had to make sure that they all made it to the path that led back to the camp and didn't take a wrong turning straight into the sea. Alcohol and the Aegean didn't mix.

The English girls Axel had picked up from the airport that morning looked particularly in need of supervision. As he watched, one of them – the one with frizzy blonde hair who reminded him of a Picasso sculpture made from two matchboxes and a piece of string he had once seen in Paris – actually fell off her bar stool. For a second, Axel panicked, thinking she may have cracked her head on the bar on the way down – a real first-aid emergency in progress. But she got back up again, giggling, and even re-enacted the fall for her friends.

'Stupid. But I must not despise them,' Axel reminded himself. These were decent, honest, hard-working people who had come to Club Aegee to relax. Some people (like Axel) relaxed by reading complicated philosophy books. Some people (the usual Club Aegee crowd) relaxed by getting so drunk they couldn't see. That didn't necessarily make them bad people. Not at all . . .

No good. Axel couldn't convince himself. He hated every single one of them.

He kissed his teeth disdainfully and sank into the shadows to smoke a cigarette. When would the selfish bastards go to bed?

12

Carrie Ann awoke to a peculiar throbbing sensation at both ends of her body. Her head was pounding from one too many all-inclusive beers. Her tailbone was also pounding as an indirect result of one too many drinks. She vaguely remembered falling off her bar stool and landing on her coccyx to discover that the soft-looking sand beneath the bar was just an inch-deep layer on top of solid concrete. Even sitting up in bed now made her want to howl in agony.

She hobbled to the bathroom to inspect her bruises, biting her bottom lip to prevent herself from crying out with each step. She needn't have bothered. Yaslyn and Rachel had managed to sleep through each other's snoring (like two jet planes taking off, as Carrie Ann had discovered). Neither would be woken by Carrie Ann's comparatively quiet scream of pain.

In the dim light of the bathroom, Carrie Ann examined her face in the mirror. This wasn't the idea at all. She had hoped to come to Turkey and spend a week reading books and drinking mineral water, allowing all the cares of her newly single world to flee her mind and the creases those cares brought with them to drop out of her face. Now six bottles of free beer sloshed about in the bags beneath her eyes. If she hadn't been a match for the Swedish Lesbian Twins the day before, they certainly weren't going to be worrying about the competition from London that morning.

'I am never, ever going to drink again,' Carrie Ann told her reflection sternly. Six bottles of beer may have made the Norwegian actuary look good enough to sleep with the night before, but it wasn't making Carrie Ann look so good now. She could only be thankful for the fact that she hadn't slept with the Norwegian after all and wasn't at that particular moment in time looking at his face on her pillow through eyes newly denuded of beer-bottle glasses.

'I am never going to drink again,' Carrie Ann repeated. Her reflection gave her a sad, knowing smile in return.

A new regime was in order. For the next six days at least, she told herself, she would make an effort to exercise every morning, read edifying books, eat health-inducing food . . . Returning to her side of the room to find something to wear, Carrie Ann picked up a half-eaten box of chocolate willies in disgust. They had been part of Rachel's hen night kit and the cause of much hilarity when Yaslyn announced that they were 'not suitable for people with nut allergies', just as Carrie Ann bit into a praline testicle. That morning, Carrie Ann's body cried out for a sugar injection. The willies had been surprisingly tasty . . .

'No.' She tossed the remains of the chocolate into the bin. This week was about detox and self-improvement. She was going for a walk.

Perhaps just one chocolate penis would give her the energy to walk for longer?

She fished the foil-wrapped bounty back out of the waste bin. It was fine but for a few strands of hair that

Rachel had cleaned out of her hairbrush the previous evening . . .

'Oh, for God's sake,' Carrie Ann hissed to herself. Is this what it had come to? Eating chocolate retrieved from a wastepaper basket? She consigned the chocolate to the bin again and covered it over with an empty fag packet and the contents of an ashtray. Not even her sugar lust could overcome that barrier.

'Who are you talking to?' came a mumble from one of the beds.

Rachel was awake.

'The chocolate,' said Carrie Ann. 'Nothing. Go back to sleep.'

Rachel rolled over and obliged.

If she was going to be miserable, Carrie Ann thought as she started her walk, at least she had fantastic surroundings to do it in. Instead of grass, the large beds in the spaces between the guest huts were filled with spiky aloe vera, cactus, trees of red, purple, pink and orange flowers that she couldn't put a name to. Mimosa, that was it. Beautiful bougainvillea poured from every window box and erupted from the wooden frames above the bar like froth from a champagne bottle. Pine trees and laburnum offered forgiving shade around the pool and along the beach. In the distance, caramel cows moved mournfully across scrubby, volcanic-looking hills. The buildings on those hills were white too, accented in blue and the palest salmon pink. Pale pink. The colour of Carrie Ann's wedding bouquet. The bouquet she had preserved and framed and saved for fifteen years. The bouquet she had mashed to dust with a hammer the previous weekend. It's impossible to get a divorce without thinking about the way the whole thing started.

Carrie Ann's wedding was going to be the wedding of the year in the small town where she grew up. Both her older sisters had already married with the kind of pomp and circumstance you'd expect for a royal wedding – the wedding of a princess bride, not the wedding of the daughter of the owner of three corner shops.

As the youngest by eight years – 'The best mistake we ever made,' her mother would say every birthday – Carrie Ann had grown up to be the darling of the family. Pampered and spoiled. Her every utterance greeted like the pronouncement of a genius. Dressed up like a little doll by her doting siblings Eithne and Trudy.

'He's not good enough for you,' said Carrie Ann's father when she first announced that she was going on a date with Greg Fisher. No one was good enough for Carrie Ann Murphy.

Carrie Ann was just seventeen years old when Greg came into her life. He was a regular in the pub where she worked at weekends, waitressing in the dining room attached to the main bar she was still too young to serve behind. Greg was twenty-four at the time and seemed quite impossibly glamorous and successful with his sales job that sometimes took him as far afield as Northern Ireland. He had a car, a proper fast car with four doors and a sun roof, when most of the guys Carrie Ann dated were still struggling to pass their driving tests or doing wheel spins round the supermarket car park in souped-up Metro hatchbacks. He seemed like a real man compared to them.

And all the girls wanted him. He looked, Carrie Ann and her best friend and fellow waitress Mairi decided, like Jon Bon Jovi from the band of the same name. Greg made the most of the alleged resemblance. When he wasn't wearing a shiny grey suit to the office, he would dress like his hero in bat-wing shirts and tight leather trousers. Once he even wore a headband around his long blond hair. Carrie Ann's father swore that he'd seen the man in eyeliner. To Carrie Ann that was just another reason to love him.

'He's so avant-garde,' she told Mairi during another interminable discussion about love when they were supposed to be revising for their A-levels.

She lost her virginity to him in the back of his Sierra while the stereo played 'Slippery When Wet'. He asked her to marry him after a row during which he told her that if she went to Reading University to study psychology, he might not be around when she came back to Gloucester during the holidays. Unable to conceive of a world without Greg Fisher, Carrie Ann snatched at his sudden proposal.

Her parents tried to talk her out of it but Carrie Ann would not go to university that year. She placated her mum and dad by merely deferring her place at first rather than turning it down altogether. She got a job as a junior with a local employment agency, filing temps' CVs and making coffee. The following summer, Carrie Ann had been promoted to junior temp coordinator and the form confirming that she should be enrolling at Reading in September was buried beneath a pile of wedding invitations.

No one tried to talk her out of it a second time.

'Well, I might not have liked him much when I first met him but at least he's stuck around,' Mr Murphy said of his prospective new son-in-law. In fact, the only objection he had was to the idea of Carrie Ann walking down the aisle to the strains of Jon BJ and his merry band of players instead of the more conventional 'Wedding March'.

On the morning of her wedding, Carrie Ann woke from a nightmare to face another one. Overnight, the tiny pimple on her chin which her mother had promised would be easy enough to conceal with some Rimmel Hide the Blemish had grown like a magic mushroom until it was so big and red that it wouldn't have been disguised by a pot of Dulux and a paint roller. Meanwhile, her dress, which had been hanging on the back of the door when she went to sleep, had fallen to the floor – the adhesive that had attached the plastic hook to the door since 1973 had finally given way. So her dress was creased, her spot was enormous, her hair wouldn't come out right no matter how much mousse and hairspray she used . . .

With half an hour to go before the wedding, Carrie Ann was crying at her reflection in the bathroom mirror.

'It's supposed to be perfect,' she said, staring in disbelief at the farmhouse loaf on top of her head that was meant to be a sophisticated chignon. 'This is an old woman's hairdo.'

Cousin Shirley, who had done the offending 'do', tried to tease out some tendrils to soften the look while

Carrie Ann's mother assured her that it was going to be a grand day. It really was.

'Anyway, don't actresses always say that a bad last rehearsal is a good sign?' Mrs Murphy tried.

'Do you think so?' Carrie Ann asked.

'Absolutely,' cooed her mother. 'You just relax, my darling. When you look back on this day in twenty years' time you'll have a good laugh about how upset you were over your hair. In fact, you'll probably be glad you had a bun instead of a shig-nun thing. Much more classic.'

At least the bridesmaids, according to tradition, looked far worse than the bride in their ruched salmon pink as they left for the church in a Roller.

No posh car for Carrie Ann, however. Mr Murphy had insisted that his youngest daughter be conveyed to the church in a horse and carriage like her sisters before her. It reminded him of his own wedding to Carrie Ann's mother, back in Ireland, he said. Anything that reminded Mr Murphy of his boyhood back in County Cork was sacred.

Mr Davenport, who ran the local riding school, was only too pleased to provide the use of his most placid nag again in return for an invite to the reception.

'I'll get horse shit on my dress like Trudy did,' Carrie Ann protested.

'Horse shit is lucky,' replied her father.

As it was, Carrie Ann managed to avoid the horse-shit issue altogether. And as they trotted to St Michael's, Carrie Ann had to admit that her father was right. This was a lovely way to get to a wedding.

Everyone stopped to look as they passed. Children pointed and waved, old ladies smiled indulgently. A builder working on a house up the road from the Murphys' house shouted, 'Don't do it, love. You'd be better off with me.'

And suddenly, it seemed that the journey Carrie Ann had been dreading all week was far too short. The half-hour trot had flashed past in what seemed like a second when the carriage drew up outside the church and Mr Davenport, the man from the stables, dismounted to help the bride down on to the square of bright red carpet he had thoughtfully provided for her pristine satin shoes.

'Are you ready?' Carrie Ann's father asked her, though it was actually he who needed a moment to dab his eyes.

Carrie Ann nodded at her father. Mairi dashed between them for a second to apply a final coat of lip gloss now that they weren't worried that Carrie Ann's hair would blow across her face and get stuck to her mouth like candy floss.

Mr Murphy offered his daughter his arm.

'I am so proud of you,' he told her. 'You may be the youngest but you're the prettiest, the cleverest and the loveliest of the lot.'

'Give over, Dad,' said Carrie Ann. 'I bet you said that to all your girls.'

She squeezed him close while the photographer took a snap. She was nervous as hell but her grin and her eyes squealed excitement.

'Are you ready?' asked the churchwarden. 'The crowd is getting a little restless.' He pushed open the door and the bridal party stepped inside.

Everyone was in that church. Everyone. As Carrie Ann processed down the aisle on her father's arm it was as though she were walking backwards through her life. There were the girls from the office, huddled together on the back row, casting their appraising eyes over her dress. There were the girls from school, Ella and Jo. They'd promised that they would never lose touch but in reality this was the first time Carrie Ann had seen either of them since they scrawled crude messages on each other's school shirts on the very last day of term. There was Carrie Ann's first employer, the landlord from the pub where she had met her future husband. There was her dentist. Her doctor. Sitting one row behind her mother was the midwife who had delivered Carrie Ann red faced into the world only nineteen years before.

Carrie Ann's mother had already ruined her make-up with proud and anxious tears. Her sister Trudy gave her the thumbs up. Eithne mouthed, 'Don't forget your lines!' Even Carrie Ann's future mother-in-law smiled with something approaching warmth.

And there was Greg. Like a film star who knows that timing is all important for dramatic impact, Greg waited until Carrie Ann was almost right behind him before he turned round to see his bride. And when he did, he smiled a beautiful crooked smile like a pre-dentistry Tom Cruise.

The world around them melted away in the magical warmth of that moment. For Carrie Ann there was only Greg and for Greg, she felt sure, there was only Carrie Ann. Holding his gaze as she took those final steps to be by his side, Carrie Ann felt like a wandering satellite being drawn in by laser beam towards her docking station. Creased dress, big spot, bad hair were all forgotten when she saw her loved one's face.

Next to Greg was his best friend Tim. They were both wearing pale grey suits, in a slightly shimmery fabric that was fashionable at the time but would look cheap and nasty when the new Mr and Mrs Fisher got the wedding album out at their anniversary party just twelve months later. Greg's straggly long hair had been highlighted specially. Mairi had done it for him. She was training to be a beautician at the local tech and was taking an option in hair colouring. Of course, in those days there wasn't actually that much choice of colour. Highlights were bright white blond or nothing, and applied via a stinking rubber skullcap that made you look like a Sindy doll who'd lost half her hair while the bleach was being applied.

Mairi had done her own highlights too. They didn't go with her complexion. But then neither did the salmon-pink dress that Carrie Ann had chosen for her ... Fortunately, the late 1980s was an era when people still didn't mind dressing in colours that made them look ill. If salmon pink was in, then you wore it. The year before it had been canary yellow. Funnily enough, that would have looked much better with Mairi's skin tone.

'Dearly beloved,' the priest began. 'We are gathered here today to witness the coming together of Greg Fisher and Carrie Ann Murphy.'

The first hymn. 'All things bright and beautiful'. Carrie Ann's favourite. She could hear her father beside her belting out the tune. In the pews behind her,

her mother's voice, adding a softly soaring descant.

I am so happy, Carrie Ann thought. So very, very happy.

It was the start of her perfect life.

Fifteen minutes later, they were signing the register. Greg used the signature he had been perfecting for months. The one that made 'Greg Fisher' look like a bit like 'Jon Bon Jovi'. The one that was essentially an illegible squiggle. Unfortunately, thirteen years later, it didn't appear that illegibility had made their marriage null and void.

'Well, Carrie Ann,' said Greg as they began their procession down the aisle as Mr and Mrs Fisher. 'We finally did it.'

They shared a smile.

'Oh, Greg,' said Carrie Ann. 'I love you.'

The new Mrs Carrie Ann Fisher felt like a fairy princess. There was so much warmth and happiness in that church, she decided, she wouldn't be at all surprised if the vaulted ceiling burst open like a flower to let that happiness go flying up to heaven.

But when Greg and Carrie Ann emerged from the rose-scented, love-packed atmosphere of the church into the sunshine on the church steps, they were not greeted as she expected by the rapturous applause of assembled onlookers. Oh, sure, there were onlookers, but for entirely the wrong reason . . .

'Don't let them out . . .' Mr Davenport was shouting.

'Too late!' said someone else. 'They're here.'

'Throw your coat over its bloody head, for heaven's sake!'

'Whose head?' Carrie Ann asked.

The little group of people gathered around the carriage that had brought Carrie Ann to the church instinctively spread out as though they might be better able to hide the awful truth. Mr Davenport opened his mac wide like a flasher for better coverage. But Carrie Ann glimpsed a horse's hoof sticking up at a very odd angle from behind Mr Davenport's coat. She glimpsed the poor creature's painfully twisted neck, frozen in a final spasm.

'Oh my God!' She rushed forward to where the horse that had brought her to the church less than an hour ago lay dead on the pavement. 'What happened?'

'She was an old horse,' said Mr Davenport. 'I guess it was all too much for her.'

Uncle Fred drove the bride and groom to the reception in the back of his blue Mercedes saloon.

Carrie Ann and Greg stared out of opposite windows for the duration of the ride, looking at each other again only when they got to the hotel. Under the circumstances the photographer had decided he would take the group photos in the gardens there rather than outside the church. When she looked back on those photos ten years later, the tears that were barely held back by Carrie Ann's forced smile seemed obvious to her.

Perhaps it was an omen. Perhaps not. Carrie Ann had never even been particularly fond of horses. It wasn't that she was devastated by the death of poor old Ginger. But there was something in the way Greg had reacted – a peevish note when he said, 'Wouldn't have happened if your dad hadn't tried to save on the hire cars,' that Carrie Ann hadn't heard in her beloved's voice before.

And Mairi, standing behind Carrie Ann in so many of the photos, wore an expression of such sweet pain. How was it that Carrie Ann hadn't guessed the real object of Mairi's affections back in 1987? It wasn't Tim, the best man, at all. It was obvious now. Mairi had even cut her own hair to be exactly like the groom's. She was besotted with Greg even then.

Which was the greater loss? The husband or the friend? Which was the greater betrayal? Not for the first time Carrie Ann wished that Mairi had been braver earlier on. She wished that Mairi had made her move on Greg that night in the pub when Carrie Ann first declared her intentions. They might have fallen out over it for a day or two. A week at the outside. Instead, Mairi tried to smother her love for Greg and ended up carrying a tiny light inside her that would smoulder for the better part of a decade and a half until Greg's heart was a dried-up husk that would burst into flames when Mairi touched him.

Fifteen years after she took her vows – thirteen years married and two endless years separated – Carrie Ann exhaled painfully as she remembered them on the shores of the Aegean. This wasn't how it was supposed to happen. She wasn't supposed to be alone again at thirty-four, wondering what she could have done differently. How she could have hung on to her man . . .

Was he worth hanging on to? That was the question her friends asked her. He was lazy, unsupportive, indifferent. He said she was boring and whiney and fat. Perhaps that was why he had been indifferent, Carrie Ann often suggested to herself. Perhaps he was right.

She threw a pebble into the waves and began the walk back to the room.

13

'Bikinis on,' said Yaslyn. 'We're missing valuable tanning time.'

She pulled out the first of her selection. It was a gold lamé number that looked as though it had been made from one of Dame Edna Everage's handkerchiefs.

'Not quite brown enough for that yet,' Yaslyn murmured. 'May have to be the pink.'

Rachel had no such decisions to make when it came to choosing between her swimwear options. It was black, black or black with white edging. And big.

'I couldn't wear any of those,' she said, nodding towards the tiny triangles that Yaslyn had laid out on her bed. 'My boobs would be all over the place.'

'You don't know how lucky you are to have boobs,' Yaslyn countered.

Rachel rolled her eyes. She'd lost count of how many times Yaslyn had tried to suggest that her 34Cs made up for the fact that she didn't have legs to her armpits and the kind of stomach you could chop lines of cocaine on (if that was your kind of thing. She knew that Yaslyn had done that at least once – before she met clean-living Euan).

'I would kill for a C cup,' Yaslyn continued blithely as she rubbed on her Factor 15.

'Well, on your body they would look fantastic,' Rachel agreed. 'But the alleged magnificence of my tits is completely cancelled out by the size of my hips and waist. I'm not so much an hourglass as a tumbler.'

Having finished her greasing up, Yaslyn pulled on her pink bikini bottoms. She looked at herself in the mirror and frowned. In the two steps she had taken across the room, they had ridden up over her buttocks. They'd never done that before.

'I really think I'm putting on weight,' she said quietly.

'Oh, for God's sake,' began Rachel. 'Don't expect any sympathy from me on that front. You've probably just shrunk your bikini bottoms in the hot wash.'

Yaslyn was fastening the bikini top around her chest now.

'And look at you!' Rachel continued. 'What are you complaining about your chest for? You've got perfect tits.'

Yaslyn stood side on to the mirror. 'I don't know where they've come from,' she said.

'Don't complain!' Rachel exclaimed. 'If I woke up with longer legs, I wouldn't be asking how it happened. I'd just get out there and strut my stuff.'

Yaslyn was still frowning at her reflection.

'Not even the Swedish Lesbian Twins could compete,' Rachel assured her. 'Now we should get out there and reserve some space by the pool before the Germans get the lot.'

'It's half past ten,' Yaslyn pointed out. 'There's no chance.'

Yaslyn was right. The poolside was already busier than the platform at Clapham Common Tube station during rush hour. The Club Aegee clientele were serious about their tanning. Rachel and Yaslyn searched in vain for three empty sun loungers together.

'Carrie Ann should have put our towels out when she went for that walk,' Yaslyn complained.

'She was probably too busy thinking,' said Rachel.

'I hope she's not going to be *thinking* all week,' said Yaslyn pointedly.

'She just got divorced.'

'So? Happens all the time. She should be celebrating the return of her freedom. There!' Yaslyn had spotted three empty sun loungers at last. They weren't side by side, though. One was separated from the others by two further loungers occupied by the couple on the bus the previous morning.

'I can't sit next to that marriage break-up in progress,' said Rachel. 'I'm sure it will bring me bad luck.'

'They'll be all right in company. Plus, if they are breaking up, Carrie Ann might want to be around to pick up the pieces. His pieces. He's not too bad looking. Soft round the middle but there's potential.'

'You are terrible,' Rachel hissed.

Yaslyn picked her way through the bodies towards the couple and introduced herself.

'Hi,' she said. 'You came in on the Gatwick flight, yeah?'

The man nodded. 'I'm Marcus,' he said. 'And this is Sally.'

Sally gave a much smaller nod of recognition.

'Yaslyn and Rachel. And we're going to steal these sunbeds,' Yaslyn announced. 'Wanted some in the shade but . . .'

'You've got to get up early to beat the Germans,'

said Marcus. 'Not that I think there are any Germans here this week.'

'Oh, there's at least one,' said Yaslyn, remembering Carrie Ann's conquest the previous night.

'He was Norwegian,' said Rachel, reading her mind.

'You been here before?' Yaslyn addressed this question to Sally.

'First time,' Marcus answered for her.

'Us too. We're on a hen week. Rachel's getting married on the twenty-seventh. And a *divorce week*,' she added as Carrie Ann came into view. 'Our friend Carrie Ann's decree absolute came through last weekend.'

'Yaslyn!' Rachel was mortified.

Carrie Ann arrived just in time to hear the word 'absolute' and knew at once to what they were referring.

'It's our duty to make her realise it's the best thing that could have happened,' Yaslyn continued blithely. 'Far better to call it a day before you end up on murder charges, I told her.'

Nobody laughed.

'There are two beds in the shade over there,' said Carrie Ann, spotting a vacancy on the other side of the pool. 'Let's just carry one of these to the other side. We won't disturb you any longer,' she muttered in the direction of the woman called Sally. She was pretending to be reading her book but clearly wasn't enjoying the interruption.

Then Carrie Ann noticed Morten the Norwegian dweeb with the limited English vocab sit down on the lounger next to the one she had been coveting for

94

herself. While everyone around him had stripped down to the scantiest swimwear imaginable, he was still wearing his short-sleeved white shirt and lace-up shoes. He took the shoes off as he sat down but left on his socks. Even more disturbingly, he had a pair of binoculars hanging around his neck, which he now used to survey the poolside crowd like a great white hunter searching for antelope on the savannah.

'Oh my God.'

Carrie Ann could almost feel him lock on to her. She froze.

'Hey! Hey! Carrie Ann!' Morten waved in her direction. He didn't bother to bring the binoculars away from his eyes.

'Oh dear. Looks like those sunbeds aren't free after all,' Carrie Ann lied. 'I guess we're going to stay here and bother you.'

'No bother,' said Marcus cheerily. 'Let me help you move that.'

Marcus lifted one of the sunbeds easily and moved it so that Yaslyn, Rachel and Carrie Ann could be side by side.

'He's not in bad shape,' Yaslyn mouthed to Carrie Ann when Marcus had sat back down. 'See those biceps.'

Rachel gestured frantically in the direction of his wife. But Sally still didn't look up. She had read the same paragraph three times.

'And then he said, perhaps we should try a cucumber!' Yaslyn found her own story so hilarious that she could hardly find the breath to finish it. 'Can you believe that?'

'I can,' said Carrie Ann. 'And this is a guy you wanted me to go out with, right?'

'At least he's adventurous,' said Rachel.

'Stop right there,' said Carrie Ann. 'Because one day you're going to suggest I go on a date with Saddam Hussein on the grounds that he has a nice moustache.'

'Do you think he dyes his hair?' asked Rachel. 'He must be in his sixties.'

Sally couldn't help but be envious of the three women chatting happily to the side of her as she tried to concentrate on her novel and ignore her bloody irritating husband.

It was crazy, she decided, to be sitting by a gorgeous pool in the gentle caress of the sunshine, wishing that she were back in her windowless office rather than sitting in that sunshine with Marcus.

When Marcus announced that he had gone ahead and booked a holiday without consulting her first, she had been furious. When she discovered that her boss had colluded with him, secretly arranging for Sally to have the week off, her anger had been white hot. But she couldn't refuse to go then. Not when David had gone to such pains to ensure that Sally's absence could be covered with no inconvenience to any of her clients.

David had been so pleased with himself. As a newly-wed, full of the joys of early matrimony, he was chuffed to be part of such a grand romantic gesture. Sally could hardly tell David that he had effectively sentenced her to a week in holiday hell, complete with a twittering hen night party to remind her how much fun life could be if you hadn't already tied the knot on your conjugal noose.

Marcus and Sally's marriage was less than five years old. If the best of their time together was already over, surely it was better to call it quits rather than try to drag this out for another ten or fifteen years? At the moment, the most optimistic Sally could bring herself to feel was when she told herself that they could get a divorce and be friends again in five years' time. In a decade, their five-year marriage wouldn't seem like such a big deal.

He had turned out to be so weak. The quietness she had once seen as evidence of his mature, laid-back nature now seemed to be a manifestation of an altogether less positive, unambitious streak. While Sally was rocketing up the career ladder like a comet, Marcus was still in the same job he had started a month before their marriage. His wages were merely inching upwards with inflation. Where was his motivation? His ambition? Where were his guts?

Sally had tried so hard to talk herself through the way she was feeling. She tried to convince herself that to have a *good* husband was more important than to have an objectively *successful* one. And Marcus was a good husband. Kind and generous and never likely to stray. But there was something horribly primeval about the disappointment she felt when her wage packet finally outgrew his. She was suddenly paying for his trousers and it made her feel as though she were wearing them.

He had changed too at that moment. He'd definitely changed. From the day she got her latest promotion he had grown submissive, she decided. Softer. She didn't want him to touch her any more. It was like being touched by a woman. She was starting to hate him for it. And hating him made her hate herself. It was every bit as uncomfortable for her to be in a vile mood as it was for Marcus to be on the receiving end of it.

'Do you fancy having a go in the hammam?' Marcus asked. There was a proper Turkish bath in the labyrinthine complex beneath the swimming pool.

Sally shook her head. 'Not now.'

'Archery?' Marcus tried.

'I don't think so.'

'We should take advantage of all the free activities while we're here. What about sailing? Didn't you once say you'd like to learn how to sail a catamaran? They've got four Hobie Cats down on the beach.'

Sally shook her head again. This time the action was accompanied by a weary sigh. 'You don't have to organise every minute of my day,' she said. 'I am perfectly happy to sit here and read my books all week.'

Not that her supply of books would last much longer, she noted. She had been so determined to spend no more time in conversation with Marcus than she had to that she had already got to the last chapter in the first of the three tomes she'd brought with her. Not that she actually remembered anything of the story she had been flicking through. She hadn't been following the narrative, just using the words to tick away time.

'You've got to do something different,' said Marcus. 'Otherwise we might just as well have stayed at home.'

'I did want to stay at home, remember?' she muttered through tightly clenched teeth.

She didn't look up from beneath her sunhat to see whether that comment had hit the mark but she heard him sigh too, as loudly as she had but more painfully. Relenting for just a second, Sally put her book down on her knees and told her husband, 'I might try and have a tennis lesson if there's time.'

'There's plenty of time. We've got nothing but time this week. Do you want me to go and book one for you?' Marcus was pathetically eager to please.

'I don't know,' said Sally. She hadn't really been intending to spend a hot hour on asphalt. But then she saw an opportunity to be alone again, even if it was only for ten minutes, while Marcus strolled over to reception and enquired about tennis tuition.

'You don't mind if I don't play with you, do you?' he asked. 'I want to have a go at windsurfing.'

'No,' Sally said. 'Of course I don't mind.'

'Then I'll put you down for tennis and see if I can get a windsurf lesson at the same time. How's that?'

'Great idea.' She nodded. 'Perfect.' Doubly perfect because she knew that just as soon as Marcus went down to the beach for his windsurf lesson, she would tell the tennis instructor that she had changed her mind and return to her sun lounger undisturbed.

Peace and quiet. That was all Sally wanted right then.

14

Unfortunately, peace and quiet wasn't on the agenda.

At 11.30 each morning, the tranquillity of life by the pool at Club Aegee was shattered. Not that any of the newly arrived guests knew that yet. Axel watched from the safety of the pool bar as Gilles led the rest of the reps, dressed as pirates in red and blue bandannas, out on to the sun terrace bearing water pistols and home-made water bombs.

The prettiest of the three English women who had arrived from Gatwick the previous day shrieked and shot off her lounger when Gilles got her straight in the centre of the stomach with a jet of ice-cold water.

Around her, more experienced guests laughed uproariously, leaving Gilles' latest victim no choice but to join in with the joke at her expense.

'It's time for your morning exercise,' said Gilles, grabbing her by the hand and hauling her to her feet.

'Let me get back to my book,' pleaded Yaslyn ineffectually.

'No way! I'm the pirate king and I'm taking you hostage,' Gilles announced. He lifted her right off her feet then.

Yaslyn let her book fall from her hand and shrugged as Gilles carried her towards the pool. Rachel and Carrie Ann cheered. There was something about

Gilles which brought out the good sport in everyone, Axel observed.

Yes, 11.30 was time for team games at Club Aegee. All of them idiotic and all of them ending in a mass dunking in the pool. Gilles' idea of a good time. Axel's idea of pure hell.

'Come on, ladies,' Gilles shouted. 'Join my team for a free kiss if we win.' He puckered his generous lips.

'Gentlemen!' yelled Delphine, the aerobics instructor and captain of the red gang. 'You can't let me be beaten by this idiot again. I will give you two free kisses if you join with me.'

Delphine pushed out her chest as she announced this and her crew's numbers were instantly doubled. They trebled when Gilles announced the rules of that morning's game. Delphine's able seamen would be expected to help her get a balloon from one end of the poolside terrace to the other without touching said balloon with their hands. The only possible way to hang on to it would be by pressing up close to Delphine, chest to chest, and squeezing the balloon in between.

Gilles' team had to deal with a balloon shaped like a sausage. No prizes for guessing the best way to transport that one.

Yaslyn grimaced in her friends' direction as Gilles held the offending balloon out towards her firmly closed thighs.

'Haven't you got anything bigger?' she asked.

Gilles, who had done two seasons at Club Aegee before and spent the winter selling skis in Colorado, had tried to explain the rules of dating guests of the village to Axel on many occasions; most recently the previous evening, as they spent the free hour between afternoon activities and dinner in their room.

'On the first day, you simply size them up,' Gilles began with authority. 'See which ones you fancy and try to make them sign up for a couple of one-to-one sessions with you on the tennis court. Or rope them into the pool games. That's not too hard. Everyone wants to be entertained when they're on holiday. And if they don't want to be entertained then you might as well forget it anyway. After that, it's important to find out whether they are staying for a week or for a fort-night before you make another move. Because timing is everything Everything. You must not get involved too early in a guest's holiday. Never. Never. Never.'

'What do you mean by too early?' Axel asked.

'If a girl arrives on a Tuesday and you're in her room on Tuesday night, you'd better be prepared for the consequences. It had better be love, is what I'm saying. She's going to be around for a whole week. If you decide you don't want a repeat performance on Wednesday night, you're going to have to find ways to avoid her for six whole days. And in a club the size of this one, that is hard. Plus,' said Gilles almost thoughtfully, 'you don't want to ruin her holiday too.

'No,' he concluded. 'The very best time to go for a guest is two nights before they leave. That way, if it's fantastic, you still get to do it more than once. And if it's terrible, you only have to find somewhere to hide for twenty-four hours or so.'

Gilles nodded. He was very pleased with his plan.

'Gilles,' Axel ventured. 'How many club guests have you actually slept with?'

'I stopped counting when I got to fifty-seven,' he said blithely. 'That was two years ago. My first season at Club Aegee.'

'Fifty-seven!' Axel breathed. 'That's . . .'

'Not as good as Pierre, I know. He's still averaging one a night. And he's been here since 1997. But I don't think many of his are queuing up for seconds. It takes time to woo a lady properly, get into her head, make her feel like you care.'

'And do you care?' asked Axel bluntly.

'Sometimes,' said Gilles. He blew a smoke ring out across the balcony of their room in the direction of the tennis court, scene of his greatest seductions. 'But it doesn't do to get too attached. My father taught me that when I was just a boy back in La Rochelle.'

'What did he do?' Axel expected to hear that Gilles' father had abandoned him at an early age, hardening his deserted son's heart and turning him into the ladykiller he was today.

'He was a slaughterman at the local abattoir. Not a great job for someone who loved cows as much as he did.'

Gilles ground out the last third of his cigarette on the whitewashed wall and got up.

'Where are you going?' Axel asked.

'Dutch girl, block E4. Leaves tomorrow morning. Wasn't going to bother but, hey, all this talk about shagging . . . I need some form of release and I don't think I want to be in a room with you when I get it.'

'Feeling's mutual,' Axel assured him.

Gilles adjusted the waistband of his faded jeans and sauntered towards the door.

'Don't wait up!'

'Sure,' said Axel.

Axel sat alone on the darkening balcony, listening to the receding sound of Gilles' whistle as he made his way through the pine trees towards the guest cottages. He was whistling the 'Marseillaise' again. His mating call.

The blue pirates won the balloon race that morning by the pool. While Delphine pushed her sorry crew into the water one by one, Gilles waved the blue flag aloft and sang the French national anthem triumphantly. Unfortunately, with the exception of Yaslyn the token Brit, the rest of Gilles' team were from Italy. Nobody but Gilles knew the words. Never mind.

The manager of the pool bar cranked up his stereo system now that team games were over and the whole of the village was officially awake. A Turkish pop song blasted from the speakers, sending Delphine and the other Go-Go girls into an impromptu belly-dance routine, much to the delight of her soggy team members. Gilles took Yaslyn by the hands and led her into a shimmy. He pulled her tight against his chest and ground his pelvis hard against hers as they moved.

'When am I going to see you on the tennis court?' he breathed hotly in her ear.

'I don't really know how to play all that well,' she said. 'I think I should stick to my books.'

'The whole point is that I will teach you things,' said Gilles.

'I don't think there's much you could teach me,' Yaslyn responded with a sigh.

Gilles released Yaslyn into a spin. As she whirled back towards him, he gave her the benefit of his very best smile. Then, in a single flowing move, he caught her, kissed her hand and bid her '*à bientôt*' with a deep and gallant bow.

Axel shook his head as he watched the English girl stagger back towards her friends and give a mock swoon with the back of her hand pressed to her forehead. She might be laughing now. They all laughed at Gilles at first, mocking his cheesy chat-up lines and all-too-knowing smiles. But by the end of the week she would be smitten. Perhaps even heartbroken. The English girl was Gilles' target for the week. Axel had seen the Club Aegee super-stud in action so many times he knew the sorry pattern of seduction by heart.

15

At a quarter to three that afternoon, Marcus went down to the beach for his first windsurfing lesson. Sally's own lesson with Gilles the tennis coach was pencilled in for quarter past. As soon as Marcus was safely out of sight, Sally started to formulate her excuse.

She was just about to tell the receptionist in pigeon French that she was feeling too dizzy from sunstroke to take up her place on the courts when she felt a tap on her shoulder. Guilt making her assume that Marcus was checking up on her, Sally jumped three feet in the air.

'Sally Mer-chant?' asked Gilles. He pronounced 'chant' as though he was saying the French word for 'sing'.

Sally nodded guiltily.

'I was just trying to tell the receptionist that . . .'

'I have been looking forward to meeting you,' said Gilles. 'Are you ready to play some tennis?'

'Well, actually, that's what I wanted to tell you . . .' Sally tried again.

Gilles cocked his head on one side, affecting not to understand that she was trying to wheedle her way out of a game.

''Old out your 'ands,' he said.

Sally could only obey. Gilles placed a tennis racket

in one hand and told her in a studiously ingenuous way, 'I think you will want to hold my balls as well.'

The girl on reception shook her head at a scene she'd witnessed a thousand times and turned to the next holidaymaker in the queue. Sally Merchant followed Gilles up towards the tennis courts like a child following the Pied Piper out of Hamelin.

It was such a cliché. Fancying the tennis instructor. But right from the start of the lesson, Gilles acted more like a porn star pretending to be a tennis coach than a bona fide sports teacher. Sally and Gilles were the only people on the court that afternoon. Gilles didn't bother to make sure that his T-shirt didn't ride up when he stripped off his Club Aegee sweatshirt, giving Sally a great view of his Athena poster abs as it did so. Such a contrast to Marcus's softly rounded stomach . . . And to begin the lesson, Gilles didn't stand across the net from his new pupil but set up a machine that would fire balls in Sally's direction so that he could stand alongside her and 'check her technique' as she missed every one.

Alongside quickly became behind. Gilles wrapped his arms right around Sally's body to show her where her hands should be on her racket for a good forehand. He moved through the swing with her, as though their bodies were one and the same. No wonder Sally continued to miss every shot. How could she be expected to keep her eye on the ball when Gilles' big brown hands were wrapped around her wrists, when his strong brown thighs were hard against the back of hers, the blond hair on his legs tickling her own bare legs in an impossibly distracting way.

'Is this how they teach tennis in France?' Sally asked with a nervous laugh. Up until that moment her experience of tennis lessons had been restricted to an after-school tennis club where thirty children between the ages of seven and twelve formed a long line to take it in turns to hit the ball back across a net to a fifty-something man who claimed he had once *nearly* played at Wimbledon. Terry Elliot, as the man's name was, looked as though he was a normal-sized man who had been hit on the head with a mallet, causing him to shrink down but spread sideways at the same time. Three years of that after-school tennis club had made it impossible for Sally to take the notion of finding a tennis coach attractive seriously. If Terry Elliot had rested his chin on her shoulder while he explained what was wrong with her forehand . . . ugh. It didn't bear thinking about.

'Slowly. More slow-ly . . .' said Gilles, dragging out the word. '*Lentement*. One more time.'

He drew her arm back as the ball machine spewed out another little yellow globe in their direction. As if she had nothing to do with the action taking place, Sally watched the head of her racket make contact with the ball for the first time in half an hour. The ball rocketed back across the net, landing just an inch inside the baseline. A perfect shot.

And instead of bringing Sally's arms back to the central position for another shot, Gilles kept turning her until her face was in his chest.

'Well done.' He squeezed her close.

Sally held her racket head awkwardly between them like a mask and stumbled back in surprise when he released her. But Gilles was still grinning as though it were perfectly natural to hold someone so close that your chest hair got up their nose when they got a decent shot in.

'Backhand,' he announced.

Sally smoothed her hair back from her eyes. The bugger was laughing at her, she was sure. Enjoying her discomfort. He did this to every woman who submitted to his coaching. No doubt about that. Well, he wasn't going to laugh at her. She wasn't like all the other women in this holiday village, desperate for a bit of frottage with a man half their age. All the same, when he told her that he thought she had 'potential' the hairs stood up all over Sally's body, and not in a bad way.

'You need to change your grip, like this,' Gilles said. And then he was back behind her again, wrapping his arms right around her body to adjust her fingers on the racket handle.

'That's better,' he murmured.

And it was.

16

Every evening at Club Aegee had a theme. Tuesday nights were black-and-white night. All the reps dressed head to toe in black or white and the cabaret was a selection of songs from the hit musical *Chess* sung by Pierre the dance instructor and Eloise, who worked the photography stand during the day.

Thursday nights were red-and-white night. All the reps wore red or white, to coordinate with the colours of the Turkish flag, and the cabaret was a display of traditional Turkish folk dancing by a local troupe that travelled from hotel to hotel. Friday night was gala night – since it was the last night of the holiday for the French visitors who generally made up most of the camp's population. The entertainment that night was a series of magic tricks, by Gilles, who often ended his show by sawing in half whichever one of the lucky guests he had been screwing the night before.

Wednesday nights were the worst. The theme at dinner on a Wednesday was the 1970s. Coq au vin. Boeuf bourguignon. Strawberry blancmange. Luckily for the chef, the dessert that time forgot was still pretty widely available in Turkey, and what the chef couldn't do with blancmange . . . The centrepiece of Wednesday evening's dinner was always a towering mountain of the stuff, decorated with green glacé cherries. Feeling queasy just at the thought of the wobbling synthetic strawberry monolith, Axel could never understand why the whole thing would be devoured before eight.

But far worse than the dinner was the seventies-night cabaret, which naturally involved dressing up in seventies-style costume. Gilles managed to look like sex on a stick in his faded flared jeans and open-fronted suede waistcoat. Let's face it, thought Axel enviously, Gilles would look like sex on a stick in a shroud. The Go-Go girls looked pretty cute too in multi-coloured flowing kaftans with great big flowers in their hair. But Axel, who had been last to arrive at the dress rehearsal at the very beginning of the season, was not so lucky. The funky clothes had already been shared out and Axel was forced to spend every Wednesday evening in a brown nylon suit that some-body had found in one of Bodrum's premier menswear outlets.

The show that evening was based around a medley of seventies tunes, which the reps would mime along to. Thus Gilles got to spend ten minutes of every Wednesday night with his arm around one of the aerobics instructors as they played at being Benny and Agnetha from Abba. Axel didn't even have the con-solation of miming words of love in the direction of Claire the cross-eyed receptionist. Examining the motley crew she had to work with that season, Melodie the choreographer had jumped up and down excitedly when the perfect role for Axel came to mind.

'You look just like him.'

Who? Axel wondered.

'Jim Morrison from The Doors?' someone

suggested a little sarcastically from the back of the room.

'Simon and Garfunkel,' said Melodie. 'Not the short one. The other one. Garfunkel. Yeah, you look just like him, Axel. How skinny you are. The way your hair recedes.'

And that was how, every Wednesday evening, Axel came to find himself miming 'Bridge Over Troubled Water' with his arm around one of the Turkish guys who worked in the kitchen – the only person in camp short enough to do a passable impression of Paul Simon – while the rest of the reps held aloft cigarette lighters and swayed in time with the music.

It made him want to cry.

Melodie wasn't to know that 'Bridge Over Troubled Water' was a song that held special significance for Axel Radanne. She wasn't to know it was the song that had been playing in the café that afternoon when he and Natalie had fallen in love.

Natalie. If he closed his eyes he could see her now as he had seen her for the very first time. She was walking up a street in Saint Germain by the back of the Sorbonne with the weak autumn sun tinting her glossy dark hair red and gold. She was wearing a green Agnès B miniskirt over thick black tights that made her legs look endless as they tapered into knee-high black suede boots. The stripy scarf wrapped around her neck was fashionably ironic. And she was smiling at Axel. That was the best part of all. He would find out later on that she needed a new prescription in her sexy round glasses.

But how could Axel resent the case of mistaken

identity that had brought them together that afternoon? When Natalie realised that Axel wasn't her friend after all, she was too polite not to apologise for waylaying him with her smile. And while she was apologising she noticed that she and Axel were carrying some of the same human biology textbooks. The textbooks that indicated they must share some classes at the University of Paris medical school Axel had recently joined as an undergraduate.

Natalie was having trouble getting to grips with her endocrine system. Axel offered to help. She told him he was too kind. He must be busy. He said it was no problem. She said she didn't know how it was possible they hadn't met before because she had been wondering where all the kind people were. When could he help her?

How about right away?

Axel, who had been on only one date in his life (with the deeply dim niece of one of his mother's colleagues), could not believe his luck. That afternoon, which he had expected to pass writing up that morning's lecture notes, was spent in a café he had hitherto felt too shy to visit, frequented as it was by the trendiest of students. 'Bridge Over Troubled Water' was playing as they stepped through the door.

Two other guys greeted Natalie by name as she led Axel through the smoky darkness to her favourite table at the back of the room. Axel had never exactly been the subject of envy before, but that was definitely the sentiment behind the looks those guys were giving him now. Beautiful and intelligent and apparently into him, Natalie was the ideal woman Axel had thought he would never find.

She ordered two black coffees. He always drank his white but was still too shy to tell her. She offered him a cigarette to smoke while he looked over the questions she had been struggling with. He didn't smoke, but decided it was about time he learned. If Natalie guessed that he had never put a cigarette in his mouth before, she didn't mention it. She didn't look at him strangely when he held the smoke in puffed-out hamster cheeks, too scared to take it down into his lungs, and blew it out again like a dolphin clearing its blowhole when he could hold it in no longer.

And then, as though the spirit of the dead poet were standing at his shoulder, Axel opened his mouth and uttered, before shyness could overwhelm him, the first line of a Baudelaire poem. 'O *toison, moutonnant, jusqu'à . . .*'

Natalie put down her pen and stared at him.

'Why did you say that?' she asked.

'Because your hair is so beautiful,' he blurted. 'I'm sorry. It just reminded me of a poem "*La Chevelure*" . . .'

'I know it. It was a Baudelaire poem. You quoted Baudelaire to me! And I was just sitting here thinking how much you look like him. I can't believe it. A medical student who knows poetry *and* looks like my favourite poet too.'

Axel had never been so thrilled to be compared to a nineteenth-century syphilitic in his life.

Natalie grasped his hands across the table and giggled.

'Axel Radanne. You could be my dream man!'

*

Their first kiss that night was by Baudelaire's tomb in the cemetery at Montparnasse. Axel felt sure his hero would have approved. It was a perfect poetic moment to begin a perfectly poetic six weeks. When Axel lost his virginity to Natalie in his little attic room three days after that first kiss, he thought he would ascend to heaven on the bat wings that decorated his Gothic hero's grave.

'I love you,' he whispered, as Natalie lay with her head on his chest.

'We'll never be apart, Axel,' she said. 'I swear it.'

Then Ed Wiseman arrived.

Ed Wiseman was an exchange student from Wisconsin via Harvard. As dark and gloomy as Axel could be, Ed was fair and shining. At first they dubbed him the Colgate Kid. His bright white teeth had never been kissed by unfiltered smoke or a strong black espresso. Natalie went along with the joke at first, laughing at Ed's neat blond hair and his tidy preppy clothes. He was a walking Lands' End catalogue, she said. But his offensively inoffensive exterior belied a brain the size of his grandfather's farm (which was, he told Natalie, roughly the size of Provence). And unlike his fellow American students he spoke fluent French. Two weeks into their acquaintanceship, he repeated, word for word, with an accent like a native's, Axel's first sniping assessment of him.

'Of course you thought I was going to be a dumb-ass,' Ed told a thoroughly humiliated Axel good-naturedly. 'Just like I thought you were going to be completely up your own ass. We're dealing with centuries of deeply ingrained racial prejudice here, Axel, old man. It's to be expected that we make these assumptions about one another. But I intend to start a new special relationship between our nations right here today.'

Axel didn't notice the discreet little smile that passed between Ed and Natalie at the suggestion.

Four weeks later, not even Axel's most heartfelt rendition of the best love poems from Baudelaire's *Fleurs du Mal* could keep Natalie's attention any more. In Ed, she would later tell him, she had found a man with the spirit and wisdom of Victor Hugo. Wrapped up in the body of Brad Pitt . . .

That was the end of Natalie and Axel.

And it was the end of Axel's academic career too. He spent the rest of the term, when he should have been working towards his important exams, shadowing Natalie and Ed about town until Natalie lodged an official complaint with the university. Axel had hoped for some sympathy – France is home of the *crime passionnel* after all – but it seemed that Natalie wasn't the only one to have fallen under Ed Wiseman's wholesome spell. Axel was asked to quit stalking his ex and leave the university. Ed was promised a research placement for the following year.

'Axel, we are running a holiday club, not a prison,' said Cherie the *chef de village* when she caught him brooding on Natalie yet again. 'You are permitted to smile at the guests.'

Axel shrugged.

'I mean it,' Cherie continued. 'This is not your own

personal foreign legion. If you want to mope about that girl back home you can do it somewhere else. Now get your brown nylon bottom over to the dining room,' she added with a grin. 'I think I hear "Bridge Over Troubled Water".'

17

Cherie didn't have to worry that Gilles might be upsetting the guests by looking miserable. Gilles loved seventies night. It may have been the decade that taste forgot but he was pretty damn pleased with the way he looked in his dressing-up-box outfit. With a towelling headband round his floppy blond locks, Gilles fancied he looked a bit like his own hero, tennis star Bjorn Borg. Only better looking. His eyes weren't so close together, for a start.

Besides, Gilles told Axel, the seventies night was an excellent one for flirting with the guests. Many of them dressed up for the occasion. The classic disco tunes were great for getting down on the dance floor. And by the end of the evening, the village would often be pervaded by an authentic seventies-style spirit of free love inspired by the silliness of it all. Gilles claimed he'd once had a threesome with two Italian girls who had come to the party as Stevie Nicks and Christine McVie because he persuaded them that it would be a very Fleetwood Mac thing to do.

'Imagine the scope if Cherie would let us have a Roman night,' Gilles mused.

That night, another Stevie Nicks was being created in guest hut B 17. As chief bridesmaid and official hen week coordinator in chief, Yaslyn had packed a number of humiliating outfits for the girls to don at some point during the holiday, including a black veil for Carrie Ann to match the white one Rachel would be wearing.

'I knew these would come in handy,' Yaslyn said as she pulled two long blond wigs out of her case. 'I'll be Stevie Nicks. You could be that one from Abba.' She handed one of the wigs to Rachel.

'I'll look more like Dougal from *The Magic Roundabout* in this,' Rachel moaned. 'Centre partings really do nothing for me.'

'There's a purple Afro here as well,' said Yaslyn, handing it straight to Carrie Ann.

'Who could I be in this?'

'The one from Boney M?' Yaslyn suggested.

'Wasn't it the bloke from Boney M who had the Afro?' Carrie Ann asked.

'Come on. It's Rachel's hen week. We've got to get a bit stupid,' Yaslyn replied. Except, of course, she didn't look stupid. She looked like Stevie Nicks's more beautiful little sister with a fabulous floaty scarf wrapped around her head and long false eyelashes that brushed her cheeks when she blinked.

'It's time for the ritual,' Rachel announced when her own transformation into seventies rock chick was complete. She filled the tooth mugs with Goldschlager and fetched the vibrator out of her suitcase. 'I wish for something really nice to eat at dinner. Mostly to get rid of the taste of this stuff.' She winced as she choked down her shot.

'Pathetic wish,' said Carrie Ann. 'I wish for the waiter to accidentally bring us one more bottle of all-inclusive wine than he's supposed to. And for gorgeous Gilles the tennis bum to get short-sighted and suddenly find me attractive,' she added as an afterthought.

'That tennis instructor is a one,' Yaslyn chuckled as she applied one more coat of mascara. 'You should have seen how he made sure I had the right grip on my racket. Wrapped his arms right round me and pressed himself up against my back. Talk about up close and personal. I could feel his balls.'

Rachel opened her mouth to exclaim.

'The tennis balls he had in his pocket,' Yaslyn elaborated.

'Ugh,' said Carrie Ann.

'I know. I don't know where he's been,' Yaslyn continued. 'But he's good for a bit of holiday flirtation.'

'As long as that's all it is,' said Rachel. 'You're not exactly single.'

'You don't have to keep reminding me.' Yaslyn sounded faintly irritated. 'We're on holiday. All normal rules of engagement are suspended on holiday. Especially on a hen week.'

'Until you pick up some nasty lurgy,' said Carrie Ann.

'Talking of which, how is your Norwegian friend?'

Carrie Ann rolled her eyes dramatically. That afternoon by the pool had turned into a game of musical sunbeds as the Oddball from Oslo moved ever closer in an effort to catch Carrie Ann's attention. He didn't seem at all fazed by the fact that every time he got two sunbeds nearer to his target Carrie Ann would get up on the pretence of going to the loo and return to move her belongings two sunbeds farther away. She wasn't the kind of woman to be snobbish about the way a man looked and she was willing to live by Margaret Mayday's 'brown paper packages' rule if it would usher true love into her life, but there had to be something inherently wrong with a man who could spend an entire day by a swimming pool in a Turkish holiday resort without feeling the need to remove his socks.

The socks were still *in situ* when the girls saw Carrie Ann's new admirer in the restaurant that evening. He seemed to have made an effort to dress in keeping with the evening's theme at least. His short-sleeved white shirt had been replaced by a tight nylon shirt patterned in brown and orange, accessorised with a matching waistcoat. Instead of his grey slacks, he was sporting a pair of brown flares. His lace-up shoes had been replaced by brown sandals.

'Why do I get the feeling that outfit wasn't supposed to be ironic when he packed it?' Carrie Ann asked. She attempted to slip past him to the buffet without making eye contact. She thought that the purple Afro might put him off the scent. It didn't.

'Hello,' he said cheerfully when he materialised beside her at the carvery.

'Hi,' said Carrie Ann. What now? 'I am not married' again? Carrie Ann didn't speak his language. He didn't speak hers. Still he continued to grin at her while Yaslyn and Rachel slipped away into the crowd, leaving Carrie Ann to her fate.

'Nice outfit,' she tried.

Her new friend smiled so broadly that Carrie Ann wondered whether she'd accidentally suggested fellatio in Norwegian.

*

Sally had refused to try to cobble together a seventies outfit for that evening. She hadn't expected so many of the guests to take the theme seriously, leaving her feeling like the one who stuck out among the flower children in her plain black shift dress.

But if she felt embarrassed that she hadn't made an effort to get seventies, Sally was mortified when Gilles joined her and Marcus for dinner. He must have noticed that they had been sitting in silence for half an hour, not even looking at each other; Sally eating her lambs' lettuce and tomato salad with the intensity of a prisoner who doesn't want to catch the eye of the hardest scrote in the jail; Marcus looking up and about him constantly as though he hoped he might persuade someone to come and join them, cover up the lack of conversation. Gilles answered his prayer.

'Mind if I join you?'

'Great,' said Marcus enthusiastically. 'It's Gilles, isn't it? Love your outfit. You look like Bjorn Borg.'

'The tennis superstar?' Gilles asked as though no one had ever suggested it before.

'That's the one.'

'Thank you. But this is the superstar.' Gilles squeezed Sally's shoulder as he sat down beside her. 'Your wife is very good at tennis,' he told Marcus.

'I knew she would be,' said Marcus proudly.

'She was a pleasure.'

'I bet you say that about all the girls,' snapped Sally.

'Say what?' asked Gilles. The crack was outside his lexicon of English phraseology.

'So,' said Marcus. 'Must be a great job this. Getting to spend the whole summer in a lovely place like

Turkey. Staying outside all day. Certainly beats working in the City, I can tell you.'

Gilles nodded.

'Have you been doing it long?'

'My third year,' said Gilles.

'Always here?'

'Yes. I like it. I like the guests.' He winked at Sally. Sally glared at the puddle of salad dressing left on her plate now the lettuce was gone.

'Must get a lot of the ladies throwing their knickers at you when you're doing the cabaret, eh?' said Marcus.

'Marcus, please.' Sally winced.

Gilles shook his head as though to deny the assumption.

'It's difficult,' he told them with his best effort at sincerity. 'I know that if I were an ordinary guy, working in an office back in La Rochelle, not many of these women would look twice at me. It's the sun. Makes everybody feel more sexy.'

Not me, thought Sally. She felt as uncomfortable as a twelve-year-old watching a sex scene in a television soap with her parents in the room.

Just then, one of the Go-Go girls squeezed by to join a table of guests from Italy. She pushed a little closer to Gilles' chair than was strictly necessary, so that her impossibly pert breasts almost brushed the top of his golden head as she passed.

''Scusez-moi, Gilles,' she breathed.

'Mon plaisir, Delphine,' said Gilles.

Yeah, I bet it is, thought Sally, as Gilles watched the girl wiggle on through the dining room.

'So, I will see you on the tennis court tomorrow morning, Sally?'

'I don't know . . .'

'Come on, Sally,' said Marcus. 'You've been saying you'd like to join the tennis club back home for years. Here's your chance. Get some practice in now and you'll wow them when we get back to Surrey.'

'You have potential,' said Gilles. He held her gaze.

'Hold that pose!' They had been joined by one of the Club Aegee photographers. The two guys wandered around the club all day with their huge cameras slung around their necks. They snapped people by the pool, on the beach, in the restaurant, and the resulting photos were displayed every evening so that guests could buy some prints to take home. Or at least get some amusement from the out-takes.

'Move in closer.' Gilles put his arm around Marcus and Sally's shoulders.

'Everybody say cheese!'

Gilles' arm slipped down to Sally's waist as he squeezed her into the frame.

'That was a good shot,' said the photographer.

'When will it be ready?' Marcus asked.

'Tonight's pictures will be posted tomorrow morning.'

'We'll have to get a copy, eh, Sally?'

'Whatever you say,' said Sally.

Gilles still hadn't moved his chair back away from hers.

At that moment, the Tannoy system began to play 'Lost In Music' by Sister Sledge.

'Excuse me,' said Gilles. 'That is my cue to get back-stage for the cabaret.'

He jumped up and joined the other reps as they

formed a whooping crocodile on their way to the audi-
torium.

'God, he's so smooth,' said Marcus half admiringly.

'Isn't he just . . .' said Sally.

'Want to watch the cabaret tonight?' Marcus asked.

'Got a bit of a stomach ache,' Sally lied. 'You can
stay up if you want to,' she added, hoping that he
would.

'Like a bridge over troubled water . . .'
Rachel, Yaslyn and Carrie Ann waved cigarette
lighters from the front row of the audience as Axel
mimed his best.

'That was bloody awful,' said Carrie Ann as the reps
filed offstage to what seemed like inexplicably loud
applause given the quality of their Jacques Tati-style
performance.

'That rep who picked us up at the airport really did
look like Art Garfunkel, though, didn't he?' commented Rachel. 'Didn't you have a huge crush on Art
Garfunkel once?'

'It was Bob Dylan,' said Carrie Ann flatly.

'Bob Dylan, Art Garfunkel. Look pretty similar to
me,' said Yaslyn. 'We going to stay up for the disco?'

'We've got to!' said Rachel. 'It's my hen week.'

That already familiar refrain. To refuse now would
seem very churlish. You couldn't be a spoilsport on a
hen week. Carrie Ann shrugged in vague agreement.

Gilles was already shimmying his way towards
them, accompanied by dancing coach Pierre and
Xavier the water-sports instructor. This was the best
part of Gilles' day – rounding up the stray single
women and herding them down to the beach bar to

strut their stuff and spend more of the club's purple drinks coupons on watered-down spirits. Now he took Yaslyn by the hand and led her in an impromptu samba.

'This is my new tennis superstar,' he informed Pierre.

'I barely hit a ball back over the net.'

'But you have potential,' Gilles assured her. 'Come and dance with me and I'll tell you more about improving your backhand.'

Yaslyn let herself be led. Pierre reached out for Rachel. Carrie Ann prepared to follow suit with Xavier but Xavier didn't seem to have noticed her. Instead, he gave a little pirouette and tangoed off in the direction of a table where three forty-something Frenchwomen were trying to preserve themselves with Armagnac and nicotine. Which left Carrie Ann alone and vulnerable again. Like a baby wildebeest separated from the rest of the herd. Perhaps it was just the Afro. Perhaps she really was unlovable.

'Hello there, Carrie Ann!'

It was Morten.

'You want to dance?'

He'd learned another four words. And a hand gesture that looked suspiciously like the international symbol for 'grope' to go with his robotics.

'Turkish tummy,' said Carrie Ann, clutching her stomach and running for the loo.

18

Marcus woke early next morning. He hadn't stayed up to watch the cabaret but had accompanied Sally back to their room and lain in silence on his single bed while she lay equally quiet and still on the other side of the room, one hand on her head, the other on her stomach. Marcus had suggested that she take the stomach upset remedy he had so carefully packed for such eventualities but she refused. She refused every offer of assistance. She didn't even want a bottle of Diet Coke to sip while she lay still and quiet. That had been all she ever needed to get over an attack of queasiness when they were travelling through India.

It seemed like an age before Sally fell asleep but eventually she began to quietly snore and Marcus dared switch on the light above his bed to read a bit more of his guidebook. There were plenty of things he wanted to see while they were in Turkey. Club Aegee offered organised day trips to Istanbul and Ephesus. Marcus read the posters next to the bar every time he passed them, but so far Sally had been uninspired. All she wanted to do was sit by the pool and read her books, she told him. The girl who had risen at four to see the Taj Mahal at dawn, climbed to the top of an Inca temple at sunset, even swum in a lake rumoured to be infested by crocs by dark, now wanted only to be left alone with the new John Grisham. Perhaps it was just that she needed a couple of days to unwind first.

With the sun just starting to make the thin brown curtains transparent, Marcus couldn't lie on that hard bed and listen to Sally snoring on her own narrow bunk any longer. He got to his feet and began to sift through the pile of clothes on the dressing table for a T-shirt to wear over his trunks. He was careful not to wake her. Let sleeping dogs lie was the thought that crossed his mind as he closed the door quietly behind him and headed for the beach. She might be a bit less fractious when she was rested.

Even at six in the morning the beach wasn't entirely empty. The Club Aegee cleaning staff were already hard at work, clearing up the beach bar before the greedy seagulls got into the bin bags and spread the rubbish all over the beach. Marcus nodded politely at one of the women. A local, he guessed from her outfit and demure headscarf. The young woman automatically covered her mouth and looked down, as though to smile back might be thought indecent. Her eyes gave her away, though.

Marcus stepped out in the direction of the German-run all-inclusive hotel at the other end of the cove. It didn't look far. But within twenty feet of the beach bar, the firm wet sand that felt so good to walk on was replaced by pebbles that were too painful to cross barefoot and difficult to negotiate even in thick rubber-soled sandals.

He would swim back, he decided. Though it was early, the sea in the cove retained heat from the whole of the summer so far and was warmer than some of the baths Marcus had taken at less expensive hotels on his travels. Besides which, Marcus loved to swim. Balmy pools or ice-cold rivers. It really didn't matter. Sometimes he just wanted to be in the water. It made him feel somehow free.

At school, he had been a champion at front crawl. His PE teacher, delighted to have such a talent in his school, had pushed him to compete at city level, then county level. Marcus came home with the silver medal in the first national competition he competed in. After that, there were murmurings to the effect that a place on the British Olympic team might not be out of the question if he was prepared to give up all his free time to prepare. He gave it his best shot. For six months. He seemed to be making some progress. Then something inside him gave up before his body did. Something inside him made him suddenly resent the time he had to put into training.

Improvements in Marcus's performance as a swimmer were directly proportional to the decrease in his popularity at school. People stopped asking him to go to parties at the weekend. He could never seem to spare the time. The county swimming team weren't exactly the most interesting bunch of people for a fifteen-year-old to socialise with. No surreptitious lager-swilling behind the youth club on a Saturday night for these people, who had to be at the pool by six o'clock the following morning.

'Just think of what you could achieve,' his mother said when he told her he was thinking about giving up. 'You could have an Olympic medal! What will your friends have when they get old? Beer bellies?'

But the argument just wasn't persuasive enough. Especially when Sarah Matthews came on the scene. Sarah was impressed by Marcus's broad back and washboard abs. Marcus was impressed by her mammaries. He skived a training weekend to try to coax her apart from her virginity while her parents were in Scotland for a funeral. Sarah did lose her virginity. And Marcus lost his place on the team.

Everyone thought it was a straightforward case of a young man being led astray by his hormones. But looking back with the benefit of hindsight, Marcus knew it was much more complicated than that. He had never been able to tell anyone how scared he was of the idea of competing at *international* level. The idea of swimming against the best people in the world filled him with a stomach-churning terror.

In reality, Marcus gave up swimming because he was a coward. He was afraid that he would do his best and discover that it just wasn't good enough. Everyone would laugh at him for having tried and failed. Better to be the boy who *could* have gone to the Olympics than the one who was remembered because he did go and came last.

These days, Marcus swam only on holiday or on business trips when he stayed in a hotel that had a pool. His power had all gone but he knew he still had technique. He cut a textbook figure as his bladed hand sliced through the salt water now. Left, right, left, right, barely making a splash as each stroke made contact with the surface. Even with the waves to contend with, he made short work of the journey back to the top end of the beach, getting there in two-thirds of the time it had taken him to walk in the opposite direction.

By the time he walked out of the surf, the other early birds were beginning to congregate on the sunbeds at last, spreading out towels to mark precious shady territory. The young woman he had greeted on the way down dared to smile at him as he passed her. He didn't notice.

When he got back to the room, Sally was still asleep. She woke up when she heard him turn on the shower and wandered into the bathroom to pee before he got in.

'You're already wet,' she said.

'I've been for a swim,' he told her.

'Oh,' she said. 'Mind if I wee before you shower?'

He duly stepped back into the main body of the room while Sally closed the door. When she had finished on the loo, Sally shuffled back to bed.

'Wake me up when you're done.' She closed her eyes again immediately.

Marcus let the shower beat down on the top of his head until it hurt. She hadn't asked him anything about his swim. Once upon a time, when they first got together, she would have asked him how fast and how far. How cold was the water? She used to encourage him to think about competing in amateur competitions again. This time she didn't ask him anything. Nothing at all.

19

Carrie Ann awoke to the unmistakable sound of vomit splattering into the toilet pan. Moments later, Yaslyn staggered back into the room, wiping her mouth clean with the scarf that had transformed her into Stevie Nicks the night before.

'Ugh. Have you just been sick?' Rachel asked nonsensically.

'I can't tell you how *glad* I am to have the bed nearest the bathroom,' said Carrie Ann. 'Drink too much Goldschlager last night?'

'I must have eaten something funny,' Yaslyn said.

'You barely ate anything at all yesterday,' said Rachel.

'Then it's probably the water.'

'You shouldn't even clean your teeth with the water here,' Rachel lectured.

Yaslyn sat down heavily on her bed. She stared into space for a second or two, then got back up again abruptly and ran for the loo. Carrie Ann covered her ears as the retching began again.

'Jesus,' shouted Carrie Ann. 'Can't you do that more quietly? It's making me want to hurl too.'

In reality, none of them was feeling particularly good that morning. Rachel's fear that the week would turn into one long hangover seemed more real than ever. Thump. Thump. Thump. And Carrie Ann was aching for yet another reason. Her tailbone had re-covered from the first night's fall from the bar stool, but overnight her shoulders had gone from slightly pink to radioactive red as the previous day's careful (in her opinion) tanning had developed into a third-degree burn. She blamed Morten. If she hadn't had to devote the entire afternoon to moving round the pool to avoid him, she might have spent more time in the shade. She asked Rachel to inspect the damage.

'Didn't you wear suntan lotion?'

'Of course I did.' Carrie Ann winced while Rachel prodded the red skin as though to test that Carrie Ann hadn't just brushed blusher all over her shoulders for a joke. 'Ow!'

'You need to stay out of the sun today. One of us had better go to the pool and save some spaces in the shade.'

'Already thought of that,' said Carrie Ann proudly. 'I put our towels out last night. By the pool bar so that we get shade from there.'

'Well done.' Yaslyn high-fived her to congratulate her on her quick thinking.

'You put on some sunblock,' Rachel told Carrie. 'You take some Imodium,' she said to Yaslyn. 'And I'll go down to the pool and make sure the towels are still there.'

Rachel soon found the spot Carrie Ann had described but there was no sign of their beach towels. Instead, the three beds nearest the sacred shade of the pool bar were already occupied by three glamorously white-haired Frenchwomen, elegantly lounging in the way that British grandmothers just can't seem to manage.

Rachel coughed to attract their attention. No one stirred. She coughed again, a little louder this time. The one who looked like a mummified version of Catherine Deneuve pushed her Chanel sunglasses up on to her forehead and nodded at Rachel expectantly.

'*Excusez-moi,*' Rachel began in her best schoolgirl French. '*Je cherche des assiettes.*'

The woman cocked her head to one side. Rachel had a vague feeling that she'd asked for help finding some plates rather than towels.

'Towels,' she said slowly. She indicated the beach towel that the woman was sitting on and did a little mime of drying herself off.

'Oh. *Serviettes.*' The woman pointed her in the direction of the swimming-pool attendant who spent all day patiently folding and handing out Club Aegee's own blue-and-white beach towels. '*Ça va?*'

'No,' said Rachel. 'My *serviette*. My friend put my towel here last night.' Rachel pointed at the woman's sunbed. 'And two others. One on each of these, I think.'

The Frenchwoman gave a shrug as only a Frenchwoman could do. And then Rachel spotted her towel, six sunbeds away, scrunched up in a pile with Yaslyn's and Carrie Ann's. She pointed over there and frowned.

'I think those towels were on these sunbeds,' she said.

'Oh, those towels?' said the Frenchwoman in impeccable English. 'They must have blown away before we got here. The sunbeds were empty.'

'Blown away?'

'It's very breezy. Anyway, you should spread them

out to dry instead of keeping me from my reading.'

Rachel opened and closed her mouth but she couldn't find the vocabulary to accuse the woman of lying. Or the guts.

'OK?' the woman asked pointedly. Then she flipped her sunglasses back down over her eyes like a protective visor and continued to read her book. She'd pulled the cover off, Rachel noted. It was probably *How to Win Friends and Influence People*.

Rachel stalked across to where their towels were heaped in a bundle. The woman had definitely been lying. There wasn't a breath of wind at the club that morning. Not enough to move a hair on Rachel's head, let alone pick up three beach towels and hurl them to the other side of the pool.

Rachel glanced back at the spot Carrie Ann had chosen for them. Her suspicion that she had been the victim of some sneaky sunbed snatching was only strengthened by the fact that two of the women were talking to each other behind their hands and looking in her direction. They were laughing at her. She was sure.

She told Yaslyn and Carrie Ann as much when she got back to the room.

'Then why didn't you say something?' asked Yaslyn.

'I tried to. I didn't know the French.'

'You didn't have to say it in French. Honestly, Rachel, sometimes you're so wet.'

'Perhaps they didn't do it.'

'They did it all right. The *wind* moved our towels? Wind, my arse. It's perfectly still here.'

Rachel felt her cheeks grow hot with indignation. 'It

might be true. Perhaps it happened while we were sleeping. Anyway, we're on holiday. I don't want to go round causing scenes.'

'You never want to cause a scene,' said Yaslyn casually. 'You don't cause a scene when you're *not* on holiday. You wouldn't cause a scene if your life depended on it. Which is why you're having the wedding your mother-in-law wants rather than the one you wanted.'

'What do you mean? My wedding is going to be exactly how I want it.'

'Of course it is,' said Yaslyn patronisingly. 'Whatever you say, Rach. We're going to have to get up earlier tomorrow morning and catch those bitches in action.'

Rachel was still bristling when she and Yaslyn got back to the poolside. If there was one thing that really touched a nerve, it was being accused of being wet. It was an accusation that Yaslyn often made of her, warning her that she missed out on what she wanted because she refused to speak up. But Rachel did speak up. She was sure she did. When it was important.

Besides, in Rachel's opinion, Yaslyn spoke up just a little too often. Surely it was better, if you didn't have a particularly strong feeling about something, to let the other person have their way? And surely it was the right thing, Rachel said to herself, to let her mother-in-law Helen have a bigger input than usual into how Rachel and Patrick planned their wedding? After all, she had given them quite a bit of money towards it and, since her own daughter had run off and got married in Las Vegas without telling anyone, she had missed out on planning a wedding as mother of the bride.

It had taken quite a while for Helen to forgive her daughter Jennifer for eloping, but Patrick was sure the relationship between his mum and Jennifer had improved even more since Rachel had given his mum carte blanche with the flower arrangements. That was a good thing. Worth giving up the lilies of her wedding fantasy for . . .

No. Rachel was not wet. She was just non-confrontational. And non-confrontational was sometimes the right way to be, wasn't it? Especially on holiday when all everybody wanted to do was relax.

She peeped up from her book at that morning's adversary. The glamour-puss was looking back in Rachel's direction. At least, Rachel thought the woman was looking at her. It was hard to tell with those oh-so-chic Jackie O sunglasses.

'You can smile all you want,' Yaslyn hissed at the woman on the other side of the pool. 'Tomorrow those sunbeds will be ours.'

Rachel ducked back behind her Marian Keyes.

Without the shade of her specially chosen place by the pool, Carrie Ann decided that she simply couldn't risk another day lying flat out in the sun. She'd have to go shopping instead.

Luckily, the layout of Club Aegee had been planned so that none of the guests need ever venture outside the village gates to get the full Turkish experience. The terracotta-tiled reception complex was surrounded by a cluster of gift shops, selling exactly the same tat as the stalls in Bodrum town at roughly four times the price. You could also buy Club Aegee branded casual wear. But only if you were the same size as one of the Club Aegee Go-Go girls, Carrie Ann noted with disgust as she picked up and quickly returned to the rack a pair of teeny lilac hot pants.

She wondered how much trade the jeweller next to the boutique did in consolatory trinkets for those women who could only guarantee a good fit in Club Aegee earrings. The jeweller's window was like Aladdin's Cave blown open by a Scud missile. Bracelets, necklaces, earrings and rings were piled haphazardly on velvet cushions. Most of it was awful – sovereign rings and brassy Creole earrings of the type that even Kate Moss couldn't make cool in a retro eighties-chic way.

Carrie Ann couldn't help grimacing when she saw one of those heart-shaped pendants that breaks into two parts so that each member of a couple can have half (the man's half on a slightly chunkier chain, of course). Carrie Ann's own half-a-heart now languished in a charity shop in Battersea, buried at the bottom of a pile of crappy plastic and silver-plated jewellery in a ballerina jewellery box she'd been given for her eleventh birthday. She wondered where Greg had hidden his.

Carrie Ann looked from the trashy pile in the shop window to her hands as they rested lightly on the sill. Her pale pink nail varnish, applied the night before they left England, was still looking pretty good. But that wasn't what caught Carrie Ann's eye.

For fifteen years she had worn three rings. The ring that Greg had given her for her eighteenth birthday – a

141

rolled-gold band set with a chip of onyx in the shape of a heart; her engagement ring, barely more expensive, more rolled gold set with synthetic rubies and cubic zirconia; and her wedding ring. Forty-five pounds it had cost him. Another piece of crap. But she would have worn them all until she died. That was the sad part.

Now those three rings were also in a broken music box in a Battersea charity shop, and all Carrie Ann had left to remind her of them was a place on the third finger of her left hand where the digit was slightly narrower. The difference wasn't immediately noticeable but to Carrie Ann it seemed quite obvious. The middle finger of her left hand reminded her of a limb that has just come out of plaster. Shrunken. Wizened. Weakened.

'Cheer up. It might never happen.'

Carrie Ann looked up from her deformed finger, into the soft brown eyes of the jewellery shop's proprietor. Gorgeous. Then she glanced down at his generous mouth and attendant cold sore. Ugh.

'You are English?' he asked.

'Irish, actually,' said Carrie Ann. 'Well, my parents are.'

'You have seen something you like here?'

'No,' said Carrie Ann. She'd seen a lot of stuff she *didn't* like but she wasn't going to tell him that.

'I have,' he said.

'It's your shop,' said Carrie Ann simply. 'You should like what you sell.'

'It is you,' he told her.

'What?'

'You,' repeated the jewellery shop owner. 'You are

more beautiful than anything I have in my shop. You have the face of an angel.'

He traced the curve of her cheek in the air.

Carrie Ann tilted her head to one side sceptically. 'Thank you. That's very kind.'

'Come inside,' he said then. 'I make you special discount.'

Of course. The 'special discount' ruse.

'I don't really want to buy anything,' Carrie Ann assured him. 'I was just looking.'

'Then just look *inside* my shop.' He took her hand. 'Try some things for size. I need to see my jewellery on a beautiful woman to know that I am getting it right.'

'I was just on my way to the pool,' she lied feebly.

'Five minutes. Yasser will be offended if you do not take his hospitality.'

What hospitality? Carrie Ann wondered. Yasser was practically kidnapping her, encircling her waist with his arm as he led her inside his stuffy little shop. She had a feeling that once she had crossed the threshold, she would be doomed. Like inviting a vampire into your home, accepting the small glass of sticky sweet mint tea that was now placed in front of her was surely asking for trouble.

'You have the right skin colour for the very finest of golds,' he began, dangling a thick gold chain in front of Carrie Ann's eyes as though he were about to attempt a spot of hypnotism.

'It is lovely,' Carrie Ann said automatically.

Yasser stepped behind her and draped it around her neck.

'It merely reflects your beauty,' he said.

Carrie Ann involuntarily snorted out a noseful of mint tea. When she had finished wiping her nose, the jeweller was still gazing at her as though she were the most fabulous woman ever to enter his store. He was very well practised. For a moment, Carrie Ann almost stopped noticing the cold sore.

'Two chains would look even better,' he assured her.

'I don't think I can afford even one,' said Carrie Ann, guesstimating the cost of the rope that already dangled at her throat. Even here in Turkey, she was surely sporting five hundred pounds' worth of the type of chain she hadn't seen since she last picked up an Argos catalogue. If she could afford to splash out, it would definitely be a triumph of spendthriftiness over taste.

'Look at this.' Yasser took her by the hand again and led her to another cabinet, arranged with the same haphazard *joie de vivre* as the window. 'You have no rings on your beautiful fingers. Every woman needs rings.'

Carrie Ann had to snort again this time.

'You have had rings in the past?' Yasser asked.

'Might as well have been handcuffs.'

'You have been badly treated by a husband?' He phrased the question like a fortune teller.

'I don't have a husband,' said Carrie Ann.

'But you did have.'

Carrie Ann set her mouth into a thin hard line. She didn't want to discuss her marital status or distinct lack of it with this man.

'He was a fool to let you go,' said Yasser. 'If I had a woman like you I would clasp her to my heart and never let her from my grasp. We would not be parted until one of us was dead.'

'A very romantic sentiment,' said Carrie Ann with just a little pinch of sarcasm. She moved to unfasten the chain around her neck. Yasser was there in a flash.

'You don't like it?'

'I told you,' said Carrie Ann. 'I think it's lovely. But I really can't afford to buy anything today.'

Carrie Ann's new friend regarded her gravely. 'I do not care that you are a rich woman or not,' said Yasser. 'What I like about you is here.' He tapped his heart. 'Not here.' He tapped his left buttock. Carrie Ann guessed that he meant he wasn't interested in her wallet. He certainly hadn't seemed to be averse to her buttocks up until now.

'Come here,' he said, taking her hand and placing it on his left breast. 'I have something special to give to you. A gift from Yasser. Close your eyes.'

Carrie Ann obliged with a shrug. There wasn't much he could get up to in full view of the village's reception desk, surely. But she felt him fiddling about with the front of her T-shirt.

'Hey!' She opened her eyes pretty promptly then. 'What are you doing?'

He was squatting a little to get to the right height. He looked up into her eyes with the kind of appealing gaze she hadn't seen since she had to have Greg's old Labrador put down. (Greg had been too pathetic to take Honey to be put out of her misery himself.)

'I am giving you a gift,' Yasser said. 'A piece of jewellery from me.'

Carrie Ann looked at the slot where he had been fiddling with her T-shirt excitedly. He hadn't given her the golden ladybird she coveted, had he? The one thing in the whole window display that she would have given house room?

No, he hadn't. Instead, where her fabulous ladybird should have been, Carrie Ann found what appeared to be a safety pin. To this safety pin was attached a misshapen blue glass bead and the tiniest gold coin imaginable. If it was gold.

'What is it?'

'It's the evil eye,' Yasser told her. 'It is to protect you from evil spirits.'

'Does it work on Turkish men?' she asked.

Yasser looked hurt.

'You will come with me to a private party later tonight?' he asked.

'I've already arranged to do something with my friends.'

'Then bring your friends,' he said. 'I will be waiting for you here.'

'Maybe,' said Carrie Ann. Then she quickly scuttled out of the shop before Yasser attempted to extract a promise. Right into the pigeon chest of Morten.

'Good morning!' he said with delight. 'Your stomach is better, Carrie Ann? You like to have a drink with me perhaps?'

Bloody hell, thought Carrie Ann. Her evil-eye pendant quite clearly didn't work on Norwegians either. Carrie Ann looked about her desperately for an escape route.

'You are going to the beach perhaps.' Morten indicated the binoculars which were once again hanging from his neck. 'Watching the birds?'

Yes, thought Carrie Ann. I bet you are.

'Perhaps you like to do that with me?'

Morten waited expectantly for her answer. He grinned. Carrie Ann spotted a piece of greenery stuck between his teeth. Then she spotted a piece of paper tacked to the door of one of the seminar rooms which led off the lobby.

'Chess tutorials here,' it said in French.

'I would love to go bird-watching,' said Carrie Ann as a flash of genius struck her. 'There's nothing I like more than spotting a good shag. As in the seabird. But I'm afraid I'll be late for my chess.'

20

'What am I doing here?' Sally asked herself, as she sat at the edge of the tennis court for a second time waiting for Gilles to finish tutoring a middle-aged woman in shorts that were really too short for anybody. Every time the woman moved, the lilac hot pants disappeared up her bum, resulting in the need to pull them out again, which meant she wasn't ready to return Gilles' shot.

Eventually the woman managed to get a single serve into the right box on the opposite side of the net. Gilles ran across the court towards her, vaulting the net, scooping her up in his arms and attempting half a lap of honour around the court before the woman's ear-splitting squealing got too much and he had to put her down.

'You will be at the French Open next year, Paulette!' Gilles gushed.

'I'll be in the bar later tonight.' Paulette winked. As she departed the court, she passed Sally and gave her a wink too. 'Your turn,' she added. 'Don't wear him out!'

'No danger of that.' Sally went to the baseline at the end of the court opposite the Club Aegee love god.

'No. Come up this end,' he said. 'We still need to work on how you hold your racket.'

'I can hear your instructions quite well from here,' Sally told him.

Gilles caught the note of harshness in her voice and raised his brows at her. Sally looked at her tennis shoes for a second. She didn't know why she felt so inordinately pissed off to see that Gilles had been lavishing the same kind of attention on that Paulette woman. He was the tennis coach. He flirted with everybody. Young, old. Male or female. It meant nothing. It was a way to pass the time with each and every punter who passed through his tennis school.

'Then I will come to you,' Gilles said. This time he was vaulting the net towards her. But rather than try his hands-on approach to coaching, he simply stood beside her and demonstrated the way he wanted her to stand in anticipation of a backhand with his own racket. Hell, there were probably three feet between them.

'You got that?' he asked seriously when he'd finished his display.

'I think so,' said Sally.

'OK. I'll go up to the other end of the court and send you some easy balls.'

He didn't even try to make the most of that double entendre.

Sally missed the first ball he sent across to her. And the second. And the third.

'Remember how I told you to stand,' he shouted. 'And don't take your eye off the ball until it hits your racket. You keep taking your eye off the ball.'

Sally missed another three balls.

Gilles crossed the net once again.

'Like this,' he said, demonstrating the swing. 'You do it.'

Sally tried to do the same.

'Like this,' said Gilles patiently. But this time he took Sally's wrists and moved her hands until they were at the right spot on the racket's handle. He continued to hold her hands as she moved through a swing with him. 'Better,' he said softly. He released his grip and straightened up. They were eye to eye. Gilles' tongue flickered out across his lips as though he were about to say something.

'I'll serve you some more balls,' he said eventually.

Sally felt her skin flush pink from her cheeks down to her navel. Flirting with her or not flirting with her. She didn't know which was worse.

Down on the beach, Marcus waited for his second hour of windsurf tuition. He'd been surprised by how easy he found it. Must have been the residual strength he had in his shoulders from all those years of swimming. He didn't struggle to raise the sail at all and soon grasped the principles that would allow him to steer the board in a wide circle around the bay while the other beginners struggled in the shallows like up-ended water beetles. Xavier, who looked after the windsurfs and catamarans in between attempting to chat up the blonde twins who lounged on the sunbeds nearest his hut, refused to believe that Marcus had never windsurfed before.

That afternoon, the sea was a little rougher than it had been the previous day. It was an offshore wind. The hardest conditions for a beginner. Marcus didn't care. An element of difficulty was exactly what he needed. While he had to think about what he was doing to stay upright on his board, it was difficult to think about anything else. More specifically, it was difficult to think about Sally.

When Marcus did manage to get up some speed, however, he did think about how good it felt. To feel that strain in his arms as he battled against the wind was like holding a guitar after ten years and discovering you can still pick out a tune. His body, which had pretty much gone into hibernation since he started to work in the City, responded to the adrenalin suddenly running through his veins like a vintage sports car purring when someone puts pedal to metal. Instantly, it was as though the Marcus who hunched over a desk all day was a different man entirely.

Once upon a time, before university and the pressure of unpaid student loans made it sound like a good idea to 'get a proper job', Sally and Marcus had talked about travelling the world, funding their progress from country to country with their skills. Sally would teach English lessons. She'd done a course in teaching English as a foreign language in preparation. Marcus would get work as a lifeguard. He would definitely have to learn to windsurf. They decided they would follow the sun around the globe. Mediterranean in the summer, overwintering in Australia, New Zealand, the Caribbean. If it worked out they could do it indefinitely. It had all seemed possible once.

In fact, the newly married Merchants still talked about the idea of a sabbatical during their first year in London. Except that now the plan was that they'd get some work experience under their belts first, then take six months' unpaid leave. Maybe extend it if things were going well. See what happened.

What happened was this. Sally got the first of her promotions. If she took time out now, the progress she had made at work might be wasted. All that effort gone for a few months in the sun, she said. She seemed to have forgotten that the idea was that they didn't make any particular effort to climb the corporate ladder, just paid off their debts and got together the first chunk of cash they needed to make their globe-trotting dream come true. Marcus had remained faithful to their vision. Sally had slipped into the corporate lifestyle of long hours and company credit cards.

Meanwhile, two of their friends from university were living Sally and Marcus's student dream. Zach and Tiff had buggered off to Thailand as soon as the ink on their finals papers was dry. Tiff set up an English school for local children. Zach was teaching waterskiing. They came back to England less and less frequently. The last time Marcus had seen the pair was at the wedding of another university match five years after graduation. Zach and Tiff were both still brown and happy. They were amused by the rain that fell on the wedding reception marquee in the way that only those people who know they don't have to live with British weather any more can be. They were so relaxed it made them seem five years younger than the rest of their old university friends.

'Don't they make you want to give everything up and run away?' Marcus asked Sally as they lay in bed that night.

'No,' she replied. 'They're living on borrowed time now. They'll have to come back one day. And what will they have to come back to? House prices aren't going to stop rising. The job market is moving along without them. They'll have to come back and live in some grotty studio flat, with no pension to look forward to either. What good is five years teaching waterskiing going to be when Zach wants a job in the City?'

Zach would never want a job in the City.

Marcus grew cold at the sound of Sally's voice as she continued to expound on the virtue of working sixty-hour weeks to service hundreds of thousands of pounds in mortgage debt to Barclays Bank while Zach and Tiff spent their evenings sipping ice-cold beer and watching the sun set over paradise. Not just for fourteen days a year. Every day . . .

'What will they have to show for all those years of messing about? Nothing,' Sally concluded.

Wouldn't that just put them on a par with the people who'd invested in a stock market in freefall? Bought a house rendered uninhabitable by flooding? Or spent five years married to someone who then decided she didn't love him after all?

Back on the beach, Xavier waved the Club Aegee 'skull and crossbones' to indicate that it was time for all those windsurfers who'd gone out at three o'clock to make their way back to the shore.

'Man, you are *good* at that,' said Xavier, when Marcus dragged his windsurf up on to the beach. 'I think I need to watch out for my job.'

'Any vacancies?' Marcus was only half joking.

21

Morten was determined. He even suggested that he join Carrie Ann for a game of chess himself. Thankfully, she managed to persuade him that the classes were strictly one on one and eventually slipped behind the safety of the door to which the poster was attached to wait for her suitor to give up and disappear.

He was taking his time about it. Carrie Ann lurked just inside the half-closed door of the seminar room, watching Morten flick through the German-language newspapers on the stand by reception. After five minutes she wondered whether she should just attempt to leg it past him while he was absorbed in a story about the German economy or something fascinating like that. While she weighed up her options – she hadn't legged it anywhere for a long time – Morten put down the paper. But then he picked up a day-old copy of the *Sun* and flicked straight to page three. He knew that much about British culture, then.

Carrie Ann sighed and sat down on a chair by the door. In the middle of the room, a chess set was already in place for the first game of the day. Who on earth signed up for chess tutorials? she wondered. It seemed such a shame to spend even five minutes in this dark, windowless room when it was so glorious outside. Even if you were suffering from heatstroke, which Carrie Ann suspected she had picked up along with her dose of sunburn. She looked at her watch. It was coming up for midday. The hottest part of the day. And lunch-time. Hopefully Morten would want to be first in the queue for lunch (though he still had half his breakfast in his teeth). Carrie Ann risked another peek. He was still there, engrossed in an article about a former Spice Girl. Or at least engrossed in the pictures of said former Spice Girl performing naked yoga on the deck of her new boyfriend's private yacht.

Carrie Ann still had her nose to the door when someone pushed his way in, sending her stumbling backwards into the room. For a second or three, she thought she was going to pull it off, maintain her balance, save herself from falling down. But she didn't. Her brief glimmer of poise ended with her landing heavily on the stone floor. Hitting her coccyx again.

'Ow!' she squealed.

She wasn't the only one who had been surprised. Axel leapt back out of the room again and counted to three before he stepped back in.

''Allo. You are OK?' he asked.

'Ow,' said Carrie Ann.

'What were you doing behind the door?'

'What were you doing just barging in here like that? You could have killed me.'

'This is my room,' said Axel. 'I am here to give the chess club.'

'Well, you should knock before you go racing through a door. You never know who is going to be on the other side of it.'

'Nobody, usually,' he told her. 'As I said, this is the

chess club.' A faint flicker of amusement lifted the right side of his mouth in a semblance of a smile. 'Are you here for the chess?'

Carrie Ann looked from Axel to the newspaper stand, where Morten was still pretending to flick through the *Sun*. In reality, he was watching the altercation at the door.

'Yes,' said Carrie Ann irritably. 'I'm here for the chess.'

'Unbelievable,' said Axel. 'You better come on in.'

Arse, thought Carrie Ann. Now she was doomed to spend an hour in a room with no windows, missing lunch to boot and possibly still having to run the gauntlet of Monstrous Morten when she came back out again.

'Not many people want to learn to play chess when they are on holiday,' Axel was saying. 'I only ever see people when it rains. Or when they're sunburned,' he added.

Carrie Ann adjusted the collar of her shirt to cover more of her bright red skin.

'English abroad, eh?' she said. 'We're just not used to the heat.'

'You 'ave to be careful of the sunstroke,' said Axel. 'It can make you crazy.'

Almost as crazy as realising that you hate your travelling companions just two days into a week-long holiday, Carrie Ann wondered. Would she be able to resist stabbing Rachel when she said 'there's someone for everyone' the five-hundredth time? Or keep herself from holding Yaslyn's head under the water in the swimming pool when she next poked her non-existent tum and complained of feeling fat? But Carrie Ann didn't burden Axel with that.

'You have played chess before, yes?' he asked.

'A long time ago,' she admitted. 'During the 1970s when all those twelve-year-old Russian grand masters were in the news, Dad had high hopes that one of us girls would become a chess superstar and save the family from bankruptcy. Unfortunately, he only knew how to play draughts. I don't know if I even know the rules. Well, I probably play chess like most people play draughts, if you know what I mean.'

'Let's just start and see how you get on,' Axel suggested. He sat down at the table next to the white pieces. 'Black or white?'

'White. I'm always white. Except when I'm a subtle shade of lobster,' she added feebly.

Axel didn't laugh. He spun the board around so that the white pieces were lined up in front of Carrie Ann.

'You start,' he said.

'Um. OK.' Carrie Ann looked at the board. All her pieces waited in their places along the bottom two lines of the board. The possible moves with which she could open the game were manifold, she knew that much. She also had a vague recollection of the traditional move to make at the start of a game. Was she right in thinking you could move a pawn two places forward to begin? She moved one of the pawns from the centre of the board two squares forward.

Axel didn't stop her but made that dismissive Gallic 'bof' noise. Eight moves later Carrie Ann found herself in checkmate.

'How did that happen?'

'You went wrong at the very beginning,' said Axel. 'Let's start again.'

Carrie Ann lined up her pieces once more.

'So how did you get to be a chess rep?' she ventured when they were ready.

'Club Aegee wanted to cater for their more intellectual guests too.'

'Oooh, does that mean I'm intellectual?' Carrie Ann joked as she moved a different pawn two places forward this time.

'You're going to fall into the same trap,' Axel observed, without answering Carrie Ann's question. 'Think ahead this time,' said her tutor. 'Concentration is what is required.'

He looked deep into her eyes as though he were trying to send her some of his own powers of the stuff. Carrie Ann looked back. Very nice eyes they were too.

22

The notion of 'getting away from it all' has been rendered nearly impossible by the advent of the mobile phone. The tranquillity of the poolside at Club Aegee was frequently rent asunder by the intrusive trill of a Motorola. The young Italians in particular seemed obsessed by text messages, to the extent of texting their companions three sunbeds away to find out who had the suntan lotion.

Carrie Ann had brought her mobile phone with her but resolved that she would leave it in her suitcase for the duration of the holiday, calling her office just twice a day to ensure that it hadn't burned down. Yaslyn was equally keen to spend a little time being incommunicado. But Rachel was unable to leave her bright red Nokia alone, constantly checking the phone's display to see whether or not she had a signal.

'Who's going to call you?' Yaslyn asked. 'The office can manage without you.'

'I don't want to miss it if Patrick calls,' was her answer.

'Patrick will be on his stag weekend in Dublin,' Yaslyn pointed out. 'The only call he might make is to the emergency services when his mates chain him up to a lamp-post.'

Rachel went pale at the thought.

'You don't think they'll do anything stupid, do you?'

'Of course they'll do something stupid. They're men.'

Yaslyn was right. Patrick didn't call. Nobody called. Until late that third afternoon by the pool. When she heard her Nokia start to play the first phrase of Dido's 'Thank you', Rachel snatched the handset up as though she had been waiting to hear the fate of a kidnap victim. Her face was momentarily a picture of expectation and optimism. Then it dropped quite abruptly. The caller was Helen. Patrick's mother.

'Thank goodness I've found you. I've been worried sick,' Helen began.

Rachel got up from her sunbed and wandered farther into the gardens to take what she knew from experience would be a long call.

'What are you worried about?' Rachel asked nervously.

'Patrick. His flight to Dublin took off from Stansted at four o'clock this evening. It should have taken less than an hour. It's a quarter past five now and he hasn't called to let me know he's landed. Has he called you?'

'No. He hasn't.'

'Then what on earth could have happened to him?' Helen cried in anguish.

'I expect he's still in the terminal, waiting for his luggage,' said Rachel. 'He'll call just as soon as he gets out. Anyway, I always say that no news is good news when it comes to travel. You would have heard something on the radio if there had been a crash.'

'Crash? Don't say that word!' Helen shrieked.

'Honestly, Rachel. Sometimes you just open your mouth without thinking.'

'I'm sorry,' said Rachel in a small voice. 'Anyway. How are you? Apart from worried about Patrick.'

'It's been a terrible week,' said Helen predictably. 'Both of you are off gadding around on holiday without a care in the world and I'm left here waiting for something to go wrong with the wedding.'

'There's nothing to go wrong, is there?' Rachel was surprised. 'I checked everything over before I left.'

'Yes, well. We'll see,' said Helen. 'At least my week hasn't been as bad as Mrs Patterson's from number fifty-four. I had her over to play cards yesterday evening. You know she's still waiting for that hip operation.'

Rachel tutted appropriately. 'Health service waiting lists.'

'She's terribly depressed about the whole thing. Could take eighteen months, they said. And this on the back of losing her husband last year.'

'Oh dear,' said Rachel.

'She says she's got nothing to look forward to. Her children hardly ever visit her. I told her she should cut them out of her will. They'd soon be visiting her then. But anyway, I mustn't keep you. I'm sure this call must be costing a fortune.'

'It probably is,' said Rachel, thinking of her own roaming charges.

'I just wanted to let you know that I've invited Mrs Patterson to the wedding reception. I knew you wouldn't mind. I told her, I have such a lovely daughter-in-law-to-be. Always keen to make other people happy. That OK, dear?'

'But I've already done the table plan,' Rachel started to protest. 'We've given the venue final numbers.'

'What's that, dear? I didn't hear you. Terrible line. Where are you standing? Next to a generator?'

'I can hear you perfectly,' said Rachel.

'So, it's OK for Mrs Patterson to come. Thank you, darling. She'll be so pleased.'

'It's OK.' Rachel sighed. It was only one extra guest after all. What difference would another old lady Rachel had never met before in her life make to a guest list that had already swelled from fifty to a hundred and fifty with Helen's various friends and acquaintances?

'Well, I'm going to get off the phone now. Patrick may well be trying to get through. You enjoy your little holiday, dear. Don't worry about the wedding arrangements. I'm managing very well on my own.'

'There's nothing for you to manage, Helen. I had everything set up exactly as I wanted it before I left. Just leave things exactly as they . . .'

'Hello?' Helen called into the other end of the line. 'Hello? I can't hear you. Rachel, are you there, dear?'

The line went dead. Rachel knew her future mother-in-law had hung up.

She dialled Patrick's mobile number at once. She was diverted straight to his answering service. He was probably talking to his mother. At least that meant he'd landed safely.

'Patrick,' she said in her message. 'Your mother has invited her next-door neighbour to our wedding. I tried to say something to her about the seating plans. But the line was pretty crackly. I suppose it doesn't really matter, does it, Patrick? Just a few extra quid on the budget. I hope you're having a good time in Dublin. Give me a call when you can.'

By the time Rachel had finished leaving a message, her phone was chirruping again to say she'd missed another call. She dialled her voicemail. It was Helen again.

'Rachel, dear. Patrick's safe. Thank goodness. And I forgot to tell you, Mrs Patterson will be bringing a gentleman friend.'

23

'Where have you been?' Yaslyn asked when Carrie Ann rejoined her at the pool that afternoon.

'Playing chess.'

Yaslyn screwed her face up.

'It was fun,' said Carrie Ann. 'I almost know what I'm doing now.'

'Who was teaching you?'

'The chap who picked us up from the airport.'

'Nice eyes,' said Yaslyn.

'Shame he never seems to smile. Do you feel any better?'

'I do. Must have been that stuff you gave me. I even felt well enough to have lunch.'

'That's a good thing.'

'In fact, I was ravenous.'

'Good.'

'Hey,' said Yaslyn when Carrie Ann sat down. 'I see you've been branded.'

'What?' Carrie Ann asked.

'The evil eye.' She pointed at the little bead dangling from Carrie Ann's breast.

'Oh, yeah. That bloke in the jewellery shop gave it to me. Doesn't look like much but it was absolutely gratis.'

'Well, you ought to take it off if you still fancy your chances with the dancing instructor.' Yaslyn smiled.

'Gilles told me when I had my tennis lesson this morning. When Yasser gives a girl the evil eye, the rest of the staff here steer clear. Nobody gets between Yasser and his wicked desires. You've been marked, Carrie Ann. Branded. You're one of Yasser's girls now.'

'Sod off!'

'It's true. But don't worry. You're among special company.'

Yaslyn jerked her head in the direction of the cryogenically preserved Frenchwoman who had been Rachel's adversary in the sunbed wars that morning.

'No.'

'Left tit,' said Yaslyn. 'The mark of Yasser. And over there.'

A similarly well-preserved – in the sense that her skin had the colour and texture of varnished wood – Italian woman was regarding her own evil-eye brooch with some affection.

'To think I thought I was special.' Carrie Ann unpinned her gift with disgust and tossed it into an ashtray with a shudder.

'Oh, but you are special,' Yaslyn assured her. 'Your Norwegian friend was looking for you earlier on.'

'He found me. That's how I ended up playing chess. Looks like I'm going to have to spend the rest of this holiday playing hide-and-seek with Mr Gorgeous. There are loads of fabulous men here and the only attention I'm getting is from the jeweller with the cold sore and the Norwegian who never takes his socks off.'

'Probably got a verruca.' Yaslyn winced.

'Please don't say that.'

'But I know how you feel about the men.'

Carrie Ann gave a disbelieving 'chuh' sound at that.

'Seriously,' Yaslyn continued. 'Men definitely don't look at me the way they used to.'

'What?' Carrie Ann exclaimed. 'Yaslyn, any man who wants a woman younger and thinner than you also wants locking up for paedophilia.'

As if on cue, the Swedish Lesbian Twins chose that moment to saunter out on to the sundeck and the thoughts of every man in the vicinity turned to joys of the barely legal kind.

'It wouldn't be so bad if they didn't hold hands the whole time,' Carrie Ann cried out in dismay when she spotted them. 'Isn't it bad enough that they look like every heterosexual man's fantasy without them having to imply that they might act like it as well? Do you think they're real lesbians?' she asked.

'Uh-uh.' Yaslyn shook her head. 'I feel pretty sure they would rather eat each other's sick than do any actual carpet-munching.'

'Ugh,' said Carrie Ann.

'I blame Cindy Crawford and k.d. lang,' Yaslyn continued. 'You never saw girls holding hands in public before that *Vanity Fair* cover. Not after the age of twelve, anyway. Now the Western world is crawling with them. Lipstick lesbians. I swear there are girls at my agency who pretend they're gay to get more jobs with hot photographers. Of course, that doesn't work with the gay male designers . . .'

On the far side of the pool, three young Italian men were gallantly offering to give up their sunbeds so that the Swedish Lesbian Twins could rest their weary young giraffe legs.

'And now for the erotic suntan lotion ritual,'

said Carrie Ann cynically. Just three days into the holiday, Carrie Ann was almost able to guess the time from the stage the Swedish girls had reached in their display. One of the girls squeezed oil into her palm and began to rub it on to the other girl's shoulders. 'Come on,' Carrie Ann groaned. 'Even I can reach my own shoulders. That's just gratuitous. It's an insult to the intelligence of those poor Italian boys.'

Insulted or not, the Italian lads were transfixed. As was just about every other man around the pool.

Except Marcus.

Marcus was watching a dragonfly flex its wings on Sally's scapula. She was asleep. He wondered whether she could feel it at all. The tiny creature must be so light and yet it looked so engineered, almost armour plated in its iridescent exoskeleton. The dragonfly's four wings folded and unfolded in perfect symmetry. Its delicately strong legs were slightly flexed, as though ready to take off again at any moment. But it had been there for almost two minutes now. Perhaps longer. Marcus wasn't sure.

Still sleeping, Sally reached her hand behind her back and scratched her waist lightly. The dragonfly moved up and down a little with the movement of her shoulder, but didn't take flight. Marcus reached out his own hand, slowly, silently, carefully. He wanted to pick the dragonfly up, as if by holding it in his hand he might be able to feel some of the heat of Sally's skin transferred to his skin by the creature's little feet.

He got within a centimetre before the dragonfly took off and he found himself touching Sally's bare back.

She felt it.

'What?' she asked. She rolled over, eyebrows creased down over her eyes against the bright sun.

'You had a . . .' Marcus stuttered. 'You had a dragonfly on your back. I was just scaring it away for you.'

'A dragonfly?' Sally clearly didn't believe him. 'They're freshwater insects, aren't they? They don't live near the sea.'

'That was what it looked like,' said Marcus. 'I suppose it might have come from inland.'

'Hmmm.' Sally rolled over on to her front again.

'Do you want me to put some suntan lotion on your back?' he chanced. 'You're going a little bit red.'

'It's OK,' said Sally. 'I was going to go back inside for a while anyway.'

She got up right away. 'Come and wake me up in time for supper, won't you?'

Supper was still four hours away.

Marcus watched her pick her way through the sun-beds towards their room. She didn't look back. Once upon a time she would always have looked back. There had been many occasions when, walking away from each other for some reason, they had both turned back to wave at exactly the same time. It was as though they were still connected.

'If she looks back before she walks down the steps, everything will be OK,' Marcus told himself.

Sally didn't look back.

24

The Swedish Lesbian Twins were putting Yaslyn off her holiday reading. Every time she glanced up from her book, one or both of them would be in the process of finding some pretext to show off her lithe, young body. Yaslyn had never before seen anyone make such a performance out of bending over to pick up a pair of dropped sunglasses or adjust the straps of a bikini as those girls. It was as though they were *acting* out every one of their moves.

She wasn't going to bring it up with Rachel or Carrie Ann again, though. If she ever voiced any concern about her appearance, Yaslyn would be treated to a lecture. 'You're so thin, so lovely, so young looking.' Or, more frequently of late from Carrie Ann, 'You've already bagged your man. Stop moaning.' As if that were the only thing that mattered. Bagging some poor sucker who wanted to marry you.

Yaslyn knew that Euan would marry her quicker than she could say 'register office'. Unfortunately, marrying Euan had never been part of the plan.

A model always had to have a plan. Yaslyn had never done anything but be a model, signing with her first agency before she even left school. But the career of a model isn't like going into accountancy. It's the difference between a snowdrop and a tree.

Yaslyn had a terrible feeling that her career had bloomed its last. The long-planned cross-over to television presenting clearly wasn't going to happen. The non-speaking role on *Friends and Family* was as good as it was going to get. Escorting contestants on to the set and handing out the gold envelope with the prize in it at the end of the show was the extent of her responsibilities there. She didn't have to say anything but 'hello', which was probably a good thing. Thinking back to the last screen test she had stuttered through could still make Yaslyn run hot and cold with shame.

No, Euan wasn't part of the plan. The plan had been to move from modelling to acting. From acting to genteel retirement. The plan had been to marry well in the traditional sense. To marry a man who would be able to look after her with his financial muscle as well as well-toned real ones. So many of her friends from her days as a model had done it; married rich older men they weren't quite in love with but who would keep them in the manner to which they wanted to be accustomed, buying the designer clothes when the freebies started to run out.

If she married Euan, what would their life be like? She couldn't live with him in his little basement flat, though she knew that pretty soon she would have to give up hers. The rent on her two-bedroom place in Chelsea was taking an increasingly large proportion of her income as the jobs got smaller and smaller and farther apart. In the last month she had been given a total of two days' work – posing for a company that sold travel accessories. Two days of grinning wildly while modelling purse-belts designed to baffle muggers. Looking with intense interest at adaptor plugs and currency converters. Purse-belts! Yaslyn wasn't even being asked to model clothes any more.

She recalled a conversation she had had with her booker just before she and the girls arranged their trip.

'You don't think I'll miss a job if I go away?' she'd asked Crispin.

Crispin cocked his head to one side. He couldn't quite disguise the pitying aspect of the look with a smile. 'Darling, you just go and have a great time. When you get back, perhaps we should go for a coffee and think about how we're going to get you out there again for the rest of the year. Tweak that look a bit.'

'Tweak that look'. Yaslyn knew only too well what that meant. Her friend and contemporary Nadia had just been for 'coffee' with Crispin and phoned Yaslyn later that same day in an unstoppable flood of tears. 'He says we need to start thinking about repositioning me in the market,' she sobbed. 'Not going for *Company* and *Elle* any more. He told me that he's got a great new contact at *Woman's Own*.'

A week later, Nadia went into the studio to have a new set of shots done for her model card. The sultry pout of Nadia's 1990 head shot was replaced by a sunny smile. The sexy-black-dress shot on the back was replaced by a picture of Nadia in a Fair Isle sweater and a pair of trousers that could properly be described as 'slacks'. Nadia had been 'mummy-fied'. It was all catalogue work from then on. And definitely no underwear shoots. Yaslyn couldn't bring herself to tell Rachel and Carrie Ann that the part she had won in a new television ad was actually the role of the mother.

Carrie Ann laughed whenever Yaslyn pointed out a new wrinkle. 'I looked like a pug before I grew into my looks and now I'm starting to look like one again. You don't need to worry, Yas. You're so beautiful, gorgeous, skinny . . .'

Yes, thought Yaslyn, that's how it looks to you. But to her model's critical eye it was obvious she was fading. The skin around her eyes was looking crêpey. Her lips were getting thinner. And the rest of her definitely wasn't.

Sitting by the pool, with the teenage Swedish Lesbian Twins reminding her how it had once been, Yaslyn pinched the skin on her stomach between thumb and forefinger and blew out her cheeks to signify how bloated she felt after a pretty meagre lunch of watercress and chopped tomatoes.

'For God's sake,' groaned Carrie Ann, catching sight of her. 'Will you stop making out like you're Mr Blobby. I fell asleep while I was doing a crossword yesterday afternoon and when I woke up I couldn't find the pen because it was lodged beneath one of my tits.'

Carrie Ann bounced her double E cups up and down to demonstrate. 'You, my girl,' she continued, 'need to eat a few more cakes.'

Yaslyn laughed dutifully. But when Carrie Ann had gone back to reading her book, she gave her stomach a sneaky prod again. She might not look 'fat' to anyone else but she was definitely bigger than she used to be. Much bigger. She couldn't see her pubic bone when she lay flat on her back and tried to look down past her stomach.

She frowned. At least this extra weight didn't seem

to be too wobbly. She was still quite firm. Must be the yoga she'd been doing. Ashtanga. Just like Gwyneth Paltrow. Talking of which . . .

'Going back to the room for a bit,' she told Carrie Ann. 'Want to get out of the sun and have a snooze.'

In the privacy of their bedroom, Yaslyn did 150 sit-ups with just a thin beach towel to protect her back from the hard, white-tiled floor beneath. When she got to 150, she decided to push herself, do a couple more. But the 152nd sit-up floored her. She felt an enormous tear of pain across her abdomen and collapsed back on to her meagre support, panting.

'Fuck.'

The first initial searing was followed by a tsunami of agony. For a moment, Yaslyn almost lost consciousness. Blackness flooded in from the corners of her eyes to obliterate her vision. She felt her body lurch downwards, though she was actually lying motionless on the floor.

Eventually she managed to get herself into a seated position, with her back against Carrie Ann's bed. That had been scary. Too much sun, she decided. Followed by too much exertion on a practically empty stomach. She hauled herself up on to her own bed and closed her eyes. She didn't wake up again until Rachel and Carrie Ann came in to shower before supper.

25

Thursday night was relatively sedate. Just four bottles of beer apiece at the beach bar, which left the girls in a sober enough state to remember to stake out their poolside territory before they went to bed.

Yaslyn weighted down her towel with a large rock from one of the flower beds.

'Let's see that get blown away by the wind,' she said.

'Perhaps we should just try to get up earlier,' Rachel suggested.

'No way,' said Yaslyn. 'We're on holiday. Besides, everybody's doing it.'

It was true. Many of the sunbeds were already staked out with brightly coloured towels and deflated Lilos.

But that didn't stop Yaslyn insisting that Rachel rush down to the poolside as soon as she woke up. Carrie Ann was still snoring on her back beneath the air con.

'I'd go myself but I just don't feel that well.'

Yaslyn leapt up and raced for the bathroom.

'You've got to sort that out,' said Rachel. 'Have you taken any of the tablets I gave you?'

'They don't seem to make any difference,' said Yaslyn. 'But I'll be OK. I'll just try to sleep a bit longer. You get down to the pool. Make the most of your tanning time.'

Rachel felt her heart begin to beat a little faster as she walked through the gardens towards the pool. It was a feeling reminiscent of that time in her fifth year at senior school when she and Yaslyn had got on the wrong side of some other girls and insults were exchanged. Joanna Roberts' parting shot had been that she would mash both Yaslyn and Rachel to a pulp the following morning. Yaslyn's retort was 'You and whose army?'. Rachel was left crying with fear when her mother refused to let her stay home the next day.

In the event, there was nothing to worry about. Joanna Roberts had managed to persuade her mother to let her stay home from school instead. So surprised had she been by Yaslyn's breezy response to her threat, she assumed that Yaslyn must know some martial arts move she didn't.

'It's all about projection,' Yaslyn told Rachel at the time (she'd been doing after-school drama classes). 'Human interaction is all about perception. If you don't want to be messed with, you have to act like you'll mess with someone back.'

Hmmm. Rachel nodded. But at the time, as now, she really wasn't convinced. Avoiding confrontation just seemed so much more sensible.

Rachel knew before she got to the pool that their towels would have been moved again. The people who planned Club Aegee Bodrum had done so in a time before sunburn and skin cancer became synonymous. There was only enough shade for three sunbeds by the pool bar and there were at least six women who wanted to sit in it. And sure enough, the same three women who had commandeered the shade the previous morning were there again, dozing like lionesses after the hunt.

Rachel didn't bother to ask the prehistoric Catherine Deneuve where the girls' towels had got to that morning. She could see them. Neatly folded and piled up on a sunbed to the right of the three French-women. To the right and right in the sun. Rachel gathered them up quickly, eager to slink away, like a female hyena who is too small and ineffectual alone to chance a nibble at the lionesses' kill.

'The pool attendant moved them,' Catherine Deneuve told Rachel with a smile. 'I saw him folding them as we arrived at the pool this morning.'

'Thank you,' said Rachel stiffly. That was definitely a lie.

'Perhaps you should just try getting up earlier in the mornings,' the woman suggested.

'Perhaps we should,' said Rachel. She turned to head back to the room with as much dignity as she could muster. As soon as she was out of sight she broke into a run.

'Your mobile phone has been ringing non-stop!' Yaslyn complained when Rachel got back. 'And what are you doing here anyway? Why aren't you out there saving our sunbeds?'

Rachel plonked the towels down on the dressing table.

'They were already taken. Apparently the pool attendant tidied our towels away for us. Perhaps we're not supposed to reserve sunbeds overnight.'

'Rubbish.' Yaslyn sat up. 'Who said that?'

'Well, no one said it but that Frenchwoman who was there yesterday morning . . .'

'You mean the same old cow pinched our sunbeds again?'

'She said we should get up earlier. And perhaps she's right.'

'She should put her towel out the night before like everybody else. I hope you said something to her. And I don't just mean "thank you"!'

'What's going on?' Carrie Ann had been awoken by the sound of Yaslyn's raised voice.

'Rachel let those bitches get our sunbeds again,' said Yaslyn.

'I didn't let them get our sunbeds. But what could I do?'

'I'd have dragged her off into the pool. What do they need the shade for anyway? They already look like a bunch of pickled walnuts. I'd have told her that for a start. I bet you just said "thank you" when she told you that the pool attendant had moved our towels. I bet that's exactly what you said.'

The sound of Dido's 'Thank You' suddenly emanated from Rachel's mobile phone. She snatched it up, grateful for the interruption to Yaslyn's rant, praying it would be Patrick, calling to wish her good morning and make the day seem worth starting again.

'Rachel.'

It was Helen.

'Where have you been? I've been trying to call you all morning.'

'I didn't take my phone with me to the pool. I'm sorry.'

'Never mind. Listen, darling, I bumped into Mrs

Patterson again yesterday afternoon. She's terribly pleased to be invited to the wedding. She's going to wear the hat she bought for Mrs Clarke's daughter's wedding last year before the car crash. Oh, that was terribly sad. Makes you realise how lucky you are, doesn't it?'

'Yes, Helen,' said Rachel as she waited for the punch line. Helen never just rang for a chat.

'Anyway, Mrs P. told me about her granddaughter Kylie. Terrible name, I know. But poor little Kylie has just had the chickenpox. Everybody's got it round here. I live in permanent fear of the shingles . . . Doctor said he had never seen anybody get the pox so bad as Kylie Patterson. Looked more like a toad than a little girl the first week. Well, she's awfully upset about the spots. Taking an age to fade they are, but she's only seven years old and she thinks she's stuck with them for ever. So I said to her grandmother, I know what will cheer little Kylie up . . .'

'She can come to the wedding,' said Rachel resignedly.

Helen didn't even pause for breath long enough to hear that generous offer. 'There's enough material left over from the bridesmaids' dresses to make a sash for a seven-year-old,' she continued. 'She can wear that around the white dress she wore to be her Auntie Christine's bridesmaid. It won't clash too much with your dress and, like I said to Mrs Patterson, it's always lovely to have a little bridesmaid as well as a couple of big ones. Not that Yaslyn is terribly big but . . .'

'What?' Rachel interrupted. 'Are you telling me that you've told Mrs Patterson that Kylie can be one of my bridesmaids?'

'Can't hear you,' mocked Patrick's mother. 'This really is a terrible line. Anyway, I hope you got all that. I'll speak to you again before you come home.'

She hung up.

'I take it from the deferential tone that was your future mother-in-law,' said Yaslyn.

'What did she want this time?' asked Carrie Ann. 'Checking we're not leading you astray?'

Rachel was too shocked to reply.

'Someone needs to get down to the pool,' muttered Yaslyn. 'Jesus, why do I feel so bloody awful?'

26

By the time the girls got back to the pool, there were just three sunbeds left. Once again, they were next to the only other British people in the village. Marcus gave them a big smile. Sally nodded and stayed behind her book.

'It's like Piccadilly Circus out here,' said Rachel.

'Believe me,' said Marcus, 'this is nothing like Piccadilly Circus. Are you having a good hen week?'

'Great,' said Rachel.

'It's a good idea to get away for a bit before the wedding, I think,' Marcus told her. 'The stress of organising everything can drive you round the bend.'

'Yes,' Rachel agreed.

'Except that Rachel has brought her stress and strain with her,' said Yaslyn, nodding towards the mobile phone Rachel still held in her hand.

'You know how it is,' said Rachel apologetically.

'Yep. And that's why I left my phone behind in England.' Marcus smiled. 'Well, I'm going to leave you lovely ladies to it. I've got a windsurfing lesson down at the beach.'

'Are they good boards?' asked Yaslyn.

'Wouldn't know if they're good or not. I've never done it before this week.'

'I used to do a bit of windsurfing,' said Yaslyn. 'Maybe I'll come down and have a look later on.

Should probably do that instead of tennis. Might keep me out of trouble.'

'So, you've met Gilles,' said Marcus knowingly.

'Oh yes. Hasn't every woman under the age of sixty-five?'

'Tells me Sally is his star pupil. Eh, Sal?'

Sally gave him a smile that was more of a grimace.

'See you later.' Marcus headed off for his lesson.

'How are you finding the tennis instruction?' Yaslyn asked Sally. 'Very hands-on, don't you think?'

'The tennis is very popular,' said Sally non-committally.

'So, what do you think of Club Aegee in general? Worth the money? What about the food? I've had food poisoning since I arrived.'

'I told her she shouldn't drink the water,' said Rachel.

'I didn't drink the water,' Yaslyn replied. 'I don't think the food hygiene standards are quite as high here as they should be. What about you? Sally, isn't it?'

Sally put down her book, inwardly cursing Marcus for making it impossible for her to carry on reading and ignore the hen party to her right.

'I just try to avoid anything that might have been washed in tap water.'

'Good idea,' said Rachel.

'Oh. You're reading *White Teeth*,' said Yaslyn, picking Sally's book up. 'What do you think? I couldn't get into it.'

'I've only just started myself.'

'Got to be better than this,' grumbled Carrie Ann.

'What are you reading?' Sally asked politely.

'*Southern Bluebell*. A story of coming of age in Carolina,' said Carrie Ann. 'Basically, it's all about a fourteen-year-old girl sleeping with most of her family members. And I don't mean because they were poor and didn't have enough bedrooms.'

'What's the plot?'

'I don't think there is one. It seems to be more an exercise in how many times you can mention anal sex in the course of one novel.'

'Sounds good. Not.' Yaslyn picked up the hardback that Rachel had momentarily set down in order to put on more suntan lotion. 'This looks more like my kind of thing.'

'You're not having it yet,' Rachel warned.

'Is that *the* book?' asked Carrie Ann.

'It is *the* book,' Rachel confirmed with a complicit glitter in her eye.

'Oh God,' Yaslyn exclaimed in mock horror. 'You've set her off again.'

'Sally,' said Carrie Ann. 'You have got to hear the story of this book. It'll make you cry.'

'Do you know the author?' Sally asked.

'Oh no,' said Rachel. 'It's better than that.'

'Let's not go mad on Christmas presents this year,' Patrick had said to Rachel one morning the previous December. 'We need to save for that deposit on our flat.'

Rachel agreed that it was a sensible idea. They were just throwing money away by renting. The rise in house prices didn't seem to be stopping for anyone, and three giddily happy years since they had first met at a Millennium Eve party, Patrick and Rachel were surely ready to make the commitment of buying a place. Together.

'What do you want, then?' Patrick asked her. 'Under twenty-five pounds, shall we say?'

Rachel chewed her lip for a moment. 'Anything,' she said.

'Be more specific,' said her boyfriend.

'A book?' she suggested at last.

'And you won't spend more than twenty-five on me?'

Rachel agreed. Though she had already bought Patrick's present. A week's wages on a gorgeous cashmere jumper. Nicole Farhi, it was. As soon as Rachel saw it in the shops at the end of August (during a heat wave), she imagined it adorning Patrick's big chest on Christmas morning. Only he wouldn't have anything to go with it, so she bought him a pair of dark brown moleskin trousers too. (The butterscotch jumper and trousers had been teamed together on the dummy in the shop window.) And then she knew that he wouldn't have the right shoes . . . He always wore black shoes and black shoes wouldn't go with the brown. Rachel bought a pair of brown loafers in Patrick Cox. In the end, she'd spent the best part of five hundred pounds.

But on Christmas morning Patrick proved as good as his word. He hadn't spent much on her Christmas present at all. Rachel tried to look pleased when she opened the solitary gift and found the glossy hardback novel she had been waiting to buy when it came out in paperback the following summer.

'You wanted that one, didn't you?' he said.

'Oh yeah,' said Rachel. 'That was really thoughtful of you, thanks.'

She handed him the first of his three big parcels. There was a stocking full of little things to go with them too. Things she had been buying on impulse and hiding away until Christmas all year. Cuff links. A pair of socks with Homer Simpson on them. A tiny Maglite torch that she thought might be useful if he ever broke down on the motorway at night . . .

Patrick opened the parcel containing his beautiful new sweater. 'You shouldn't have,' he told her. But he didn't seem unduly embarrassed by the discrepancy between the amount she had spent on him and the altogether smaller sum he'd spent on her.

Rachel tried not to let it bother her. They did need to save for a deposit on a flat. Patrick was being sensible. But a book? A hardback book? It was hardly very romantic. When he'd first suggested this 'not spending too much cash' thing, Rachel had thought that he might be making her a present instead. He was very good at woodwork. He'd made his mother a wonderful card table for her sixtieth birthday. He was always telling Rachel that one day he would make her a rocking chair.

'What did Patrick get you?' was the first thing Yaslyn asked when she called on New Year's Eve, just back from her Christmas in the Canaries.

'Er, this and that,' said Rachel evasively.

'Naughty undies? Are they so bad you'll have to take them back to the shop as soon as the sales start?'

'He bought me a copy of *Sushi for Beginners*,' said Rachel flatly.

'And . . .'

'That's it.'

'He bought you a book?'

'Yes. A book. A hardback one.'

'That's not much of a Christmas present, is it?'

Rachel defended him diligently. Explained that they were saving up.

'Oh my God,' said Yaslyn. 'I can't believe you want to buy a flat with such a tightwad. He'll make you reuse the tea bags.'

Rachel batted Yaslyn's comment away at the time but an hour later it was ringing in her ears again. Maybe Patrick was a tightwad. Maybe he was spending his spare cash on somebody else! By the time Patrick arrived at Rachel's flat that evening, she was simmering like a steamed pudding that had been left on the hotplate all day. She barely said a word on the drive to the pub where they would be celebrating the New Year with friends.

Rachel's anger grew like a little tumour as she listened to the other women in the group describe their wonderful Christmas presents. Amy was wearing a real cashmere cardigan. Right shape, right size and colour! Sarah flashed a tennis bracelet that must have cost her boyfriend half a month's wages. Lizzie confided that she was terrified of her Christmas present from Rob. A block of ten driving lessons. She'd already failed her test three times.

When Rachel told the girls that Patrick had bought her a book, they cooed over his thoughtfulness at getting the exact title she wanted. But Rachel was sure she could see pity in their eyes. A hardback book. Was that really it? Her boyfriend was a tightwad. Yaslyn was absolutely right.

By ten to midnight, the old year wasn't the only thing on the verge of ending. Patrick had finally noticed that Rachel wasn't actually speaking to him. He tackled her. Asked what the problem was.

'All you bought me for Christmas was a sodding book!' she said. 'One sodding hardback book. I spent a bloody fortune on you. I feel like an idiot,' she added.

'But you agreed we'd only spend twenty-five pounds on each other,' said Patrick.

'I didn't think you meant it.'

'We're saving for a deposit.'

'Sarah and Ian are saving for a deposit too and he bought her a diamond bracelet!'

'I can't believe you're comparing us to Sarah and Ian.'

'I can't believe I'm going out with such a tightwad.'

Rachel spat the words out with such violence that Patrick looked as though she had hit him across the face.

'Then you won't be wanting this,' he said.

He put the little velvet box on the table between them and stalked out of the pub.

For a second, Rachel was confused. Then she was horrified. She snatched up the little box and opened it hurriedly. Inside was a ring set with a diamond as big as a peanut.

'Oh my God . . . Patrick . . .'

She leapt up to follow him outside into the snow. The wind had picked up and the flakes that fell now were as big as first-class stamps. Every car was covered with an inch-thick layer as though an ermine cloak had been spread across the car park by a benevolent giant. Patrick's footprints headed in the direction of his car then stopped quite abruptly. The smart Ford Puma was still there but Patrick was nowhere to be seen.

'Pat!' Rachel called. 'Patrick!' She was reluctant to step away from the shelter of the pub doorway. 'Pat! I'm sorry! Of course I want this! And of course I want to marry you!'

'What makes you think I was asking?'

Patrick stepped out of the shadows to the left of the porch. Rachel hiccuped with shock.

'Weren't you?' she asked.

'I was going to ask the Rachel who would have been happy to get a book for Christmas. But I don't know where she's gone to.'

'Oh, Pat. I'm sorry. You know I'm sorry for everything I said just then. It's just that when you said you weren't going to spend very much on me this Christmas, I didn't think you meant it . . .'

'Well, the ring is only cubic zirconia,' he joked. 'Have you tried it on?' he asked more seriously.

'I rushed straight out here after you,' she said.

'Good. Give me the box.'

She handed it back to him. He tucked it straight into his pocket.

'What are you doing?' she asked, terrified that whatever he was going to offer her might have been withdrawn because of her stupid, childish outburst.

'Ssssssh,' he said. 'I want to do this how I was going to do it before you had a strop.'

Inside the pub, the master of ceremonies was instructing everybody to charge their glasses to toast the birth of the New Year. Outside in the porch, Patrick cleared his throat. He sank to one knee, ligaments popping in protest as he did so. Inside, the television was switched to BBC1, volume cranked up loud so that everyone could listen to Big Ben.

'Dong.' The first big chime.

'Rachel Louise Buckley . . .'

'Dong.'

'Will you do me the honour . . .'

'Dong.'

'Of consenting . . .'

'Dong.'

'To become . . .'

'Dong.'

'My wife?'

'Dong.'

Rachel waited six more dongs before she said yes.

Everyone in the pub was in on the secret. Yaslyn too had known that Patrick was going to propose and that no amount of name-calling on Rachel's part would have stopped him. But the feeling that she had come close to losing Patrick with her outburst stayed with Rachel for quite a while after that night. Even repeating the story by a poolside in the heat of a Turkish summer day, Rachel felt a chill as she remembered the hurt on Patrick's face when she accused him of being a tightwad at top volume in a pub full of their friends. She never wanted to see him look like that again. She never wanted to hurt him.

It was a wonderful thing to have met someone she felt so very strongly for, but at the same time to have such strength of feeling for Patrick was sometimes terrifying. In preparation for the wedding, they had to attend several sessions with the vicar of the church they hoped to be married in. At the first of these sessions, the vicar read through the marriage service and asked the engaged couples, who had not thought much beyond having a pretty backdrop for their wedding photos, to meditate on each part of the vows they were about to take.

'Till death us do part' was the one that got to Rachel. She found herself crying when they got to that bit. Right there in front of the vicar and three other couples she had never met before that Saturday afternoon, Rachel opened her mouth and wailed. Until that moment her life with Patrick had seemed like a bud about to burst open into a single beautiful, perfect bloom. Now she could see a winter ahead for them. A time when, no matter how hard they loved each other, one of them would be left alone.

Her eyes misted again by the pool that sunny morning.

'That's a really nice story,' said Sally, relieved it was over.

'Yeah. What are you crying for, you soft thing?' Carrie Ann asked.

'Because . . . you know . . . it's just . . .' She turned to Sally. 'You know what it's like when you love someone so much you could just die . . .'

27

The slightly sombre mood brought on by Rachel's recollections was destroyed, absolutely promptly, when the 11.30 lunacy hour began. That morning the game involved the somewhat blasphemous 'search for a new messiah'. Gilles and Delphine strung a rope across the pool, to which were attached several children's swimming floats. The idea was that the lucky competitors should try to walk on water, racing across the pool using the floats as stepping stones.

'We need some volunteers,' Gilles shouted. Sally shrank down behind her book. 'Come on.' He started to stalk around the poolside. 'Paulette? I know you will come and join my team.'

Paulette was only too delighted.

'Here he comes,' said Rachel. Rachel, Carrie Ann and Yaslyn joined Sally in hiding behind their books like school kids trying to avoid a teacher.

'Yaslyn! No hiding behind that book,' Gilles cried. 'Come and join me.' He started to tug her leg. 'Bring your friends.'

Rachel and Carrie Ann looked horrified. Sally put down her own book and got up as quietly as she could. While Gilles tried to pull Yaslyn off her sunbed, Sally slipped silently away from the fray.

'Sally!'

Too late. He'd spotted her.

She prepared her excuses. But she didn't need to use them.

'I'll see you for your tennis class this afternoon?' He sounded almost shy.

She nodded and carried on.

Sally was glad that the 11.30 games had given her the opportunity to get away from the other British girls. Bloody hell. It was as though that Rachel woman had been sent by God to drive her crazy with her proposal story and the subsequent tears about loving her man too much. As if Sally wasn't already feeling guilty that she didn't appear to love her husband enough to lay down in the same bed as him any more, let alone lay down her life.

'If you want to stay married you've got to have an affair' was the advice her best friend Victoria gave. 'It's the only way to keep a marriage going in my opinion.' She poured herself another gin and tonic in the immaculate fitted kitchen of her Surrey farmhouse (no farm animals to go with it, of course).

It seemed wrong to be having that conversation. Not just wrong from a moral standpoint either, but because they were only thirty. In fact, Victoria was just twenty-nine. More than half the women Sally knew were still scrabbling about in the clubs and bars of London trying to find a man who would marry them, not contemplating tearing a marriage apart already. Having an affair seemed like the territory of a much older woman. A woman who wanted to prove to herself that, despite her husband's lack of interest, she was still a fabulous, sexual being worth lusting after. It was as though Sally and Victoria had skipped a few pages in a script and were suddenly acting out a scene that shouldn't have followed on so quickly from the excitement of a wedding.

The day after Victoria first suggested a little bit of extra-curricular activity for her friend, Sally found herself shaking hands with the opportunity. Her department had just been assigned to offer consultancy services to the Ministry of Defence. The sites Sally had to visit for this project would take her away from home for days at a stretch, and for the first time Sally didn't argue for working out of the London office so that she could spend every evening at home.

Sally's counterpart at the MOD, the man she would have to liaise with, was called Squadron Leader Timothy Webster. She had an idea what he would be like. A fifty-something man with a paunch and an old-fashioned moustache. She certainly hadn't envisaged the man who stood before her on the morning the project began. He was maybe five years older than her. Definitely no paunch. He looked as though he lived at the gym when he wasn't charming young management consultants into a swoon. Sally's assistant Kerry decided instantly that she wasn't so bothered about having to work away from home after all.

Unfortunately for Kerry, her role was to keep her in the office, making Power Point presentations out of the scrappy notes Sally e-mailed back after each meeting. Sally was the one who got to spend an evening in Preston with the dashing squadron leader later that week. A day touring local MOD sites was followed by dinner at the hotel where they were staying. When they finished talking about work, Squadron Leader Webster – 'call me Tim' – answered

Sally's polite questions about his background. He told her about the time he had spent in the Gulf and the Balkans. Sally was quietly impressed by the matter-of-fact manner in which he regaled stories that lesser men might have elaborated to make themselves seem more heroic and perhaps lower Sally's resistance to later advances.

Tim didn't do that. Instead, he told Sally how hard it had been on his wife and kids that he spent such a lot of time away. They were glad that he was office-bound now. Even if he did resent the fact that the only time he got to jump out of a helicopter these days was when raising funds for cancer research. Sally asked how long he had been married. Five years, he said. Five years and a month exactly. And he showed her a picture of the woman he had promised to love and honour until death.

Sally made the requisite murmurings of approval about the passably pretty woman and slid the picture back across the table towards him. Her own passport photo of Marcus remained firmly tucked inside her wallet behind a clutch of receipts and a supermarket reward card. She hadn't looked at it in months. Had forgotten it was there. Not that he looked much like the man in the picture these days anyway.

After dinner, Sally went up to her hotel room and tried to watch television. Nothing caught her interest so she attempted instead to make sense of that day's notes to the background noise of MTV. Too distracted to pay them the proper attention they required, she sank back into the over-plump hotel pillows and watched a couple of music videos. A soft-metal band sang about a tragic love affair over sepia-toned footage of a long-haired girl frolicking on the beach in what were presumably meant to be happier times for the angst-ridden singer.

Sally's mobile phone buzzed on the bedside table. She flipped the phone's case open and saw her own home number on the display. Marcus calling to wish her goodnight, no doubt. She flipped the phone closed again without answering his call. She turned the television off. Thought about going to sleep.

Less than half an hour after retiring to her room for the evening, Sally found herself back downstairs in the hotel bar. Just as her vodka tonic appeared, Squadron Leader Webster arrived to join her.

'Couldn't sleep,' he said.

'Me neither,' said Sally.

He ordered a vodka tonic for himself and they moved from the bar to a table in a quiet corner of the room. Not that the barman cared. You don't have to work in a hotel for long before you realise that the couples looking deeply into each other's eyes are less likely to be newly-weds than married to other people entirely.

Sally felt her heart banging in her chest. The conversation, which had been so easy earlier that evening, was suddenly stilted and awkward. Was he wondering whether she had come downstairs again to find him? Had he come back to the bar to find her? They talked for a bit about different brands of vodka. Sally knew several he'd never even heard of thanks to Victoria's hen weekend in New York. They'd made an almost scientific study of the stuff in Manhattan's better bars.

'As long as it gets me drunk,' said Tim.

'But doesn't get you into trouble,' Sally replied without thinking.

He looked at her questioningly. She blushed, not sure where that last comment had come from. Then, in a moment so charged it could have powered the whole of London, they simultaneously reached for the single beer mat on the table between them. Both looking for something to occupy nervous hands, only to find each other's fingers.

They withdrew their hands at once, like a couple of anemones pulling in their tentacles. Tim coughed a 'sorry' that was lost to Sally as she coughed her own 'sorry' back. They both knew that this was the moment around which everything pivoted. They could bid each other goodnight and go to bed separately or . . .

Sally chewed her bottom lip as she studied the man across the table from her. There was no doubt that she was attracted to him. The heat remaining in her cheeks after the blush over the beer mat was testament to that. And he was obviously attracted to her. Why else the peculiar reaction to her 'getting into trouble' comment?

'We could . . .' he began.

Go upstairs? Sally finished the sentence in her head but said nothing out loud. They could. It didn't have to be complicated. They were both married. They both had the same amount to lose if word got out. She could trust him to keep it a secret because he would definitely want it kept that way too.

Tim's hand snaked back on to the table. He took the beer mat and started flipping it between his fingers as though he were performing a card trick. It was a certain signal. He was touching the one item on the table they had both grabbed for because what he really wanted to do was touch her. She wanted him to touch her.

'Mrs Merchant?'

The barman interrupted them.

'Mrs Merchant?'

Sally didn't look up at once. It was as though the name didn't belong to her that night.

'Mrs Merchant?' The barman leaned over the bar so that his voice carried farther.

Sally turned to him with a slightly startled air.

'Yes?'

'Telephone call for you.'

'Oh. Right. Thanks.'

He held the receiver towards her.

Marcus was worried. He said he'd called her mobile several times and got no answer. After that he called the hotel and got no answer from her room. By the time Sally got Marcus off the phone, Tim had finished his drink. She considered just for a second asking him whether he wanted another. But the flame that had flickered between them was all smoke again now.

'Early start,' said Tim. 'Think I'll turn in now.'

'Good idea,' said Sally.

She excused herself to the ladies' room so that they didn't even travel upstairs in the same elevator. And next day, it was business as usual.

Victoria's response had been that Sally should have pushed it. Should have gone for it on their second night at the hotel, instead of ordering dinner on room service and eating it alone with *Coronation Street* for company. But Sally adopted the air of a penitent. She told herself that she wouldn't drink on business trips any more. When she got back home, she made a conscious effort to be nicer to her husband. She greeted him with a hug, cooked his favourite meal (though he was actually a far better cook than she was).

'What's the matter with you?' Marcus asked, when she told him that he could choose the video at Blockbuster that night. 'Got a guilty conscience?'

She laughed it off.

But it was already too late. Even without kissing Tim Webster, Sally had taken a step towards unfaithfulness. She had mentally prepared herself to sleep with someone else. As though she had taken a filter from in front of a lens, she had started to look at people differently. The men she encountered became potential lovers once more. She wondered whether she had started to look different too. Men certainly seemed to be acting differently towards her.

Like Gilles. But then she shouldn't think anything of the way Gilles acted, should she? He was just playing a game.

Sally stepped into the bathroom and studied her reflection in the mirror. She'd got some colour over the past couple of days. She was lucky enough to have the kind of olive-toned skin that browned easily without going red first. She wasn't a typical English rose. In fact, several people had addressed her in French or Italian that week, assuming that she must be one or the other.

She combed her hair back from her face and attempted a smile at the woman in the mirror. She was only thirty. That wasn't old. Jesus, she knew women of her age who still collected 'Hello Kitty' stationery. She'd heard somewhere that a woman who divorces by thirty is more likely to marry again than a single woman aged thirty is to get married for the first time. In any case, why should that be holding Sally back? She didn't need a man to support her. She was bringing most of the income into the home. Marcus would be the one who found himself worse off. Unless he found some woman-hating lawyer to take Sally for the difference.

The door to the room opened. Sally stopped her easy divorce fantasy abruptly.

'Nice windsurfing lesson?' she asked Marcus. She knew that she was over-compensating by trying to take an interest.

'Rough out there today. Xavier says there will probably be a storm tonight or tomorrow.'

'Really?'

'Yeah. If it's going to be shitty weather tomorrow, might be the perfect day to get on a bus and go to Ephesus. There's a coach leaves from the car park at half past nine.'

'What's at Ephesus?' Sally asked.

'Ruins and stuff.'

She pulled a face.

'You don't have to come.'

'No. I'll come if you want. I mean, I want to.'

'Good,' said Marcus, stepping past her to shower off the salt water. 'That'd be nice.'

28

Sally wasn't the only one who found an excuse to get away from the poolside when the 11.30 shenanigans started. She may have stumbled upon Axel's chess class only by accident, but Carrie Ann was surprised by how much she enjoyed herself in the hour they were together. It turned out that many of the rules she had been playing did belong to draughts and not to chess at all. When Axel explained how the game really worked, however, it all seemed much more interesting.

Besides, there was only so much time Carrie Ann could spend by the pool, reading books about anal sex in South Carolina and providing dutiful responses when Rachel asked whether the groom's aunt should sit on the same table as her ex-husband, or Yaslyn bemoaned her fading beauty compared to the Swedish Lesbian Twins. Carrie Ann didn't want to spend an hour falling off a windsurf or putting her back out trying to shoot arrows at a target. It suddenly seemed like a very good idea to spend the hottest part of the day stretching her brain instead. And a little part of her looked forward to a winter's evening back in London, playing chess in front of a roaring fire with an as yet unspecified intellectual hunk.

'You're back.' Axel looked surprised. Carrie Ann caught him sitting with his feet on the table, flicking through a book.

'Sorry,' she said. 'I'm interrupting your reading.'

Axel shrugged. 'It's OK. I have read this book too many times. And I am supposed to be here to give chess lessons.'

Carrie Ann looked at the book cover. '*Fleurs du Mal*,' she pronounced badly. 'Flowers of evil? Is that right? What is it?'

'Poetry. Love poetry,' said Axel. 'By Charles Baudelaire.'

'Is that your kind of thing?' Carrie Ann asked.

'It was.' Something clouded Axel's expression. 'I was just looking for a quote to put in a letter back to France. To my . . . friend.' He stumbled on the word.

Carrie Ann picked the book up. Axel immediately relieved her of it. The first embarrassing draft of letter eighteen to Natalie was tucked inside the cover.

'Did you study literature?' Carrie Ann asked.

'No. I was a medical student.'

'Really?'

'You look surprised. Does that stop me from enjoying poetry?'

'No. It's just . . .Well, I didn't expect to meet a rep who had studied medicine. Or even been to college at all. I didn't think they had to. Why aren't you working as a doctor?'

'I haven't yet qualified,' said Axel.

'Oh. You're taking a sabbatical.'

Axel nodded curtly. Sabbatical. That was a laugh. He wondered whether a single university in France would take him after he had broken down in the principal's office and then threatened the poor man with a letter-opening knife when he asked Axel to leave his university.

'Perhaps you're not cut out for medicine after all,' the principal had said. 'You need to be harder, Mr Radanne. There is no place for a romantic poet in the accident and emergency department.'

'So,' Axel closed the subject that morning in the chess room. 'Do you think you can remember what I told you yesterday?'

'I think so. I can move the knight like this, right?' Carrie Ann made one of her little ivory horsemen leap over a pawn.

'You can. Shall we start? You can move first.'

'That's my move,' said Carrie Ann, leaving her knight in its new position. 'You'll have to excuse me if I don't get things right straight away. I know I'm not terribly clever.'

'Just take your time.' Axel moved a pawn.

Carrie Ann reached for a pawn of her own, moved it two spaces forward then hesitated. 'Oh, hang on. I don't think I meant to do that.'

'Take your time.'

'I'm not cut out for this intellectual stuff.' She put the pawn back in its starting position and made the same move with a pawn farther along the board. Axel nodded. Carrie Ann relaxed. 'So, why have you taken a sabbatical?' she asked casually. 'Too much like hard work being a student, eh?'

'Something like that,' said Axel.

'The students near where I live seem to spend all their time in Starbucks. But I'm in awe of you lot really,' she told him. 'Students. I'm totally in awe of anyone who goes to university. I know it isn't all sitting around drinking coffee.'

Axel made his move in silence.

'You must get frustrated by some of the other reps,' Carrie Ann ventured. 'I mean, they're not exactly the brainiest bunch of people. Nice personalities, I'm sure. But who do you have to talk to when you want to talk poetry? Not that I can talk. I couldn't possibly talk poetry with someone like you. They have a very thorough education system in France, don't they? Don't you have to take seven subjects in your last year at school? I suppose that's why you're a poetry lover and a scientist.'

'You can't do that move,' Axel interrupted. 'Bishops always have to travel in diagonal lines.'

'I'm sorry. I wasn't concentrating.'

'I noticed,' said Axel dryly.

Carrie Ann clammed up. She had been rambling. Probably saying the exact same things that every person who sat across the chessboard from Axel said. But then he broke the silence.

'Are you enjoying your holiday here in Bodrum, Carrie Ann?'

'Oh yes,' she answered instantly, wondering why the question felt like a reprieve. 'I really needed to get away.'

'Working too hard?'

'That and my divorce.'

'Divorce?'

It had just slipped out. And after she had promised herself that she wouldn't mention it. Not talking about it seemed to be the best way to forget it had ever happened.

'I thought that you were celebrating a marriage.'

'Well, Rachel's getting married in three weeks. I am very much divorced. He ran off with my best friend.' She gave a little laugh when she said it, as though it had happened to someone else entirely and could thus be considered one of those funny things.

'That is not good.'

'I should have known.' Carrie Ann sighed. 'She fell in love with him at the exact same time I did but at the time he fancied me and not her. She never said anything. Never gave me an inkling that she fancied my husband. I think I just wish she had said something because we might all still be friends. We used to have a great time. Going out all three of us together . . .'

Three of us together . . . Axel's mind was suddenly hijacked by a memory of a lost afternoon in a café with Ed and Natalie. How happy he had been. The woman he loved on one side. On his other side a man, an intellectual, who considered Axel to be his equal and friend. At least, that was how it seemed at the time. That afternoon, Axel had almost had a physical sensation of blossoming. Ed actually asked Axel's opinion on things. No one had ever wanted Axel's view before. Natalie had beamed with pride when Axel made a particularly good point about the 2000 American presidential election.

Now, looking back, Axel could see that Natalie's smiles had not been for him at all. The blossoming he felt that day had been brought to an abrupt end, as when a late-blooming rose is spoiled by an early frost. For that one afternoon in the café by the Sorbonne, Axel had truly felt that he might one day become a man people should justifiably feel in awe of. A medical student, near the top of his class, with a beautiful girl-friend and a fantastic new friend. Where was he now? Chess rep at Club Aegee, Bodrum. Entertaining women of a certain age who didn't know their chess from their draughts.

Lost in his painful reverie, Axel was utterly unconscious of the change of expression that had come over his face. His mouth turned down at the corners as though he had caught the scent of something bad.

Carrie Ann, who had been elaborating a little on the circumstances of her divorce, looked up and, seeing Axel's grimace, assumed quite automatically that his expression was a reflection on her conversation.

'I'm sorry,' she said. 'You didn't need to know.'

Face to face across a table in the half-light, it was so easy to let your lips move and say everything you'd been so careful to keep inside. It must happen all the time, thought Carrie Ann. Especially at Club Aegee Bodrum. So much for the club's reputation as a singles paradise. Perhaps once upon a time Club Aegee had been the place to go to meet an eligible man. Now it was like a car maintenance class, full of women hoping to meet lots of men. Carrie Ann had watched them drifting about for three days. The single women of a certain age. Older than her, for the most part. But she recognised their look of disappointment. Knew that the only men they really talked to these days were their hairdressers. Axel must have heard every hard love story in the village.

Axel flipped back from his memories to the present.

'You can't do that with your queen,' he said.

It was too late. Carrie Ann felt too uncomfortable to play on.

'I'm sorry. I think I'm going to give up for today,' she said.

'Really?' Axel looked surprisingly surprised.

'Yeah. I think my brain's gone soft from the heat.'

A knock at the door interrupted them in any case.

'Come in.'

It was Morten.

'Carrie Ann! You are playing the chess as well. Perhaps we can play together?'

'You could do,' said Axel. 'You're about the same level. I'll referee.'

Morten looked thrilled by the idea. 'Yeah. We play chess. Battle of the minds.' He mimed a little bit of boxing action to illustrate the 'battle'. 'Loser has to buy the winner a drink.'

'I'd love to,' said Carrie Ann. 'But I think I feel another attack of diarrhoea coming on.'

She pushed past Morten in her haste to be away from the room. Axel's pity and Morten's attentions made her feel desperate. This was the reality of her predicament as a divorcee. Pitied by the attractive men and hopelessly pursued by the ones that only a mother could love.

'I have medicine!' Morten called after her. 'I'll bring it to your room!'

'Yeah, sure,' she called back. Thank God he didn't know where her room was.

29

So much for a week of bacchanalian pleasures that would make the ancient Romans blush. That evening found Yaslyn, Rachel and Carrie Ann sitting on the balcony of their room, comparing strap marks, belly ache and insect bites.

Yaslyn was unusually grumpy.

'You should take some more Imodium,' Rachel suggested.

'I haven't got diarrhoea,' Yaslyn told her for the fifth time since Rachel had come back from the pool to find her groaning on her bed again. 'I just feel strange all over. Tired. Achy.'

'My mum always used to give us a cup of tea and a couple of Trebor mints when we got ill,' said Carrie Ann. 'It worked on the dog as well.'

'This is a disaster,' said Yaslyn. 'We're meant to be celebrating Rachel's last week as a spinster and your return to the world of the single girl. We could sit around and moan like this in Clapham.'

'I'm having a great time,' Rachel lied.

'Rubbish. You spend half the day looking at your watch, trying to work out what time it is in Dublin and whether Patrick's friends will have accidentally drowned him in the Liffey by now.'

'What time is it in Dublin?' Carrie Ann asked.

'Five in the afternoon,' said Rachel. 'I wonder if I should give him a call. They won't be at the pub now, surely.'

'Don't call him!' Yaslyn insisted. 'You're on your hen night.'

'Let her call him if she wants. Have you phoned Euan yet?' Carrie Ann asked.

'No, I haven't.'

'Won't he be worried about you?'

'Why should he be? He'll have checked the flights on the Net. Like he always does. And now he'll be in Dublin as well.'

'I don't know why you have to sound so disdainful. I wish someone cared enough about me to check that my plane had landed. You don't know how . . .'

'Lucky you are?' Yaslyn chimed in.

'Well, yes,' said Carrie Ann. 'He's kind, thoughtful, gorgeous . . .'

Yaslyn picked up the vibrator that had caused Rachel such trouble at customs and pointed it at Carrie Ann as though it were a gun. Since their arrival in Bodrum the black plastic penis had been given pride of place in the middle of their patio table like a totem between 'going out' rituals. Heaven knows what the cleaners thought went on.

Rachel sighed. 'I can't believe you brought that thing out here.'

Thought it might come in useful for Carrie Ann. As long as she doesn't keep me awake at night with the buzzing . . .'

'Will I ever get the opportunity to keep anyone awake all night again?' Carrie Ann wondered aloud.

'If you want to. You've had loads of attention this

holiday. Yasser. The Norwegian guy. Yasser . . .' Rachel tailed off.

'Here. You can take this back to London if you want.' Yaslyn passed Carrie Ann the vibrator.

'Have you ever owned one of these for real?' Carrie Ann asked as she twisted the vibrator's base to start it up.

'You mean you haven't?' said Yaslyn.

'I wouldn't have the guts to go and buy one,' Rachel replied. 'Where did you get it from?'

'Where do you think? Marks and Spencer's.'

'Wasn't it horrible having to go into a sex shop with all those dirty-mac-wearing old perverts?'

Carrie Ann placed the vibrator on its end on the wall that encircled the balcony. It vibrated itself along the top of the wall in a whirligig fashion as though it were a child's toy or something to amuse the cat with. The girls watched its unsteady progress dispassionately.

'I wonder who thought these things up,' said Carrie Ann.

'They were invented as a cure for hysteria,' Yaslyn told her. 'Doctors used to bring female patients to orgasm to cure them of their neuroses. Took too long to do it by hand. Vibrators were the original labour-saving device.'

'Oh God. That's just awful,' breathed Rachel.

'Imagine getting orgasms on the National Health . . .'

'Imagine getting orgasms.' Carrie Ann sighed.

The thought was interrupted by the sound of a mobile phone trilling inside the room. It was Rachel's.

'It's not going to be him,' Yaslyn mocked as Rachel rushed to catch the call. 'Patrick is probably tied to a lamp-post in Temple Bar right now. Euan and the others will have covered him in Guinness and persuaded some of the local girls to lick him clean.'

'Don't tease her like that,' said Carrie Ann. 'You know she's worried sick he won't come home in one piece as it is.'

'Hey, Patrick!' Yaslyn shouted so that the caller would be able to hear. 'Let Rachel get off the phone so she can come and take the handcuffs off the gigolo.'

Rachel appeared very briefly in the doorway to the balcony. Her expression made it clear that she wasn't talking to Patrick. She put a finger to her lips to make double sure Yaslyn knew to shut up.

'Yes, Helen,' said Rachel. 'I've already booked cars to take us all from the church to the reception. No, I don't think a horse and carriage would be a better idea. Especially not a shire horse.'

Carrie Ann groaned at the thought. Rachel mouthed 'Sorry' and disappeared into the room to continue her conversation.

'You wait for it,' said Yaslyn. 'Rachel will be arriving at that wedding behind Shergar.'

'She doesn't want a horse and carriage,' said Carrie Ann. 'She's terrified of horses.'

'But Old Ma Hewson wants a horse and carriage and if that's what Patrick's mother wants that's what Rachel will get. Particularly if she won't stand up for herself.'

'Give her a break. It's a difficult thing to do. Arrange a wedding. Doubtless you and Euan will just jet off to Las Vegas and tie the knot in some Elvis theme place. Or are you just bitter because he hasn't asked you?' Carrie Ann pried.

'I think I'll go inside and get a cardigan,' said

Yaslyn, without answering. 'It's getting a bit nippy out here.'

'OK,' said Carrie Ann, as she was left alone on the balcony with only the electric penis for company.

What a depressing little thing it was. All hard and shiny and not at all like the real thing . . . Not so likely to tear your heart in two either, though. Ever ready as long as the batteries were. No one ever lost their vibrator to their best friend.

Perhaps Carrie Ann would have to get one when she got home . . .

She picked the vibrator up again and held it against the tip of her nose. Somewhere in the back of her mind she had a feeling she'd once read that was the best way to test them. Wasn't doing much for her, except making her eyes water. Carrie Ann turned it up to top speed and placed it back on the wall again, where it jittered along even faster than before. The noise was horrific. There was no way you could use one of these in a semi-detached house. You would have to pretend it was the washing machine on spin cycle. Carrie Ann shuddered as she realised she was already preparing excuses for when her neighbours popped round to complain. Was this really the future of her sex life?

Before she could answer that question for herself, the little black bullet of pleasure buzzed itself off the wall and into oblivion.

'Fuck!'

Carrie Ann jumped up to see where it had landed.

Morten looked back up at her. It had landed in his lap.

If he hadn't known where her room was before, he most definitely did know now.

30

'Go back downstairs and ask for it!' said Yaslyn, when Carrie Ann came hurtling into the room to describe the horrific accident that had just taken place.

'It's not a bloody tennis ball,' Carrie Ann reminded her.

'No,' said Rachel. 'It's a vibrator. *My* vibrator. My special hen week vibrator and I want it back!'

'No you don't,' said Carrie Ann in a low voice.

'I do,' said Rachel. There was a wicked look in her eyes. She needed some light relief after her conversation with Helen about horses.

'I'm not going,' Carrie Ann said firmly. 'I am not going downstairs to ask the Norwegian nerd if I can have that vibrator back. He's a freak. He looked up at me through those bloody binoculars. I'm going to pretend the whole incident never happened and, if he's a gentleman, he'll react in exactly the same way.'

'You'll have to do a forfeit,' Yaslyn warned her. 'That vibrator, that sacred vibrator, was like the Olympic torch of this holiday, and you've let it fall into the hands of a man.'

'You must reclaim the sacred vibrator by sacrificing yourself in its stead,' Rachel suggested.

'Fuck off,' said Carrie Ann succinctly.

*

As it happened, no terrible forfeit Yaslyn and Rachel could have thought up could have been quite so humiliating as the events that were to unfold the next morning. After four days of glorious, unbroken sunshine, the girls awoke to an overcast sky. With the cloudy weather for once negating the need to race down to the swimming pool to bag those all-important sunbeds in the shade, the girls were enjoying a late and leisurely breakfast. The restaurant was busy. Yasser the jewellery shop owner was cruising around the holidaymakers, bestowing kisses upon those women sporting the mark of the evil eye (and a few who didn't as well). Carrie Ann was standing in the queue for eggs. Each morning, two chefs stood at a huge range, preparing eggs exactly how the holidaymakers liked them. Carrie Ann thought a boiled egg might be just the thing she needed.

Still slightly sleepy, she didn't notice Yasser approaching from the left. Or Morten, making a bee-line straight through the breakfast crowds towards her. They arrived at either side of Carrie Ann at exactly the same time, as though they had planned the horrifying pincer movement beforehand in a military briefing. Carrie Ann was like a gazelle at the watering hole which doesn't know anything about the two crocs just under the surface until it is too late. The choreography continued as Yasser planted a smacker on her lips (never mind about his cold sore) and Morten simultaneously placed the sacred vibrator of doom in Carrie Ann's free hand.

'You are forgetting your belongings this morning,' said Morten. 'Your vibrator,' he added helpfully, in case there was anyone in the queue who wasn't sure what it was.

'Hey, hey!' said Yasser, snatching the thing from Carrie Ann's hand. 'What is this for?'

As if he didn't know either.

'It isn't mine,' Carrie Ann protested, as she tried to snatch it back.

'I can give you something more realistic than that,' Yasser assured her. He turned the thing on and danced towards her with it, as though he were fencing.

'And I can be doing the same too,' said Morten.

Blush wasn't the word for it. The feeling in Carrie Ann's cheeks right then was something more akin to the blistering, cracking heat that peels paint from woodwork in a house fire. 'This isn't mine,' she continued to protest feebly as she regained possession of the vibrator and looked for somewhere to hide the damn thing. She didn't have any pockets in her bikini and sarong ensemble. Her beach bag was being used as a place marker at the table the girls had chosen to sit at. She turned beseechingly to Rachel, who merely shrugged as she remembered her own humiliation at Gatwick. Yaslyn was laughing so hard she was on the point of suffocating.

By now, Carrie Ann had reached the front of the queue for eggs. She was still flanked by Yasser and Morten.

'Why are you needing this?' asked Yasser. 'There are so many good men around Club Aegee.'

'That is what I am thinking,' Morten replied.

Unable to think of anything to say that didn't sound like the over-the-top protestation of someone who is thoroughly guilty, Carrie Ann decided that her best strategy at this point was to ignore the men beside her and the crowd gathering behind her, grab her breakfast with as much dignity as she could muster, and leave.

'Good morning,' said the chef, with one eye on Carrie Ann's unusual accessory as he took her plate (he had those eyes that go in slightly different directions, as seems to be compulsory for at least one teacher in every school). 'How would you like your eggs?' he asked.

'Fertilised!' shouted Yaslyn from farther down the line.

Carrie Ann knew she should have been able to find more of her sense of humour in the face of the vibrator debacle, but try as she might, she couldn't bring herself to see the funny side that morning.

She knew that Yaslyn and Rachel loved her and would never intentionally hurt her, but the constant ribbing she'd been subject to since their arrival in Turkey was beginning to grate. It was all very well for them to try to force her into the arms of any passing thing with a penis. They were both happily attached to wonderful men. It was safe for them to flirt. For Carrie Ann, every flirtation carried so much more meaning. Every little knock-back hurt so much more because it seemed to take her that much closer to the final rejection that would condemn her to a miserable old age on her own.

She'd been very brave about her divorce, her friends told her. That was only because she let them think that, always careful not to break down in company. The reward was that everyone thought she was a trooper. She was still invited to dinner parties and on holidays like this one because nobody thought she would be a miserable drag talking of nothing but her last failed relationship.

Carrie Ann had seen it happen to other women. For the first few weeks after a break-up, the girlfriends would rally round with support. But it was never long before people decided that you really should be 'over it' and simply dropped you from their 'friends and family' calling circle if they suspected you might want to whinge about the Bastard Ex long after you should have dusted yourself off and started throwing yourself into the search for a new one.

Though sometimes Carrie Ann wondered whether being dropped from the social whirl wouldn't be preferable to the alternative. Her new single status gave her access to a nightmare world she had hitherto only read about in the problem pages of women's magazines. As 'spare woman' she had been pair-matched to a dizzying succession of unsuitable men.

'You'll like this one' was always the promise, as Carrie Ann hopefully dolled herself up for another dinner party only to find that she had been seated next to the world's most boring man. There had been Neil, who drove a Porsche but was still living with his parents at thirty-four. Then Jasper, who referred to girls as 'fillies' and suggested that they were finished as 'breeders' after the age of twenty-nine. Then Peter, the whizz-kid IT consultant who may well have had a flat in London's Docklands and an apartment in San Francisco, but made Morten look like a master of social niceties. 'Your teeth are very yellow,' he told Carrie Ann as he sat next to her at dinner, then later had the gall to look surprised when she declined the offer of a date.

They were the kind of stories that made Yaslyn and Rachel roar with laughter, but Carrie Ann was tired of her love life as a stand-up comedy routine. That morning she had surpassed herself. More than a hundred assorted Europeans had a wonderful holiday anecdote to take back to their workmates. Carrie Ann had another reason to want to throw herself into the Aegean and hope for a strong rip-tide.

She resolved to spend the rest of that morning in exile on the balcony. Staying way back from the edge, of course. There was just one more necessary trip into the outside world to make before she pulled up the drawbridge. She had almost run out of reading material. She'd seen a copy of *Hello!* in the resort gift shop the previous day. A morning spent poring over the tasteless wedding photos of the rich and famous would be just the thing to convince her that she wasn't quite so sad after all. If she was really lucky, there might be a 'stars and their cellulite' supplement too.

Carrie Ann braved the stares and sniggers on her way to the gift shop. Assuming it was all about the vibrator, she wouldn't realise until much later that her sarong was tucked into the back of her bikini knickers. She found the solitary copy of *Hello!* and handed over three billion or so Turkish lira in exchange. Before leaving the shop she scanned the terrain for possible hazards. Yasser was busy making a phone call. He hadn't spotted her. There was no sign of Morten. Carrie Ann prepared to make a dash back to the room.

She was halfway between the shop and the next available cover when Morten jogged into view.

'Carrie Ann!' he called.

Carrie Ann dived for the first available door.

It was Axel's chess room. She startled him in the act of picking his nose but was far too flustered to notice his embarrassment.

'You are back for more?' Axel asked when he had regained his composure. He hadn't really expected to see Carrie Ann again after the previous day's strange exit.

'I suppose I am,' said Carrie Ann, sitting opposite him at the chessboard. 'Don't think anything of it. Shall we begin?'

She hopped one of her knights towards the centre of the board.

31

Sally pulled back the thin brown curtains and looked across the valley outside the window to the hills beyond. She shivered instinctively when she looked at the sky. The clouds that had gathered over the mountains behind the club were so dark they seemed almost too heavy to stay aloft.

She looked back into the room. Marcus was already up and about somewhere. His bed was empty and no sound came from the bathroom to suggest he might be in there. Sally felt a guilty sense of relief as she padded across to the bathroom herself, stripping off her nightshirt as she went. It was much too bloody hot to wear a nightshirt, especially since the only one Sally had was a big thick Wee Willie Winkie affair with a picture of Mickey Mouse on the back. Marcus's mother had given it to Sally as a Christmas gift when they were first going out.

'To make sure we don't have sex before marriage,' Sally had joked then. The joke wasn't quite so funny now that she really was wearing the nightshirt for exactly that purpose. To send clear, unequivocal signals to her husband that she wasn't in the mood.

In fact, Sally couldn't really remember the last time she'd had sex with her husband. Before Christmas perhaps, when they were both drunk from office parties. It wasn't that Sally had lost her sex drive altogether. If only that were the case. No, her libido was still hanging around like a ghost, brushing past from time to time to remind her of the difference between the way she felt about Marcus now and the way it used to be.

She was lazily combing conditioner through her hair when Marcus burst into the bedroom.

'Sally?' He banged on the bathroom door. 'Are you ready? The coach is about to leave.'

'What coach?' she asked.

'The coach for Ephesus. Come on. I thought you'd be done by now. You said you were going to get up and get dressed while I went to get the packed lunches.'

'I don't remember saying anything,' Sally lied. Now that she thought about it she had a vague recollection of muttering the words to Marcus, then rolling over and going straight back to sleep when he left to order a packed lunch for their trip from the kitchen.

'Come on.'

'Christ. Give me a bloody minute.'

Sally rinsed the conditioner straight back out again. She jumped out of the shower and grabbed a towel. She hadn't rinsed the conditioner out properly. A drip ran down her forehead and straight into her eye, stinging like crazy.

'Ow!' she complained.

'What have you done?' Marcus asked.

'I got conditioner in my eye.'

He opened the bathroom door to find her trying to rinse her eyes clean with fresh water.

'Are you OK?'

'No. It bloody hurts like fuck. I can't see anything.'

She sat down on the toilet seat and screwed her eyes tight shut to lessen the pain.

'The coach is about to go.'

'I can't get on the coach now,' said Sally. 'I can't bloody see anything, can I?'

'But we're booked on the coach to Ephesus . . .'

'You go. Don't wait for me. You'll have a good time.'

She waved him away.

'Sally, I . . .'

'I'm not going to be ready in time. I can't see a thing and I don't know what I'm going to wear and I've got to put my suntan lotion on. I won't be ready. Go without me.'

'But I wanted to go with you.'

'Please don't make me feel guilty,' she pleaded. 'Go without me. I'll go some other time.'

'Fine. OK.'

Marcus closed the bathroom door on her. She heard the main door to their room open and close behind him as he headed back out for the car park.

'Oh God.'

A wave of guilt overwhelmed her. She opened her eyes and sighed, waited sixty seconds, then threw on a sundress and ran after him.

Sally hadn't made them late for the coach trip to Ephesus deliberately. In fact, she told Marcus, according to her watch, they weren't late at all. But the car park was empty. The coach had gone. The girl on reception shrugged when Marcus asked whether there would be another opportunity to get to the ancient ruins.

'Not this week,' she said. 'The trip only goes on a Saturday.'

'Fine,' said Marcus. He turned to Sally. 'We've missed our chance.'

'Guess we should go and get some breakfast, then,' Sally suggested.

Marcus nodded. 'You go and save a table. I'll be with you in a minute.'

Sally headed for the restaurant with a guilty lightness in her step. The ruins at Ephesus had been there for many hundreds of years. They'd be around for a few more. Marcus would get his chance to see them. Perhaps with someone else in reluctant tow.

She draped her cardigan across the back of a chair to mark a table as saved. It was late. There wasn't much left on the breakfast buffet. She was just helping herself to the last slice of pineapple when Marcus reappeared. He was smiling.

'I've sorted it out,' he said.

'What?'

'We can go to Ephesus after all.'

'How?'

'I've hired a car. We'll probably beat the coach party to it if we get started quickly.'

'Marcus . . .'

'I know. I'm blowing the budget. But it's only fifty quid or so, and what's the point of coming all the way to Turkey if the only thing we get to see is the bloody swimming pool at Club Aegee?'

'You don't want to drive on these roads,' Sally tried. 'They're ridiculous.'

'Nothing can be worse than the roads in India. Besides, we'll probably be safer than we would be on the coach with no seat belts and a driver who has a bit too much raki at lunch-time. Anyway' – Marcus now delivered the killer blow – 'I won't be the only designated driver. There was another woman at reception who missed the coach as well. I said she could come with us. And then your friend was walking by and he said that he wouldn't mind taking a trip out to Ephesus too.'

'My friend?'

'Yeah. Gilles. The tennis bloke. It's his day off. Can you believe he's spent every summer in Turkey for the past three years and he's never been any farther afield than Bodrum? Having too much fun here, I suppose. I told them we'd meet them both by reception in fifteen minutes. That long enough for you?'

'Oh, yeah. Great.' Sally didn't feel much like eating any more.

32

It seemed that the miserable weather had inspired just about everybody who would ordinarily have spent the day by the pool to chance a trip outside the village. Most were heading into Bodrum, the nearest big town. For the convenience of its guests, Club Aegee had arranged for local buses to stop right outside the village. When Yaslyn and Rachel saw a luxury, air-conditioned coach gliding smoothly up the hill towards the stop, they were pleasantly impressed. Less so when the beautiful coach continued straight past, already full of tourists from the even swankier resort a little farther down the coast.

The bus that eventually pulled up at the Club Aegee stop was altogether different. It was tiny. A truly mini minibus.

'Looks like we'll be waiting for the next one,' said Rachel, as the rest of the guests who had been at the stop abandoned the queue and went for the Continental European system of piling on in a random fashion with no regard for anyone who may have been waiting longer.

But no. Like a Tardis, the bus had far more capacity than Rachel and Yaslyn imagined. They filed on and took the last two seats. When all the seats were full, two local guys who worked shifts in the Club Aegee kitchen climbed aboard and sat on a plank of wood that had been made into a bench down the aisle.

'They've got to be kidding,' said Yaslyn, when she saw the men perch on the board. 'That's never safe.'

'Perhaps they're only going down the road,' said Rachel.

The minibus did indeed stop at the bottom of the hill. But not to let the two local lads off. At this bus stop, two old men wearing black berets at jaunty angles were waiting for a lift into Bodrum too. They climbed on board. One sat on the end of the makeshift bench. The other sat on an upturned bucket he had been carrying.

'I dread to think what would happen if we crashed,' said Rachel. 'That must be full capacity.'

No. It wasn't. The bus began to slow ominously as they approached a crossroads where a man and woman waited with their small child. The driver shouted something out of his window to them.

'We're full, I hope,' ventured Yaslyn.

And it did seem that they were going to drive past. Then, suddenly, as though a cow had run out into the road ahead of him, the driver pulled the bus to a dramatic handbrake stop on the dangerously wet road. Yaslyn and Rachel just about managed to remain in their seats. The man on the bucket wasn't quite so lucky. But he didn't complain. When he had managed to lever himself upright again, he simply made room for the next people to board.

'This is ridiculous,' muttered Yaslyn as the man who had been waiting at the stop sat on the armrest between the driver and the front passenger's seat, facing the back of the bus. His wife sat upon his knee. Then the little boy clambered on to her lap, using

Yaslyn's knee as a convenient step to help him get up there. Once seated, the little prince gave her a gap-toothed grin. His face was as round as a watermelon. Moon faced, that was what he was. His mother kissed him on the top of the head.

Yaslyn was rendered silent with disbelief. The cramped conditions on the bus were bad enough, but the sticky little handprint on the knee of her trousers had turned this retail therapy trip into the shopping equivalent of ECT.

The Turkish passengers on the bus laughed at the little boy as he turned to his mother and lisped something into her ear that was meant to be discreet but clearly wasn't. Rachel turned to Yaslyn. Yaslyn attempted a smile in return. But she wasn't quite sure what was funny. It wasn't simply that it was lost in translation. Yaslyn didn't see why everything someone said was cause for hilarity just because he was a small human being.

The little boy turned back to face her and gave another smile. Yaslyn stared at the gap where the little boy's front teeth had been. She stared at his chubby hands on his knees. The chubby hands that had touched *her* knees as he made himself comfortable. He'd used Yaslyn's knee as though she were part of the furniture, Yaslyn remembered in outrage. This boy was utterly without the invisible barriers of an adult. Adults were simply there to help him make his way through the world.

'What a sweet little boy,' said someone travelling behind her.

Yaslyn couldn't help thinking about the horrible wasp that lays its eggs inside caterpillars so that the larvae have to eat their way out of the unfortunate creature when they hatch.

Everyone kept telling Yaslyn that she would make a fantastic mother. She was great fun, everyone said. Creative, exciting. She would raise a truly free-spirited and individual child. If not five of them. But they didn't see that Yaslyn's happy-go-lucky nature was based on the fact that she had no responsibilities; no one to worry about but herself. How much fun would she be with no sleep at night, no money to spend on shoes, no waistline?

Yaslyn decided she had become *anti*-broody. While her girlfriends had started to coo over the tiny jump-suits in the children's department of Harvey Nichols, Yaslyn had considered writing a letter to the management, telling them that by situating their chi-chi baby-wear so near to the seductive lingerie they were putting her off sex. She seemed to lack the hormone that made her able to see the beauty in the angry, red-faced little maggots that passed for newborn human beings.

However, like cats and dogs that seem to make a beeline for the one person that is scared of them, children seemed to home in on Yaslyn Stimpson. She rubbed the place where the little boy's clammy hand had been moments before. He'd left behind some sort of sticky mess. She wanted to reach into her handbag and bring out one of her cleansing wipes. Bloody hell, if she couldn't put up with a sticky handprint on her knee then she wasn't ready for poo and sick and vomit all over her designer wardrobe. No thanks.

Now the little boy was singing a song. His parents were delighted. One of the old guys at the back of the bus started clapping along and pretty soon everyone was clapping, even Rachel. Yaslyn put her hands together too. As you're supposed to when a child brings everyone together. It was just like being in an audience with Stalin.

The song seemed to last for ever. It was tuneless. Every time Yaslyn thought it was about to end there was another verse. The kid was still singing as the driver swung the bus sharply round a corner and into the car park in the centre of Bodrum. Only the spectacle of the old man falling off his bucket again made the little boy quit singing and chortle.

'Cute kid,' said Rachel, as they climbed off the bus.

'Mmmm.' Yaslyn nodded vaguely. 'Which way do we want to go?'

They had reached the edge of the car park, where a dozen or so assorted tourists were wondering exactly the same thing. The rain earlier that day had turned the road ahead of them into a series of fast-flowing rivulets. Bad drainage, Yaslyn noted. As they hesitated on the kerb, trying to work out where the harbour might be, a couple of lads on a scooter took the corner just a little too close and splattered dull brown water all over the girls' legs.

'Arse!' shouted Rachel.

'Arseholes!' Yaslyn elaborated. She flicked a finger in the direction of the retreating bike. 'For fuck's sake.' She stepped back and bent down to wipe the water from her shins. 'It's probably full of parasites that are going to give me the squits and make me feel worse than I already do. And they've ruined my trousers. Not that they weren't ruined before by that kid and his stupid filthy hands.'

Her white cropped trousers were spotted with brown.

'It'll wash out,' said Rachel.

'No, it won't. Fucking Turks.'

Rachel was more than a little taken aback. 'They were probably just holidaymakers like us,' she said reasonably.

'Well, they've ruined my trousers.'

Yaslyn was examining the marks.

'They'll wash. What are they made of?'

'They won't bloody wash,' Yaslyn snapped. 'They've got to be fucking dry cleaned, and by the time we get back to the UK it will be too late. The stains will have set for good.'

She jerked upright again. Her teeth were clenched together so hard that the sinews down the side of her neck stood out like bone.

'Yaslyn, are you OK?' Rachel ventured.

'I'm fine.'

'Are you sure?'

'I'm fine,' Yaslyn barked. 'Let's find some bloody shops.'

The lights changed. The traffic almost stopped. Yaslyn stormed across the road. In completely the wrong direction.

Oh dear. It soon transpired that the waterlogging of the car park was a relatively minor civic disaster by Bodrum standards. When the girls got as far as the harbour, they discovered that an overloaded sewer had also flooded and covered what might otherwise have been a charming marketplace with a thin layer of liquid shit.

It was not the kind of terrain you really wanted to be crossing in your canvas espadrilles.

Rachel hadn't seen Yaslyn in such a bad mood for a long time. It was quite spectacular when Yaslyn decided to get angry. She had the kind of face that could eclipse the sun on a good day. On a bad day, she could also stop traffic. And turn all the drivers who looked at her to stone.

'There's supposed to be a great bazaar around here somewhere,' Rachel said hopefully. 'Loads of good jewellery shops.'

'I doubt it,' said Yaslyn.

'We could go and see the castle, if you like. The castle has been here since the Crusades, I think.'

'Rachel, you've known me for fifteen years. During that time, have I ever expressed an interest in bloody castles?'

'I'm just trying to make the best of a bad day,' said Rachel tightly.

'Are you sure we can't get a bus back to the resort for another hour?'

'Well, we could get a cab. I won't be going on a Turkish bus again unless I have to. That little kid we saw this morning was cute, though.'

'Will you stop going on about that little boy?'

'What?'

'Stop going on about him.'

'I wasn't.'

'You were. *Isn't he cute?*' Yaslyn mimicked. 'He wasn't cute, Rachel. He had a head like a squashed grapefruit. And he was showing off. He was a complete pain in the arse.'

'Yaslyn. How can you be so nasty? He was only

small. They don't know they're showing off at that age. He was trying to entertain us. My nephews, Jake and Harry . . .'

'Please don't start with the Jake and Harry anecdotes,' Yaslyn interrupted. 'They don't make me think "how cute". They make me want to send a United Nations peacekeeping force round to liberate your sister from their vile oppression.'

'She doesn't feel oppressed,' Rachel protested.

'How do you know?'

'She just doesn't. She's never complained. Well, she's complained about being tired and losing her waistline from time to time. But she never wishes she hadn't had the twins.'

Yaslyn snorted.

'I don't know why you pretend you hate children so much, Yas. You'll feel differently when you have some of your own.'

'That old chestnut.'

'It's true.'

'How do you know? You haven't had any of your own yet.'

'But I want to . . .'

'Yeah. Well, I don't.'

'Not now. But think about how sad it would be to get old and not have any family around you. No one ever dropping in to visit. No grandchildren.'

'Who's to say that your grandchildren would visit you anyway? Look at Patrick's sister and his mother. They can't stand each other. What if you ended up like that with one of your kids? Why put yourself through it? You lose your figure, your freedom . . .' Yaslyn counted off the losses on her fingers. 'You lose your mind through lack of sleep. And all in the hope of ending up with a couple of grandchildren who'll only visit you when they want some money.'

Rachel was visibly pained by Yaslyn's cynicism.

'You'll change your mind about children when you see Jake and Harry at my wedding. They're worth it. They look so sweet in their little knickerbocker outfits . . .'

'Stop!' Yaslyn raised both her hands in disgust. 'Did you just say knickerbocker outfits?'

'Yes. I told you. Helen made them.'

'It's bad enough that you're having pageboys. But knickerbockers? What next, Rachel? Are you actually trying for the most tasteless wedding of the year award?'

'What do you mean?'

'Pink roses. A string quartet at the reception. Sugared almonds for place settings.'

'They're not tasteless.'

'You couldn't get much more boring.'

'Yaslyn. What is wrong with you today?'

'Oh, come on. What is wrong with *you*? Are you going to promise to love, honour, obey and start dressing from the Boden catalogue? The transformation obviously began at the engagement. You're turning into Patrick's mother. You're having the most boring wedding on earth to mark the start of the most boring life.'

'I don't know what's wrong with you. I don't want to hear any more of this.'

Rachel turned and started to walk away. Within two steps she had broken into a jog and was crying. Yaslyn remained in the middle of the square, filthy brown water sloshing around her feet. A honey-mooning British couple who'd caught the tail-end of the argument stared aghast.

'You better go after her,' said the woman. 'Unless you really are that much of a bitch.'

Yaslyn snarled back. 'Oh, mind your own fucking business.'

But she did go after Rachel. She had to run to catch her up. When she caught hold of Rachel's sleeve at last, Rachel shrugged her off with some violence.

'I don't want to speak to you,' she said. 'Why have you suddenly got so nasty?'

'I'm sorry,' Yaslyn blurted out. 'I wasn't thinking. I'm sorry, I'm sorry, I'm sorry.'

Rachel stopped running. Her face was already blotchy from crying.

'I'm sorry,' Yaslyn said again.

'Why did you say all that stuff about my having a boring wedding?' Rachel asked plaintively.

'I don't know,' Yaslyn told her. 'You know it isn't even what I really think. You're going to have a lovely wedding, Rachel. I think pageboys are really sweet. I only said what I did because I'm having a bad day. I'm having a bad week. I don't know what's wrong with me. I've been feeling really strange since we got here.'
Slowly, Rachel's face softened.

'I was having a really bad time before I came away,' Yaslyn continued. 'Work has been really quiet and I've been wondering what I should do about that.'

'You got that new ad,' Rachel pointed out.

'Playing the mother,' Yaslyn admitted to her.

'Isn't that good?'

'No, it isn't. My days as a model are over.'

She sniffed and wiped her hand across her cheek.

'Oh God, here come the waterworks,' said Rachel. 'I'm the one who should be upset. You just insulted my choice of flowers.'

'I'm sorry. I'm really sorry. I've upset you and I didn't want to and I feel so awful and I don't know what's wrong with me.' Yaslyn clutched her stomach. 'Christ, when this week is over I am never eating Turkish food again.'

'It's not the food. Carrie Ann and I have both been fine since we stopped drinking the water. You've got to use bottled water to clean your teeth,' Rachel told her matter-of-factly. 'Otherwise you'll end up with Turkey tummy every time.'

'I know,' said Yaslyn. 'I'm sorry. I'm sorry I was such a bitch.'

'It's OK,' said Rachel. She threw her arm around Yaslyn's shaking shoulders. The tear taps were definitely on full now. 'I vote we go over there for a mint tea to settle your stomach.' She pointed to a smart little coffee shop on the far side of the square. 'Then,' she added with a tiny drop of sarcasm, 'you can tell me exactly how the fashionable people are going to be married this year.'

'You're the best, Rach,' said Yaslyn. 'Sometimes I don't know why you're my friend.'

'It is a mystery,' Rachel admitted.

33

Rachel and Yaslyn hadn't always been best friends. They hadn't been friends at all. Not for a long time after they first met in Mrs Griffiths' reception class at the Church of England primary school they both attended. Yaslyn was a star from the very beginning. She arrived at school with the stage-school confidence of a little girl who had been singing into a hairbrush since she uttered her first words and embraced her new schoolmates as a new captive audience.

Rachel, by contrast, hated school from that very first morning. She clung to her mother's legs as they waited at the school gates for the attendance bell to ring, and then cowered at the back of the classroom, terrified that she was going to wet herself but too scared to ask to go to the bathroom, until it was home-time again. In the six years that followed that first horrible day, she very rarely felt any better.

Yaslyn Stimpson was not one of the girls Rachel hoped would go on to the secondary school she had chosen. The feeling was absolutely mutual. When they were put into the same first-year class at Ribston Road High School for Girls, Yaslyn affected not to know her former stable-mate from St Edward's primary. She quickly became the most popular girl in this new class too. People would fight to sit next to her. She had to introduce a sort of rota. Tanya for English, Debbie for

History, and so on . . . Rachel always chose to sit at least ten desks away from Ribston Road's answer to Winona Ryder's 'Heathers'.

Which was why Rachel was somewhat shocked when her mother announced one evening that Yaslyn would be staying with them for the weekend. Mrs Buckley worked in the same office as Yaslyn's mum down at the City Council buildings. Despite their daughters' open dislike of one another, Cherry Stimpson and Megan Buckley were great friends, but Rachel didn't think that her mum would ever try to force a bond between her and Yaslyn. Never.

Yaslyn's parents were 'having difficulties,' said Mrs Buckley. They wanted to go away for the weekend to talk things through and didn't want to have to take Yaslyn with them.

'Can't she stay with her grandma or something?' Rachel asked.

'She hasn't got a grandma. She's staying with us,' said Mrs Buckley firmly. 'And you're not to go round school telling everybody why. You've got to be a good friend to her now. She needs you.'

The news that she would be staying with Rachel over the weekend didn't seem to have made a difference to Yaslyn that week. She still didn't speak to Rachel until they found themselves side by side at the dinner table that Friday night. The first thing Yaslyn said to Rachel after ten years of ignoring her at school was, 'Pass the ketchup, please.'

Rachel was furious that Yaslyn could even make her feel uncomfortable in her own home now too. She slammed the tomato sauce bottle down next to Yaslyn. Yaslyn picked the bottle up and began to shake it with equally violent malevolence, only to discover that Rachel hadn't screwed the lid back on properly when she had finished with the sauce herself.

Rachel was covered from head to waist when the lid flew away from the bottle. Her new top, bought just that day at River Island because she wanted to look as cool as possible when the interloper arrived, was saturated with thick red goo. It would never recover, she was sure of it. Not even the fact that ketchup was reputed to tone down the brassiness of highlights gone wrong (of which Rachel had a headful) was any consolation. She closed her eyes. A drop of sauce fell from her nose on to the tablecloth.

The stunned silence that had fallen immediately after the accident was now broken by a single snort. Rachel's father couldn't help himself. And Mrs Buckley, catching sight of her husband's gently jiggling shoulders, was soon biting her bottom lip too. Yaslyn and Rachel just stared at each other. Rachel thought she was about to cry. If Yaslyn laughed then she would have to hit her. The tension was unbearable. Then Mr Buckley let out a gigantic 'Ha!', and in doing so gave his wife the permission she needed to laugh so hard she almost choked.

'It isn't funny!' Rachel protested. And for the first time ever, Yaslyn was on her side. They remained stony-faced comrades, defending their teenage seriousness about matters such as having to sit at the dinner table with your worst enemy and remain completely cool even though both you and the dog have been covered in goo. (The dog at least didn't mind licking himself clean.)

'It isn't funny!' Rachel shrieked again.

She slammed her fists down on the Formica table, making her plate jump and sending all her peas rolling off the edge (the dog thought it was his lucky day). Then she got to her feet and flew from the kitchen. Yaslyn, to Mr and Mrs Buckley's amazement, followed their daughter and found her at the bottom of the stairs.

'I'm really sorry, Rach.'

Yaslyn proffered a balled-up tissue that had been living up her sleeve.

'They never take me seriously,' sobbed Rachel.

'You think *your* parents don't take you seriously. At least yours don't send you to stay with your worst enemy while they try to kiss and make up. I didn't want to come here, you know.'

'I didn't want you to come here either,' Rachel confirmed.

'I could have stayed at home on my own. I can look after myself.'

'Yeah.' Rachel sniffed as she started to dab at the splodges on her new shirt. 'We're fourteen, goddam it. We're not children any more.'

'I don't even know why they're bothering,' Yaslyn said. 'I don't know why they just don't get on with getting a divorce.'

'Don't you want your parents to stay together?' Rachel asked.

'I don't care any more.'

But it was clear that she did. Yaslyn looked away quickly, but not quickly enough to hide the tear that glittered in the corner of her eye. Rachel had never seen Yaslyn Stimpson cry. Not even when the hardest girl in the fifth form dragged her across the school car park by her ponytail after Yaslyn 'looked at her funny' one lunch-time. That incident had resulted in a reputation for hardness that had gone unchallenged for years. But now Yaslyn was crying. And in front of Rachel 'Buck-teeth' Buckley, who had no vested interest in keeping Yaslyn's vulnerability a secret after all those years of frostiness and disdain.

'I'm really sorry about your top, Rach. I'll give you one of mine,' Yaslyn snorted into another grotty piece of tissue.

'I should have put the lid on the bottle properly in the first place,' Rachel countered.

'But I shook the bottle.'

'Everyone shakes the ketchup bottle before they open it.'

'I suppose.'

'Shall we go up to my room?' Rachel asked. 'I've got some fags. Benson and Hedges.'

They spent the rest of that evening sitting on the window sill of Rachel's bedroom, blowing smoke out into the garden and furiously sucking mints when Mrs Buckley called up the stairs to say she was bringing them some tea and biscuits since they hadn't eaten their supper.

By the end of that weekend, Rachel and Yaslyn had embarked on what could tentatively be called a friendship. Yaslyn's parents had decided to file for divorce.

It didn't feel that bad. Yaslyn was surprised. When her father moved out, she actually saw more of him. Instead of spending all his spare time in some bar or other, trying to avoid coming home to his long-suffering wife, Pete Stimpson concentrated on making up for his absence. There were meals out, trips to the cinema, shopping expeditions. And he often let her bring along a friend. Rachel almost wished her own parents would separate when she saw Yaslyn's father handing over his credit card for two hundred pounds' worth of fashionable tat in Top Shop.

Even the day of the divorce itself was painless. Yaslyn went home from school to the Buckley family house that night. By the time she saw her mother again the following day, the former Mrs Stimpson had patched up her puffy eyes quite admirably with a combination of cucumber slices and expensive eye cream. Yaslyn got presents from both her parents that week. Her mother bought her the CD Walkman Yaslyn had thought prohibitively expensive. Her father sent a card containing a hundred pounds' worth of vouchers from Next. Being the child of divorced parents really wasn't so bad at all.

Things changed when other people became involved.

Yaslyn was racked with guilt when she accepted the presents from Tanya, her father's first girlfriend post-divorce. Torn between wanting to refuse to have anything to do with her out of loyalty to her mum and wanting the things that Tanya offered. Lipstick, eyeshadow, perfume. Even stockings. These were the kinds of things that Yaslyn's mother thought she was still too young to have.

It was Tanya who encouraged Yaslyn to take a chance on becoming a model. It was Tanya who helped her to do her hair, encouraging her away from the nasty poodle perm that had afflicted every girl in the fourth form that year and towards the sleek, long swathe that was to become Yaslyn's trademark. Tanya drove Yaslyn to London to see a model agency. Yaslyn's mother didn't even know they were going. She would have tried to stop them if she had.

But Yaslyn wanted desperately to be a model. She wanted London, Paris, New York, Milan. She wanted to be wanted for the way she looked. There was no point having a beautiful personality, she decided. Having a beautiful personality had not helped her mother hold on to her father. In Yaslyn's eyes, her mother had failed. She had let herself get fat, old and boring by forty. Game over. According to fifteen-year-old Yaslyn, the family split up because Mrs Stimpson had made no effort to hold back time or move with it.

Four years later, while Yaslyn was in Japan, making a small fortune (for a nineteen-year-old girl) in the lucrative commercials market, Tanya phoned in tears to say that Yaslyn's father was leaving her too.

'He . . . he . . . he's got a younger woman!' Tanya stuttered.

Yaslyn tried to sound sympathetic down the long-distance line. But while she spent that evening mourning the end of Dad and Tanya almost as much as she had mourned the split between her parents, Yaslyn never spoke to Tanya again.

'Was that it, Dad?' she asked her father, next time she was at his house. 'Is it because she let herself go?'

'Don't be ridiculous, petal,' her father told her. 'It's about more than the way a woman looks.' He winked at Laura, the new incumbent. She smiled indulgently. But there was something in her eyes that told Yaslyn that Laura knew he was probably lying. Even to himself. For the time being, though, she was too young to worry that one day the axe would fall on her too.

By the time she was twenty, Yaslyn had as much belief in love as she did in Father Christmas. She believed instead that all relationships were a business contract. The man put in the money. The woman put in the beauty. And when the beauty faded, if the woman got fat after having the kids or started to pay them more attention than she did her husband (as Yaslyn's mother once suggested was Pete Stimpson's problem), then the man withdrew the cash. Kids equalled fat and boring equalled divorce. That was the way it happened.

34

'Road trip! Yeah!' Gilles gave Marcus a high five when they found him at reception with Paulette, the smart Parisian woman in her late forties who was holidaying alone and had been Sally's rival for Gilles' attention on the tennis court.

'Thank you so much for letting us go to the ruins with you,' said Paulette to Sally. 'Your husband is a very lovely man.'

'Thank you.'

Right then, Sally could think of many adjectives to describe her husband and none of them was 'lovely'.

'Who is driving first?' asked Gilles. 'Shall I do it, Marcus? I've been here for three years, remember?'

'Yes, but you haven't driven a car in all that time.'

'No, but I am used to traffic being on the right side of the road.'

'I think you'll find that's the wrong side,' said Marcus jovially. 'I'll drive first,' he decided. 'You can swap over halfway if you want. Sally, would you like to navigate?'

'No chance,' said Sally. 'Remember Lake Garda?'

Marcus smiled pleasantly at the memory. Sally just remembered the shouting that had ensued when she got her right and her left mixed up a couple of times. OK. *Every* time. Marcus may have been a sensitive new man on the surface (and a little bit too far below the surface, as far as Sally was concerned these days), but stick him behind a wheel and he was 110 per cent caveman, swearing and swerving with the worst of them.

'Navigator gets to sit in the front,' Marcus offered to tempt her.

'I'll navigate,' said Paulette quickly. 'I've been to Turkey before. I think I might even remember the way from here to Ephesus without a map.'

'Brilliant,' said Marcus. 'Then we're set.'

' "Ephesus is one of the most spectacular archaeological sites anywhere in the world," ' Paulette read aloud from the guidebook. ' "The ancient city was founded by the Ionians in the eleventh century BC and quickly became a thriving trading port and sacred centre for worshippers of the cult of Artemis, goddess of the moon, the hunt and chastity." '

Sally involuntarily glanced at Gilles when chastity was mentioned. They were sitting together in the back of the car, which was hardly the whale of a Cadillac you see when people road-trip in the movies. This hire car was a two-door Japanese hot hatch, and the back seat was so small that, even by wedging herself against the wall, Sally couldn't make more than a space of an inch between her thigh and that of her erstwhile tennis instructor. Matters worsened when Marcus shifted his seat back so that he could find a better driving position. Gilles had to open his legs wide to accommodate the back of Marcus's seat, pressing his thigh more firmly against Sally's in the process.

' "The Ionian settlers built a great temple in honour of the goddess," ' Paulette continued. ' "That became

254

one of the Seven Wonders of the Ancient World. Other splendours that can still be seen in the city today include an amphitheatre which seats more than twenty-five thousand spectators." Perhaps we should throw Gilles to the lions when we get there,' Paulette joked. 'He's a very naughty boy.' She looked back fondly at the man of her middle-aged single dreams, then down with just the flicker of a frown at the place where his thigh rested against Sally's. Sally subtly wedged her handbag between them to make it clear she wasn't playing.

'Isn't this great?' said Gilles. 'I'm so glad I got the day off today.'

'Yeah,' said Marcus. 'It's good to have some company. But you're still here as the entertainment, Gilles, you know that. We want to hear all the insider gossip about life as a Club Aegee rep. Is it really as bad as it's cracked up to be?'

'Do you mean "bad" in a good way?' Gilles asked. 'Isn't that what you English say?'

'He loves his work!' Paulette interrupted. 'Why wouldn't he? A young man like him, in a country like this, surrounded by beautiful women. He's having the time of his life. With all of them,' Paulette added with a meaningful glance back at Sally.

'Now, now, Paulette,' Gilles protested. 'It really isn't like that.'

'That's not what I heard. Pierre the dancing instructor told me they call you the Prince of Broken Hearts for all the poor female guests you seduce and so brutally cast aside when you're done with them.'

'Good title,' said Marcus.

'That's not true,' Gilles insisted. 'Paulette, Pierre

just told you that to make himself seem less dangerous. It was his way of getting into your knickers. You
should watch him. He's the real Prince of Broken
Hearts in Club Aegee Bodrum.'

'That's right. You just shift the focus to poor Pierre,'
said Paulette. 'Make him out to be the bounder and
the scoundrel. He told me that was one of *your* tactics.
Must work pretty well, though,' Paulette continued. 'I
heard you had to stop making notches in your bedpost
after the headboard fell off.'

Paulette laughed so hard Sally could see all her
fillings.

'Pierre's just a bullshitter.' Gilles addressed this
comment to Sally. 'He's the one that can't keep his
hands off the female guests. I've hardly seen any of
them romantically. I don't believe in one-night stands.
I'm not that shallow.'

'Doesn't matter to me, Gilles,' Sally said quietly.
'You can sleep with as many women as you like. You
are a single man, after all.'

'But I don't . . .'

'Marcus, how long is this drive going to take today?'
Sally asked.

'Shouldn't be much longer than three hours.
Provided we don't run into a flock of goats en route.'

'You're a naughty young man.' Paulette was still
ribbing Gilles. She reached round to squeeze his knee.

'I've put all that behind me,' Gilles protested.

'Why put it behind you when you could bring so
much pleasure to the women of the world?'

'Yeah, Gilles. Get it while you can!' Marcus chimed
in. 'One day, one of them will snare you good and
proper and you really will want to turn over a new

leaf.' Marcus reached behind his seat to give Sally's knee a friendly squeeze. The knee he grabbed hold of was a little bigger and hairier than he expected.

'Whatever they say about me, I'm not going gay.' Gilles laughed.

'That would really break my heart!' shrieked Paulette from the passenger seat.

Sally sank as deep as she could into her side of the back seat and leaned her cheek against the cool glass. A day at Ephesus with her husband, the born-again stud, and Paulette, the desperate ex-diva. On her side of the car, the verge dropped away sharply to a ravine. Perhaps, if they were lucky, Marcus would misjudge the next corner and put everyone out of their misery.

In the end, they did beat the Club Aegee bus to it. They'd known they were going to half an hour into the journey when they actually passed the bus in a lay-by. The driver was standing next to the front wheel on the driver's side, scratching his head. They'd clearly had a blow-out.

'Should we stop and help?' asked Paulette. 'Gilles, you're probably expected to be on duty in an emergency situation like this, aren't you?'

'Probably,' said Gilles. 'But we're having so much fun. I want to keep playing truant with you, Paulette.'

Paulette blushed girlishly. That was good enough for her.

'Looks like you were right to be late after all,' Marcus told his wife.

Perhaps there had been a lot of flat tyres on the road from Bodrum that morning. Ephesus was surprisingly quiet. There were just a couple of coaches in the car park. One other car. Standing almost alone for a minute or two on the long white marble road grooved with chariot tracks that ran through the centre of the city, Sally felt as though she had entered a ghostly realm, expecting at any moment to feel the rush of wind as a spectral soldier swept by on his horse. Ahead of her, the grand façade of what must once have been the house of a nobleman gleamed like the bleached remains of a skeleton in the sun. A feral dog held Sally's eye for a second before it darted through a doorway that might once have been reserved for a prince.

The illusion of having slipped through time was soon over.

Paulette screeched, 'The brothel is still standing, Gilles! Not that you ever need to pay for it!'

And then Sally found herself surrounded again. Marcus was pedantically planning a circular route round the city to ensure that they saw every point of interest without having to double back. Paulette kept asking whether he'd found the brothel yet. Gilles continued to protest his chastity.

'Where we're standing right now,' said Marcus authoritatively, 'used to be the port. The harbour filled up with silt over the centuries and now Ephesus is two miles inland.'

Sally nodded.

'I think we should start by walking down here. We'll go past the Library of Celsus on our left, then on towards the amphitheatre. We'll see the municipal baths and the brothel on our way back.'

Sally couldn't stand it. Marcus being tour guide. Paulette being plain annoying. And Gilles being . . . well, Gilles just being Gilles.

'I'm going to the loo,' she said. 'I'll catch you up.'

'I thought you didn't want to go,' said Marcus. She had stolen her few moments alone on the marble road while the others visited the restrooms.

'Well, I do now,' she said. 'I'm not a schoolgirl. Don't wait for me. I know where you're going.'

Paulette shrugged. 'Come on,' she said, linking her arm through Gilles'. 'She'll be all right on her own.' Marcus led the way. Sally slunk back towards the entrance to the city. She glanced over her shoulder just once. Gilles was looking back at her.

Sally spent less than a minute in the restroom, splashing water on to her face. Her only real intention had been to let Marcus and his little tour group get so far ahead of her that she could not catch them up at all. Even better if she lived up to Marcus's opinion of her map-reading skills and took the wrong turn at the earliest opportunity.

When she emerged into the sunlight again, she could still see her happy band of fellow travellers in the distance as they dawdled and paused to look at something interesting. She waited in the shade of a scrubby-looking tree until they turned a corner.

Now she could see Ephesus as she wanted to. Without Marcus's BBC-correspondent-style commentary straight from the guidebook. Without Paulette's inane and ineffective flirtatious chatter. Without Gilles continually trying to catch her eye.

Seeing Ephesus wasn't the only thing to make Sally feel as though she had taken a step back in time. Sitting in the back of the car with Gilles for three hours had sent her straight back to 1986, when, as a fifteen-year-old, she had taken a trip to London with her teenage boyfriend Nick and his parents. They had shared the back seat of the car with Nick's younger brother. He had insisted on having a window seat. Sally found herself sitting on the armrest, surreptitiously holding Nick's hand beneath the cover of her anorak spread across their laps. Every time the car travelled over a bump they were thrown a little closer together. The thrill of the sudden contact was intense.

But the last thing Sally wanted was to spend another three hours blushing her way back to Bodrum. She would insist that Gilles took the front passenger seat on the way home. And when they did get back to the village, she would cancel the rest of her tennis lessons. That was what she was thinking as she followed the little feral dog down a narrow street that would once have led straight to the harbour. It was the kind of street where prostitutes might have plied their trade to passing sailors. She imagined drinking dens full of the kind of people that poor chaste Artemis would have frowned upon.

She stepped across the threshold into the wide open space that had once been someone's home and sat down upon a low wall. She closed her eyes and tipped her head back. The sun caressed her face like a truly tender lover. Away from the crowds, she could hear only the insistent chirping of invisible cicadas. Away from Marcus and the confusion that was Gilles, Sally felt relaxed for the first time that holiday. She lay back on the wall. If only it could always be like this. Quiet. Alone.

Sally must have fallen asleep. She awoke only when a shadow passed across her face. Her eyes flickered open to see a face. Gilles. Sally wasn't sure whether she was still dreaming.

'You have a red nose,' said Gilles. He touched it gently. 'You need some more suntan lotion.'

Sally sat up abruptly. She straightened herself. Shortly before dozing off, she had opened the top three buttons of her shirt. A tender pink triangle on her breastbone where the sun had caught her suggested how long she had been dozing.

'Where are the others?'

'They're around here somewhere,' he told her. 'When you didn't catch us up, Marcus was worried. We decided to look for you. He and Paulette have gone that way.' Gilles jerked his head in the direction of the car park. He looked at his watch. 'The plan is that we will meet again by the car in twenty minutes. Did you get lost?' he asked.

'Sort of,' said Sally. 'Deliberately,' she added, embarrassed.

Gilles smiled. Sally avoided his eyes by fiddling with the buckle on her sandal.

'I bet Marcus is doing his head in.'

'What?'

'I bet he's upset with me,' Sally clarified.

'It seems more often that you are upset with him,' said Gilles.

'What do you mean?'

'I have noticed it,' said Gilles. 'I know about these

things. I meet a lot of people in my job. You are so often somewhere else when you are with him, Sally. I think that you have grown apart.'

'All marriages have their ups and downs,' she told him in an attempt to bring the conversation to a close before it started.

'You can talk to me about it if you want,' said Gilles.

'Yeah, right.' Sally buttoned her shirt up to the neck. 'No thanks.'

'I'm serious.'

'So am I,' Sally rejoined.

'Holidays are one of the most stressful life events a person can go through,' said Gilles. He'd read that in one of Axel's psychology books during a week when he thought he might have a chance to sleep with a clinical psychologist from La Rochelle. Unfortunately, she was still too clever for him. (And too much of a lesbian, according to Xavier.) 'Marcus told me that he arranged this holiday as a surprise. He is trying very hard to make you happy. You should be pleased about that.'

'I know.' Sally's mood swung from sleepy to irritable. Why was Gilles acting like a marriage counsellor all of a sudden?

'I don't like to see two such nice people being so unhappy.'

'We've established that,' said Sally. 'Let's go and find Marcus and Paulette, shall we?'

'Sally,' said Gilles then, 'I know you think I am just another stupid rep, but I know how to keep a secret. Whatever you want to tell me will not go any farther. But perhaps it will help you to get it out in the open. I know about love,' he assured her.

'You do?'

She wasn't about to go for his sensitive act and fall straight into his arms. Sally had no doubt that, nine times out of ten, if Gilles asked a woman whether she was disappointed in her husband, the answer would be in the affirmative and Gilles would offer the perfect solution. Just as nine out of ten husbands faced with the prospect of casual sex with a woman whose physical attributes outweighed her brains and personality would resort to the 'my wife doesn't understand me' line. Gilles didn't know about love. Perhaps he knew about lust, but love – definitely not. Because people who have loved properly always have a touch of melancholy about them. That's what Sally thought.

'Let's get back to the car park,' she repeated. 'Come on. Before Marcus sends out a search party.'

Marcus and Paulette were leaning against the car. Paulette was smoking a cigarette. When she took a drag, her already pinched expression became almost rat-like. She must have been imagining all sorts of misbehaviour between Sally and Gilles beneath the pomegranate trees. Seeing her hero emerge from the ruined city with a safe three feet between him and Sally, Paulette's face was transformed by a yellow-toothed grin. A piece of loose tobacco was wedged between her two front teeth.

'You bad girl!' said Paulette. 'Abandoning your lovely husband like that! He was an excellent tour guide.' Paulette squeezed Marcus's arm flirtatiously, but it was clear that Sally had nothing to worry about. Paulette had eyes only for Gilles. 'You must sit with him in the back of the car on the way home to make up for your neglect.'

'You all right to drive, Gilles?' Marcus asked.

Gilles confirmed that he would be happy to take them back to Club Aegee.

'Then I'll navigate again!' Paulette said happily. 'I was just saying to Marcus that we should stop for a drink in Aphrodisias on the way back to Bodrum. Now there was a goddess for you, Gilles ... Aphrodite. Far more interesting than boring old Artemis.'

'I'm sorry,' Sally whispered to Marcus as they took their places in the hire car. 'I got lost.'

'I thought that might happen,' said Marcus with a sad sort of smile.

35

After their disastrous day in Bodrum, Yaslyn and Rachel decided that it was time to act like real girls on a hen night. Enough of this sipping mint tea after dinner at Club Aegee. It was time to find a real club and get absolutely hammered.

The Halikarnassus nightclub on the harbour front at Bodrum was almost as legendary as the ancient city that gave the place its name. Built to resemble an ancient Greek temple, the club centred around a dance floor that became a foam-filled play-pit every evening at ten.

'We have got to go to that,' said Yaslyn, as she and Rachel passed the club on their way back to the bus station.

'Really?' said Rachel sceptically.

'Don't you think it looks like fun?'

'Hmmm.'

Carrie Ann also needed convincing. 'A foam party? It'll be full of kids on 18-30s holidays out of their heads on raki and trying to shag their way into double figures.'

'Don't be such a spoilsport,' said Yaslyn. 'We can just go and watch.'

Carrie Ann eventually agreed. With that morning's humiliation still in the back of her mind, she decided that it might not be such a bad idea to get out of the confines of Club Aegee anyway. Yasser and Morten had been like two monitor lizards who, having got their teeth into their prey, were determined to hang around until she succumbed to their poisonous bite. Even staying in the room was no way to escape Morten any more. He spent the entire afternoon on his balcony, scanning the distance with his binoculars and whistling loudly, as if to remind Carrie Ann that if she wanted to throw herself off her own balcony in misery, he had a fine lap she could land on. Just as the vibrator had.

So, foam party it was. Though, more accurately, Carrie Ann and Rachel agreed to watch the foam party from a safe distance while sipping cocktails. Yaslyn assured them that the enthusiasm of the 18-30s bunch would be infectious. She made a bet that all three of them would be in the bubbles by midnight. The Goldschlager ritual followed, complete with the retrieved vibrator. Carrie Ann could hardly bear to look at the damn thing any more.

The entrance fee to the Halikarnassus nightclub was pretty steep. Even taking into account the exchange rate of sixty billion Turkish lira to the pound, it came out at twenty quid per person. This included, the girl on the desk reminded them, a 'welcome' drink.

'This certainly isn't bloody welcome,' said Carrie Ann, as she looked around for a flower pot in which to dispose of another predictably aniseed-flavoured concoction. 'Why do holiday shots always taste of aniseed?' she moaned.

'This is more like a proper hen night,' said Yaslyn.

At nine o'clock the club was already heaving. Another group of hens were playing an extravagant drinking game at the bar. They sported T-shirts printed with the names of Bond movie heroines. The bride was 'Pussy Galore', of course.

Rachel had got off lightly, she decided. Carrie Ann and Yaslyn had threatened to have her wearing a veil and L-plates like poor Pussy. Yaslyn had the requisite kit in her suitcase. But in the end she got away with a plastic tiara from Claire's Accessories trimmed with pale purple marabou.

'This may actually be worse than wearing a comedy veil,' said Rachel, as she clocked herself in the mirror behind the bar. 'People might think I'm wearing this tiara for real. I just look like a clueless teen on her way to a post-GCSEs ball.'

'That look is very *en vogue* at the moment,' Yaslyn assured her.

'Are we going to get some proper drinks now?' Carrie Ann asked. She was eager to find something that would wash the taste of aniseed from her mouth.

'Oh yes,' said Yaslyn. 'But we're not going to buy it.'

'What are we going to do?' Carrie Ann retorted. 'Lean over the bar and drink straight from the taps? I'm just not that acrobatic any more.'

'We're going to get some men to buy drinks for us,' Yaslyn told her. 'We'll take it in turns. If you have to buy your own drink, the forfeit is that you have to down it in one.'

'Do we have to play drinking games?' Rachel whined.

'Yes,' said Yaslyn. 'If you don't do your hen night

properly then I'm sure it's unlucky for your wedding or something like that.'

Rachel's mouth dropped open in horror. 'Is that true?'

'Of course it isn't bloody true,' said Carrie Ann. 'On my hen night, I played so many drinking games I didn't know I had a tattoo of Bugs Bunny on my arse until Greg saw it on my wedding night.'

Rachel and Yaslyn looked shocked.

'You're having a laugh,' said Rachel.

'Show us,' said Yaslyn. 'Show us now!'

'What, here? In front of the whole bar?'

The other girls nodded.

'OK.' Carrie Ann took the waistband of her skirt and began to inch it down towards the top of her knickers. Yaslyn and Rachel were transfixed.

'How come you never told us about this before?' Rachel asked. 'How come we've never seen it?'

'Because I haven't got one, you idiots,' said Carrie Ann, abruptly pulling her skirt back up. 'Though I did nearly get one. My chief bridesmaid . . .'

'She whose name shall not be mentioned,' Yaslyn and Rachel chimed at the reference to the adulterous traitor Mairi.

'Yes. Her,' Carrie Ann spat. 'Well, she dragged me into a tattoo parlour on the way home from the night-club where I was dancing away my last day as Carrie Ann Murphy. We were both going to get tattoos. Mairi was going to get a little devil stealing a heart on her hip bone.'

'How appropriate,' said Rachel.

'And I was going to get Wile E. Coyote on my left buttock.'

'Why Wile E. Coyote?' Yaslyn asked. 'Why not something a bit . . . prettier?'

'Because Greg had "Road Runner" tattooed on the right cheek of his backside. Mairi thought it would be a really good wedding surprise for Greg if I had the other half of the partnership on my bottom.'

'But Road Runner is always trying to get away from Wile E.,' Rachel pointed out. 'Or dropping something heavy on his head. They're hardly the cartoon world's greatest love story.'

'How did you get out of it?' asked Yaslyn.

'I was next in line to have the tattoo done. I remember sitting in that waiting room, just about half conscious, looking at the designs on the wall and trying to find one that matched what I wanted. There were lots of cartoon characters. Tom and Jerry, Betty Boop. My heart sank when I saw Betty Boop. You know how she's meant to have those great big eyes? Well, this version looked half Chinese. Perhaps she was meant to be winking, but it was slowly becoming clear to me that this particular tattoo artist wasn't terribly good at cartoons. His Tweety-Pie looked like a yellow beach ball with bananas sticking out of its sides instead of wings.'

'Mairi was going to let you have a tattoo done by an artist who couldn't draw?' Rachel breathed.

'She kept insisting she was going to have one done too. After I had mine. Even offered to pay for it.'

'I bet she did,' said Yaslyn. 'She wanted to ruin your body.' With the benefit of hindsight into Mairi's husband-stealing ways, all her actions were open to reinterpretation.

'So, there I was, sitting in the waiting room,

listening to the screams of the poor soul already on the table, waiting to have Wile E. Coyote tattooed on my bottom by a man who probably didn't know the difference between Wile E. Coyote and Pluto . . .'

Carrie Ann went green at the memory.

'I assumed that Mairi would buckle. The sounds coming from the tattoo parlour were horrendous. Drilling and screaming and swearing and drilling. I thought she would change her mind and drag me out of there. I didn't want to be the one to wimp out first. But Mairi wasn't wimping out. And then the drilling stopped. There was one last squeal of anguish and the tattooist shouted "Next" in his big, booming voice.'

'Did you run away?' Rachel asked.

'God, no. A Murphy girl always stands her ground,' Carrie Ann said proudly. 'Not that I could stand terribly well by this point. I got up and walked across the room on legs that would barely carry me. I was saying Hail Marys under my breath the whole time, praying that something would save me.'

'And something did,' said Yaslyn.

'Oh, yeah. The Virgin Mary answered my prayers all right. I was still wearing the comedy veil that Mairi had insisted I wear all night. I put it over my face for the walk into the parlour. Seemed symbolic somehow. I was going to take it off when the tattoo was finally done. But I could hardly see where I was going. I didn't see the sign that said "Mind the step". I tripped over the bloody thing and landed straight on my head. I was out cold for two whole minutes apparently. The tattooist wouldn't touch me after that. Said it wasn't worth his licence to tattoo someone who might have concussion.'

'Did Mairi get her tattoo?'

'She had the perfect opportunity to wimp out. But when Mairi gets drunk she gets kind of proud. There were two other girls from my hen night there with us. They suggested that she never intended to get one. She was just saying she would to get me in the chair. Mairi got all defensive. She comes from a long line of fighters from Dublin. And before any of us could stop her, she had climbed on to the table. She got her devil holding a little heart – though the heart looked like it had melted. The devil was crap. I think he was based on the tattooist's version of Betty Boop.'

'Serves her right,' said Rachel.

'Yeah. Except when Greg and I split up, he cited that bloody tattoo as evidence that Mairi was more adventurous than I was . . . It was only a little thing,' Carrie Ann concluded.

'Bet it's bigger now,' said Yaslyn. 'If it's stretched with the size of her arse!'

The girls cracked up.

'Girls.' Rachel interrupted the hilarity to address them solemnly. 'You have got to make me a promise. Whatever happens tonight, no matter how drunk we get or how much you hate the dresses I'm making you wear as bridesmaids, you have got to promise me that you will not make me get a tattoo.'

'Of course not,' said Carrie Ann with a wink to Yaslyn.

'Or shave both my eyebrows off if I fall asleep before you.'

'I hadn't even thought of that!' said Yaslyn. 'What a brilliant idea!'

'No!' Rachel ducked away from her.

'It'll seem like an even better idea once we've had a few drinks,' Carrie Ann pointed out. 'Who's first to beg, steal or borrow some booze? Yaslyn. Seeing as it was your idea . . .'

Yaslyn accepted the challenge gracefully. 'Watch this.' She approached the bar and positioned herself between two men. Both automatically turned to check her out. She gave them both the benefit of the smile that had got her on to magazine covers all over the world. The man to Yaslyn's right immediately took the bait and called the barman over for her. Yaslyn ordered a bottle of champagne and made a big show of searching for her purse in her handbag. Before she could flip open the pop-stud that held her purse shut, the guy on Yaslyn's left had placed his credit card on the bar in front of her. The man on her right placed his card on top of it, as though they were playing American Express/Visa snap.

'I couldn't possibly,' mouthed Yaslyn, pushing the cards back towards their respective owners.

Both men insisted. Both wanted to be the one Yaslyn chose to do the honours. It was becoming a matter of pride.

'Don't ask me to choose,' she said playfully. 'I'm a Libran.'

She returned to the girls moments later with two bottles of champagne. 'And an invitation to a party on a yacht after this place has closed. Beat that.'

'You do have the unfair advantage of being stunningly attractive,' Carrie Ann pointed out.

'I'm not everybody's type,' said Yaslyn. 'Champagne?' She poured out three glasses. 'To Rachel's wedding.'

'Rachel's wedding,' replied Carrie Ann.

'Thanks, girls,' said Rachel.

'Wonder what Patrick's doing now,' Yaslyn teased. 'All innocent and vulnerable on the streets of Dublin, surrounded by girl gangs like that.' She jerked her head in the direction of the Bond Girls, who had surrounded some poor, unsuspecting lads from Newcastle (judging by the football strip they were wearing). The Bond Girls were shouting 'get 'em off' with rising excitement, making them look like a pack of hyenas surrounding a freshly killed wildebeest. The Newcastle boys were trapped. They could see no means of escape. If they didn't want to get their kit off, it didn't matter. A hundred manicured hands decorated with huge fake engagement rings from Claire's Accessories were already pulling at their shirts.

'They don't stand a chance,' Carrie Ann commented.

'Patrick's mates wouldn't let that happen to him,' said Rachel firmly. 'Euan definitely wouldn't.'

'I can see him now,' said Yaslyn. 'Stripped of his football shirt, shivering in a back alley, catching chronic pneumonia . . .'

'Table!' Carrie Ann shouted then. Rachel and Yaslyn followed like well-trained infantrymen to the vacant spot before anyone else in the club tried their luck. It was a good spot too. On a balcony overlooking the main dance floor and the stage, where a Turkish MC was trying to get all P Diddy.

The whole place was really rather glamorous. Rachel's experience of holiday resort nightclubs prior to this one was limited to the kind of places that still played the macarena. Halikarnassus was a nightclub on the scale of and in the style of the super-clubs in Ibiza, with super-glam clientele to match. If you looked beyond the British hen nights and the packs of young men in football strip, you saw clusters of those beautiful people of indeterminate European origin. French, Italian, Turkish, Spanish. Shabby chic had passed them by. They looked effortlessly cool. Rachel, on the other hand, wondered whether she had ever looked cool in her life.

Yaslyn was lucky enough to be able to do any 'look' she wanted. Her success as a model was partly due to her ability to look like a Scandinavian ice queen, an all-American girl or an ephemeral English rose. She could hold her own with the best of Eurotrash and was attracting plenty of admiring glances now. Dressed in a pair of shorts that she didn't mind ruining if they did end up in the foam pit after all, Rachel felt distinctly invisible. Even with her tiara.

She hoped it wasn't going to be like that on the big day. When she announced that Carrie Ann and Yaslyn were to be her bridesmaids, one of Patrick's work-mates had snorted, 'The bridesmaids are supposed to make the bride look good by being awful, Rachel,' before she realised quite what she was saying.

Rachel laughed the comment off by assuring Rhian that she fully intended to have Yaslyn wear a dress fashioned from a marquee.

In the end, Rachel had chosen to dress her brides-maids in beautiful deep pink silk shift dresses. She had thought they were tasteful. Devoid of frills and flat-tering. But that afternoon's spat with Yaslyn had left Rachel feeling unsure about her choice. God only knew what Yaslyn would think of the wedding dress itself. Helen was making it and had insisted that it wouldn't be as plain as the bridesmaids'.

The fact was Rachel rather liked the dress that Helen was making for her. She liked the way the big skirt made her waist look relatively tiny. She liked the feeling of all those metres of fabric swishing around her legs as she walked. And if you couldn't wear a huge dress on your wedding day . . . It was up to her. If she wanted to wear a meringue . . .

Rachel failed to convince herself. She stared at the glass in front of her on the table, feeling almost exactly as she had felt when Yaslyn had laughed at the leather blouson jacket Rachel had bought with her first-ever wage packet. How was it possible that Yaslyn could still make her feel this way fifteen years down the line?

'What's up with you?' Carrie Ann interrupted Rachel's contemplation. 'I'm the one who's supposed to be depressed by the lack of talent!'

'I'm fine,' Rachel lied. 'I was just thinking about the catering.'

'Catering!' Carrie Ann exclaimed. 'Forget the catering. The hens haven't even laid the eggs that are going to be made into your quiches yet.'

'Ugh! You're not really having quiche at your wedding?' said Yaslyn.

'Ladies and gentlemen, the foam party is about to begin!!!!'

The announcement was greeted by much whooping and cheering from the crowd. The music that blasted out from speakers on all sides was suitably triumphal. There was a sudden rush of movement as people took their positions. Those who had spent too much money on their clothes to risk getting their dry-clean designer classics wet made a dash for the bar. The Bond girl hen party made a dash for the middle of the foam pit.

'Are we going to go for it?' Yaslyn asked.

Rachel and Carrie Ann looked at each other doubtfully. The Bond girl hens seemed to have formed themselves into a rugby scrum. There was no telling whether they had some poor bloke trapped beneath them.

'I don't know if I want to be in the vicinity when that lot go wild,' said Carrie Ann.

'We should be going wild with them. Come on.'

The foam machines had been wheeled into place. They looked like huge fans but while they were making plenty of noise, they didn't appear to be making many bubbles. Eventually, one of them sputtered out a little gobbet of white.

'They haven't used enough Fairy Liquid,' Carrie Ann commented.

'Perhaps we should go down there and have a bit of a dance,' said Rachel. The foam machine had been on for five minutes and the bubbles had yet to reach ankle height. It seemed a pretty safe bet.

Watching the foam machines splutter away, Carrie Ann was reminded of disappointing snowstorms from her childhood, when the weatherman promised a white Wednesday and everyone under the age of eighteen waited hopefully to hear that school had been cancelled. Perhaps the foam machines were broken, Carrie Ann thought. In which case it would be perfectly safe for her to agree that they should get up and dance. They wouldn't get particularly wet and Yaslyn couldn't accuse her of being a killjoy.

They made their way down to the dance floor, careful to position themselves as far away from the Bond Girls, who had extricated themselves from their scrummage and were now attempting the can-can, as possible. A dangerous exercise, since what little foam there was had already made the marble floor somewhat slippery.

'This is pathetic,' said Yaslyn, as she reached up to catch a snowflake of foam.

'I quite like it,' said Rachel. It was easy to get funky on the slippery surface beneath them. Carrie Ann was equally happy with the low bubble quotient and the groove assistance offered by the combination of foam and marble tiling. The DJ had put on a Turkish pop song with a hard-core garage bass line. The three girls moved into mock belly dancer mode.

Then, like a sudden hailstorm that catches you out when you're dashing across the car park in the spitty, spotty rain, somebody *really* turned the foam machines on.

'Oh my God!' Carrie Ann had the misfortune to be standing right in the line of fire. The force of the jet that suddenly shot out behind her almost toppled her over. Regaining her balance by grabbing hold of Rachel, she brought Rachel down with her instead. The two girls looked at each other in shock. Yaslyn laughed above them as Carrie Ann helped Rachel to her feet. But before Carrie Ann could point out that landing on your arse on a marble floor for the third time in a week was far from funny, the joker in charge of the foam jet swivelled it around on its base like a machine gun and took Yaslyn out as well.

In the time it took Yaslyn to recover from her fall,

start laughing again and get back to her feet, the foam was as high as their waists.

'So much for staying dry,' Carrie Ann shouted over the music.

'I'm getting out,' said Rachel. It seemed that no matter where she moved the foam jet followed her. 'I can't see anything. I think I might have gone blind.'

'Hold my hand,' said Yaslyn, reaching out for her. 'But you're not going anywhere yet. What's the point? Our clothes are ruined. Our hair is ruined.'

'I bet my make-up's ruined,' said Carrie Ann.

'Oh yes,' Yaslyn confirmed.

'I've lost a shoe,' Rachel wailed then. She got back down in the foam to feel around for it.

'This is yours?' A man popped up beside the girls brandishing a random flip-flop.

'Nope,' said Rachel. 'I don't believe it. These are my favourite sandals.'

'We'll help you look,' said the flip-flop guy. He was joined by a couple of men who might have been his brothers. They were all very similar looking, with curly, jet-black hair framing large round faces. They dived eagerly into the foam. Seconds later, Yaslyn felt a hand moving slowly up her leg.

'Hey!' She slapped it away.

'I am sorry.' One of the men popped out of the foam at belly height in front of her. 'I was getting lost.'

'Perhaps you *should* get lost,' said Yaslyn irritably.

'I think I have your shoe!' A second guy emerged from the foam, brandishing Rachel's sandal like the Lady of the Lake brandishing Excalibur.

'Thank you,' she said gratefully. 'I'm going to take

'my shoe and get out of here,' she told the girls. She reached for the sandal. Her saviour deftly moved so that it was out of her reach again.

'Where is my reward?' he said, pursing his lips in her direction.

Rachel looked to Carrie Ann and Yaslyn for reassurance. The girls were having their own trouble. Carrie Ann was grimacing wildly as the first guy took her by the wrists and made her dance like a freakish human puppet.

'You are here from England, yes?' the man asked her. Carrie Ann nodded.

'You are having a nice holiday.'

It was rapidly turning into a 'hell-i-day'. It was quickly becoming clear that the only women in the foam were tourists. The Turkish women, in their immaculate outfits, watched from the balconies that surrounded the dance floor as their men plunged right in and took advantage of the cover afforded by the foam to goose loose foreign women to their hearts' content. While Carrie Ann was safely disarmed with her hands held high in the air, yet another guy came up behind her and rubbed his groin against her buttocks in the pretext of a dance.

'You are here for the sex,' he asked her straightforwardly.

'Absolutely not,' she said in her best schoolmarmish voice. 'Let me go, please.'

'Come on. Jiggy jiggy. We're having fun.'

'I'm not. Let me go.'

She stepped forward and aimed for her captor's foot.

'Let's get out of here,' Yaslyn yelled.

'I'm trying to,' Carrie Ann yelled back. 'I seem to be surrounded.'

The boys from Istanbul had indeed corralled them.

But the cavalry was at hand. At the other end of the dance floor, the Bond Girls were laying waste to every man who ventured within grabbing distance. One of the former hard men from Newcastle was stark naked and fishing about in the foam for his underpants. When his mate had the temerity to laugh, the Bond Girls relieved him of his clothes too and took his boxer shorts as a souvenir. Their end of the dance floor was almost entirely man free now as every male still able to run decided it was probably best to do so. Like a swarm of locusts looking for the next field to devastate, they turned their attention on the gang of Turkish guys that had surrounded Carrie Ann, Rachel and Yaslyn.

'Men ahoy!' shouted the Chief Bridesmaid Bond Girl as she led the charge through the foam.

The boys from Istanbul didn't know what hit them and stripped them. Each experienced a brief moment of ecstasy as a pair of foreign female hands fumbled around their flies. They were good, these girls. Clinically fast. And the fashion for baggy trousers was very much in their favour.

Yaslyn, Rachel and Carrie Ann had their chance to scramble clear. When the bubbles finally subsided that night, the dance floor would be like a battlefield.

In the ladies' restroom, the girls attempted to clean themselves up before leaving for the village. The foam was nothing like bubble bath or even washing-up liquid at all. The special formulation that gave the bubbles their staying power also gave them a slightly greasy feel. It was effective, though. Even after walking across the entire nightclub, Carrie Ann still looked like a snowman, with bubbles that simply refused to burst throughout her curly hair.

'The horror. The horror,' was all she could say as she surveyed the damage in a mirror.

'It was like being in *Logan's Run*,' said Rachel. 'You know that bit where he walks through a sort of sex shop and there are all those hands coming out of the walls?'

'Thank God for the Bond Girls,' said Yaslyn.

They were joined at the mirror by one of the junior members of that gang. She had the legend 'Pola Ivanova' in glittery lettering on the back of her black hen-night T-shirt. She was wearing a pair of pants on her head. Men's underpants.

'I hope you checked those for skid marks before you put them on,' commented Carrie Ann.

Pola promptly ripped the offending headgear off and dropped it on the floor.

'It's brilliant here, isn't it?' she said. 'I've had fifteen snogs tonight.'

Yaslyn and Carrie Ann smiled indulgently. When Pola left to rejoin her comrades, they looked at each other and shared a complicit smile.

'Fifteen snogs,' said Carrie Ann with admiration. 'And our little hen here hasn't had a single one.'

'Are you thinking what I'm thinking?' asked Yaslyn.

'Oh, yeah. We haven't been doing this properly at all.'

They linked their arms through Rachel's like a pair of policemen escorting a prisoner to the cells.

'I think the tradition is one snog for every year you want to stay married, isn't it?' Carrie Ann made the facts up as they went along. 'And here's number one.'

Like a monster from the deep, Yasser the jewellery seller chose exactly that moment to rise from the foam pond.

'Carrie Ann!' he shouted. 'You want to come and have a good time with me?'

'No, but Rachel definitely does.'

Yaslyn and Carrie Ann gave their hen a firm push in Yasser's direction.

'A snog for every year you want to stay married,' Yaslyn reminded her.

Yasser cut through the foam like a shark's fin. Cold sore glinting . . .

36

'Good cabaret tonight,' Marcus ventured. After their day at Ephesus, Paulette had insisted that Marcus and Sally join her for dinner and to watch the Turkish dancing.

'It was good,' Sally agreed. At least Paulette's presence that evening had saved her and Marcus from having to sit in silence while thinking of something to say to each other. Paulette rarely drew breath long enough for Sally and Marcus to have a chance to speak anyway.

'You looked really sexy, you know,' Marcus continued. 'Dancing with the dance instructor bloke.'

'Thanks.'

Paulette had insisted that they accompany her to the Club Aegee nightclub as well. Sally had found herself being whisked around the floor by Pierre while Paulette ground her pelvis against Gilles' as though they were engaged in a frenzied fertility dance. Gilles didn't seem to mind, though at one point he had mouthed 'help me' to Sally across Paulette's shoulder.

'I'd forgotten how good a dancer you are,' said Marcus. 'We should do more of it when we get back to England. Charlie says they do salsa classes at the Mexican restaurant that's just opened in town.'

'Yeah. Maybe,' said Sally. 'Those kinds of classes are usually cattle markets for single Sloanes.'

'Perfect for Charlie. He's always on the hunt. Perhaps we should try to fix him up with one of your friends when we get back. What about Jenny? She's desperate to find a man before her eggs are completely fried. We could have them both round for dinner. See what happens.'

Sally shuddered at the thought of a double date. And not because it would mean spending the evening with Charlie the Chump and Jenny Desperate, as the unfortunate girl had become known to her friends, if not to her face.

Sally lay down upon her bed and picked up her book. For the past four nights of the holiday, Marcus had taken this as his cue to give up and get into his own bed. That night, however, Marcus sat down beside his wife on her bed and began to run his fingers lightly along her long brown legs.

'What are you doing?' Sally asked suspiciously.

'Smooth legs,' he murmured.

'I'm not in the mood,' she said, sensing what might be coming next.

'Come on,' said Marcus. He kissed her on the dent just below each knee.

Sally tucked her legs right up under her bottom so that they were out of his range. Marcus pulled them out again.

'However you want it, Sal,' he whispered. 'What do you want me to do to you? Shall I go down on you? Would you like that?'

Sally's face creased into a grimace behind the cover of her paperback.

'I don't want you to do anything,' she told him flatly.

'You must want something. Go on. Tell me what to do.'

'How about . . . I just want to finish this chapter and go to sleep.'

'What do you need to sleep for? You don't have to get up in the morning. There's no six forty-five to Waterloo to catch here. We're on holiday.'

'I'm tired,' Sally insisted.

'This might wake you up,' said Marcus, attempting a cheeky wink. He pushed Sally back into the pillows, lifted her nightshirt armour out of the way and began to kiss his way down her body, from her sternum, across her ribcage to her flat, tanned stomach. Sally stiffened every time his lips touched her skin.

'Marcus,' she said, hoping that the tone of her voice would be warning enough that she really wasn't pleased by the attention.

'You're so lovely and brown,' he said without taking his mouth off her stomach. 'You look beautiful with a tan. Have I told you often enough how beautiful I think you are . . . ?' He was still kissing.

'Marcus,' Sally tried again.

Another kiss.

'Marcus. Please.' Sally took her husband's head in both her hands and lifted it gently away from her belly button in a gesture she assumed was unequivocal. 'I'm *tired.*'

Marcus merely brushed her hands away and was straight back down again, this time heading lower.

'Marcus! Will you stop it?' Sally pleaded. 'I said I'm tired. What part of that sentence don't you understand?'

'I just want to show you how much I love you. I

really, really love you, Sally Merchant. I love you as much as the day we first met.'

'You're drunk,' she accused him.

'Only on you.'

He made to remove the bikini bottoms she was still wearing beneath her nightshirt.

'I just want to make you happy.'

'And I just want to fucking sleep.'

Sally rolled out of the way, rearranging her clothes as she did so. 'Is that OK with you? I don't want you to maul me like you're a fucking dog and I'm some piece of meat. Leave me alone.'

'What?'

'Just give it a rest. I don't want to have sex with you tonight. OK?'

'You don't have to do anything.' Marcus made a final grab for her. 'Sally.' His voice was wheedling. Marcus had reached for Sally's shoulders but she struggled so much to get away from him that he in- advertently ended up holding her wrists as though she were his prisoner.

'Get off. Get off!' she shouted this time.

'Sally.'

Wrenching her hands free at last, Sally shoved her husband so hard that he fell off the mattress and on to the bedside table.

'What the . . . Sally!'

Marcus stood up in a hurry, catching his shin on the side of the bed as he did so.

'Fuck!'

He stared down at her in shock. In the five years of their marriage they had never before come to blows.

Now Sally was looking at him as though she was scared of him, pressing herself against the wall as though she hoped she might press herself through it. And the truth was Marcus was scared of her too. He didn't recognise the frightened wildcat look in her eyes. He had never seen her look so frightened *and* angry.

'Look, I'm sorry,' she stuttered suddenly. 'I'm sorry.' She covered her face with her hands. 'I didn't mean to shove you like that.' She was right up against the wall now and pulled her nightshirt tighter around her. 'I just . . . I just . . . I don't know.'

'Sally, what is wrong with us?' Marcus pleaded.

'Nothing. I don't know. I don't know. I . . . It's nothing. I'm just stressed out, that's all. It'll be OK in the morning. Please. Let's forget it happened.'

She got up abruptly and started looking for the sundress she had worn to dinner among the pile of discarded clothes on the floor.

'What are you doing?' Marcus asked her when she had put the dress back on.

'I'm going to go to the bar and get a bottle of water.'

'What?'

'Some water. I'm going to get some.'

'Now? Don't be ridiculous. Stay there. I'll go for you. You just get into bed.'

'No. I *want* to go.' Sally was already by the door. 'I need some air,' she told him, before adding almost inaudibly, 'I need some space.'

She let the door slam shut behind her and ran down the dark path to the pool bar.

Marcus stood where she had left him. When the

echo of the slamming door had faded, he could hear nothing but the rush of his blood pumping round his brain. It sounded as though it were escaping from somewhere. His life was seeping out of him as surely as if Sally had shot him in the heart.

37

It was three o'clock in the morning before the hen party girls got back to Club Aegee. It had been next to impossible to find a cab when Halikarnassus closed its doors on the bubbly bacchanalians. In the end, the girls had to submit to a long walk home or a ride back to the village in the back of Yasser's car with Carrie Ann sitting in the front like a sacrificial lamb. Yasser touched her knee every time he reached for the gear stick. And when they finally pulled into the car park, he insisted on a kiss for payment.

Carrie Ann closed her eyes and puckered up, aiming for the cold-sore-free side of his mouth and hoping that, if she kept it brief enough, she wouldn't be in danger of picking up anything nasty.

'Goodnight, then,' said Carrie Ann, wriggling free of Yasser's inevitable bear hug.

'You're not going to bed now,' Yasser insisted. 'The night is still young.'

'But we're not,' quipped Carrie Ann.

'I insist that you join us for some more drinks. Yasser will be offended if you don't accept his hospitality. It is the Turkish way,' he added. It was always the Turkish way with Yasser.

'After hours in your room again?'

They had been joined by Gilles.

'What a fantastic idea,' Yaslyn suddenly decided for the girls. Carrie Ann and Rachel could only watch in horror as Yaslyn went into top-gear flirt mode, and they realised that they wouldn't be going to bed after all. 'Just the one drink, eh?'

'I thought we might see you at the nightclub tonight,' Yaslyn told Gilles.

'I was tired,' he said. 'I went to Ephesus today.'

'Didn't know you were into history.'

'He isn't,' said Yasser. 'Which piece of tail did you chase out to Ephesus, Gilles? Not that Paulette woman from Paris. She's old enough to be your mother.'

'You know he's joking,' Gilles said to Yaslyn. 'I only have eyes for you, Yaslyn, and when I didn't see you by the pool this morning, there didn't seem much point in hanging around.'

'It was raining,' Carrie Ann pointed out. 'Nobody was by the pool this morning.'

'Hey, Gilles! Yasser!'

Carrie Ann's heart headed straight for her flip-flops. Now they were joined by her Norwegian nightmare.

'Morten.' Yasser slapped his new friend on the back. 'We thought we'd lost you back in Bodrum.' Yasser gave Gilles an unsubtle wink.

'I tried to look for you when I came out of the club,' Morten explained breathlessly. 'I had to get a taxi on my own. I don't know how I am losing you.'

'You should have taken your binoculars.' Yasser laughed. 'Never mind. You're with us now. Come on.' Yasser linked his arm through Carrie Ann's. Morten linked his arm through the other side. 'I have some very special stuff for you people in my room.'

Yaslyn linked her arm through Gilles'. He brought her in close to him and leaned down to whisper something in her ear. Yaslyn laughed. In response, Gilles kissed the soft bare curve where Yaslyn's neck swept down into her shoulder. He placed his hand flat on her smooth brown back, naked in her low-cut dress, eliciting another little giggle. Yaslyn snaked her arm around Gilles' waist and tucked her hand into the back pocket of his jeans.

Rachel narrowed her eyes as she followed behind them with Yasser's cross-eyed young shop assistant, Oscar, ensuring that he kept a very safe distance from her own bare shoulders. Rachel didn't really want to join the boys for a late-night drink in Yasser's dingy quarters. She was pretty sure Carrie Ann felt the same – especially since Morten had joined them – but Yaslyn was clearly determined that the night would not end before sunrise, and it had become a matter of making sure that she didn't get into trouble.

It was well over two hours since Rachel had had her last drink at the Halikarnassus. Looking for a taxi, giving up the search and then taking a precarious journey to the village in the back of Yasser's old BMW had taken that much time. As a result, Rachel had long since lost the fuzzy glow of drunkenness that makes everything seem all right. The world had come back into focus and swiftly become just a little too focused. Why is it, Rachel wondered, that danger always seems so much easier to spot when you are descending into a hangover?

Rachel didn't like Gilles. She suspected that he had heard 'yes' too many times to take 'no' for an answer if he got it. And Yaslyn would say 'no', wouldn't she? Of course she would, with lovely Euan waiting for her back home.

Rachel couldn't quite believe the way Yaslyn took her boyfriend for granted. As far as she knew, Yaslyn hadn't called Euan once the whole trip. Not even to let him know that they had landed safely, let alone to say that she was missing him. Rachel missed Patrick dreadfully whenever they were apart. In actual fact, this hen week was the longest they had spent apart since the start of their relationship on Millennium Eve. Rachel knew that she was in love with Patrick because every time she saw something wonderful she wanted only to be able to point it out to him. Sunsets and sunrises were wasted without Patrick beside her to see them. There had been plenty of fabulous wasted moments on this trip.

Yaslyn, on the other hand, had never been particularly romantic. She put it down to her parents' divorce. It made her cautious, she said. And rightly so. When Yaslyn first became a model, she found herself exposed to a whole new world where *all* the men were rich and charming and handsome but ultimately shallow. She reasoned that her pragmatic approach to love in those circumstances saved her from bottomless unhappiness. She saw the pain all around her. Young girls would be swept up by the glamour and romance of the high-rolling *modelisers* – candlelit dinners, diamonds, yachts – only to be dropped like last season's skirt length when someone younger and prettier came along.

But she didn't need to be so hard now, Rachel kept

reminding her. Euan wasn't a modeliser. Though he could have used his job title to sleep with any number of naive young wannabes (he'd quickly got freelance work as a photographer from plenty of newspapers), Euan didn't capitalise on the opportunity. He was a decent bloke. All Patrick's friends were. And yet it seemed Yaslyn was treating Euan the way she treated the scumbags she had met on the way to meeting her Mr Right.

Rachel felt like Yaslyn's mother every time she suggested she might consider settling down with this one. But it would be too awful if Yaslyn didn't realise what a diamond she had in Euan until she pushed him away for the last time. The kind of indifference that might have kept more fickle men interested beyond the third date would ultimately be too much for a genuinely good guy. Patrick had often said so.

And now Yaslyn was sitting on Gilles' lap, flirting as if Euan didn't exist again. 'Defensive dating', Yaslyn had once called it, spreading your affections wide so that when one man let you down – as she claimed they inevitably would – only half your heart would be bruised. Rachel hated the idea. She hated the way Yaslyn assumed that anyone who believed in being faithful and honest was stupid; trotting out her statistics about the percentage of married men who had affairs as evidence why the women should get in there first with the infidelity. There was no room for trust in Yaslyn's world. And right now it was as though Yaslyn's towering distrust of relationships were casting a shadow over Rachel's perfect little love kingdom. Especially this close to the wedding.

'You must have a boyfriend,' Yasser was saying to Yaslyn.

'No one special,' she said.

Gilles squeezed her tighter.

Yaslyn ignored Rachel's glare.

38

The fact was that, right then, Yaslyn wasn't entirely sure that she was lying to Gilles and Yasser at all. The real reason she hadn't called Euan's mobile while he whooped it up with Patrick in Dublin was because she couldn't be sure that he would pick up the phone to her if she did ring. Last time she'd seen him, Euan had been trudging from Yaslyn's house towards his motorbike without even glancing back over his shoulder to wave farewell.

Yaslyn hadn't intended that to happen. When Euan arrived at her house early on Sunday evening, to spend one last night with her before she headed off to Turkey for the hen week and he went with Patrick's gang to Dublin, she had been looking forward to seeing him. She'd uncorked a bottle of half-decent red wine to get it breathing, fetched a video from the shop on the corner (a romantic comedy which he probably wouldn't want to watch but would feign interest in for her sake), and Euan for his part was going to pick up a pizza on his way round. God, Yaslyn thought when she saw the size of the pizza box he brought out of his pannier, there goes my career.

'I asked them not to put cheese on your half,' he told her, as a concession to her continual diet.

They watched the film. It was all going perfectly. Euan actually laughed out loud at jokes Yaslyn had thought only a girl could appreciate. Curled up on the sofa in his big warm arms, Yaslyn felt supremely contented. Like a cat on a cashmere jumper. She even shed a tiny tear of happiness when the girl on the screen finally got her man and dragged him up the aisle.

Then he spoiled it.

'Is that going to be us any time soon?' he asked.

'What?' Yaslyn sat up abruptly, feigning confusion but knowing instantly exactly what he was referring to.

'Walking up the aisle, Yas. You and me. Is it ever going to happen?'

'I don't know if we're allowed,' said Yaslyn lightly. 'Isn't there a rule about transsexuals getting married?'

It was one of their private jokes. Yaslyn often teased Euan that he was so sweet and sensitive he must really be a woman who'd undergone a sex change. But this time he didn't try to match her banter by accusing her of being the transsexual in the relationship, with her legs far too long to belong to a real girl.

'We could do it,' he said, looking into her eyes with an intensity that suddenly disturbed her as much as it had turned her on the first time she saw it that afternoon in the New Forest.

'My father just spent my dowry money on a patio,' Yaslyn quipped.

'Will you be serious?' Euan asked. 'Just once. Just for a minute. Just for me.'

He took both her hands in his and looked so deep into her eyes it was as though he could really see into the mind that was hiding behind them.

'I am being serious,' said Yaslyn desperately. 'York

stone, water features. The works. These things add up, you know. Patios.'

But Euan was not to be deflected. Not this time.

'Yaslyn, where is this going?' he asked with a sigh. 'I mean, where do you see us in another year's time? Five years' time? Ten years? Because I know where I see us, Yas. I see me with you. I want to be with you. You know that. I want to live with you in a nice house in the country and have dogs and horses and maybe one day a couple of children . . .' He paused to search her eyes again for a response.

'You really want that?' Yaslyn croaked.

'I really do,' he said, reaching out to gently brush her trembling bottom lip with his thumb.

This wasn't meant to happen. This was so much the opposite of the way it was supposed to be. Yaslyn was the girl. She was supposed to be the one begging for more commitment. She was supposed to be the one bringing up the possibility of having a big house in the country and dogs and cats and *kids* in a tiny shame-faced voice as if she were suggesting anal sex.

'Do you want the same thing?' Euan pushed her.

'I . . . I . . .' Yaslyn stuttered. She turned her face away so that Euan couldn't stare at her any more. 'I don't know. I mean, this is all really sudden. I've never really thought about it before. I didn't think you were into that kind of thing either . . . You're only thirty.'

The intensity in his eyes was already darkening into disappointment.

'You mean *you're* not into that kind of thing,' he translated.

'I don't mean that,' Yaslyn tried. 'It's just that . . . I'm not sure. I just can't really picture . . .'

'What? Us? Together? With a family?'

She didn't have to shake her head for him to know that he had hit the mark.

'That's what you mean, isn't it?'

'I don't know,' she said. Her voice was a whisper. 'What's wrong with the way we are now?'

He got up from the sofa silently and walked into the kitchen. When she heard him turn on the tap, she assumed that he was going to make a pot of tea to drink while they forgot that this strange, uncomfortable exchange about love and marriage had just happened. But Euan wasn't filling the kettle. Leaning as far back as she could on the sofa, Yaslyn saw him gulping down a glass of water as though he were trying to clear the taste of something bitter from his mouth, then he snatched up his leather jacket from the back of the chair he had hung it from. He tucked his motorbike helmet under his arm and headed for the door.

'Euan, where are you going?'

He didn't answer. He just carried on walking.

'Euan! Wait.' Yaslyn got to the sitting-room door in time to hear him slam the front one and shout, 'It's make-your-mind-up time.'

She decided to let him go. Passivity seemed the only answer right then. Least said, soonest mended, she thought. He hadn't really just given her an ultimatum, had he? She assumed that he would call later that evening and didn't worry too much until closing time passed. But he didn't call that evening. Eventually, she did phone him but got his answerphone. She didn't leave a message. She didn't speak to him again before she caught the flight to Turkey.

Yaslyn wasn't sure why she hadn't told Carrie Ann and Rachel about the row. Partly it was because she didn't want a lecture. Sometimes it seemed Rachel loved Euan almost as much as she loved her own fiancé, and she would find it difficult to listen to the story without coming down firmly on Euan's side. As for Carrie Ann, since splitting from her husband she had become increasingly focused on her own misery. Every time someone else tried to talk about something that was worrying them, Carrie Ann would bring the conversation back round to her own tale of woe.

Besides, Yaslyn still wasn't sure whether it would be a good or a bad thing if she never saw Euan again. If he had given her an ultimatum, then perhaps she needed to call his bluff. If she really loved him, she should have been delighted when he suggested marriage, not seen it as a big black door that would slam shut on her life so far, forcing her to spend the rest of it in the cell of one person's affection. What if she devoted herself to one person and that one person let her down? He wouldn't even have to be unfaithful to her. What if some accident happened that took her one special person away? Yaslyn wasn't sure she would be able to survive the pain. Better not to risk the jump at all than have her parachute fail when she was already hurtling towards the ground.

Not that Yaslyn wasn't a thrill-seeker. And perhaps that was the other problem. Would one man's attention ever be enough for her? Getting married would put a stop to the flirting that had kept her confidence in her own attractiveness afloat for years. Because despite, or perhaps because of, the nature of her work,

Yaslyn always needed to be told that she was beautiful, wonderful, a girl in a million . . . Gilles was looking at Yaslyn with something approaching awe right then and that felt good to her. Like a shot of her favourite drug. The dilated pupils of a new admirer were the only mirror in which Yaslyn could really see just how beautiful she was.

'I need some matches for my cigarettes,' Gilles told her in a murmur. 'Would you like to come outside with me to get some?'

'Sure, I could do with some air,' said Yaslyn.

'Me too,' said Carrie Ann, catching Rachel's disapproving look and seizing the opportunity to extricate them both from an evening with Bodrum's most wanted. Alcohol had been making Morten increasingly bold and he was edging ever nearer to Carrie Ann's side. Yasser was closing in from the other direction.

'Gilles can walk us all back to our room.'

39

Sharing a room with Gilles hadn't turned out to be quite the nightmare Axel was sure it would be when he first discovered that he was to be billeted with the Club Aegee Casanova. At least four nights out of seven, Gilles wouldn't come back to the room at all, instead spending the hours of darkness in the room of his chosen victim for the evening.

In keeping with his rule about not sleeping with guests until their penultimate night at the village to avoid heartache for them and minimise possible inconvenience to himself, Mondays were Italian night (the Italians left on Wednesday). Wednesdays were French night (the flight to Paris departed on Friday morning) and Sundays were English night, assuming there were any English guests on-site at all.

Axel was surprised to be woken by the sound of Gilles coming back to the room in the early hours of Sunday morning. By definition, the hours between 8 p.m. Saturday and 7 a.m. Sunday comprised Dutch night, and that week there were definitely Dutch guests around. As usual when he did come back before dawn, Gilles reached instinctively for the light switch, blasting Axel with blinding brightness for a second before he remembered that he wasn't supposed to switch the light on when he got back after ten in case Axel was already tucked up in bed and asleep.

'Sorry!' Gilles whispered loudly. He'd also forgotten that he wasn't supposed to say anything either. Not even make an apology for fear of making it even harder for Axel to roll over and carry on sleeping.

However, Axel could hardly sleep as Gilles made his way across the room in the dark. By day, Gilles' side of the tiny room was an eyesore. By night it was a veritable minefield. Gilles scoffed at Axel's daily suggestion that he should take empty beer bottles down to the recycling unit when he had finished with them, preferring instead to build elaborate beer-bottle sculptures as shrines to his ability to drink five Budvar at any one sitting. Now the bottles were having their revenge as one of the sculptures collapsed, sending Gilles skidding across the room to crack his shins against the concrete-hard base of his bed.

'Ow.' He couldn't keep his annoyance quiet.

'Put the light on,' said Axel resignedly.

'It's OK,' said Gilles. 'No need. I think I'm on the bed now.'

'Great. Go to sleep before you do yourself any more damage.'

Axel closed his eyes again and tried to drift back to dreamland. The fact that he had been dreaming about Natalie made him even more disgruntled. He wanted to snatch every moment with her. Even if those moments existed only in his imagination. But Gilles wasn't about to let Axel sink back into a world where Natalie Leclerc still loved him and Ed Wiseman was a midget with no hair.

Gilles gave a sigh. It was a sigh as deep and vast as any man in love ever sighed.

Axel rolled towards the wall, burying one ear in his pillow and covering the other with his hand.

Gilles gave another sigh. Axel could still hear him.

'What?' Axel asked irritably.

'It is a nightmare,' said Gilles.

'Oh good,' said Axel. 'Thank goodness it's only a nightmare. Because for one terrible moment I thought you really had come bursting into the room, making lots of noise and keeping me awake when all I want to do is go to sleep because tomorrow morning I am on six o'clock litter supervision duty.'

'Sorry,' said Gilles. 'I'll try to go to sleep too.'

'Goodnight.'

The room was silent but for the sound of Axel's eighteenth-birthday-present wristwatch ticking on his nightstand. For two whole minutes. Axel counted the seconds. Then Gilles sighed again.

'What?' Axel sat up in bed this time. 'What is wrong with you now?'

'I think there is something wrong with me,' said Gilles. 'I should have been with that Dutch girl.'

'But you're back in the room tonight. The Dutch girl didn't want you. So what? Maybe she's got a boyfriend back home. Maybe she's the kind of person who doesn't believe in having casual sex just because she's a thousand miles away from the man she loves. There's nothing wrong with you except you picked a girl with morals.'

'Oh no,' said Gilles defensively. 'I could have had her.'

'Of course,' said Axel.

'I didn't want to.'

'Sure.'

'I mean it, Axel. I just didn't want to. She came up to me after the cabaret tonight and I knew right then I could do anything I wanted. She told me that her room-mate was going to be spending the night with Pierre in his room. How much bigger a green light can you get than that?'

'Might have been making conversation.'

'She wanted me,' said Gilles a little irritably. He didn't like the idea that anyone doubted his attractiveness, even if it was only Axel and Axel hardly counted.

'And you didn't want her,' Axel responded. 'Big deal. We all meet women who are more interested in us than we are in them.' He shuddered as he remembered Sonia and her big cow eyes searching for the truth in his as he endured their daily chess tutorials.

'But she was exactly my type,' Gilles continued. 'Long hair, long legs, big . . .' He made the shape of a pair of huge knockers in the air with his hands. Axel couldn't see, of course. It was still dark. 'Something has happened to me,' Gilles whispered. 'I don't want casual sex any more. I can see just how meaningless my existence really is.'

'I could have told you that weeks ago,' said Axel.

'I think I may have fallen in love.'

Axel turned on his bedside lamp to get a good look at Gilles' face. 'You are joking, aren't you?'

'I'm not. It's one of the English girls who arrived on Tuesday. She's been coming to me for tennis lessons. She's just so beautiful. I see her in her tennis skirt and I just want to put my hand . . .'

'You haven't undergone a real epiphany, then,' Axel snorted, guessing what was going to come next.

'I just want to put my hand in her hand,' said Gilles unexpectedly.

'And lead her round the back of the tennis shed.'

'It's not like that,' Gilles protested. 'It's making me feel really strange. A bit unhappy. It didn't even cheer me up that Delphine has split up with Xavier.'

'She has?'

'He wanted anal sex,' said Gilles matter-of-factly. 'It didn't bother him so much that she said no. But when Pierre told Xavier she'd let me have a go at it two weeks into the season . . .'

Axel gritted his teeth at the thought.

'What can I do?' Gilles asked.

'Tell Xavier it isn't true,' Axel suggested.

'What are you talking about?'

'The anal sex.'

'Jesus, Axel. I'm talking about true love here and all you can think about is giving it up the bum.'

'You were the one who brought that up.'

'Did I?' Gilles was miles away in his romantic dream-world. 'I can't remember. I can't think about anything except her. When am I going to stop feeling like this? Is this really love?'

'It'll pass,' said Axel, somewhat bitterly.

'Axel,' Gilles began cautiously, 'how did you know you were in love with what's-her-name? The one back in Paris.'

'With Natalie?'

'Yeah. Tell me about it.'

'You're always telling me to forget about it,' said Axel.

'Well, tonight I'm not. I need your help, man. I need to compare what happened to you with what's happening to me right now. I need to make sure I'm not going to end up like you are. All sad and lonely . . .'

Axel shook his head. 'I'm definitely not telling you now.'

'Please, man. Just tell me,' Gilles insisted.

'I can't tell you . . .'

'Come on, man.'

'You wouldn't understand.'

'Give me credit for some sensitivity, would you, Axel? Everyone just assumes I'm a meathead with no feelings but . . .' He sighed again.

'OK.' Axel took a deep breath and began. 'You have to promise not to laugh at me.'

'Axel, have I ever laughed at you?'

'Three times today,' Axel pointed out.

'I swear I will never laugh at you again.'

Axel knew that was an empty promise. But even though he also knew that everything he was about to say would at some point be used against him, Axel had a need to unburden himself. He wanted to tell the story of Axel and Natalie out loud one more time. It was as though telling it was a way of keeping it real. Somewhere, in a parallel universe, Axel Radanne and Natalie Leclerc were meeting and falling in love again and again and again.

'How did you know you were in love with her?'

'I knew I was in love with Natalie because the rest of the world went soft focus,' Axel began. 'It was as though my life had become a film and Natalie was the heroine. Every scene of my life played in reference to her from that moment onwards. I was just a supporting character in her story. And the strange thing was, I didn't care.

'When Natalie was with me, everything seemed so much better. The filthy place where I lived became charmingly shabby. The concierge who made my life a misery seemed like an altogether friendlier witch. Natalie's presence cast a soft glow over everything. Everything was blurred and yet somehow sharper. I'd never experienced it before and I haven't felt it since.'

Gilles nodded. 'That's exactly what it feels like!' he said.

Axel smiled indulgently.

'But I don't want to be in some pissy Meg Ryan film.'

Axel stopped smiling. He hadn't exactly been thinking of a Meg Ryan film himself. Gilles had ruined his romantic image. 'Like I said,' Axel told him, 'it'll pass. It always does. By the end of this girl's stay you'll have persuaded her to sleep with you and you'll be bored and on the hunt again.'

'Do you think so?' Gilles looked at his room-mate as though Axel had just told him the most reassuring truth in the world in that last sentence.

'I do.'

'It's so good to hear you say that. She will give it up to me eventually, won't she? And then I'll be cured of this . . . this thing.'

'Inevitably.' Axel sighed.

'You know, Axel,' Gilles concluded, 'I don't care what everyone else says about you. I think you're a good guy. *Bonne nuit, mon ami.*'

'*Bonne nuit.* Hey, hang on . . .!'

The thought that love wouldn't last was enough to send Gilles off to sleep like an innocent child. But Axel had no chance whatsoever of having any more sweet dreams that night. What did everybody else say about him? What? He felt an irritating need to know.

Not that he should have cared. After all, apart from the grudging affection he occasionally felt for Gilles (in the way that one cares for a dumb animal) there was no love lost between Axel and his fellow Club Aegee reps. He had studied medicine at the best university in Paris, for heaven's sake. But he wasn't just a scientist. He knew about politics and philosophy. He knew that Seneca wasn't something you took for constipation. What the likes of Pierre and Celine and Xavier had to say about him was hardly likely to come from a well-thought-out philosophical standpoint . . .

But maybe what they thought was the answer. It was occurring to Axel on an increasingly frequent basis that those things that made him different from other men were perhaps what made him unattractive to Natalie. He had no doubt that were Ed Wiseman a rep at Club Aegee he would be one of the most popular guys on the team. As painful as it was, perhaps it was time that Axel found out why Ed was a good guy and everyone thought he was a prat.

'What do they say about me?' Axel asked Gilles. But Gilles was sleeping. He answered with a snore.

40

The bad weather seemed like a distant memory when Rachel awoke on Sunday morning. The soundtrack to her awakening, however, had become disturbingly familiar. Yaslyn was vomiting again.

'Christ,' she muttered as she staggered out of the bathroom, wiping her mouth on a clean white towel. 'Never mix raki and Babycham.'

Raki and Babycham had been Yasser's idea of a sophisticated cocktail. After Gilles said that he needed to get some matches and Carrie Ann tried to use the opportunity to end the evening's revelry early, Yasser had insisted on just one more drink before bedtime. Rachel didn't want one. Carrie Ann didn't want one. But Yaslyn did. And since Yaslyn was such a force of nature, it seemed that her one vote vetoed both of theirs. Especially since Yaslyn played the killjoy card.

'This is the last time we'll all be single together,' she said to Rachel. 'You can go to bed early when you're married.'

At least she was paying for it now, Rachel thought. Chucking up Yasser's Turkish hospitality all over the bathroom. Not that there was much joy to be had in that. Hearing Yaslyn vomiting made Rachel acutely aware of just how unstable her own digestive system was feeling that morning as well. Babycham and raki. My God.

'Is she throwing up again?' Carrie Ann groaned from her bed beneath the air conditioner.

'Uh-huh.' Rachel nodded.

'Serves her right.'

Relations between Carrie Ann and Yaslyn were understandably frosty that morning. Rachel shivered at the memory of the walk back to the room. When Carrie Ann said that Gilles should walk them all home, Yaslyn understood at once that she was being chaperoned and she didn't like the idea at all. As soon as they left Yasser's room, Rachel, who had been monosyllabic for much of the drinking session, was chatty again. So was Carrie Ann. It was obvious they were mightily relieved.

'You could have left at any time, you know,' Yaslyn pointed out. 'I'm perfectly able to look after myself.'

'Not when you're drunk. We didn't want to leave you on your own with those guys. Gilles is a creep,' said Carrie Ann.

'I bet he sleeps with a different girl every week,' said Rachel.

'Every night,' corrected Carrie Ann.

'And I wasn't necessarily going to be the next one,' Yaslyn pointed out.

'You certainly gave him the impression you were gagging for it,' said Carrie Ann in an offhand manner. 'With your legs wrapped around his and your tongue practically down his throat every time he talked to you.'

Yaslyn held her hand up in protest. 'Fuck off,' she said to her room-mate. 'Since when was the law passed that says you're not allowed to flirt with a man?'

'I don't know why you need to flirt with the likes of him when you've got a fantastic boyfriend back home. I don't know how Euan puts up with it. Do you have to try to seduce every man who crosses your path?'

'I don't have to *try*,' Yaslyn told her. 'I'm just being myself.'

'Yeah, right.'

'That's a problem for you, isn't it, Carrie Ann? The way I can get on with guys.'

'It's your problem, Yaslyn. If you're really so insecure that you need to know every man you meet would go to bed with you . . .'

'What's wrong with being friendly? You're so fucked up about Greg that you don't even know how to be civil to a man any more. You act like you're too good to talk to the likes of Yasser and that Norwegian bloke downstairs. Well, wake up, Carrie Ann. There are millions of divorced women out there and your *sunny* countenance hardly sets you apart from the rest of them.'

'Oh dear.' Carrie Ann pulled a face of mock horror. 'You think that's lost me my chance with Yasser and Morten? Feels like I'm really missing out.'

Carrie Ann brought her nightshirt out from beneath her pillow and started to change out of her still-damp clubbing clothes. She had her T-shirt over her head when Yaslyn fired her next shot.

'You know what, I wasn't sure I wanted to come away with you this week, Carrie Ann. I thought, can I really stand a whole week with Miss Havisham, moaning about the one that got away? But Rachel insisted that you'd loosen up once we got on the aeroplane. She said you'd soon be back to being a laugh again. Well, she was wrong. You've been a miserable pain in the arse all week, moping about like you're the only woman on earth who ever lost a man to someone else. You're like a black widow spider. You don't want anyone else to have any fun because you're not. You haven't loosened up at all.'

'Well, at least I'm not loose in all the wrong ways,' Carrie Ann retorted. 'What do you think your *flirting* looks like, Yaslyn? It may have been cute once but the way you fawn all over guys like Gilles is just starting to look old. Next to girls like the Swedish Lesbian Twins, Yaslyn, you look just as old and desperate as I do. Only I'm not still trying to work it. You need to find some dignity.'

'Dignity? *You* need to find some fucking Botox.'

'What? Like you did?'

'Who told you I had Botox? That's a lie.'

Rachel was the only other person who knew Yaslyn had submitted to the needle after Crispin the model agency booker freaked out about Yaslyn having a wrinkle that no one without a magnifying lens could see.

'She just guessed,' Rachel pleaded. 'Because you look so good and rested.'

'Well, I may have had Botox,' Yaslyn bristled. 'So what? One lousy shot of Botox. That's got to be better than letting it all hang out as soon as you hit thirty. It's better than having a fucking moustache.'

'Yaslyn!' Rachel could see the argument escalating into full-scale war.

But Carrie Ann was surprisingly sanguine. She just raised her hands as though in surrender and headed for the bathroom.

'Don't take for ever in there!' Yaslyn shrieked after her. 'You always take ages!'

'Got a lot of imperfections to deal with,' Carrie Ann shouted back.

It had defused the moment.

Rachel was pathetically grateful. She hated conflict. Really hated it. Hearing raised voices could make her physically ill.

'What time is it?' Carrie Ann groaned.

'Eight in the morning,' said Rachel.

'Jeez . . .'

'Fantastic,' said Yaslyn from her new position face down in her pillows. 'Still early. Someone should go and save those sunbeds in the shade.'

It fell to Rachel, of course. She gathered up their three beach towels and set out for the pool like a soldier on a top-secret bombing mission. She scuttled through the gardens, praying that it was early enough to avoid the enemy. Her heart slowed a little closer to normal speed when she saw that the poolside was deserted but for the guy whose job it was to strain dead leaves and bugs from the surface of the water. (He didn't always do such a great job. The dragonfly that had rested so briefly on Sally's shoulder had ended up in a hapless swimmer's mouth the following morning.)

Rachel spotted the three coveted sunbeds in the shadow of the pool bar's stripy canopy. All three were empty of towels or any other signs of occupation.

Rachel increased her speed just a notch to get to her target. She flung down her beach towels on the first bed. She collapsed with grateful relief on to the second.

Together with Carrie Ann and Yaslyn's bickering, sunbed bagging was another part of this holiday that she definitely would not miss when she was back in London. Each morning she had felt like an England player taking a penalty kick against France in the World Cup, such was the pressure to secure the territory by the pool before the French trio did.

Just one more day of this, she thought with relief as she spread their beach towels out properly. She arranged the contents of her beach bag on two of them to anchor them down. Suntan lotion on one, book on another. Then she took her place in the middle of the three beds and waited for the time when Yaslyn or Carrie Ann would come to relieve her so that she could grab some breakfast.

It was a bloody boring wait. Rachel got out her mobile phone, turned it on and checked for messages. Nothing. It was too early to try ringing Patrick in Dublin. She put the phone back in her bag. But Rachel still felt her dialling finger itching. Perhaps it wasn't too early to call him. He would have turned his phone off before he went to bed. In which case she wouldn't have to worry about waking him. It wouldn't hurt to give him a ring and listen to his answer-machine message. Just to hear his voice . . . Rachel reached into her bag but, just as she did so, the phone rang of its own accord. She was so shocked she jerked her hand back out of her bag as though she had just dived in there and felt the soft furry body of a pointy-toothed rat.

'Bloody hell.' She recovered herself and answered the call.

'Rachel.' It was Helen. 'Were you swearing? You sound shocked. What on earth are you doing out there?'

'Nothing,' said Rachel. 'Honestly. The ring just took me by surprise.'

'Really?'

After policemen and customs officers, Helen Hewson was the person most likely to make Rachel feel as though she were up to something when she wasn't.

'Is everything OK?' Rachel ventured. Helen was ringing at half past seven in the morning her time.

'Well, it is now . . .'

That ominous phrase.

'What do you mean?' Rachel asked slowly.

'I'm sure it was just an oversight on your part, dear. I know you've been terribly busy with all the other arrangements. And of course, you've been away enjoying yourself with your friends all week and probably haven't given very much thought to how things are progressing here.'

'Helen, what's happened? How are things progressing?'

'It's the caterers.'

'I paid the deposit before I left. I wrote the cheque out on Wednesday and sent it by first-class post. They should have got it on Thursday morning.'

'Well, I expect we've lost that now.' Helen sighed.

'Lost what?'

'The deposit. I suppose they're within their rights to

keep it whether it was their mistake or not. Since you put your signature on the order form.'

'Helen . . .' Rachel tried hard to keep the exasperation out of her voice. 'Who's made a mistake? What mistake are you talking about? Exactly what have you said to whom?'

'I had them fax the menu over to Jennifer's office so I could have a look at it and she dropped it in here on her way home from work. I can't believe you didn't notice, dear. The problem simply leapt out at me. It was obvious.'

Rachel counted to ten. 'What problem?'

It was probably just a spelling mistake, Rachel told herself. An ex-secondary school teacher of the old-fashioned kind, Helen was a stickler for good grammar and spelling. She frequently pointed out the inappropriate use of apostrophes to hapless market-stall owners – 'There's no excuse for it,' she said – and then wondered why there was inevitably a mouldy fruit at the bottom of her paper bag full of apples.

There was clearly no excuse for whatever was riling Helen that morning either.

'I'm sure there isn't,' Rachel agreed. 'But could you please tell me what there's no excuse for?'

'I don't know how they have the gall to charge thirty pounds a head when there isn't a scrap of it on the menu. Not a scrap. Not so much as a smoked salmon canapé. Just who do they think they're kidding? That's what I want to know. Thirty pounds a head for mushroom risotto and a tian of avocado? They must think we were born yesterday. You could put that lot together for three pounds fifty and have three pounds twenty-five left over.'

'Helen,' Rachel interrupted. 'Tian of avocado was what we asked for. And mushroom risotto. That was the menu we chose.'

'You mean you *chose* for there to be no meat on the menu?'

'Yes.' Rachel laughed with relief. 'Of course there's no meat. Patrick and I are vegetarians, remember? We specifically chose a vegetarian catering company. They were acting exactly as we instructed, Helen. Everything is fine.'

'Patrick isn't a vegetarian,' Helen protested.

'He hasn't eaten any meat for the past three years.'

'I've seen him eat chicken.'

'Not since the year 2000 you haven't.'

'Rubbish. He's just saying that to please you, dear. I know you're into this eco-warrior business, which is all very commendable, I'm sure . . . but Patrick is a real man and a real man can't survive on tian of avocado.'

'We chose a vegetarian menu,' Rachel persisted. 'Together. Me and Patrick.'

'You can't choose a vegetarian menu for a wedding!' Helen exclaimed. 'People will expect to be fed properly. You're going to send them home feeling hungry! Anyway, I've sorted it out for you. I called the caterers who were booked for Mrs Clarke's daughter's wedding before the terrible accident. It's very short notice but luckily they've just had a cancellation. Anyway, they suggested roast lamb, which is nice for the older people who don't have all their own teeth, and a fish course for the vegetarians . . .'

'Vegetarians don't eat fish!' Rachel exclaimed.

'The only difficult choice was deciding whether to have tiramisu or pavlova for pudding. I went for pavlova. Not everybody likes tiramisu. But the pavlova's got raspberries and . . .'

'Helen, stop! You can't . . .'

'What's that, dear? You know, the line to Turkey really is quite terrible. I can't hear anything except crackle. Are you still there, dear? I really can't hear you. Oh well. I'll speak to you later I expect.'

Helen made a swift telephonic getaway.

Rachel jumped up from her sunbed and jabbed last number redial.

'Helen, you can't . . .' she began as soon as the ringing stopped.

'The mobile phone you are calling may be switched off,' announced the clipped tones of Ms Orange Network.

'Rubbish,' said Rachel. Helen never turned her mobile phone off if Patrick was out of the country.

Rachel dialled again.

'The mobile phone you are calling . . .'

'Aaaarggh.'

Rachel would have to call Helen's home number. Which meant going back to the room to find her diary with the number scribbled in the back of it. Which meant leaving the precious sunbeds unattended . . .

That morning, Marcus was the first person on the beach again. He bumped into Xavier in the queue for eggs at breakfast and managed to persuade the water-sports instructor, against strict Club Aegee policy, to let him take a windsurf out before the water-sports hut was manned.

'Hey, man, I trust you not to go drowning yourself,' said Xavier, throwing him the keys to the hut before returning to the table where the Swedish Lesbian Twins awaited his bronzed, beach-blond appearance.

Xavier usually helped guests to carry their wind-surfs down to the edge of the water, but that morning Marcus had to do the work on his own. He didn't notice the weight of the board at all. His body was still infused with adrenalin from the previous night. There had been no further argument. When Sally returned from the bar with her bottle of water, Marcus was already pretending to be asleep. It had seemed like the best idea at the time. What were they going to say to each other if he did stay up and wait for her? Worse still, what was he going to hear?

Marcus waded out into the water, pulling his board along with him, until the waves reached waist height. The sea was a little choppier today. The wind a little faster. Marcus couldn't wait until he was on his board and concentrating on following that wind. He wanted the churning thoughts in his brain to stop just for a moment. But that morning, even when he was standing on his board and flashing through the waves like a fisherman's float being reeled in, Marcus couldn't clear his mind.

The situation between him and Sally was clearly worse than he had dared imagine. Before last night's argument, he had caught her looking at him dispassionately, sure. Sometimes he'd even seen her regard him with pity. But he had never seen her look so scared and angry and disgusted. Disgusted. The realisation that Marcus disgusted his wife made him feel physically ill. And there could be no hiding that this was the way she felt any more. It was as though they had peeled back a bandage and discovered gangrene underneath. They could cover the wound back up again but now that they knew what was beneath . . . It was a case of act now or face total amputation.

What was he going to do? Marcus had never loved anyone but Sally. As soon as she came into his life he realised that every girl who had passed through his bed before her was just a place-holder for the day when Sally Tyrrell would arrive. Knowing that Sally loved him had made him feel stronger, better than before. And even when it became clear that she wasn't going to follow him to India or Thailand and set up a beach bar in paradise, it didn't really matter. Paradise without Sally wouldn't have been such a paradise anyway.

And now it seemed she had fallen out of love with him. What had he done wrong? Had he been ambitious enough for her? He remembered the

Christmas party her company had thrown the previous year; the hurried and almost embarrassed way she had introduced him and muttered his job title for the benefit of the twenty-four-year-old office wunderkind who had already been performing the same role at Sally's firm for six months.

Had he listened to Sally properly when she talked about her work? Marcus found Sally's brand of consultancy about as interesting as his own (that is, almost as much fun as watching condensation form on the inside of a window) but she took her job very seriously. Marcus should at least try to remember the name of some of the businesses she consulted for, or nod wisely when she talked about office politics.

Or was it because he had let himself get out of shape? Marcus looked down at his stomach as he battled to hold his board's sail upright. After his first windsurfing session his stomach muscles had felt as though they had been tied between two donkeys who were racing in opposite directions. But within three short days he had felt a definite improvement. If his muscles still responded that quickly to a bit of effort, he could start going to the gym again when they got back to Surrey and be in better shape than Gilles or Xavier by the end of three months.

If lack of ambition, interest and muscle tone were really his flaws, thought Marcus, then at least they could all be rectified. He could be her perfect man again.

The onshore wind picked up. Marcus found himself heading towards a larger wave than he had ever tackled before on a windsurf. He tensed his stomach muscles, his shoulders. His forearms became like steel as they held the sail upright in front of him. The nose of his board hit the wave and went aerial. Without even thinking the move through, Marcus had executed his first jump. The board smacked down on the other side of the wave with Marcus still standing proud, as though he had been windsurfing since the sport was invented.

'Go, Marcus!' came a shout from the beach.

When he brought the board in, Xavier and the Swedish Lesbian Twins were standing at the water's edge. Xavier was clapping and whooping. The girls giggled behind their hands and regarded Marcus shyly, as though he were every bit as gorgeous as their water-sports rep friend.

'Man,' said Xavier. 'That jump was just ludicrous! Amazing. I was all ready to have to head out there and rescue you when you took the fall but . . . Man . . .' Xavier punched Marcus playfully on the arm. 'You took it like a pro, man. You are magnificent. You're my hero. Have you met Charlotte and Marie?'

The Swedish Lesbian Twins looked up at Marcus from beneath lowered lashes, as shy as the schoolgirls they had only recently finished being.

'We think you look like James Bond,' they said in unison.

'Pussy Galore, man.' Xavier grinned as he nudged Marcus subtly in the ribs.

He still had it, Marcus convinced himself. The Swedish twins proved that to him. Marcus towel-dried his hair with studied nonchalance. He felt sexy again. Full of potential. He was going to give his marriage one more try.

42

Sally had been waiting for this opportunity for most of the week. Carrie Ann was alone by the pool, engrossed in her paperback. There was an empty sunbed to the side of her. With Marcus windsurfing down on the beach, Sally knew she had the best part of an hour to start the conversation she needed.

'Hi.' She sat down on the empty sunbed.

'Hi,' said Carrie Ann. She smiled in a fairly neutral way then went straight back to her book. There was no precedent for these two women to chat. In fact, Carrie Ann rather got the impression that she bored the pinched-looking divorcee-in-waiting.

'Good book?' Sally asked. 'Better than anal sex in South Carolina?'

'Well . . . It's a bit unbelievable really,' said Carrie Ann.

'How so?'

'The heroine gets back with her ex. Exes, eh?' Carrie Ann breathed.

'Impossible to get to our age without having a couple.'

'If only it were legal to shoot them,' Carrie Ann mused.

'You just got divorced, didn't you?'

Carrie Ann nodded. 'How could you tell? This is my divorce week, apparently. As well as Rachel's hen week. Odd idea, don't you think? Like having a christening and a funeral . . .'

'How's it been so far?'

'Better than my hen night was.'

'Only without so much to look forward to at the end of it,' Sally ventured.

'On the contrary,' said Carrie Ann. 'I may not get to wear a big white dress next weekend and have everybody buy me presents for my kitchen, but at least I don't have to spend the rest of my life with a man whose idea of oral sex is biting me on the bottom through my knickers.'

'That sounds like good sex to me.' Sally sighed.

They were silent for a moment, regarding the action by the pool in the calm before the 11.30 rumpus.

One of the Go-Go girls had decided to take a dip. She sauntered to the edge of the pool with the confidence of a catwalk model and struck a pose that suggested she was about to make an Olympic medal-winning dive into the water. Both Carrie Ann and Sally were transfixed. As, of course, was every man in the village.

'Oh my God,' said Sally, realising just as Carrie Ann did that the girl was about to do her picture-perfect plunge into the shallow end of the pool.

'She'll crack her head open!' said Carrie Ann.

But she didn't. The girl squinted down into the water and straightened up from her preparatory lunge with a little frown. Noticing just in time that she was about to go head first into three feet of water, she instead sat down on the edge of the pool and slipped in feet first, as though that was what she had intended all along.

'Thank goodness for that,' said Sally, before giving in to the laughter that told Carrie Ann she wouldn't have been so disappointed to see blood. Fortunately, Carrie Ann was utterly of the same mind. 'I'm so glad she's stupid as well as beautiful.'

'What do you mean?' said Carrie Ann. 'That just makes her even closer to every man's perfect girl!'

'Christ,' Sally muttered. 'Women really are women's worst enemies, don't you think?'

Carrie Ann nodded, remembering Mairi.

'So.' Sally steeled herself to ask the big question.

'Yes?' Carrie Ann asked.

'How do you go about getting a divorce?'

'What do you mean?'

'Where do you start when you decide you need to get one?'

'Do *you* want to know?' Carrie Ann asked pointedly.

'Not for me,' said Sally unconvincingly. 'For my friend. She's in a similar situation to you, you see. Her husband wants to be with someone else.'

'In that case, she needs to get on to a lawyer double quick. I won't recommend mine, since he might as well have been working for my husband. But if she's the injured party, she needs to start claiming those assets now. If, on the other hand, she's really the one who has been having an affair . . .'

'She hasn't,' said Sally hurriedly. 'And neither has he. I don't think.'

'Then I would advise them to try to patch it up first.' Carrie Ann looked at Sally closely. 'If they're both the kind of people I imagine they are. All marriages have their down times. Sometimes those down times seem to last for years. But if you loved each other enough to be so serious about your commitment that you wanted to get married in the first place in a society that hardly demands it any more, then you must have had something really special.'

'You think that's the truth?'

'Yes. Yes, I do. And if you work at it you might be able to get it back again.'

Sally shook her head without realising she was doing it.

'You don't think it's better to go for the fastest, most painless ending possible?'

'No,' said Carrie Ann. 'I don't. Because it's never painless. A marriage might feel like a life sentence, but divorce is an execution.

'I can't help thinking that the divorce rate we have isn't a positive sign of personal freedom at all,' Carrie Ann continued. 'It's a sign that everybody wants something for nothing. We want perfect lives without having to work at them just like the magazines promise we can have perfect bodies without going to the gym. It isn't possible. There's no magic potion to get rid of cellulite. There's no magic potion to keep a marriage as exciting as it was at the start. But if you work at it you might be surprised at what you can claw back. Love is a muscle. You can make it stronger. That's what I think.'

The barman at the pool bar cranked up the volume on a funky Turkish track. Delphine and her Go-Go girls appeared beside the pool wearing bikinis and black bowler hats. Delphine began the shouting.

'Ladies and gentlemen! It's time to get funky!'

'Shit. It's eleven thirty already,' said Sally.

'Chess class,' said Carrie Ann, gathering up her stuff.

'Me too,' said Sally. 'I mean, I'm washing my hair. Anything but this!'

The women parted at the poolside. Carrie Ann glanced back to see Sally wandering slowly through the gardens. She was a nice woman. Far nicer than Carrie Ann had expected when Sally had sat scowling at the back of the bus from the airport, reminding her of the way Greg had looked when Carrie Ann had dragged him to Crete. Sally wasn't Greg, though. Sometimes Carrie Ann thought Greg had married her with the sole intention of ruining her life, not because he loved her. There had never been any chance that Greg would meet Carrie Ann halfway to save their marriage because there was so little love on his side to save.

The only love muscle Greg was interested in was the one Mairi had gone down on in Carrie Ann's marital bedroom. Sally didn't strike Carrie Ann as the sort of woman who would line up a new lover before she had left her husband, though.

Carrie Ann hoped she had said the right thing.

43

When Carrie Ann arrived at the chess room, Axel was already waiting for her in front of the board.

''Allo, Carrie Ann.'

She liked the way he said her name. She liked the way he said anything. Anything said in a French accent immediately sounds sexier, she thought. It sounds as though it is being murmured from beneath the duvet.

'Hi, Axel,' she said, wondering whether her accent did anything for him in return.

Probably not.

'Shall we begin?' he asked.

She nodded and sat down opposite him at the table. He let her start. She'd come a long way with just a couple of days' instruction. She no longer laid herself open to attack within three moves, that was sure. This time, she even managed to remove a couple of Axel's pieces from the board before he said the dreaded 'Checkmate'.

Nevertheless, Carrie Ann's automatic reaction to her defeat was to mutter, 'I'm so stupid.'

'You are not stupid,' said Axel, as he set the pieces up again. 'You are much better than you were when we first met. You just need more experience.'

'No. I am stupid,' said Carrie Ann. 'Trust me.'

She knew a little about Axel from their chats before

and after each tutorial, and it was obvious that he had a brain the size of Boulogne. He had told her about his time in Paris, studying medicine but using his spare time to read philosophy. The French had great respect for philosophers, he told her. In fact, there were philosophers working (or should that be thinking) in France at the moment who were considered by some to be the great sex symbols of the age. Axel thought that was rather frivolous, of course.

Axel didn't tell Carrie Ann that he didn't think he would be finishing his degree. He continued to let her think he was taking a sabbatical. She, for her part, didn't tell him the real reason she had never even started one. It was easier to have him think that she was too stupid to get into university rather than hear the truth, which was that she had given up a place at university to marry a man whose greatest intellectual achievement was memorising all the winners of the Eurovision Song Contest from 1970 onwards for a pub quiz challenge. Yes, not taking up her place at university to marry Greg definitely made her more stupid than someone who couldn't get the necessary A-levels to go in the first place.

'Lunch-time,' Axel announced, when they finished their second brief game.

'Can I come again tomorrow?' Carrie Ann ventured.

'Tomorrow is my day off.'

'And I go home the day after that. Oh well. I guess I'll just have to remember what you taught me and try to find someone I can play against back in London.'

Axel nodded. Carrie Ann was disappointed. She realised that she had been hoping he would make an exception for her, squeeze in one more lesson before the end of her holiday. But he didn't suggest it. Ah well. Just because he worked in a holiday village didn't mean that Axel wasn't entitled to guard his days off with the intensity Carrie Ann felt for her own time away from the office back in London.

'You know, Axel,' she told him then, 'I've really enjoyed our chess lessons. It's been great to do something different. Stretch my brain a bit. In fact, I'd say it's been the best part of the week.'

'*Mon plaisir*,' said Axel.

'Well,' said Carrie Ann, 'I'd better go and make the most of the weather. Not going to get much sunshine back home. Er, good luck with everything you do,' she added. 'Good luck with your studies when you go back to them. I'm sure you'll make a fantastic surgeon one day.'

'Thank you.' Axel nodded.

''Bye.' Carrie Ann lingered by the door.

There was a moment when she thought Axel might be about to say something. But then his mouth settled into one of those straight-line smiles that signal the end of the conversation.

'Thanks,' Carrie Ann said one more time before she scuttled away in the direction of the restaurant.

44

For their own separate reasons, by lunch-time Sally and Marcus had both decided that it was best not to talk about the previous evening's row. They met for the first time that day in the lunch queue. Sally had saved Marcus a place.

'Good windsurfing lesson?' she asked lightly.

'Yeah,' said Marcus. He didn't tell her about the jump.

Charlotte and Marie passed the Merchants on their way out of the restaurant.

'Hey, Marcus,' they chimed.

'You've got some new friends,' Sally observed.

'They're always hanging out with Xavier down on the beach,' said Marcus casually. But inside he felt anything but casual about the Swedish Lesbian Twins' attentions. It wasn't that he fancied either of them. But if they fancied him . . . If perhaps their interest would help remind Sally that he wasn't such an unfanciable lump after all . . .

Unfortunately, Sally had her own Club Aegee admirer to cancel out Marcus's advantage on that front.

Gilles tapped Marcus on the top of his head with a tennis racket as he squeezed into the lunch queue beside them.

'You coming to play this afternoon?' he asked Sally.

'It's too hot,' she said.

'You should come down to the beach,' Marcus told her. 'There's a nice breeze there.'

'I thought I might do some souvenir shopping,' said Sally. So both Marcus and Gilles were disappointed. Gilles turned his attention to Paulette instead. She would be only too happy to squeeze in an extra tennis lesson that afternoon.

The Merchants ate lunch with more conversation than they had managed all week. Marcus told Sally some of the things Xavier had told him about weather conditions down on the beach. Apparently there were some weeks when Xavier could guarantee that everyone who wanted to learn to windsurf would leave Club Aegee an expert. Other weeks, when there was a relentless offshore wind, it might be all but impossible to turn amateurs into competent surfers.

'I think I'm going to look up a windsurfing club when we get home,' Marcus concluded.

'Good,' said Sally. 'I'm glad you've found something that inspires you.'

There was a lull in the conversation for a moment. Their eyes met.

'Sally . . .' Marcus began.

They both drew breath anxiously.

'Cheese!'

They were interrupted by the Club Aegee photographer who had taken their picture with Gilles at dinner on that second night in Turkey. Marcus had bought that photo even though he had his eyes shut in the shot.

Marcus and Sally dutifully lowered their cutlery and

smiled. By the time the photographer had finished, Paulette and Gilles had arrived to take the remaining spare seats at the Merchants' table.

'I wish you guys were staying here for two weeks,' Paulette told them. 'When you leave on Tuesday, I'll have lost all my friends here. Gilles, you will have to console me!'

Paulette draped herself over Gilles' broad shoulders.

Marcus and Sally both found themselves laughing. Both knowing it was less about Paulette's antics than a huge sense of relief.

On the other side of the restaurant terrace, Carrie Ann joined Rachel and Yaslyn. Rachel was staring down at her plate, deep in thought.

'Helen has cancelled the vegetarian caterers,' Yaslyn explained. 'And now Rachel can't get hold of her to tell her to change the arrangements back.'

'Have you told Patrick what his mother's been doing?' Carrie Ann asked.

'Every time I get hold of him he's in a pub,' Rachel cried. 'He can't hear what I'm saying because of the noise in the background and, in any case, it sounds like he's too drunk to do anything about it if he could hear what the problem was.'

'Then sort it out yourself,' said Yaslyn. 'Call the original caterers, put them back on the job and deal with Helen when you get back to London. Except that you'll never deal with Helen. Just like you never dealt with those sunbed-stealing witches.'

'Why should I always be the one that has to deal with them?'

'No one wants to get into a row on holiday,' Carrie Ann interrupted.

'I'm just going to be glad to get home at this rate,' Rachel sobbed over her vegetarian moussaka.

'You're not the only one,' said Yaslyn under her breath.

Carrie Ann poured herself another glass of all-inclusive rosé and made it drinkable with the addition of a few ice cubes. How much longer did they have to go before they caught that plane back home?

'Carrie Ann!' Morten waved at her from several tables away. Carrie Ann pretended not to see him.

'Dive, dive!' joked Yaslyn, as Carrie Ann ducked under the tablecloth.

'Tying my shoelace,' she explained when she surfaced to discover that Morten was standing right in front of her.

'Your shoelace is often coming undone,' Morten commented. 'Every time I see you, you are going under the table like this.'

'We'll see you by the pool, Caz.'

Once again Rachel and Yaslyn abandoned her.

'I will stay here with you while you are eating,' said Morten.

She had been afraid he was going to say that.

Axel saw it all from his shady table in the corner. He couldn't help but envy the Norwegian guy for his confidence. Always just marching up to women and striking up conversation. As Axel watched, Carrie Ann smiled prettily at something that Morten had said. She had a nice smile. Axel had noticed it when they were playing chess. It was one of those smiles where the top lip stays straight and the bottom lip curves extravagantly like a perfect melon slice.

'Hey!'

Gilles slapped Axel so hard on the back that Axel spat a mouthful of beetroot salad out all over the white tablecloth.

'What are you doing over here in the shade, watching that English girl like you're some kind of stalker?'

'I was not,' Axel insisted.

'I've been watching you for ages. You can't take your eyes off her.'

'I think I must be going short-sighted,' said Axel. 'I was just trying to work out how far I can see before everything goes blurred. Do you think the club doctor can get me an eye test?'

'Stop changing the subject,' said Gilles. 'She's one of your chess students, isn't she?'

'She was. She said it was the best part of her holiday.' Axel was still astounded by that.

'What? She fancies you.'

'No.' Axel didn't think so.

'Wake up, Axel,' said Gilles. 'She wants you. Definitely.'

'She doesn't want me.'

'Take it from me. If a chess class is the highlight of a woman's holiday in this place, it isn't because she has enjoyed "stretching her brain". It's because she's enjoyed looking at you across the chessboard. Jesus. How you ever got it on with that Natalie girl is beyond me. Did she stick a poster on her forehead saying "I fancy Axel Radanne"? Have you learned nothing from me since you've been here? Are you really that blind to the signals?'

Axel shrugged.

'That Carrie Ann woman fancies you. She near as dammit said so. She's the first girl under forty who's looked at you since you got here. She's not a dog. In fact, she's quite reasonable,' Gilles added generously. 'And she's going home the day after tomorrow?'

'Yes.'

'Just in time for the penultimate-night rule.' The tennis coach grinned. 'Not only that, but you've got tomorrow off. If it's really bloody terrible you don't even have to hang around the camp avoiding her. You can go down to Bodrum. Even stay in the room reading *philosophy*,' Gilles conceded. 'It is, as the Americans say, a "no-brainer". Do it. Shag her. Get yourself laid.'

At that moment, Carrie Ann got up from the table and made her excuses to Morten. She glanced over in Axel's direction. She didn't see him but Axel shrank a little farther back into the shade just in case.

'OK.' He said it so quietly it was almost lost in his exhalation.

'What did you just say?'

'I said OK.'

Gilles looked at Axel in surprise. He hadn't really expected to be able to convince him.

Axel took a deep breath as though he had just agreed to do a skydive. 'You're right, Gilles. You are so very right. In fact, I've been thinking about it for some time now. I need to put Natalie behind me and the only way to do it is to convince myself that I can make love to another woman. Carrie Ann is as good as any woman I've met so far to start with. I'll make love to her tonight.'

'You don't have to *make love* to her,' said Gilles. 'Just give the old todger a taste of what he's been missing. Make sure it still works.'

Axel grimaced.

'Glad you've come to your senses at last,' Gilles told him, giving him another hearty slap on the back. 'Bloody glad. You have no idea . . . I've had fifty euros riding on the fact that you're not gay since the beginning of the season.'

'What?'

'Hey, don't take offence, man. It wasn't me that suggested the bet. I've been telling everybody that you're not. I mean, I wouldn't share a room with you if I thought you were, would I? But you have to admit it looks a bit strange. You're out here in Turkey, surrounded by beautiful women – beautiful women who are out to get laid – and all you do is mope around reading your poetry books. What do you expect people to think?'

'That I'm a man of integrity! That I was absolutely in love with Natalie and I am not prepared to denigrate her memory or myself by . . .'

Gilles' expression had begun to glaze over. 'Yeah, yeah.'

He picked up the book Axel had been reading that lunch-time – another book of impenetrable poetry – and absent-mindedly ripped off a corner from the title page to make a roach for his roll-up cigarette. It was a week till pay day and Gilles couldn't afford to buy any more proper fags before then. Even Paulette had been too stingy to give him more than two of hers. At this rate he would have to break into the emergency packet in his bedside table.

'Hey!' Axel snatched the book from Gilles' hand. 'That's a first edition.' Gilles gave a groan from the depths of his very being.

'And it is probably a book you got from Natalie . . .'

'Forget it,' said Axel. He let the book fall back on to the table. 'You can burn the whole thing, if you like. Tonight I will put Natalie Leclerc behind me for ever. Tonight I will sleep with Carrie Ann.'

45

'It sounds stupid now,' Carrie Ann said in a whisper. 'But I came on this holiday determined to get laid. I was determined that by the time I got back to Battersea I would be able to hold my head up and say that Greg Fisher was not the last man I slept with. Or the only man . . .' Carrie Ann pondered what she had just said for a moment then added hurriedly, 'Not that I would go around telling everybody about it, of course. It was just going to be my secret. My special secret that stopped me from feeling such a mug.'

'Your secret's safe with me,' said Rachel.

'Yeah, but only because there's not much chance of you having anything to keep quiet.' Carrie Ann sighed. 'I can't believe we picked the only Club Aegee resort in the world where everyone is getting less sex than I get back home. Choosing between the single men here has been like choosing between a smear test and a rectal examination. You avoid them both but can't help thinking you should have had one. And I don't want to go back to England thinking I should have had one . . .'

Rachel frowned as she tried to work out the analogy.

'I mean, all I'm after is a casual shag to break the ice. I haven't slept with anybody for the past two years and the longer it goes on, the more I think that I'll never pluck up the courage to take my clothes off in front of a man again. I'm rapidly becoming a born-again virgin. Do you think perhaps I'm being too picky?'

Morten had just hauled himself out on to the side of the pool. Rachel got another glimpse of his Speedos and assured Carrie Ann that she hadn't been too picky at all.

'What about a rep?' suggested Yaslyn. Both Rachel and Carrie Ann had assumed that she was asleep beneath her paperback.

'Are you joking? Do you know how many girls they sleep with every season? I overheard one of them in the laundry complaining to his friend that he only managed three girls last week.'

'But if all you want is a no-strings-attached roll on the sand . . . Get yourself some girl power and use a condom. What does it matter?'

Rachel was shocked. But Carrie Ann couldn't help smiling.

'The windsurfing coach or the guy who teaches archery are both good bets, I reckon.'

'Please!' exclaimed Carrie Ann. 'That's a ridiculous idea. They're both about twelve years old. Besides, you can't get anywhere near them for panting Go-Go girls and septuagenarian Brigitte Bardot types.'

'Ah-ha! So you would give it a go if you thought you'd succeed!' said Yaslyn with a detective's perception. 'I knew it.'

'Well, who wouldn't,' said Carrie Ann. Her view of the Norwegian in his Speedos had been momentarily blocked by the vision of loveliness that was Pierre the dance instructor's bottom in his pristine white shorts as he fished a sweet wrapper out of the swimming pool.

'What about the chess rep?' asked Rachel. 'He doesn't seem like the others.'

'Axel?' said Carrie Ann.

'Yes. I think he's rather good looking.'

'He is. Never smiles, though.'

'But if he did?'

'No. He wouldn't be interested in me.'

'How do you know?' Rachel asked.

'Because whenever I went for a chess lesson he looked so bored I thought he was about to keel over and die. He could barely bring himself to say "hello" if I interrupted him reading one of his philosophy books. And that's the other thing. He's way too brainy to go for a quick shag with one of the guests. He thinks we're all stupid. He definitely thinks I'm stupid.'

'What?' Yaslyn exclaimed. 'How could anyone think you're stupid? You run your own business, for God's sake.'

'Yeah. But I don't know anything about philosophy or poetry, do I?'

'Join the majority of the population,' said Yaslyn. 'Most people couldn't even spell philosophy, and do you think that stops them getting laid?'

'Just because most people don't know anything about philosophy doesn't stop me from wishing I knew more. You know, I had a place to read psychology at university once.'

Rachel looked at her in surprise. 'Why didn't you go?'

'Why do you think?'

'Greg,' Yaslyn and Rachel chorused.

343

'Yes, Greg. I gave it up because he didn't think he could wait three years for me. That should have been the big red flag. I mean, how on earth could I have promised to love someone for the rest of my life when he couldn't promise to love me for three years, even if I did come home every weekend?'

'Patrick's mother gave up a place at university to get married too,' said Rachel. 'But she did her Open University degree while Patrick and Jennifer were at school.'

'Of course she did,' said Yaslyn. 'She's Super-woman. Have you spoken to her yet?'

'Not yet,' Rachel admitted.

'And have you spoken to Patrick?'

'Not yet,' Rachel lied.

In fact she had spoken to Patrick. Not that she could hear anything he said back. She had caught him in the middle of a drinking game again. Every time Patrick replied to one of Rachel's questions, his voice was drowned out by the roar of his mates as one of them got a complicated limerick wrong and had to down another short.

And so, once more, Rachel didn't get around to telling Patrick that his mother had ordered fish for the vegetarians and that, even as he was getting drunk in a Dublin pub, fifty fluffy white lambs were being slaughtered for the guests with false teeth. The guests with false teeth being for the most part Helen's old friends, neighbours and acquaintances. The guests that Patrick and Rachel didn't even know.

As the day passed, Rachel began to wonder whether she was making too much of a fuss. Those fluffy white lambs were bred for the slaughter, after all. The fish had probably been caught and frozen in the Atlantic before Patrick and Rachel had even set a date.

It was just one day in her life. It was meant to be the best day of her life, sure, but Rachel had always secretly hated that sentiment anyway. Far better for the best day of her life to come later, during her long happy marriage. Who wanted their wedding day to mark the beginning of a downhill slope?

And Helen didn't mean any harm by interfering with the wedding arrangements. Rachel should at least be grateful that Helen was interested in the wedding at all. As Rachel's own mother had pointed out when she called her for sympathy, Helen was probably right about the vegetarian thing. There were plenty of people on Rachel's own side of the family who would rather eat lamb than an avocado tian.

'When your gran and granddad got married,' said Rachel's mother, 'they couldn't even have a proper cake. They could only get the ingredients for one tier of fruit cake by pooling ration books from everybody in the family. The other two tiers were made of card-board. And they were the happiest couple you ever saw.'

That made Rachel feel particularly childish and selfish. It wasn't the party which mattered. It was the vows you took beforehand. There was no part of the wedding service that said 'Until your mother interferes'.

The poolside was all but empty. The village guests were retiring to their rooms to dress for dinner. That evening the theme was Moulin Rouge.

'Time to get ready,' Yaslyn announced.

'I'll have first shower,' said Carrie Ann, springing up from her sunbed.

'Don't be in that bathroom for ever!' said Yaslyn.

'Well, it takes a bit of time to bleach my moustache.'

Carrie Ann stood in front of the bathroom mirror and surveyed the damage. Her skin, usually translucent Irish pale, was tender pink with a smattering of freckles across her nose. Her hair, on which she spent half an hour with the straightening irons every morning before work, stuck out around her head like a frizzy halo. Greg had always liked her with straight hair, like Yasmin Le Bon's. Though not even sleeping with her head on an ironing board could have transformed this Celtic blonde into a sleek Persian brunette. By contrast, every other man who had ever commented on Carrie Ann's hair said they preferred it curly. She remembered a morning when she had to go to work looking like Raggedy Ann because engineers working in the road outside her house had accidentally cut through a cable and plunged three streets into darkness. That day, Carrie Ann had received a number of comments about her hair. In retrospect, all of them were positive.

'You look younger,' said her assistant Jane.

Unfortunately, Carrie Ann was equating younger with incompetent at that point. Next day, the electricity was back on and the straightening irons were back in service. The only time Carrie Ann could ever be seen with curls was on holiday or when she was ill.

Thinking about Jane her assistant inevitably brought Carrie Ann back to thinking about her office. Since opening Fisher Temps, after five years at the Office Angels bureau where she had first met Rachel, Carrie Ann had found it difficult to enjoy going on holiday. She never took more than a week off, except when she and Greg were trying to patch their marriage up. After that fortnight away, she had returned with the sure knowledge that her marriage was over to find that the office bathroom had flooded on her first day away and had been left like that because her assistant at the time didn't know how to find a plumber in the Yellow Pages.

After that, Carrie Ann had got herself an assistant with more than one GCSE (Jane) and refused to go away for longer than five working days to minimise damage. Those five days would still be spent worrying and calling back home. Last year, holidaying in southern Spain, Carrie Ann had spent a sweltering afternoon climbing to the top of a hill to get a mobile phone signal so that she could call Jane and hear the words 'Everything's OK' before the line went dead again.

This trip, Carrie Ann had been less bothered. She phoned Jane every other day and left instructions that she should send a text message if there was a crisis. No crisis warning had occurred and, unusually, Carrie Ann didn't call to probe and check that Jane wasn't hiding something from her that would have morphed into a full-blown disaster by the time she got back. For now it seemed that all their temps were working and happy. All their clients were paying on time.

But Carrie Ann was bored of the employment agency business. When she had started out on her own, every day at the office had required 110 per cent of her effort. Now contracts were renewed like clock-work. She was able to recognise within sixty seconds whether the young girl who walked in off the street to sign up would be a reliable worker or take a day off to cry if her boyfriend uttered a harsh word. It had all become so easy. And perhaps that was why she found it difficult to believe it when Yaslyn suggested that running a business was something to be proud of.

Carrie Ann needed a new challenge. She could hold her own with any businessman she had ever met on profit margins and personnel management. But she wanted to be able to understand why modern thinkers still referred to the men who'd worn togas. She wanted to know more. Meeting Axel had made her realise how much there was left to learn outside her narrow world.

It struck Carrie Ann then that what she regretted most about her marriage wasn't that she had been betrayed by her husband and best friend at all.

'What are you doing in there?' Yaslyn hammered on the bathroom door.

'I'm nearly finished,' Carrie Ann lied.

She slicked on some lip gloss and stepped out into the bedroom.

The vibrator of doom was already on the coffee table in preparation for the ritual. The Goldschlager was already poured out.

'OK,' said Yaslyn. 'We're doing it differently tonight. Instead of making a wish for ourselves, we have to make wishes for each other. Carrie Ann, you wish for Rachel. Rachel for me. And me for Carrie Ann.'

Carrie Ann's wish for Rachel was easy.

'That your wedding goes perfectly. Lamb chops or no.'

Rachel's wish for Yaslyn: 'That you get many more Marmite jobs. Or their equivalent. For more glamorous products.'

Yaslyn's for Carrie Ann: 'That you get a shag tonight!'

Rachel and Yaslyn cheered. Carrie Ann looked at her toes.

'With the man of your choice,' Yaslyn added.

'Did George Clooney arrive this afternoon?' Carrie Ann quipped.

'That Axel has similar eyes.'

'What, you mean in the way that they have the same number?'

'You'll need this,' said Rachel, tucking a big silk rose behind Carrie Ann's ear. 'It's my lucky rose. I was wearing it the night I met Patrick.'

46

On the other side of the village, Gilles did his best to help Axel accomplish his own newly stated mission by lending him his 'lucky' shirt.

'But it isn't clean,' said Axel, as he held the pale blue denim shirt at arm's length.

'Of course it isn't. It is impregnated with my pheromones,' said Gilles. 'I don't want to wash them all away.'

'Just smells like sweat to me.'

'To you, yes, because you are a man. But to a woman . . .' Gilles kissed the tips of his thumb and first two fingers. 'Irresistible. Like honey to a bee. Put it on.'

'It won't work for me,' Axel grumbled. 'Anyway, don't you need it yourself? If you're going to go for that English girl you've fallen in love with?'

'I am fortunate enough to have talent as well as luck,' said Gilles. 'I won't need my shirt tonight.'

'Which one is she? Your target,' Axel asked.

'That would be telling.'

'You know who I am going for. And you've never been exactly shy about your conquests before.'

'This one is different,' said Gilles mysteriously. 'Put the shirt on.'

Axel thought Gilles had forgotten. But Gilles wasn't

going to let him step outside without the vile rag. Axel tried not to breathe in as he slipped the stinking shirt over his head and buttoned it up to the collar.

'Not like that.' Gilles tutted. 'You look like a school kid. You need to have some buttons open. Show off your muscle tone.'

Gilles arranged the shirt like a master stylist, leaving the top four buttons undone.

'You can see all the way to my navel!' Axel complained.

'OK. Perhaps not.' Gilles buttoned him back up. 'You haven't really got the chest for it. That's better.'

'I look like an idiot.'

'If you pull that face you will. You've got to stand up tall.'

Gilles snapped his room-mate upright.

'Suck your stomach in. Not that you've got a stomach. Jeez, Axel. How'd you get so skinny? You look like a little girl. Then you've got to work on your facial expression. Smile, smile, smile. Moody might work, but only if you're James Dean. If you haven't got the physical assets to go with a frown you've got to look like you're going to be fun.'

Axel attempted a grin in front of the mirror.

'Hopeless,' said his guru. 'Lucky you've got no competition.'

'What about that Norwegian guy?'

'Morten? I'll have him seen to.'

'And Yasser?'

'Yasser has evil-eyed four new arrivals from France since last night. He can spare you Carrie Ann. Axel, this woman wants you. It's in the bag. All you have to do is show up, keep smiling and don't mention

Natalie. Oh, and don't drink too much so you're ready when the moment presents itself.'

Gilles nodded meaningfully towards Axel's groin.

Axel looked down at the front of his trousers with a grimace.

'Think of anything you have to to make it happen,' said Gilles. 'It'll come. OK?' He grabbed his after-shave off the nightstand and slapped some on to his unshaven cheeks. He never actually used aftershave when he was clean shaven, Axel had noticed.

'We're all set,' Gilles announced. 'I'll divert Yasser and the guy from Norway. You do your bit and I'll see you back here tomorrow morning.'

'You're not coming back tonight?'

'Of course not. Not if I'm lucky. But even if I'm not, I promise I won't disturb you. I'll sleep in a hammock if I have to because tonight, Axel Radanne, is going to be *your* lucky night.'

It seemed Axel's luck didn't last long. Carrie Ann was nowhere to be seen. On every other night of her holiday she had been in the bar by eight o'clock, usually with those other English girls, the shy one and the over-confident brunette. They were there, in their usual place. But no Carrie Ann.

Axel was secretly relieved. If she didn't come down to the bar, then he didn't have to try to seduce her. The idea had been becoming less and less palatable since Gilles put it into his head over lunch.

Now Axel lurked in the dark corner of the pool bar, over by the kitchen doors, holding his breath every time someone new walked in. If Carrie Ann wasn't there by 8.30 he would go back to his room and take off this stupid shirt. Every time he lifted his glass of rum and Coke to his lips he got an overwhelming blast of Gilles' manliness from his armpit. Did Gilles really think women went for that stink? The only possible explanation was that it worked on their brains like nerve gas.

The confidence that Gilles had tried to instil in Axel before they headed out for 'the kill' had quickly evaporated when Axel got to the pool bar. Though he had been at Club Aegee for almost three months now, Axel still felt like the new boy every time he ventured out of his room. The other reps were like the trendy students who had intimidated him into keeping away from the best cafés in Paris until Natalie had dragged him along with her. Axel wondered how they did it. How were they able to make small talk with strangers night after night after night? Small talk to Axel was like a foreign language. How did you even start?

Gilles had been kind enough to give Axel a few of his own best opening lines but most of them seemed to involve the phrase 'hey, babycakes', and that wasn't a combination of words Axel could ever imagine passing his lips.

'Hey, babycakes,' he had at least tried in the privacy of the bedroom he shared with his new guru.

'No, no, no,' said Gilles. 'You need to be more Barry White and less Woody Allen.'

But, oh boy, did Axel feel like something out of a Woody Allen film right then. Waiting in a dark corner like a spider for Carrie Ann to appear while confident love machine Gilles cleared the field of obstacles (from where Axel was hiding, he had seen Gilles introducing Morten to one of that day's new arrivals – an inelegant divorcee called Madeleine from Charleville in Ardennes. Which was where the romantic poet Arthur Rimbaud had grown up. Did she know that? Axel asked her during the welcome meeting. Did she hell).

Morten and Madeleine were still chatting happily, though in what language was anyone's guess. In fact, as Axel watched, Morten put his hand on Madeleine's left buttock. She swatted at him playfully then put her own hand straight on the front of Morten's trousers. Axel averted his eyes in horror.

When he could bring himself to look again, Axel saw that Gilles was now talking to Yasser. He put his arm around Yasser's shoulders and whispered something into his ear which made Yasser respond with a lewd display of hip-thrusting that left Axel in no doubt as to what had been said. Gilles and Yasser parted with much back-slapping and laughter. And with the exchange of a number of rolled-up banknotes. Was Gilles already collecting the winnings on his bet that Axel wasn't a fairy?

It really was too much. The thought of every rep in Club Aegee speculating on his sexual orientation made Axel blush the colour of his favourite beetroot salad. In every wave of laughter that emanated from the pool bar that evening, Axel heard a joke about himself. This was the way it was destined to be. Always had been. Always would be. Always the butt of everyone's jokes. No one would ever laugh *with* Axel.

Axel downed the last of his Dutch courage – the rum and Coke that Gilles had sneakily made a triple – and left his shady hiding place. He swayed out into the main part of the pool bar, and was preparing to sway right on through it. Let Gilles lose his stupid bet . . . Axel Radanne would go to his grave having loved and lost only one woman. He had a box of aspirin back in the room and he was prepared to take the lot to get rid of his pain once and for all. Perhaps Natalie would cry as they carried his coffin slowly down the street where she lived. He would let her know he forgave her in the letter he would write to be read at his funeral. The pain would be over. Hopefully the guilt would be with Natalie for the rest of her life and make it impossible for her to continue seeing Ed Wiseman, but . . .

Then he saw her. Carrie Ann.

'Watch out!' she said, as Axel practically shoulder-barged her in his haste to be away from the bar.

Carrie Ann's bright pink cocktail made a glittering arc through the air before splattering like a Jackson Pollock all over the front of her pretty white dress.

'I guess you owe me a drink,' she said sanguinely.

There was no way Axel couldn't talk to her now.

47

From their table by the poolside, Yaslyn and Rachel saw Carrie Ann make dramatic contact with her prey.

'He spilt her drink over her.' Rachel was disappointed. 'What an idiot.'

'That means he's nervous as hell. He's definitely into her. Carrie Ann won't be sleeping on her own tonight.'

'Wouldn't it be fantastic if this was the start of something special? I can just see Carrie Ann with someone like that chess rep. Someone a bit intellectual and sensitive. Wouldn't it be great if we could tell this story to their grandkids one day, about how he was so excited he soaked her in Planter's Punch?'

Yaslyn sighed. 'Rachel, this isn't going to end with a wedding. Sometimes you are romantic to the point of ridiculous.'

'And sometimes you're too cynical. I believe in true love.'

'Talking of which, here comes love's young dream.'

Marcus and Sally were picking their way through the bar in the girls' direction. After their night with Paulette, they had cottoned on to the fact that spending the evening with other people was a lot less painful than spending it alone together.

'Mind if we join you?' Marcus asked.

'Feel free,' said Yaslyn, gesturing them towards the empty seats. From her point of view it was a fair swap. She and Rachel would keep them from having to talk to each other. And Marcus and Sally would keep Yaslyn from having to listen to Rachel twittering on about love and marriage.

'Where's your friend?'

'Over there.' Rachel pointed Carrie Ann out. 'She's making a move on the chess instructor.'

'Looks like it's going well,' said Sally somewhat sarcastically.

Axel had fetched Carrie Ann another cocktail and himself another rum and Coke. Now they stood facing each other in silence as they sipped their new drinks. Carrie Ann was starting to shiver as the Planter's Punch dried on the front of her dress.

Axel's rendezvous with Carrie Ann had started badly and was getting worse. Correctly anticipating that Axel would be struck dumb by nerves when face to face with his target, Gilles had tried to forearm him with a series of conversational gambits that were guaranteed to work on any girl of any nationality. Unfortunately, Axel couldn't remember any of them.

'Nice weather,' he tried.

'What? Now?' said Carrie Ann. 'It's dark.'

Every time Axel looked over Carrie Ann's shoulder he saw Gilles giving him the 'thumbs up' or Yasser giving him a hard stare which was probably intended to put him off his stroke and lose Gilles the gay/not gay bet. The silence between exchanges seemed interminable. And when Axel did think of something to say, he almost inevitably mumbled it so that Carrie

Ann had to ask him to repeat himself a little louder over the pumping club music.

He couldn't understand why she hadn't already given up. Why was she still standing in front of him three-quarters of an hour after he spilled her drink? An hour later, Gilles was certainly getting exasperated. He made some stabbing gestures that Axel assumed meant he should go for the kill. It seemed unlikely that it would work.

'Will you excuse me for a minute?' said Carrie Ann suddenly.

She handed Axel her glass and left him alone by the bar. Gilles was at his side in an instant.

'What are you doing? You look like you're at the buffet for some funeral. You've hardly said anything to her for the past hour and now she's gone.'

'She went to the bathroom, I think,' said Axel.

'Yeah.' Gilles sighed. 'And if she comes back, I'll eat my tennis shorts. You blew it.'

'I did.'

'Almost definitely. But just supposing she proves me wrong, you have got to make the killer move now. If you don't invite her back to your room in the next ten minutes you have lost it. She'll think you're not interested. Plus, Yasser said he would give you until ten o'clock then he's moving in himself. I couldn't buy him off for any longer, I'm sorry.'

'You had to buy him off? This is all so sordid,' Axel complained.

'I'm going to give you bloody sordid if I lose this bet,' said Gilles. 'Fifty euros, Axel. That's a lot of cigarettes.'

*

Seeing Carrie Ann leave Axel's side and head for the loos, Yaslyn and Rachel had headed over there themselves for a debrief.

'How's it going?' they asked.

'It isn't going to work,' said Carrie Ann.

'He looks nervous,' said Rachel.

'He looks bored as hell from where I'm standing. He's probably only talking to me because there's some Club Aegee rule that says a rep can't walk away from a conversation with a guest first. I bet he'll have moved on when I get back to the bar. In fact, I'm not going back to the bar. I'm going to come and sit with you guys.'

'You can't give up now,' Rachel protested.

'Watch me.'

'You've just got to make a bold move,' Yaslyn suggested. 'There's no point fannying around like you would back home. The rules don't apply here. You don't have to worry that he'll think you're a slapper if you make all the running because you're not lining him up as a future husband. You just want a piece of young stud muffin. You'll never see him again after tonight.'

Carrie Ann chewed her lip.

'Get back out there or I'm going to tell Morten you were looking for him,' Yaslyn threatened. 'And don't forget to hang your bikini bottoms on the outside of the door if you decide to go back to our room.'

Carrie Ann smeared on some lipstick. 'Well, it won't have been much of a hen week if none of us gets a shag.'

*

'Oh my God,' breathed Gilles. 'You were right. She is coming back. Come on, Axel. Smile!'

He melted back into the crowd.

Carrie Ann took up her position opposite Axel again and relieved him of her glass.

It was time to go for it, she told herself. The clock above the bar read five to ten.

Axel also glanced at the clock. Five to ten. It was now or never. Yasser was circling ever closer.

'Do you want to come back to my room?' They said it simultaneously.

'For a game of chess.' They said that simultaneously too.

They regarded each other nervously. The suggestion was out there now. Game of chess? That was a laugh.

'Your room or mine?' Carrie Ann asked eventually.

Axel swallowed, his Adam's apple bobbing up and down in comedy panic.

'Your room, I think.' Carrie Ann made the executive decision. She put her glass down on the bar. 'Come on,' she said. 'Tell me where I'm going.'

Axel put his glass down too. At least, he tried to. In his nervousness he missed the bar and his glass ended up smashing on the floor. Carrie Ann continued to walk away in the direction of the staff huts while Axel panicked over what to do next. He crouched down to pick up some of the bigger shards. Gilles towered over him.

'Fifty euros!' he reminded Axel. 'Get back to the room.' Gilles grabbed the collar of the lucky shirt and pulled Axel to his feet. 'Get after her.'

He pointed him in the right direction. Axel stumbled

after Carrie Ann. Every male and female rep he passed and several of the guests patted him heartily on the back as he set out on his quest.

Xavier whistled. 'Go, Axel! He really is going to get laid,' the water-sports rep breathed in admiration.

'Come on, everybody. Clearly not gay. Time to cough up your cash,' said Gilles.

48

An hour later, the conversation at the poolside table was starting to wind down. Rachel, Yaslyn and the Merchants had exhausted all the polite South-East England topics. House prices, traffic, the hell of commuting into London from the Home Counties. Rachel had described her wedding plans. Sally had, somewhat reluctantly, Yaslyn thought, described her own wedding day five years earlier. She'd been slightly happier on the subject of honeymoon destinations. Rachel had no idea where she was going yet. According to tradition, Patrick was organising the honeymoon as a surprise for his future wife.

'I don't mind where I go,' said Rachel. 'Except India.'

Marcus looked at Sally to see whether she would leap to the country's defence. She was too busy fishing a bug out of her mint tea.

'I don't want to get Delhi belly,' Rachel elaborated.

Marcus pulled a face as if on cue. 'Or Turkey tummy. Will you ladies excuse me?'

'Are you feeling ill? I'll come with you,' said Sally.

'No need,' Marcus told her. 'You stay and have another drink with the girls.'

'I'd feel guilty.'

'Good,' said Marcus. But his smile was the seal of

approval on Sally staying in the bar. He bid Rachel and Yaslyn 'goodnight' and left.

'I'll be here if you need me,' Sally called after him. Then she turned back to the other women. The thought of staying up with them didn't exactly thrill her but it was a way of avoiding a repeat of last night's bedroom disaster. She wouldn't go back until she thought Marcus would be asleep.

'Another round, then?' Yaslyn suggested.

'My turn, I think,' said Sally.

'It's great this, isn't it?' said Rachel. 'You can safely say you'll get a round when everything's all-inclusive.'

'We paid enough to come here in the first place,' Yaslyn reminded her. 'And I'm sure they water all this stuff down.'

'Same again?' Sally asked her.

'Yes, please. Make it a double. Do you need help carrying it?'

'I think I can manage three glasses.'

Sally headed for a spot at the pool bar where the punters were only two deep.

'See,' said Yaslyn when Sally had left her alone with Rachel again. 'He's got tummy trouble too. It's not just me. The food here *is* terrible.'

For once Rachel wasn't interested in lecturing Yaslyn on her bowel movements. 'I can't see Carrie Ann any more,' she said. 'Or that Axel! Do you think she's done it? Do you think she's gone back to his room?'

'Well, I hope she hasn't taken him back to ours!' said Yaslyn.

'She must have done it. Here's a toast to Carrie Ann!'

'To the loss of her born-again virginity,' Yaslyn agreed.

The bar was still busy. When the cabaret ended each evening, the poolside nightclub began, with a resident DJ making a mess of the links between that summer's top hits.

'Oh yay, oh yay, oh yay, oh yay,' ran the chorus to a song that Sally could only imagine was quite big on the Continent. It was certainly familiar to the forty-something French guests gyrating along the edge of the pool like extras from a 1980s Black Lace video dressed by Karl Lagerfeld. Paulette was leading the dance.

Sally was full of envy as she watched them. They looked stupid but they were definitely enjoying themselves. Sally, in contrast, was limping towards the end of one of the worst weeks of her life. It was as though an invisible barrier prevented her from crossing the dance floor and joining in their happiness. Like Christmas, holidays were either the best time or the worst time, never in between. Being unhappy on holiday was so much worse than being unhappy back home. So much worse.

Sally's unconscious frown was preventing her from getting served at the bar.

''Allo.' She felt a hand on her shoulder. It was Gilles. He insinuated himself between Sally and the holidaymaker next to her. 'I thought you went to bed.'

'No. Marcus did. He's got a dodgy stomach,' Sally explained. 'Club Aegee food. Doesn't agree with him.'

Gilles nodded. 'Need to drink more spirits to kill the bugs.'

'The barman doesn't seem to have noticed me,' Sally continued.

'Perhaps it is because you are not smiling your beautiful smile,' said Gilles. He put two fingers in his mouth and whistled. 'Madam requires service,' he said.

'Madam? That makes me sound so old.'

'I didn't want to offend you by calling you "mademoiselle". I seem to find it very easy to offend you.' Gilles raised a brow.

The barman strolled over to Sally and took her order.

'Who is having the water?' Gilles asked when the three glasses arrived.

'I am.'

'Water is no good for a night out. How about a proper nightcap?'

'I don't think so. I don't want to wake up in the morning with a headache. Water will do fine.'

'You English. You don't know how to enjoy yourselves,' Gilles teased. 'You're either too drunk to stand up or too sober to dance. One little nightcap. With me.' Gilles raised his eyebrows again to catch the attention of one of the barmen and raised two fingers. Seconds later the barman placed two brandies down in front of Gilles and Sally.

'Very smooth,' said Sally sarcastically. 'How do you know if I even like brandy?'

'Everybody likes this,' Gilles assured her as he handed her one of the luxurious round glasses. 'Cheers.'

'Cheers,' said Sally. 'I'd better take these back to the girls.'

'And will I see you again?'

'I've got my last tennis lesson tomorrow, so I guess you will.'

'I mean before then,' Gilles clarified. 'I am going to go for a walk down on the beach now.'

'Have a nice walk,' said Sally.

'You could come with me. To talk. You look like you need to talk.'

'A walk to talk?' Sally looked Gilles straight in the eye. She knew he wasn't really suggesting it out of concern for her psychological well-being. He wasn't suggesting they go somewhere private so she could unburden her heart. She knew it was part of a routine. The brandy. The walk. The barman only had to see Gilles' hand gesture to know what was required of him. And Sally knew what in all probability was required of her at the moment too.

She glanced around her. There was no one present who might have cared or noticed that she was having a drink with someone other than her husband. Or that she was seriously considering setting out into the darkness with the tennis instructor.

'People in England make a lot of fuss about staying faithful to the one they married,' Gilles suddenly observed.

'Well, that's what the marriage service is supposed to be about. Till death us do part.' Sally thought of that girl Rachel, blubbing by the pool when she considered the vows she was about to take.

'Death. Or divorce,' said Gilles. 'And you have more divorce in your country, I think, than we have in France.'

'Then please tell me the secret of a happy marriage,' Sally challenged.

'*Cinq à sept*,' Gilles told her. 'A little afternoon affair. Everybody does it. Nobody expects to find passion in marriage. Nobody minds when you get passion elsewhere. Everybody goes home happy and carries on with their lives.'

'Five to seven? It's almost midnight now,' Sally half joked.

'*Cinq à sept. Sept à minuit.*' Gilles shrugged. 'There's no strict timetable.'

'So, it's just about sex,' Sally clarified.

'Not always,' said Gilles. 'Not all the time. Let's take that walk. I'll meet you on the beach path.'

Sally walked as steadily as she could back to the table where Rachel and Yaslyn were waiting for their drinks. She placed the double vodka tonics in front of them but didn't sit down this time.

'I feel really guilty about leaving Marcus on his own,' she lied. 'I'm going to go back to the room and see how he's feeling.'

'If you need some Imodium,' said Rachel, 'we've got plenty.'

'Thanks. I may take you up on that.'

'Tell him I hope he feels better soon.' Rachel smiled. 'I will.'

'Goodnight,' said Yaslyn.

Sally nodded her goodnight back. She couldn't quite look Yaslyn in the eye. Rachel was clearly the naive one. She thought the best of everybody. But if anyone could guess what Sally was about to do, it was Yaslyn.

She clipped away from the table in her wooden-soled sandals without looking back. Neither had she checked to see whether Gilles had set off for their rendezvous. Her heart was gathering speed in her chest. She got within twenty feet of the room she had been sharing with Marcus that week. Close enough to see that the light was out. He must be sleeping. Sally took the wrong fork in the path and headed on towards the beach.

Gilles was waiting exactly where he had said he would be. He was sitting on a low wall halfway down the beach path. The moon high in the sky and reflected on the calm sea behind him threw him into silhouette. Sally could just about make out the glowing red tip of a cigarette which he extinguished as she got closer.

It's not inevitable, she told herself. It wasn't inevitable that they would do anything more than flirt again. But when she got close enough, Gilles reached out and took her hand. Then he vanquished what little resolve she had left within her with the most astonishing thing she had ever heard from the mouth of a man.

'Sally,' Gilles began. 'Since I first saw you step off that bus last Tuesday, I have finally known what it's like to love someone so much that the rest of the world goes soft focus . . .'

49

While Axel fiddled with his key in the door to the room he shared with Gilles, Carrie Ann had a brief urge to turn on her heel and run as fast as she could in the opposite direction. What was she doing? Allowing herself to be seduced by a man who was too young to remember the Wombles (not to mention too French)?

When Axel finally got the door to his room open, Carrie Ann almost swooned in the blast of young male hormones the action released; a veritable tsunami of rampaging pheromones. It reminded Carrie Ann of the smell that hung around the corridors of the boys' school that was brother to her own girls' grammar. She tried not to wrinkle her nose in disgust. Had they never opened a window?

'I share with Gilles,' Axel explained.

It was easy to see which was Axel's side of the room. A neatly made bed. A pile of worthy books on the bedside table. In contrast, Gilles' bed looked like an explosion in the laundry room. A pathway of grubby white underpants and tennis shorts connected the bed and Gilles' washbasin like entrails spilling from a punctured mattress. Axel surreptitiously kicked a pair of recently worn Calvin Kleins back over the imaginary dividing line.

What now? wondered Carrie Ann.

'Er, would you like a drink?' he asked.

'That would be nice. What have you got?'

Axel looked about him as though searching for inspiration. 'Er, nothing,' he said, embarrassed. 'But I could go back to the bar. No. Wait.' He dived on to the floor next to Gilles' bed, rummaged about in the dangerous darkness beneath and emerged with a bottle of tequila and a tooth mug from which to drink it.

'I think I'm OK for alcohol,' said Carrie Ann, subconsciously taking a step backwards in the direction of the door. Filth and tequila. It was all a bit too much like being seventeen again. Perhaps this was a mistake . . .

'Wait,' said Axel. He dived under the bed once more. This time he emerged with a bottle of Sol. 'It isn't cold,' he added apologetically.

'But it is hermetically sealed,' said Carrie Ann. 'Can I sit down?' she asked, looking about her for a chair.

There may have been a chair under the huge pile of tennis whites and wet towels on Gilles' side of the room but she couldn't be sure. Axel started the excavation for her.

'Don't bother with that,' said Carrie Ann, when it became clear that Axel was intending to fold every piece of fabric he removed from Gilles' hidden chair. 'I'll be OK here.' She perched on the edge of Axel's bed. 'And you can sit next to me,' she said. No point pretending they weren't both intending to end up there . . .

Axel paused in his folding. He looked at Carrie Ann. Carrie Ann looked back. For the first time in almost a year Axel had a woman in his bedroom (he wasn't counting the ones that had squeezed into Gilles' single bed while Axel pretended to sleep) and now he was frightened. Carrie Ann cocked her head to one side expectantly. Smoothing the bedspread beside her, she subtly invited him to join her. Axel clutched one of Gilles' stinky T-shirts like a security blanket. Carrie Ann went for the less subtle 'pat on the mattress' gesture to indicate once more where Axel should be headed.

Axel let the T-shirt fall from his grip and stepped towards the bed.

'At last,' said Carrie Ann.

'Hold on.' He froze again.

Axel went over to Gilles' bedside table and started rifling through the top drawer. He tried to conceal what he had found there with a swift bit of sleight of hand, but Carrie Ann guessed at once. He'd found a condom. He thought he was in with a chance, then. About to get lucky. Axel sat down on the bed beside Carrie Ann and reached out to brush her hair from her face.

'You have lovely hair,' he said.

Perhaps he was.

50

Sally was frozen in her tracks. Had Gilles really just come out with all that? Had he really just described love as a film where every scene was played out in reference to the beloved? Sally didn't think she had ever heard such a beautiful description of the way love made you feel. And hearing it from Gilles' lips? That was confusing.

'I think I know what you mean,' said Sally.

Gilles nodded.

'You're quite a poet underneath that meathead exterior,' Sally joked to break the mood. But the mood wouldn't be broken. Gilles continued to look at her intently. Sally felt that empty-stomached, hollow feeling of fear. It was like the moment before you make a parachute jump. Fear and excitement and anticipation. The moment before you kiss someone for the very first time . . .

In the darkness, Sally saw Gilles' eyes glint, reflecting the distant light of the moon and the stars. He smiled slowly, one side of his mouth preceding the other in its upward curve. He had great teeth. Someone must have told him that before. His slow smile made the very best of them. He started to move his hand up towards Sally's cheek.

Sally felt her heartbeat speed up instantly. Even before he touched her, she could feel the warmth of that touch. She closed her eyes and tilted her face up towards his. A shiver of electricity ran through her body; a sensation long forgotten. She had thought at times that perhaps she wouldn't ever feel this way again. Was this how it was going to happen? The first unfaithful kiss of her life?

'Oh God,' Sally murmured.

'You are so beautiful,' Gilles told her. His mouth was so close to her face she could feel the rhythm of his breath on her cheekbone as he talked.

'We shouldn't be doing this.' Her conscience gave one last squeak.

'This is different. It isn't just about sex,' said Gilles.

Sally felt herself lean in towards him.

'Sally,' he murmured.

Gilles' fingertips hovered millimetres from Sally's jaw-line. He stared at her lips intently and licked his own.

'Sally!'

It wasn't Gilles' voice which was calling her this time.

'Sally?'

'Fuck.'

Gilles let his hand fall back to his side. Abruptly jolted out of her romantic dream by Gilles' sudden withdrawal, Sally stepped backwards in surprise and turned to find herself face to face with Marcus.

'Oh,' he said, half in surprise. 'It *is* you.'

'I was just walking her back to you,' said Gilles hurriedly. Too hurriedly. His usual laid-back calm had utterly deserted him.

'Via the beach?' Marcus asked. He looked back at his wife. 'I wondered what had happened to you, Sal.

I was worried. I went back to the bar to join you for a last drink and Yaslyn said you'd gone back to the room.'

'I didn't say that,' Sally stuttered. 'I said I was going for a walk.'

'In the dark?'

The three of them stood in a silent triangle until Gilles cleared his throat and said, 'Well, I must bid you both farewell. I have to teach a class at eight o'clock tomorrow morning. Tennis,' he added nonsensically.

Marcus glared at him. Gilles sprinted off down the path as though following an invisible ball to the baseline.

'Thanks for walking her back,' Marcus called after him. His voice was heavy with sarcasm. 'Still want to walk on the beach?' he asked his wife.

'No,' said Sally. 'I'm fine now.'

'Yeah,' said Marcus.

'Are you feeling better, then?' Sally tried.

'I'm fine. I just want to go to bed.'

They walked back to their room in silence.

Marcus didn't even try to kiss her goodnight.

Oh God. Sally stared at the plain white ceiling above her head. What had Marcus seen? What had he heard? How long had he been standing right behind them on that path? Perhaps he hadn't seen anything. It was dark down by the beach. And though Gilles had definitely been about to kiss her, their lips hadn't actually touched. Perhaps Marcus thought Gilles was trying to get a lash out of her eye?

Should they talk about it?

Sally rolled on to her side to look at her husband.

He was on his side, facing away from her. Perhaps he was asleep.

'Marcus,' she half whispered. A half-hearted attempt to start a dialogue.

He didn't respond. Either he was asleep or he didn't want to talk to her. It was more likely to be the former. Since the day they first met, Marcus had never actually refused to speak to his wife, though she would stop talking to him at the slightest provocation. But if he didn't want to talk to her, then he must be very angry indeed. Angry enough to have the row that would finally set Sally free? The thought fluttered up inside her, half hope and half despair.

There was never going to be a good time to tell him what she wanted. Never. And, Sally thought with a sad, secret smile, the holiday had been so bloody awful anyway that choosing to make the revelation that she wanted a divorce now would probably seem like just another drop in an ocean of unhappiness.

She started to plan it out in her head, as coolly and methodically as if she were planning a Sunday barbecue. She would tell him the following morning, while they still had twenty-four hours left in Turkey; twenty-four hours left on neutral ground in which to talk, or rather for her to tell him why it was no longer working and why it just wasn't worth giving it a try when they got back to England.

Then she would call Victoria. Victoria, her best friend since her teenage years, who had promised to back her up no matter what she did. Well, she'd kept her promise so far, respecting Sally's counsel regarding her doubts about Marcus and their marriage. During one long whispered telephone conversation while Marcus was asleep on the sofa in the next room, Victoria had also told Sally that if she ever decided to do anything drastic she could count on a place to lay her head at Victoria's lovely farmhouse back in Surrey.

'And if you can do it, maybe I'll gather up the courage to leave my ball and chain too,' Victoria had added with a giggle. 'Then we could get a flat together in London. Just like old times. Wouldn't it be great?'

Sally murmured her agreement. Except she knew Victoria was looking back on their carefree, single past through extremely opaque rose-tinted spectacles. The time they had spent in a shared flat, during their second year at university, had been one of the low points of their friendship. Endless arguments about cleaning rotas and pilfered make-up and running out of milk. Endless angst about not having bagged the men they were so bloody bored of now. Sally knew that Victoria was just trying to make her feel better. There was no way she would really give up her Aga just because Sally had shown her that it was possible to walk out on a moribund marriage and live on a solitary income. The thought of giving up her brand-new Mitsubishi Shogun would get Victoria in the end. She would be married to her husband Rob until one of them died. Sally knew that.

But she would have to call on Victoria and take up the offer of the spare room for a while. And assuming Victoria came through, she wouldn't even have to go back to the house she shared with Marcus as soon as they got back to England. She figured she had enough clothes in her case to last her for a week or so. And if the weather wasn't as good as it should be in the UK in late July, then she could always ransack Victoria's extensive designer wardrobe for something warmer.

Sally chewed her lip as she tested her latest plan in her head. Did she have everything she needed to go into the office on Wednesday? Luckily she had left her laptop safely locked in the top drawer of her desk instead of taking it home as she often did. Lucky also that the dress code in her office was relatively casual.

Yes. In the morning she would tell him. She felt lighter just thinking about the freedom that would be hers again by the following evening. And it would be better for Marcus too. He would have to see that eventually. He would find someone who really loved him and be happy again. Not that Sally *didn't* love him. She would probably always love him for the things they had shared in the past. She just wasn't *in love* with him any more, and she was too young to live without that kind of passion.

In less than twenty-four hours they would be preparing to separate. Sally nodded to herself at the rightness of her decision. But her eyes felt hot when she closed them. She rubbed away a tear before it started.

Marcus sighed in his sleep.

51

'Stop!'

Carrie Ann pushed Axel off and glared at him.

'What do you think you're doing?' she asked.

'I am making love to you,' said Axel, somewhat defensively.

'Making love? Is that what you call it? You were kneading my tits like you were trying to make bloody focaccia. I'm a woman, Axel. Not a dough ball.' Carrie Ann rearranged her bra so that it covered her nipples once more. 'And you called me Natalie,' she added almost as an afterthought.

Axel sat up and looked at Carrie Ann innocently.

'Yes, Axel. You called me Natalie. In fact, you called me Natalie not once, not twice, but three times in as many minutes.'

'Oh God.' Axel buried his face in his hands.

Great, thought Carrie Ann. Now he's going to cry. I'm the one who should be crying.

'Oh God,' he said again.

'Forget it. You're not the first person to get my name wrong,' Carrie Ann assured him, thinking back to a particularly painful moment when Greg had called out 'Mairi' at exactly the wrong time. She picked up her sundress from where it lay in a crumpled heap next to the remains of Gilles' latest house of beer bottles and pulled it over her head. Once she was dressed again she felt instantly less vulnerable and subsequently less inclined to be harsh.

'I'm sorry,' Axel cried.

'It's OK.' She patted him on the shoulder.

'My heart is broken,' said Axel.

'Certainly looks that way. Do you want to tell me about it?' Carrie Ann asked dutifully.

'Do you really want to listen?'

Carrie Ann let out a long sigh. 'Well, this isn't exactly how I thought I would spend my last but one night in Turkey. But go on. Tell me all about bloody Natalie and your broken heart. God knows I've bent enough ears in my time.'

'Bent ears?' Axel was confused.

'I mean I've cried on plenty of shoulders myself since my divorce came through. Bored the pants off people with my problems.'

'I don't want to bore you.'

'Just get on with it. It had better be good.'

Axel got up and went to rifle through Gilles' bedside table again.

'I don't think we need another condom, do you?' said Carrie Ann.

Axel blushed like a girl. 'I wasn't looking for a condom,' he stuttered. This time he came out of Gilles' bedside drawer with a packet of cigarettes – Gilles' secret emergency end-of-the-month pack – from which he purloined two.

'Do you smoke?' he asked.

'I do now,' said Carrie Ann, taking the fag he offered her in anticipation of the long night ahead.

*

Safely away from the beach path, Gilles lit up a cigarette and took a long, lazy drag that filled his lungs and instantly relaxed him. He was irritated. Sally was something different. He'd enjoyed sparring with her that week.

By the swimming pool, the late-night revels continued. A handful of guests desperate to make the most of their few days away from their ordinary lives drank and gyrated themselves silly. The other good-looking English girl was still around. Gilles had got her departure date wrong. He had thought she was staying for a fortnight but in fact she and her friends were flying back to the UK in two days as well. Right now she was sitting at the table near the bar watching her friend and room-mate getting down and dirty with the dance instructor, adding some very unorthodox moves to the routine he had been teaching that afternoon. Yaslyn looked bored. She was swirling her ice round in her glass, staring at the melting cubes as though they might reveal the eternal truth about humanity.

As Gilles approached, Yaslyn's whole demeanour changed. She sat up straighter, taller, pushing her chest out to maximum effect. Her frown was gone. She glanced suggestively at the empty seat beside her. Gilles took his place at the table. Sally Merchant was quickly forgotten.

The music ended. Even at Club Aegee, the party couldn't go on all night. The pool bar manager pulled down the blinds that prevented guests from pilfering booze under cover of darkness. Another cover was pulled over the pool to prevent any accidental drownings.

Pierre the dancing instructor returned Rachel to the table, where her mint tea was almost cold. Rachel sat down and watched the crowd finish last drinks and disperse to their rooms. She couldn't see Yaslyn anywhere.

Eventually, Rachel was entirely alone at the poolside. One of the bar staff started to go around the tables, stacking chairs on top of them to make his job of sweeping the floor beneath easier. He piled chairs on the tables to either side of the place where Rachel sat.

'I'm in your way,' she said. 'I'll go.' But he motioned her to stay.

'Your tea,' he said.

It was undrinkably cold by now.

Where was Yaslyn? Rachel wasn't exactly worried, but she was starting to get a bit irritated. Being left alone in the middle of Club Aegee wasn't like being left alone in the middle of Brixton after midnight, but, all the same, the walk back to their room was a thoroughly spooky one which Rachel preferred not to do on her own. Yaslyn might at least have let her know she was going.

Ah well. There wasn't much choice now. Unless she really was going to sit by the pool bar until daylight. At least that would save the trouble of having to get up early to save the sunbeds. Rachel pushed her teacup away and got unsteadily to her feet. She didn't think she'd drunk that much.

The village was quiet now except for the chirping of the cicadas and the occasional French or Italian expletive as someone tripped over on the pitch-black walk back to their room. Rachel wished she had taken Patrick's advice and packed a torch for the holiday. When he had suggested it, she had pooh-poohed the idea. It would just add to the weight of her luggage. And Rachel was always terrified of getting into trouble for going over the luggage allowance.

She took baby steps along the rough path around the back of reception. When they had first arrived at the village, it had seemed like a good thing that they were so far away from the brightly lit public areas. Good if you liked dead quiet for a night's sleep. Not so good if you wanted to get back to your bed at night without a broken ankle.

Ahead of her she could hear a new sound. The sound of giggling. It seemed to be coming from the laundry room, where guests who had packed more lightly than Rachel were free to rinse through their smalls. The smell of the laundry room took Rachel straight back to university, where she and her friends had spent many winter afternoons watching their knickers dry in the luxurious warmth of the laundry rather than going back to their freezing accommodation-hall rooms.

The door to the laundry was ajar, casting a sliver of welcome light on to the path so that Rachel could see and avoid a pothole that might otherwise have floored her. From what she could hear, Rachel guessed that a couple of late-night revellers were using the room as a trysting place. She ducked her head to scuttle on past inconspicuously. But just as she was passing the half-open door, she was brought to a halt by a familiar voice.

'Stop it, you dirty beast!'

Rachel turned automatically towards the voice she knew. And caught an eyeful of the last thing she wanted to see.

Yaslyn was sitting on top of a dryer. Her black gypsy skirt was ruched up around her waist like a swimming ring. Her slender bare brown calves were resting on the shoulders of a faceless man. Faceless because he had his face buried between Yaslyn's thighs.

Throwing her head back in a gasp of unalloyed delight, Yaslyn grabbed her companion by a hank of beach-blond hair and pull him up from his knees so he could kiss her on the mouth again.

'Don't you like that?' asked Gilles.

'I love it,' Yaslyn growled at him. She kissed his lips as though she was trying to bite them off. 'Now get back down, you naughty boy.' In a single, flowing movement, she pushed Gilles back to his knees and kicked the open door to the laundry shut with her foot, as though she had sensed they had an audience. She didn't bother to see who the audience might be.

52

Carrie Ann propped herself up on her elbow and looked down into Axel Radanne's face. The first light of a new day was filtering in beneath the curtains, picking out his profile against the pillow. She realised she'd never asked him how old he was. He'd never said. She had guessed that he was probably in his early twenties but now, in the dim light of dawn, he looked much younger.

So much for Carrie Ann's liberating night of passion with a rampant rep. Once he had started on the subject of Natalie, Axel kept talking for three hours straight about the girl. By the time he had finished, Carrie Ann felt as though she had been there throughout their entire relationship. Axel seemed to have remembered every single conversation he and Natalie had ever had and wanted to run through them word for word in the search for clues as to why she had abandoned him.

'She said she loved me,' he told Carrie Ann plaintively. It was a pitifully familiar refrain.

But Carrie Ann couldn't blame Axel for hanging on to the sweet things Natalie had whispered in the early days. Even when Greg moved out of their home into Mairi's flat for the duration of the divorce proceedings, Carrie Ann found herself going back to conversations she and her husband had had at the very start of their marriage. He had promised that they would always be together. Then suddenly they weren't. It was as though a light had gone out. Someone had flicked a switch somewhere.

'Was she lying to me?' Axel asked.

'No,' Carrie Ann assured him. 'I am sure that she did love you. But feelings change. And eventually your feelings for Natalie will change too.'

With Axel's head on her lap, Carrie Ann couldn't help the little sad smile that settled on her lips as she assured him that everything would be OK. How trite the very same words had sounded when she had heard them from her friends in the aftermath of her breakup. They didn't understand the depth of the love she and Greg had was what she thought then. It could never be replaced.

But time was beginning to prove her wrong. How disappointingly normal her feelings were turning out to be. Every week that went by made the status quo feel a little easier to handle. The rest of her life had expanded to fill the hole left by her husband's desertion, just as people promised it would.

When she thought about Greg now, Carrie Ann thought in snapshots. Literally, in snapshots. She remembered his face in their wedding photos. Or holiday snaps. She could only accurately recall his voice mumbling the greeting on their old answering machine. He was fading. Becoming a part of her past that would eventually be jumbled up with and indistinguishable from memories of films she had seen or songs she had heard on the radio.

Axel had known Natalie for just a few months. How much more quickly she would become a painless part of his history. But only if Axel made the decision not to keep picking at the scar she had left behind on his heart and stop shying away from the things that reminded him of their relationship for fear of the pain they might cause him. Running away didn't work. Carrie Ann knew that. Axel had come to Club Aegee to escape from his memories but the distance had served only to magnify those memories into hideous ghosts that threatened to stay with him his whole life.

Carrie Ann could just imagine Natalie. Axel had described her as though she were as beautiful as Botticelli's Venus. Carrie Ann imagined someone altogether less attractive. Self-consciously intellectual. Pretentious. Even cruel. How could she have left someone in such tatters otherwise? Why hadn't she tried to talk some sense into him before he lost his treasured place at university?

Axel had a choice, Carrie Ann told him as they sat on his bed in the dark. Natalie's memory only had as much power over him as he granted it. If he went back to Paris and finished his studies, Carrie Ann promised, then he would be happy in himself again within a year. There was a possibility he might bump into Natalie and Ed and that would hurt like hell the first couple of times but if he never went back, if he allowed his sabbatical to become permanent and didn't become the doctor he had dreamed of becoming, the pain would eventually get worse. He would begin to despise himself for allowing Natalie to keep him from the future he wanted. There was a very real danger that he might never be happy again.

In the course of Carrie Ann's midnight advice

session, Axel had somehow managed to curl up under her arm. She had wrapped her arm around him naturally, lovingly, because she recognised the pain he was going through and responded with the one thing she always wanted in the same circumstances. Physical comfort. Axel may have been fond of fancy words describing high emotions, but Carrie Ann knew that in the final analysis we are all the same when we are hurt. We all go back to being the little children who ran in from scraping their knees in the playground to have the pain made better with a hug.

'You know, Axel,' she had murmured, 'you are a very special guy and somewhere out there is someone who will recognise you for what you really are. I know it sounds like I'm just saying that. God knows I've heard it enough times myself. But I really believe it. You're unique and funny and clever and handsome and . . .'

Axel gave an enormous snorting snore. And Carrie Ann was trapped for the night, with his head resting heavily on her arm.

Carrie Ann's arm was still slightly numb now, the following morning. She tried to rub some life into it as she searched the floor around Axel's bed for her sandals. She eventually found them beneath a pile of Gilles' T-shirts, knocked to the floor during that first frenzied attempt to make love.

In retrospect, Carrie Ann was glad nothing much had happened beyond a fumble. Axel needed more in his life than sex. Carrie Ann needed more in her life too. Friendship. Companionship. Support. That was what she had got from their midnight conversation.

Counselling Axel about his ambitions had stirred up some old ones of her own.

'Sweet dreams, Axel.' The chess rep was still sleeping. She kissed him on the cheek and stepped into the sunshine outside his room nursing a tiny new kernel of optimism in her mind.

53

Rachel woke to find herself alone in the girls' room. She sat up and stretched. No retching from the bathroom. No snoring drowning out the noisy air conditioner. She was alone. And what was more, neither of the other beds in the room had been slept in *at all* that night. Not Carrie Ann's. Or Yaslyn's.

After a moment of blissful forgetfulness as she came round from her dreams, the image of Yaslyn and Gilles in the laundry room hit Rachel again like a wave of physical nausea.

How could she have done it? Cheating on Euan was bad enough. But cheating on him with a holiday rep? It was all so very tacky. Gilles was the human equivalent of a burger. Momentarily satisfying but ultimately cheap, nasty and not very good for you. Worse still, that was almost certainly how he viewed Yaslyn.

Rachel could imagine Euan in Dublin. With his effortlessly charming manner, there would have been no shortage of women queuing up for his attentions. But he would stop short at flirting with them. Rachel knew he would. What would he think if he knew what had been going on in Turkey?

Rachel was surprised by just how angry she felt. Whether or not she had intended to, Yaslyn had burdened Rachel with a secret that she really didn't want to know. Now, every time she saw Euan, Rachel would have that picture of Yaslyn in the laundry room at the back of her mind. When Rachel had last spoken to Patrick, she had heard Euan in the background shouting, 'Make sure you keep Yaslyn out of trouble!'

Well, she had hardly managed that, had she?

Angrily, Rachel turned the shower on full blast and fumed while she waited for the water to get hot. Just as she stepped into the cubicle, Yaslyn tumbled into the room and headed straight for the toilet bowl. Dropping to her knees, she swayed over it. Nothing came out. She stayed there for a few moments before she realised she wasn't alone.

'Sorry!' she called to Rachel. 'Didn't see you there.'

'Where were you last night?'

'Who are you?' Yaslyn asked with an air of amusement. 'My mother?'

'You don't actually need to answer. I know exactly where you were. I saw you,' said Rachel. 'With Gilles.'

Yaslyn shrugged and grinned. 'You did?'

'In the laundry room.'

'Whoops,' said Yaslyn.

'What about Euan?'

'What about him? He doesn't need to know. God, I need to get some sleep. I am shattered.'

Yaslyn left Rachel alone in the bathroom.

Rachel cut short her shower and followed Yaslyn out.

'I'm not happy about it.'

'About what?'

'About you being unfaithful to Euan. You preached for hours about how Carrie Ann should leave Greg as soon as she found out he was cheating and then you go and do the same. I find it more than slightly hypo-critical.'

'Do you really?' said Yaslyn flatly.

'Yes, I do.'

'Since when did you have the right to comment on the way I live my life?'

'Since you cheated on one of my friends.'

'One of *your* friends?'

'Yes. Euan is one of my friends. He's going to be best man at my wedding. He's my husband's *best* friend. And what am I supposed to do when Euan comes round and starts telling me how much he loves you? Act like nothing happened out here? It feels so hypocritical. I'll feel guilty. Every time I look at Euan I'll think of you and that horrible man in the laundry room.'

Yaslyn's lip curled upwards into a smile at the memory. She couldn't help it. 'I'm not going to live my life like a nun just so that you feel comfortable when you're throwing one of your happily married dinner parties,' was her reply.

'Fine. Well, I'm not sure if I want you as my brides-maid any more,' said Rachel quietly.

'For God's sake.'

'I'm not happy with it. I'm not happy with the idea of being followed down the aisle by an adulterer.'

'I think that technically you have to be married before you can be an adulterer,' Yaslyn pointed out.

'That's so you,' Rachel said in exasperation. 'To have a technical get-out clause. If it isn't bad enough that you cheated on Euan in the first place. Why can't you take my feelings seriously either?'

'Because they're irrational. Infidelity is a fact of life.

Birds do it. Bees do it. Even educated fleas do it . . .'

'But I don't. And neither does Carrie Ann. And even in your own life you've seen how much unhappiness it can bring. What about your father?'

'Like father, like daughter, I guess. Look, Rachel, I really don't need this lecture. I'm tired now. Gilles wasn't actually that good when it came down to it and I won't be going back for seconds. It was just a bit of holiday madness, and if you could just take your prissy head out of your own arse for a moment, I'm sure you would see that too. No one needs to know. No harm done.'

'No. There is harm done,' Rachel insisted. 'I don't want the start of my marriage to be blighted by your sordid little games.'

'For Christ's sake . . . What are you talking about?'

'Commitment actually means something to me. Euan's commitment should mean something to you.'

'You're drifting along in a big romantic cloud,' Yaslyn muttered in exasperation.

'I believe in honesty.'

'You believe in fairy tales. You think you're going to get married to Patrick and have 2.4 children and buy a Labrador and everything will be hunky-dory. Well, wake up. Real life isn't like that. Two out of three marriages end in divorce these days. What makes you think you'll be any different? I give you a two-in-three chance of ending up just as disappointed as everybody else whether or not I follow you down the aisle in a fucking terrible dress.'

Rachel stepped back as though Yaslyn had physically attacked her.

'I can't believe you just said that.' Her face

crumpled. 'We're here on my hen week and you just wished me a divorce! How could you say that? You bitch!'

'I'm sorry,' Yaslyn said unconvincingly.

'No you're not. You're never sorry. Not really. You treat everyone else like they were put here on earth for your benefit and you don't care about anybody's feelings but your own and . . .'

Yaslyn sat down on the bed, abruptly, as though she wasn't controlling her movements at all. It was as if an angry puppeteer had suddenly dropped her strings and dumped her there. Her eyes were momentarily glazed with pain.

'Rachel,' she whispered. 'Please, stop shouting at me.'

'You've always looked down on me. You think we're all stupid . . .'

'Rachel,' Yaslyn tried again. 'Please stop. I think I'm going to pass out.'

'Oh, for God's sake,' Rachel snarled this time. 'You can't even have the runs without turning it into a terminal illness.'

'No, really. I am.'

'Yeah, right. Everybody's got the same thing. Just get over it. You're trying to make me feel sorry for you because you don't want to deal with how I'm feeling about what you did last night.'

Yaslyn lowered herself backwards on to the bed.

Rachel was standing at the window now, arms crossed defensively, too busy dealing with her own pain to worry about Yaslyn's doubtless exaggerated ones.

'Why don't you take some more of my painkillers,'

she continued. 'Just help yourself. Like you do to everything in my life. After all, what's mine is yours, isn't it?'

Rachel was on to another big bugbear.

'And I've always been happy to give it to you. Good old Rachel. Rachel can spare her best moisturiser for my hands because I can't be bothered to look through my luggage for my own. Rachel can spare her white towels to dry me off when my fake tan is running. Rachel can spare the dress she's been saving to wear to the gala dinner because I've spilt ice cream down my own. Do you have any idea how often I have had to bite my lip and stop myself from screaming at you over the past fifteen years? Of course you don't. It wouldn't even cross your mind. It never did. You're a breed apart. Mere mortals like me and Carrie Ann and Euan are just here to smooth your passage through life. Well, perhaps all that is coming to an end. Perhaps you'll have to spend some time in the real world now your career's going down the pan. Have to start taking other people into consideration. Act like a friend if you really want to keep some. Euan deserves someone better than you. I bloody hope he has met somebody in Dublin.'

And with that Rachel left the room, not bothering to look back because, while she had just delivered the speech she had never expected to find the strength to utter, she wasn't sure that she was strong enough not to apologise for it as soon as she saw Yaslyn's perfect pained expression. She'd seen it a hundred times, but it never failed to get to her. The downturned mouth. The sadly beautiful glitter of tears in her big round eyes.

'Rachel!' Yaslyn shouted feebly as her best friend strode purposefully to the door.

Rachel held her head up and kept walking. Sod sunbed duty by the pool. She was going to sit down on the beach and have a cocktail. She was going to read her book and enjoy her last day in Turkey and plan how different life was going to be when they got back to England. She was going to enjoy the feeling of having the last word for once.

'Rachel!'

Rachel broke into a run as soon as she was outside the room and just about managed to get down to the beach before she started crying.

'Fuck.'

It was the worst cramping session so far. Yaslyn forced down another two painkillers then lay on her bed in the dark for a while. She couldn't remember when she had last felt so sorry for herself.

She gave herself a mental ticking off. 'Pull yourself together, Yas. It's just another bout of Turkey tummy. And speaking of tummy . . .'

She prodded her abdominal muscles in disgust. A week of eating too much food and drinking too many sticky sweet cocktails and doing nowhere near enough exercise wasn't going to help her convince the model agency that she was still a contender for the fashion mags rather than the thermal underwear catalogues when she got back to London. She was going to have to put together a serious regime when she got home. Circuit training. Lots of crunches. Bit of yoga perhaps.

The cramping started to fade away. Yaslyn sat back up.

Windsurfing was very good exercise for the abdominals. She would go and do an hour down at the beach. Start as she meant to go on and give Rachel time to cool down a bit. Things would be OK between them again eventually, wouldn't they? There was no way she really would stop Yaslyn from being her bridesmaid. The dresses had already been made.

Yaslyn pulled on her bikini and looked at herself in the mirror. Considering she had spent a week lazing in the sun, she didn't look exactly rested. An uncomfortable night on a nest of soggy towels in the laundry room had probably contributed to that. She hadn't intended to stay there on the laundry floor all night. She certainly hadn't intended to wake up there on her own when the cleaners came in the next morning.

Gilles must have fucked off at some point during the night. Probably for the best. What a mistake that had been. When he finally took his trousers down, Yaslyn had to bite her hand not to laugh at what little he kept inside them. The sex was terrible. Nowhere near as good as it had been with Euan.

Euan. What was she going to do about him?

Yaslyn turned her mobile on at least once a day to check for messages but so far there had been none. She thought he would have called by now. It was more than a week since he had stormed out of her flat. Admittedly, she hadn't called him but that was the way it worked in their relationship. Yaslyn was the cool one. Euan danced attendance. Only he wasn't any more. And Yaslyn was surprised. And scared . . .

54

Marcus and Sally returned to their room straight after breakfast.

Sally breathed in deeply through her nose and let the breath out again with an audible sigh just as Marcus wandered out on to the balcony. He was holding a crumpled tube of Factor 15 sunscreen.

'We're almost out of this,' he said. 'Though I guess it won't matter if I go down to Factor Eight now that we're just a day from going home. I've got quite a good base tan.'

Sally nodded her head distractedly.

'You OK?' he asked.

She turned to face him. Marcus. Her husband. He had his glasses on. He bloody would do. She hated the little-boy-lost look they gave him. Hated that look almost as much as she had once adored it.

'Sally,' Marcus said suddenly, 'I don't quite know how to say this so you'll have to forgive me if it comes out wrong.'

'What?'

'Sit down.'

'I'm fine like this, thanks.'

Sally looked down at her hands. 'What is it?' she asked, struggling to keep her voice light. Was he going to bring up the incident on the beach path? She was gripping the handrail around the balcony so tight she could see her knuckle bones quite clearly through her skin.

'Sally, I know that you didn't want to come on this holiday . . .'

'That's not true,' Sally began.

'Sally.' Marcus put his head on one side. 'You don't have to pretend any more. I know you didn't want to come away. I didn't give you a choice. I even got your boss involved, which wasn't very sensible. But I thought this holiday might help us to put aside some of the differences we've had lately. I thought that a bit of time together away from work and the office and the bloody DIY might help us rediscover each other. Get back to being the people we were before things started to get us down. Before . . .' He took a deep breath and looked down at his own hands, gripping the balcony rail just a few inches from Sally's now.

'But the thing is, the people we were don't exist any more. Not even under all the layers of stress and the arguing. Not even if we won the lottery tomorrow and never had to go to work again. We've changed, Sally. Both of us. Grown up perhaps. But I don't think we've been growing in the same direction.'

'Marcus, I . . .' Sally felt an urge to disagree, to make things better. It was a terrible, terrible habit.

'Don't,' said Marcus again, putting a finger to her lips. 'Don't say it. I love you, Sally. I loved you from the first time I met you and I think I always will. But I know that I can't make you happy any more. I've tried everything I can think of but nothing seems to work. So, I've decided to let you go. When we get back to England, I won't be going back to the house. You know Charlie's got a flat in London he sometimes uses during the week? Well, I called him yesterday and he says that I can stay there for as long as I need to. Maybe we should stay out of each other's way for a month or so to start with, then we can get together for lunch or something and talk about what to do with the house and how to set about making things official.'

Marcus squirted the last of the suntan lotion on to his hand and rubbed it into his leg. He had his head down now. He couldn't look at her.

'No need to say anything,' he said. She could tell he was forcing himself to sound businesslike. 'I'll be down by the beach if you need me today.'

'Marcus . . .'

'Don't say anything now,' he reiterated. 'Give yourself a few minutes.'

He picked up his beach towel and left.

From her position on the balcony, Sally watched her husband walk down the path towards the beach and felt suddenly as though she was seeing him for the very last time. The farther away he walked, the more he became like a ghost, the heat shimmer from the hot ground beneath his feet blurring his outline like a picture seen through tears.

Oh God. What had just happened? Sally felt the pressure building behind her eyes. What had just happened?

He had given her everything she wanted, that was what. He had offered her a way out of their marriage that didn't even require her to say goodbye to her walk-in wardrobe. He had saved her the humiliation of having to admit that she had wanted someone else.

She should have been elated. He had opened the door to the cage and shown her the way to fly.

Then why did it feel so wrong?

It was inevitable, she supposed. After all, she had never stopped loving him. And by offering her a get-out in such a decent, gentlemanly manner, he had robbed her of some of her justification. He hadn't given her anything to get angry about; to hold up as a reason why she was better off without him. She couldn't turn up on Victoria's doorstep now, saying 'The bastard threw me out'. Somehow that made her guilt seem a little heavier.

He had handled the ending as he had handled everything about their relationship from the start. Calmly, quietly, fairly. Because he was a calm, quiet, fair sort of man.

'Oh God, Marcus!' Sally shocked herself with her exclamation. But he was already too far away to hear.

55

Carrie Ann didn't go straight back to the girls' room after she left Axel. Instead, she headed for the viewpoint on the path above the beach, wanting to watch the sun climb the sky over the water and hold on to the strange sense of peace that was with her that morning for just a little bit longer. The last thing she wanted was to go back to the room and face a teasing post-mortem about her 'night of passion'. She hadn't yet decided whether she was going to tell Yaslyn and Rachel the truth. After all, Axel had fifty euros riding on her discretion. Poor sod.

All the same, Carrie Ann was surprised and a little disappointed when Rachel stomped past her without saying good morning. She had her sunhat pulled down over her eyes. Carrie Ann assumed (and hoped) that Rachel just hadn't noticed her sitting on the bench. Half an hour later, Yaslyn came by too. She looked equally distracted.

'Morning,' Carrie Ann called pointedly as Yaslyn almost passed her by.

'Oh, hi,' said Yaslyn. 'Going to do a bit of windsurfing before it gets crowded,' she added. Then she too was gone.

'Good morning to you too,' Carrie Ann muttered. What was wrong with her room-mates? Carrie Ann leaned over the wooden barrier that prevented holidaymakers from getting down to the beach the fast way and watched with interest as Yaslyn walked straight past Rachel on her way to the water sports hut. Rachel, for her part, held her holiday reading right up to her face to make it clear that she wasn't in the mood for talking either.

They must have fallen out. And badly too, if neither of them could be bothered to ask whether Carrie Ann had got laid after the fuss they had made in anticipation.

'Carrie Ann!'

Unfortunately, there was one person at Club Aegee who still very much wanted to talk to her that morning. Morten settled himself and his binoculars down beside her on the bench.

'You are leaving the bar early last night, I see. For a game of chess?'

He gave her a nudge in the ribs.

Carrie Ann felt her cheeks colour furiously.

'He is gay, you know,' Morten told her matter-of-factly. 'Yasser is saying so.'

'Yasser doesn't know everything,' said Carrie Ann.

Morten shrugged. He didn't believe her. He took his binoculars from around his neck.

'This is the best spot you are sitting in. I can see everything from up here,' he said. It immediately sounded sinister. 'Do you want to have a look?'

Morten put the glasses up to his eyes and zoomed in on something down on the sand. 'I think I can see your friend. The one who is with Gilles in the laundry room last night.'

'What?'

'Oh yes. She is taking out a windsurf board.'

Morten adjusted his focus.

'My friend was with Gilles in the laundry room?' Carrie Ann probed. 'Which one? You must have got the wrong girl.'

'No. This one. She is your friend. Look.'

Morten held the binoculars steady so that Carrie Ann could put her eyes to the eyepieces and see exactly what he had been focusing on. Her field of vision was filled with toned brown flesh and pink Lycra as the particular bird Morten had been watching bent over to adjust her sandal strap.

It was Yaslyn's bottom.

Carrie Ann handed back the binoculars in disgust. She didn't need to see such a perfect bottom that early in the morning and Morten really shouldn't have been looking. Carrie Ann assumed that her expression said everything about her opinion of his brand of 'bird watching' but Morten was unfazed. He was Scandinavian, she supposed.

'I'll see you around,' Carrie Ann told him, though she really had no intention of speaking to Morten again. She scuttled off down the beach path. The one time she glanced back, she caught Morten focusing on her bottom instead.

Carrie Ann plonked herself down on the sand beside Rachel.

'You walked straight past me,' she said accusingly.

'Did I?' Rachel was surprised. 'Sorry.'

'I just got cornered by Morten again. He was watching Yaslyn through his binoculars. He said he saw her with Gilles in the laundry room last night. What on earth does that mean?'

Rachel put down her book. 'You don't want to know.'

'Of course I want to know,' said Carrie Ann.

By the water's edge, Yaslyn was ready to take her board out to sea. Xavier had insisted that she take a life jacket but she sneakily discarded it now. Yaslyn had done plenty of windsurfing as a teenager. A course of windsurf lessons had been one of the best bribes she had received in the aftermath of her parents' divorce. Yaslyn didn't think she needed a life jacket. It was hardly the most flattering thing she'd ever worn.

Xavier was too busy chatting to the Swedish Lesbian Twins to notice whether or not the other holidaymakers were flouting the rules. Yaslyn began to wade through the waves, stopping just once to look back towards the shore and find a landmark she could use to take her bearings. She saw Carrie Ann sitting in the sand next to Rachel's sunbed. Rachel was leaning down towards Carrie Ann, as though she was imparting some great secret. Yaslyn had a pretty good idea what they were talking about.

She hoped that Carrie Ann would stick up for her when Rachel told the story. Carrie Ann was less naive than Rachel. More reasonable. She knew that people were flawed but that this didn't necessarily mean they were irredeemably bad. Rachel didn't understand the need Yaslyn felt to do something terrible before somebody did the same thing to her. Every man Yaslyn had ever met had been unfaithful to her eventually, just as her father had been unfaithful to her mother. Knowing that she hadn't been an angel herself helped Yaslyn to survive the hurt.

She would have given anything to have Rachel's shining confidence in the future. She would have loved to have been able to put her trust in one man, just as Rachel was about to with Patrick. If she had been scathing about the wedding, it was at least in part because she was jealous. Perhaps Yaslyn should have told her that.

Rachel shot an angry glance in Yaslyn's direction. Not ready to kiss and make up yet by the look of things. Not at all. Yaslyn turned back towards the horizon and pushed her windsurf board farther out to sea.

Marcus was already out there, zipping across the waves like a stone thrown by an expert skimmer. He was pushing himself to the limits of his ability, trying once again to block out the teeming thoughts in his mind. But that morning's conversation played again and again and again. How had Sally looked when he had told her he knew it was over? Was she sad? Or was she relieved?

It was a question he had asked himself the previous night as well, when he came across her on the beach path with that scumbag Gilles. Marcus had been watching them for a few minutes before he revealed himself. He was only grateful that he hadn't been able to hear the platitudes that accompanied the caress.

Why Gilles? Before this Turkish holiday disaster, it had crossed Marcus's mind that Sally might be thinking about having an affair. She'd talked a lot about that squadron leader guy she had been working with. It sounded as though she admired him. And Marcus could grudgingly admit that he sounded like the kind of bloke who should be admired. But Gilles? Was Sally really so desperate for sex?

Or was she just desperate to be caught? And then set free for ever.

Marcus gritted his teeth and hit the next wave with desperate aggression.

'Nice jump,' someone shouted as they passed him at speed. It was Yaslyn. Bloody hell, she was good. She sailed on as though the board were part of her body.

56

Axel dreamed he was suffocating. He couldn't breathe. He was fighting for his life while an incubus sat on his chest and drained the essence of his soul out with his breath. When he opened his eyes, he found Gilles' white-shorted bum cheeks hovering over his face.

The tennis rep let out a fart.

'For God's sake.'

Axel battled his way upright.

'So?' asked Gilles. 'Where is she?'

'Who?'

'Who d'you think? What was it like? Did she know a few tricks you hadn't done before?'

Axel pushed Gilles out of the way and headed across to the basin. He splashed water on his face.

'Come on, Axel! I need something to take back to the lads. Did she leave any evidence? Knickers? Bra? Even a hair on your pillow would do. What happened?'

'Whatever you want to think,' Axel told him.

'Fantastic.' Gilles slapped him on the back. 'You did it. Might make it easier to read this.'

Gilles tossed a pale pink envelope on to Axel's bed and left.

*

Axel picked the letter up with shaking hands. There, in the handwriting that had written 'not known at this address' on every letter he had sent to Natalie, was his own name and address. On the back of the envelope, the neatly printed return address. 'N. Leclerc, 135 rue Descamps, Apt 3.'

57

Down on the beach, the morning was passing as every other morning that week had passed. Xavier sat in the shade of the water sports hut allowing the Swedish Lesbian Twins to take turns at feeling his muscles. In the shallow water, other holidaymakers played rowdy games with inflatable balls. Beneath the sun umbrellas, less energetic guests read holiday books and sipped lurid-coloured cocktails from plastic cups. The breeze coming in from the water was warm, like a lover's breath. Carrie Ann closed her eyes and allowed herself to slip into a doze.

Beside her, Rachel was turning the pages of her beach novel furiously, eager to know before lunch-time what would happen to the heroine. Sitting on the bench high above the sand, Morten trained his binoculars on the bodies beneath. He allowed his eyes to skim lazily over Carrie Ann's curves, up Rachel's legs, over the beautiful shoulders of the two Swedish girls . . .

As though he sensed Morten's gaze upon him, but in reality because he had seen a flash of light reflected on the glass, Xavier turned suddenly to face the Norwegian's lenses. Morten swiftly moved his sights, panning out over the waves instead. He saw Marcus. Marcus had just taken a tumble and was hauling himself back on to his board. Farther out, Carrie

Ann's other travelling companion was holding a steady line out across the sea in the direction of Kos, which was visible to the naked eye on a day such as today.

Morten adjusted his binoculars, but even then the figure on the windsurf board continued to become smaller at remarkable speed. Morten wished he could be out there with her. But he had never been what one might call an impressive physical specimen. That kind of activity was beyond him. At school, he had always been the last to be chosen during games lessons, pilloried in the playground for his thick-lensed glasses and his clumsiness. As an adult, he was still the last to be chosen. He knew that women found him repulsive on the whole.

Morten just wanted to be like the reps at Club Aegee; physically beautiful and with none of the social awkwardness that meant the women he fell for didn't stick around long enough to hear about his multi-million-dollar lumber business and his fabulous but empty house on the fjords.

Morten heaved a sigh as he watched the Amazon on the windsurf board continue her journey to Greece. He put his binoculars down in his lap as he wiped away the beginnings of a tear from behind his glasses. Was it always going to be like this? he wondered. Year after year holidaying at Club Aegee, pretending to enjoy the cattle-market atmosphere of the pool-bar disco when he would much rather have been walking round a museum, holding hands with a woman he loved. All he had ever wanted was someone to share his life with . . .

Sniffing back his unhappiness, Morten resumed his

surveillance of the beach. Carrie Ann had rolled on to her front. How he would have loved to have rubbed suntan lotion into those shoulder blades. Her friend Rachel had finished her book. Out on the water, Yaslyn was still breasting the waves like a professional. Except . . . Hang on . . .

Had she moved such a distance in such a short time? Morten couldn't see her any more. He focused his binoculars on the horizon, scanned the water for her pink-and-yellow sail. Morten could see nothing. Yaslyn appeared to have gone.

Yaslyn felt as if she were flying. The waves beneath her, the wind behind her. All the elements were working together to take her away from the beach, her friends and the little irritations that had made her feel so bad. If only she could keep sailing like this for ever. If only she didn't have to go back to the shore and make apologies and decisions. Life was so much easier if you didn't care about other people, Yaslyn thought.

She was turning her board when the blackout came. First she felt the cramping, just like every day since the start of this disappointing holiday. She tried not to let the pain make her lose her balance, tried to move a little faster towards the beach. Then the blackness started creeping in from the corners of her eyes, like curtains being drawn at the end of a play. Her grip loosened around the bar by which she held the sail upright. Her knees softened and soon she slipped backwards.

Out on the waves, Yaslyn let herself drift on her back for a while, as if she were lounging in a warm, soapy bath. The board, which she had been trying so hard to hang on to, was already out of reach. She stretched an arm towards it, but it was as though her nerves and muscles had been replaced by skeins of cotton wool. She was floating. Then she was sinking. Floating and sinking. Floating and sinking. Then the edges of her vision became fuzzy again. Then black.

58

'I've finished that book,' said Rachel.

'Happy ending?' asked Carrie Ann.

'Of course.'

'You certainly look happier. Feeling a little more generous about our dear friend Yaslyn yet?'

A frown passed over Rachel's forehead like a cloud.

'I think she's the one that needs to apologise.'

Carrie Ann sat up from her prone position on the sand. 'You really don't want her as your bridesmaid?'

'I don't think I even want her as my friend any more.'

'I think you should cut her some slack.' Carrie Ann surprised even herself with the pronouncement. 'I don't think things have been as easy for her as you imagine over the past few months. Have you ever considered that she might be jealous of what you have with Patrick?'

'She's got a fabulous boyfriend of her own. She practically told me she wished my marriage would break up.'

'We say the worst things out of fear, not hate,' said Carrie Ann quietly.

'You don't understand how long I've had to put up with Yaslyn,' Rachel retorted. 'You don't know how many years I've been in that girl's shadow. It's probably for the best that she isn't my bridesmaid. I have no doubt she would try to overshadow me on my wedding day as well.'

'Carrie Ann!'

Carrie Ann heard the familiar call before Morten saw her. Quick as a flash she lay down flat in the sand and covered her face with a sunhat as though that could make her invisible.

'Carrie Ann!'

'Bloody hell,' said Rachel. 'He sounds like he wants you pretty desperately. Haven't you told him you're shagging the chess rep? I assume you did shag him last night?'

'Sssshhhh,' said Carrie Ann desperately. 'Pretend I'm asleep.'

Morten fell to his knees on the sand in front of her. He lifted the sunhat straight off her face. 'Carrie Ann. Thank goodness I have found you.'

'I was trying to sleep,' she said testily.

'Your friend on the windsurf,' Morten told her desperately. 'I think she has drowned.'

Carrie Ann sat up again.

'What are you talking about?'

Morten took Carrie Ann by the elbow and pulled her somewhat roughly to her feet. He slapped his binoculars into her hands.

'Out there.' He gestured towards the horizon. 'I saw her sailing in the direction of the Greek islands then suddenly she is gone. I look closer and see her board but not your friend.'

Carrie Ann tried to get a focus on anything but failed.

'Here.' Morten took the binoculars back, focused

on something far in the distance and then held the binoculars carefully in position so that Carrie Ann could look through them. Just as he had done when he was focusing on Yaslyn's bottom as she prepared for her hour on the surf.

'You see?' Morten asked.

'I can't see anything.'

'It is her windsurf board. But she is gone. Right?'

Carrie Ann could see nothing but the grey-blue of the distant water. But then there was something. The undulation of a wave momentarily held a pink-and-yellow sail far enough in the air for Carrie Ann to catch sight of it.

'I think I can see the board she was on,' Carrie Ann told Morten nervously. 'Rachel. Get up and have a look at this, will you? Your eyesight's far better than mine.'

'She'll be OK.'

'What would you do if she wasn't? I can see her board but I can't see Yaslyn, Rach.'

Rachel got grudgingly to her feet and took her turn at Morten's binoculars. 'God almighty. That girl always has to be at the centre of a drama. Even when she's not consciously creating one. She'll be dunking her hair in the water to make it go blonder, that's all . . .'

Carrie Ann shaded her eyes and peered out in the direction of Yaslyn's windsurf board again. The changing tide was already bringing it closer in. The board was bobbing quite dramatically now. The waves that rippled like tiny meringue peaks on the fringes of the beach were much bigger farther out.

Carrie Ann thought she could see Yaslyn hanging on to the back of her board, trying to haul herself back on. Then she couldn't . . .

'Help!'

When Rachel and Carrie Ann finally agreed with Morten that Yaslyn's windsurf technique was seriously flawed, the girls abandoned their reading and dozing and hared across the sand and pebbles to the windsurf rep's beach hut. The pair of binoculars the reps were supposed to glance through every couple of minutes to check that no one was getting into difficulties hung on a hook beside the emergency lifebelt. Xavier was letting one of the Swedish Lesbian Twins feel his muscles again in the shadow of a spare sail.

Furious and frightened, Carrie Ann grabbed the boy by his bicep and spun him around to look at her. The Swedish Lesbian Twin put her hands on her hips huffily.

'He hasn't got time to see to you now, dear,' Carrie Ann spat. 'There's somebody drowning out there.'

'Where?' Xavier squinted. He was too vain to wear glasses and had run out of disposable contact lenses for the season.

'Beyond the rock there,' said Morten helpfully.

'Who is it?'

'Yaslyn,' said Carrie Ann. 'She went out on a windsurf about forty minutes ago.'

'She should have come in by now,' said the rep. 'You're only supposed to have a board for half an hour when it's busy.'

'For God's sake,' said Carrie Ann. 'She hasn't come in because she can't. She hasn't had her sail up for the past ten minutes. Someone needs to go and bring her back. Where's your emergency boat?'

The emergency boat was undergoing emergency repairs in a hut a little farther down the beach.

'What are you going to do?' Rachel asked Xavier. His Gallic shrug was far from charming now. Xavier considered his options, growing increasingly agitated as he did so. The emergency boat was out of action. All three of the catamarans were already halfway to Greece. The only windsurf remaining on the beach was the one that had come out worse off in a nose-to-nose collision with the emergency boat the week before. He would have to swim it. But he hadn't exactly been doing a lot of swimming that year. The water was choppy. The English girl was a long way out.

'What are you going to do?' Morten asked him again.

'I don't know,' Xavier admitted. 'I don't know.' He shook his head and scrunched his hair up in his hands. 'This has never happened here before!'

'You should have been keeping an eye on her,' said Rachel.

'There's no time for recriminations,' said Carrie Ann. 'Isn't there someone you can call?'

'The battery on the walkie-talkie has run out.' Xavier looked as though he was about to cry.

'Hey! Hey!' Morten waded as far as he could out into the water, still wearing his clothes except for his white shirt which he waved above his head like a flag. 'Somebody help us. There's somebody in trouble over there.'

Marcus just about caught every other word of Morten's shout on the breeze. He was zipping across the waves at thirty miles an hour, concentrating hard on his course back to the beach hut. He knew that he'd been out for longer than he was supposed to be but didn't think the little Norwegian guy was really desperate for a board. He'd find out what the fuss was about when he got back, he thought. But then he saw Yaslyn's board. And no Yaslyn. And realised.

59

Sally knew from the first night she and Marcus spent together that this man would one day ask to marry her. They were at her place, beneath the clean sheets she had prepared that afternoon just in case. They hadn't had sex yet. Just kissing. Sally hadn't even taken her knickers off in her new boyfriend's presence. Marcus was still in his boxers.

He must have thought she was asleep. She lay with her back against his stomach, his arm across her belly. Spooning. That was what it was called. Sally was the little spoon. She had her eyes closed but she wasn't sleeping. She was listening to him breathing, waiting for the slowing down in his breath pattern that would tell her he had nodded off.

Sally didn't want to be the one to go to sleep first. They had had two bottles of wine between them that night and when Sally got drunk, Sally snored. She was terrified Marcus would find out too soon and be put off. That afternoon, getting ready for the night ahead, she had promised herself she would send him home before it got to the moment of truth. But she had changed the sheets in any case. And now, at half past two in the morning, she didn't think he would appreciate it if she suddenly called for a cab. Besides, she was comfortable too. So comfortable inside his embrace.

So she had to wait, fighting off sleep until she was

sure that he would be too deep in REM to hear the first trumpet of the snore concerto her last boyfriend had sworn took place almost every night. But Marcus's breathing wasn't slowing down. He was savouring the moment too. And when he thought, from Sally's breathing, that she had finally tripped off to the Land of Nod herself, he said it.

'Sally.'

Just her name. That was all he said. But Sally knew he was trying it on for size. Not saying 'Sally' to help him remember what she was called in the morning. Not trying to wake her up. But saying her name as though it was the first word in an incantation that would bind them together for ever. Sally gave up the pretence of sleeping and turned to face him. She kissed him lightly on the eyelids and murmured back, 'I suppose I should warn you. I snore.'

He claimed she didn't snore at all and, after that, they spent every night of the week together. Sometimes at his place, but mostly at hers, since, like most boys, he didn't see the need to change bed linen until it threatened to walk off on its own.

Months later, when he said 'I love you' for the first time, it almost didn't have the same impact as the night he said only her name. Because she knew as soon as he whispered her name in the dark that he loved her.

And now she was letting him go.

60

'Does anybody know any first aid?' Carrie Ann shouted. 'Anybody?'

Marcus knew mouth-to-mouth but he was barely able to breathe for himself. The reps had all received first-aid training but none of them seemed able to recall the fact right then, when they were faced with their first real emergency.

'Clear her airways,' Marcus spluttered before coughing to clear the salt water out of his own. 'I think that's how you start.'

'Come on.' Carrie Ann looked around them. 'One of you must know something more. Help me!'

She opened Yaslyn's mouth but wasn't sure where to go from there. She had a vague notion that blowing straight into a drowning patient's lungs was not the correct procedure and might actually cause more damage. And yet she couldn't *not* do anything. The reps stood in a semicircle like stone monkeys. Rachel was hysterical. Marcus was too exhausted from his heroic swim back to the shore with Yaslyn to help her out again now. Morten tried clumsily to help Carrie Ann roll her friend into the recovery position. Yaslyn kept flopping over on to her back.

'Come on!' Carrie Ann screamed.

*

'Carrie Ann, I behaved very badly towards you. I tried to seduce you last night to help Gilles win a bet. I made assumptions about you based on prejudices that really just aren't true. I realise now that you are a highly intelligent woman . . .'

Axel thought he just about had his speech right as he got to the bottom of the path to the beach. Now to find Carrie Ann among all the semi-naked bodies. He wanted to tell her so much. About the letter from Natalie and the phone call he had just made.

He hesitated at the beach bar. Something appeared to be going on by the boathouse. There was shouting. Another team game, Axel thought. He may have been feeling lighter than he had in a long time but Axel Radanne still hated team games. He hoped to God that Carrie Ann wasn't involved . . .

He spotted her through the crowd. She was kneeling on the ground, her extravagantly curly blonde hair whipping across her face in the sea breeze. Axel gave her a wave when he thought she'd caught his eye. She didn't respond at first. Then . . .

'Axel!!!!' Carrie Ann suddenly screamed his name. 'Axel! I need you now. Thank God you're here!'

It was an even better reception than he had hoped for. She needed him now? Axel shifted gear into a leisurely jog across the sand. He brushed his hair back from his eyes and plastered on his best smile. Carrie Ann was running to meet him halfway. She grabbed his hand.

'Carrie Ann, I want to tell you . . .'

'No time to tell me anything,' she said, and pulled him over to where her friend lay dying on the sand.

'What?' Axel paled.

'She needs mouth-to-mouth. She was nearly drowned out there. You know what to do, don't you, Axel? You did do first aid, didn't you? When you were training to be a doctor?'

For a moment, fear swept through Axel's body like the rip-tide that had finally parted Yaslyn from her board. But in its immediate wake came a lull. A moment of calm when the shouting around him seemed to grow distant, the background became a little hazy. Axel shrugged off his jacket. Too bloody hot for a jacket in this place anyway, let alone when he was being called upon to save a life.

'Move out of the way,' he told the people who had crowded around to witness the excitement. He hauled Yaslyn over on to her side, into the recovery position, and began.

Axel's unexpected calmness galvanised the other reps into action. Delphine asked guests for the loan of a mobile phone while Xavier ran in the direction of reception, in case a phone might not be forthcoming in time. The Swedish Lesbian Twins wrapped their beach towels around a shivering Marcus. Rachel was led to a seat.

Carrie Ann refused the same offer, insisting instead on remaining on her knees at Axel's side while he alternately blew into Yaslyn's mouth and pummelled her chest to get her heart beating again.

'Is she breathing?'

'Yes, she's breathing.'

'Oh, thank God.'

Carrie Ann clasped one of Axel's hands and one of Morten's. 'Thank God. Thank God. Thank God.'

*

The commotion caused when Yaslyn was carried up the beach path to reception spread through the village more quickly than a cold sore passed round the reps. Sally hadn't moved from the balcony where Marcus had left her until the moment the woman in the room next to theirs banged on the door and shouted, 'Engleesh. An Engleesh person has been drowned.'

Knowing no more than that, Sally immediately feared the worst. Marcus had been going for a wind-surf. Had he been too upset by their argument to get himself out of trouble in a rip-tide? Had he tried to kill himself?

As she ran to the car park, Sally bargained with God. For Marcus to be safe she would sacrifice her freedom.

She pushed her way to the front of the crowd which parted naturally as soon as they heard her English accent. They were all there. All the women who had been on the bus from the airport that first morning. Every English-speaking person holidaying at the village that week. The weedy dark-haired rep was struggling to keep enough space around his patient to administer first aid. Sally could see Carrie Ann and Rachel but she couldn't see her husband. Carrie Ann turned towards her. She had Marcus's beach towel draped over her arm.

'No! Marcus!'

When he stood up from the bumper of Yasser's car, it was as though he had been resurrected from the dead. He was wet, certainly, but not drowned. Sally immediately wrapped herself around him in the tightest embrace she had given him for years.

Sally felt elation and guilt flood through her when

she realised that the body on the floor was Yaslyn. The chess rep was kneeling at her head, trying to tell Xavier and Gilles something as they lifted the girl into the back of Yasser's car in preparation for the bumpy ride to the hospital. Yaslyn's friends went with her. The crowd watched the car leave the village then started to disperse. Sally and Marcus were left alone. She still had her arms around him. She couldn't let him go.

Carrie Ann and Rachel spent the rest of the day at the hospital with Axel and Yasser, anxiously watching the white swing-doors through which Yaslyn had been admitted to an emergency ward. Eventually, the doctor who had taken Yaslyn's details, with Yasser acting as translator, came back into the waiting room. He looked worried and far too young to be saving people's lives.

'He needs to speak to her husband,' Yasser translated again.

'Her husband?' said Rachel. 'She hasn't got one. Is it serious?'

'It's very serious,' said Yasser on the doctor's behalf. 'He needs to speak to the father of her child.'

Euan and Patrick arrived in Bodrum in the early hours of Monday morning, having flown via most of the European capitals en route. By the time Euan got to the hospital, Yaslyn was sitting up in bed, sipping water quietly, trying to take in everything the doctor had told her since she had woken up. At first she wouldn't believe it and assumed that Yasser was getting his terms mixed up as he translated quickly from Turkish to English and back again like an interpreter at the United Nations. In the end, Yasser had the doctor draw a diagram of a woman with a child nestling inside her stomach. There was no mistaking the meaning of that.

Carrie Ann and Rachel sat on either side of Yaslyn as she stared at the picture that lay on her lap. She held their hands so tightly that she left nail marks in their palms.

'Euan's on his way. It'll be all right,' said Carrie Ann when Yaslyn started crying.

'I know,' she said. She pushed away a tear. She'd never wanted to see someone so much in her life.

Rachel had been right. Euan proposed at Yaslyn's hospital bedside when the rest of the crowd had returned to the Club Aegee village and they finally found themselves alone. He had been intending to propose at the wedding the following Saturday, but it didn't seem worth waiting now. That moment seemed like the right time.

He didn't have the ring with him. That was the only problem. He wasn't due to pick it up from the shop until the Friday afternoon.

Yaslyn smiled a little sadly. 'No point picking it up at all,' she told him. 'I just don't think I can marry you.'

'But what about the baby?' he asked.

'It's OK,' said Yaslyn. 'I'm having that.'

She laid her hands on her stomach protectively. The doctor estimated that she might be as much as three months pregnant already. It was still impossible to tell that she was pregnant at all by looking at her rock-hard abdominal muscles. Talking of which, she'd have to lay off the sit-up marathons for a while.

'I am having a baby.'

She never thought she'd hear herself say the words. Until that day, having a child had always seemed to be about the things she would lose in the process. Her waistline. Her freedom. Euan.

There was no holding on to the waistline. But here was Euan, having flown across a continent to be with her. And he swore that he would always want to be with her. No matter whether she got fat or frumpy or preferred to iron school shirts rather than give him a blowjob. He would prove it to her by marrying her when she was as round as a house and almost ready to have her baby on the register office floor, he said. Yaslyn believed him but she still refused his proposal.

'I'm going to be a mum,' she said. 'I don't think I'm quite ready to be a *missus* as well.'

Ah well. It didn't matter. It didn't matter if they *never* made it official. They were going to be a family their way. Yaslyn, Euan and the baby. History didn't have to repeat itself this time.

Club Aegee was dark when the other girls and their companions got back from the hospital. They hadn't said much on the drive back in Yasser's car. Yasser did squeeze Carrie Ann's knee once – she was sitting in the passenger seat beside him – but she let him do it this time. It was a squeeze devoid of the wicked intentions he had had towards her before.

On the back seat, Rachel's sleepy head lolled against Patrick's shoulder. Now that he was in town, they would need an extra room. Axel thought he might be able to arrange that with Cherie. As they stood in reception waiting for the *chef de village* to come down from her office (she often worked late into the night) Axel told Carrie Ann about the letter from his long-lost love. Ed had called the relationship off. Would Axel give her another chance?

Carrie Ann smiled. 'She knows she let a good thing slip through her fingers.'

'But it's too late,' Axel said. 'I know now that everything you said was true. She's not the goddess I thought she was. She doesn't really want me. She feels sorry for herself. That's all. She's just an ordinary girl.'

Carrie Ann nodded. 'There're a lot of us about.'

'You're not an ordinary girl,' said Axel.

'Thanks.'

'I'm going back to medical school,' Axel continued. 'After I got the letter this morning, I called my old tutor and asked him what he thought my chances were

433

of getting back on the course. He said he would do his best to make sure that I was back in his classroom by September. He said I was one of the best students he'd ever had and he missed having me to teach. That was one of the things I was going to tell you when I came down to the beach this morning.'

'What was the other thing?'

Axel blushed. 'Just that meeting you has made everything different,' he said.

Then, tentatively, he reached for Carrie Ann's hands. When they were holding hands he started to pull her towards him. He inclined his head to one side. She inclined her head to the other. Their mouths were so close Carrie Ann could feel Axel's breath tickling her top lip. They were about to kiss.

Suddenly, she pulled away and kissed him in the middle of his forehead.

'Meeting you has changed things for me as well,' she murmured back. 'You're not the only one who's going back to school. I've decided I'm going to take some time out from my business and apply for a place at university again. I'm going to be the Carrie Ann I was before love got in the way.'

'And you don't want to . . .' Axel was still holding her hands.

Carrie Ann looked at him seriously. Then one corner of her mouth crept up in a smile. This time she took Axel's head in both her hands and planted a huge smacker right on his lips.

'Hooray!'

The cheer went up all around them.

All that time they had been quietly talking in

reception, pretty much the entire population of Club Aegee had been lurking in a room just off the main hall, waiting for the moment to start the party. Axel Radanne was hero of the hour. And rep of the year, as well.

A congo line danced through reception and out in the direction of the pool bar. Morten was at the head of it, drunk as a lord and covered in lipstick kisses after his afternoon as the centre of attention, telling the story of how his binoculars played their part in the saving of the English girl.

'Carrie Ann!' he called.

She joined the line right behind him. Axel joined the line between two of the Go-Go girls. One of them pinched his bottom.

In their room on the other side of the village, Marcus and Sally weren't in quite the same party mood. Returning from the hospital after a check-up to make sure that Marcus wasn't suffering too much from the after-effects of dragging a half-drowned woman back to shore, the Merchants circumnavigated the fuss and excitement by the pool in favour of an afternoon on their balcony.

They spent it talking. Talking about their marriage and what had gone wrong with it, their hopes and dreams and what they had become. And now they lay side by side on the single bed that had been Sally's for the duration of the holiday. Their fingers were entwined. Their heads were touching. Sally turned to face her husband. He felt the butterfly touch of her lashes on his cheek.

'We're going to be all right, aren't we?' she asked him.

'Yes,' said Marcus. 'We're going to be all right.'

'It's not all right,' said Rachel, flinging her mobile phone on to the single bed she would be sharing with Patrick that night. Helen had called while Rachel was at the hospital. She'd just received the order of service from the printers and was disappointed to find that Rachel hadn't chosen 'I vow to thee my country' as one of the hymns after all. Helen had taken the liberty of having the service order changed.

'It's supposed to be our wedding day,' Rachel yelled at her fiancé. 'We're supposed to be celebrating our love exactly as we want to. But she's invited all her cronies, swapped my Rolls-Royce for a horse and carriage. She's sacked the vegetarian caterers and now she's choosing the hymns.

'I'm not going to stand for this any longer,' she continued. 'I've had enough of being a mouse. Everyone thinks they can walk all over me. Your mother. Yaslyn. Those stupid women by the pool. Well, not any more they can't.'

Patrick tried to calm her down with a platitude.

'What do you mean, it doesn't matter?' Rachel glared at him. 'That's it,' she announced. 'This whole stupid wedding is off.'

Epilogue

Three in the afternoon. July 27. And the bride who should at that very moment have been walking down the aisle at St Mary's Church in Washport was once again worrying whether a WH Smith bag would count as a second item of hand luggage when she tried to board the plane.

'Next, please.' The security guard called her forward from the queue of excited holidaymakers. Rachel put her smart little wheelie case on to the conveyor belt and stepped with trepidation through the metal detector arch.

'I'm afraid we're going to have to open this up,' said the security guard, when she got to the other side.

Rachel felt the blood make a dash from her head to her feet. The security guard began to unzip her luggage on the carpeted bench.

'You can't!' she protested.

'We must. There's an object we can't identify,' the guard told her flatly.

Rachel sighed. 'Then at least let me do it in private.'

The guard carried her case to a little screened-off area. Rachel followed him obediently and couldn't stop the smile crossing her face when he finally opened the wheelie case up. The guard started smiling too when he saw Rachel's carefully packed holiday outfit. Six long metres of fluffy white taffeta. A carefully embroidered bodice. A sparkling tiara. Slightly squashed.

'We're getting married in Jamaica. Didn't want my fiancé to see my wedding dress,' Rachel explained.

The security guard nodded. 'That's understandable.' Then he frowned. 'Don't suppose you really wanted him to see this thing either,' he said.

The guard reached under the table for a box full of rubber gloves . . .

'Oh my God,' said Rachel. 'I swear I didn't pack that. It's my friend's . . . It's from my hen night . . . I mean, I've never even seen one before . . .'